# Lucky Woman

Patricia Finney

Hi – my name is Patricia Finney and I want to bribe you to sign up for my email list.

Even if you've already signed up for my list through my website or a Carey novel, I want you to sign up again because this is a different list.

LUCKY WOMAN is a romantic comedy thriller, sort of thing – and more or less contemporary. No, I don't count the early 2000s as historical. Sorry.

The Carey, Enys and Elizabethan Noir books are historical novels.

So – two lists. One for historical novels, one for everything else. I hesitate to use the word "contemporary" because I might write SF or fantasy or something. I don't know what the Interstellar Idea Bats are planning, do I?

You know I won't anxiously spam you with loads of emails – if I send you one it'll be because I think you might be genuinely interested in it.

So if you want to sign up for my everything-else fiction list, go to this URL (you'll have to type it in!)

https://www.subscribepage.com/ambrosestory

You'll also get exclusive access to a short story called AMBROSE THE GAY POSTMAN. I dare you!

Also, when you've finished the book of course, could you please write a review?

Thank you.

# Prologue

Lying there in hospital, with two black eyes and a broken nose, along with painful other damage, I was actually wondering how the hell I got so lucky.

In fact, when you got right down to it, the person I should really have thanked was Mr Very Respectable Wife-beater who beat me up about eight years before the two black eyes etc. If it hadn't been for him, none of the rest of it could ever have happened.

At the time, of course, I didn't know that's what he was. All I knew was that his wife had cancer – I can't honestly remember what kind – and I was supposed to help her in my bright shiny new job of Terminal Care In The Community Nursing Officer. Being a lot more naïve then, I never questioned why her nose was slightly squashed-looking, or why there were scars around her eyes, or why she had a permanently scared look and said practically nothing when her husband was around. She seemed colourless even before she started fading away, not resisting very much. Her husband, of course, was frantic about her.

She lay propped up to help her breathing and he sat next to her, vibrating with fury, holding her hand so tightly her fingers were going blue.

I was wondering whether I should say anything about that, but she did it for me. She had been letting him have her limp hand and when his grip slackened, she removed it, quickly, neatly. I can't tell you Mr Wife-beater's name, he was quite a well-known local accountant, Rotary member and school governor and People would be upset.

"Look at her!" he accused me for the fourth time. "She's dying!"

I didn't know what to say. Certainly not the smart aleck comment that instantly sprang to mind about how long had it taken him to notice that? I'd already learned that there isn't a lot you can usefully say in those circumstances.

"Look at her!" He turned on me, in his suit, late for work, very small knot for his tie, square black glasses on, grey hair neatly combed back. They had two children, now both at college, who visited during the day when their father was at work. They had various carers popping in and out, among them, me. "She's leaving me!" he shouted. "She's going! You've got to *do* something!"

Wife-beater's Wife's eyelids opened at that, her washed-out blue eyes suddenly sparkling with something new.

"I wish I could," I said, sincerely, thinking how selfish he was, bellowing about it while she was lying there.

"No, you don't," sneered Mr Wife-beater. "It's just a job to you, isn't it? Why would you care that she's leaving me?"

He was leaning forwards, both his fists bunched. His wife sighed, so he turned back to her.

"What will I do without you?" he whispered, eyes filling with tears.

Wife's eyes narrowed.

"Actually, dear," she breathed in her very polite middle-class voice, "I rather hope you rot."

There was one of those little silences that happen when someone says the unspeakable and nobody can think what to do next. Wife-beater scowled. Wife blinked at him.

"Um... drugs," I said brightly. "Drugs affect the brain you know, a bit like booze..."

"My mind is quite clear, thank you, Anna," said Wife. "I've wanted to say this to you for a very long time, dear, you know, but I was always afraid to. But there's nothing to be afraid of any more now, is there? So may I say that I hope you stew in your own selfish juices. I hope you live a long, lonely, squalid life and die in an old people's home because your children hate you. They do, you know, dear." She smiled at him, closed her eyes again. "And I really hope they take the time to find one of those places where they beat up the residents, so you'll find out what that's like."

I thought he looked completely gormless, staring at her with his mouth open. However, I must have had very little gorm myself because all I could think of was that maybe I should be going now. So I coughed.

"I'll just... er..." I said, sliding sideways to the door, "I'm due in Lyonesse in twenty minutes, must be going..."

I'd actually made it to the front door before he caught up with me.

"Wait! You can't go. You've got to help her."

There was no crisis, nothing to do. Wife probably wasn't going to die for a week or two yet. All the emergency was inside him because he'd just worked it out or, more likely, been told by someone tactless. He was breathing hard and looked white.

"I'm sorry," I said firmly, wondering why my own heart was thumping, "but I really must go now. Your... um... wife will be quite comfortable until Mell comes in at..."

"You don't understand!" he was hissing at me through his teeth, fists bunched again, "She can't leave me, she's mine, you've got to stop her..."

Grow up, I thought. "I'm sorry," I said, "I've got a little boy with muscular..."

Bam! There it was. Right out of the blue. What makes real violence so shocking and terrifying is that you never ever expect it.

He'd slapped me.

And I froze. I just stood there, staring stupidly. Didn't try to hit him, didn't even have the sense to run like hell, just rocked in my sensible shoes and gawped at him with my mouth open and my face prickling and stinging all over.

"*Don't you ever interrupt me, you useless little bitch!*" shrieked the accountant, right in my face, his square glasses almost touching my eyebrows.

My knees were trembling. I tried to totter away down the neat garden path...

He caught my shoulder, shoved me so I reeled, caught the front of my uniform and rammed me against the white pebbledash and punched me hard in the left breast. It hurt so much I couldn't scream, only gasp. He punched me again in the face and everything went foggy and whirling. I ineffectually tried to fight back, part of me still refusing adamantly to believe that this was actually happening, managed to claw his face with my nails and that really upset him.

Next thing I was on the ground, gravel in my mouth, somebody kicking me and shrieking at me, fading in and out. Reflexively I curled up and felt one of the kicks bust a rib.

Then there was the shocked voice of Ambrose the gay postman. Apparently he whacked Mr Wife-beater over the head with a magazine tube. The thudding of feet on my ribs stopped at last and the accountant staggered back indoors, crying that he didn't mean to, he was sorry. And Ambrose was cradling my head and weeping ineffectual tears all over me, which I could have done without, frankly.

It hurt unbelievably badly. And the shock, the sheer total uncomprehending surprise of it... I just couldn't compute. I couldn't work out what I'd done to set him off, or why he'd done it or anything. In movies, the heroine would get up, wipe off the blood and swagger back indoors to deal with the accountant. Me, I could only lie there, breathing very carefully because of my cracked ribs while Ambrose rang the ambulance and the police.

Ambrose was only too delighted to tell them exactly what he'd seen the accountant doing and offered his services as a witness.

It was his moment of glory, he was all over the papers the following week and four months later for the trial.

The ambulance scooped me up, the police scooped up the accountant who they already knew as a nasty drunk, and since they were friends of mine, they dropped him several times on the way to the cells. Once their father was safely out of the house, both of Mr Wife-beater's kids moved back home to look after their mum.

And I lay in bed, in hospital, still shaking for days after. My own husband, Jim, was furious about it and turned up drunk that night at the copshop offering to fight the accountant personally. My two little boys were desperately upset, Simon even offered to lend me his teddy bear to make me feel better.

Then it all got better and faded away and became a story you tell to people to show how dangerous nursing can be.

Except for one thing. While I lay shaking in bed with solicitous nurses bringing me cups of tea and offering therapists, I made a decision. It was never going to happen again. Never ever again would I stand and stare helplessly at some violent nutcase. And so, as soon as my ribs and face were healed, I went and signed up for a self-defence class at the Lyonesse Dance Palace.

Which brings me to the real start of the story about how I got so bloody lucky. Bear in mind that it all happened around the Millennium (remember that?) so we're back in the prehistoric era before smartphones, Facebook, Twitter. Oldsters can reminisce. Youngsters can gasp at the primitive conditions. Some things have stayed the same though.

# Chapter 1





Dealing with death and dying all the time – I suppose it *might* make you saintly. However it just made me paranoid and bad-tempered. Young men who roared past my car in narrow country lanes on their shiny motorbikes got short shrift.

"Fucking organ donor!" I shrieked at the departing leather back, to be rewarded with a coolly upraised middle finger.

Still muttering, I carried on with my appointments for that morning – Mrs Tredurgan with terminal mouth cancer and Robbie who hadn't been born when she was diagnosed, fighting Muscular Dystrophy every step of his way out.

Then I headed for the hill overlooking the little South Cornwall town of Lyonesse, where St Jude's lighthouse looks down like the citadel of a technowizard. My patient was living… well, squatting… in a derelict tourist trap. The forms said she had a mobile home but it was a lot smaller and less glamorous than a trailer – what we Brits call a caravan.

Thinking back to that time, I realise I was so tired, so generally overstressed and under-rested, I was twitchy, barely functioning. But I was too tired even to know that – had no idea how I felt. There was a brittle shell all around me, like a cast. It had grown slowly, to protect me, and I no longer even knew it was there. I just carried on through the days, keeping going, very careful not to feel anything.

So I sighed and climbed out of the car, not seeing anything of the magnificent black cliffs where the clouds rocket in from the Atlantic, bronco-riding the Gulf Stream that keeps Cornwall subtropical and wet. They generally make their first hasty dump of rain right there, often while the sun is still shining.

MiniWonders had been one of those World in Miniature follies built in the Thirties, in very pretty gardens, now exuberantly overgrown. They had the Eiffel Tower, Leaning Tower of Pisa (collapsed), the White House, the Pyramids and, of course, the Taj Mahal. They added a restaurant, so called, they added a children's play area for dry days, they added an indoor play area for the other 360 days of the year, they advertised, they did special offers and in the end, of course, they still went bust. Back in the days when going to France was an adventure, people would pay to gawp at small scale fakes of places they could never hope to see. Nowadays… tourists know when they're being trapped.

But the surfers love the place because something about the shape of the cove puts enormous reliable waves that have come all the way from the Bahamas right in on the sandy beach at the north side of the peninsula. And Onion's caravan was perched on the cliff above the cove, near the Taj Mahal, as close to the edge as she could get, with surfers' tents scattered around her. Lyonesse one side, surf the other, St Jude ahead of her and, as she boasted, freedom all around.

I had parked my car in the essential secondary car-park, built so that the English tourists could sit safely in their cars and look through their windscreens at the fantastic Atlantic. As I went towards Onion's caravan, I paused. There was an extremely scary-looking motorbike parked next to it. I assumed it was one of those Harley Davisons and wondered if it belonged to the fucking organ-donor.

I could see that Benjy, the young surfer currently on duty, was pottering around outside doing something mysterious with Onion's herb garden. When she'd been less ill, Onion had been a busy gardener and now bright blue lobelias and hot pink and white petunias exploded all around her caravan in that vulgar Cornish way.

"Hi Benj."

"Oh… ah… hi." Benjy never recognised anyone because his brain was completely blasted by chemicals, partly dope. Where did he get it? Well, he grew it because Onion needed it so badly for the pain. At that time, the pillocks who run the world still classified marijuana as a dangerous drug which was so evilly terrible that a doctor who could prescribe heroin if he wanted, had to apply to the Home Office in order to prescribe marijuana.

Sorry about the soap box. "Who's that?" I asked him, gesturing at the Harley.

Benjy looked puzzled. "Oh… yeah… some guy. Turned up this morning. Caravan was getting crowded, so I… uh…"

He waved at the nice five-fronded plants he was treating with bright blue slug pellets. You have to, in Cornwall, we have the biggest and greediest slugs in the world here.

"She all right?"

Benjy shook his head. "I suppose."

Most people are shocked by what an ugly business it is to die of cancer. That's why most people like it tidied away into hospitals so they don't have to look at it. But not Onion's surfer brigade. They were shocked, they were frightened and disgusted, but they kept coming back when they said they would, and doing things their parents would have fainted dead away on the spot even to watch. Which parents probably gave them hell every time they met for not having a proper job in marketing or something.

I looked at the Harley, then I went back to my car, put drugs bag in the boot, locked everything up tight. Oh yes, there are people scummy enough to mug nurses and social workers.

My stomach tightened as I went up to the caravan, and even though I was telling myself not to be so paranoid, I still listened before I went in. Yes, there are even people scummy enough to steal drugs from terminal cancer patients.

Which is how I heard his voice before I actually met him personally. You could say that everything else stemmed from that, because his voice was beautiful. Deep, quite soft, tinged with a hard-to-place flavour of something that I thought at first was Essex.

"Come on, Lily," he was saying, "I can get you out of this place, looked after properly…"

"Why would I want to get out of the most beautiful place in the world?" said Onion's breathless voice. "And it's Onion, I told you."

"But it's a bloody trailer!"

"So what, it's mine."

"Who's looking after you?"

"The boys. They take it in turns, I'm never alone unless I ask to be."

"What, like that wasted specimen outside?"

"Yes. He's Benjy, and he's sweet."

"Lily, you need round the clock nursing…"

"Call me Onion or I'll kick you out."

"I never realised… I never knew. I wish you'd…"

"Oh shut up, you silly great git, I'd have told you if I'd wanted you to know. I don't know who put my picture in the paper but when I find out…"

"It was me, Li… Onion. Me, I did it. I wondered where you were. And then one of your boys rang me. I couldn't fucking believe it when he said… When he told me… You. You were…"

"Dying? Well, he shouldn't have rung. I don't want you and I don't want your help."

Silence. I wished I hadn't listened now, it was all a bit personal. I turned around and lit a cigarette. Yes, I know, I know. I tell people, I do it so I won't be a burden on what's left of the National Health Service when I get old. In my family, you generally have to shoot us once we roll past 100, totally marble-less but fighting fit.

It was Onion's voice again. She was sounding very breathless, worse than she should have done.

"All right. I'm sorry. I do want you, I'm pleased to see you, really. I just don't want your help. OK? You can stick around, so long as you promise, no helping."

"I promise," said that deep velvet voice. "No helping."

"Now just sit there and be decorative, like you used to say. And I can't believe what you did to your face."

"Good, isn't it?"

"No, it's horrible."

"It's all for you, darling Lily."

"I'll throw something."

"All right. I'll be good."

I stamped on the fag-end, knocked and opened the door. I expected to see Onion disposed on her couch like Snow White and Cleopatra rolled into one – and she was. Postcards of flowers, paintings and tourist sites covered the walls. Great rolls and swags of material draped over the bed, hung with herbs and little bottles of essential oils and crystals and feathered Amerindian dream-catchers, all in dramatic shades of purple and crimson interspersed with white muslin. Onion herself was in a purple crushed velvet robe. Her fine blonde hair and bone structure said that she was once thoroughly beautiful, but since then the cancer had swelled her up here and sucked her out there so you couldn't call her even presentable. She still wore a lot of make-up, sometimes built up in layers like an archaeological site until one of the boys rebelled and took a swipe at it with baby lotion.

She liked to hold court, so there was a slightly broken managing director's chair saved from the dump, also draped with crimson to hide the boring brown knit covers and the moth-eaten foam seat, crammed in next to her bed with the various machines she needed behind it. And in the hotseat was... Well, I honestly didn't expect the owner of that voice to look like that.

He was big, not just tall but broad, wide shoulders, wearing the mixture of oily denim, horrible faded black t-shirt and scuffed leather jacket that I'd expect of someone with a Harley. Quite fit, though there was an incipient gut giving his big silver belt buckle a bit of work. He had something… what do you call it? Presence? Charisma? He filled up the caravan, even with Onion in it who was not a shrinking violet of a personality herself. No wonder gentle wasted Benjy had felt threatened.

He was bald, shaved not fallen out. And he had a tattoo over the whole of his face which was either some kind of swirly psychedelic spiderweb or something Celtic. Or maybe Maori. Or something. Horrible. Mesmerisingly horrible. You were so distracted by the thing, you simply couldn't work out what the face underneath might look like, which was obviously the intention. And this was back when bald heads were generally natural and tattoos were much rarer.

He looked at me, clocked the uniform, then my expression and stood up quite politely, ducking his head under the roof, which didn't help him look less threatening, not at all.

"Oh, it's Anna," said Onion brightly, "I told you about her, she's my dealer."

Ha ha, funny joke. Well, it isn't a joke really. Onion had a pump so she could self-medicate with diamorphine which I came every day to supervise. It had taken one hell of a fight to get it for her, during which her boys had scored the illegal stuff for her to stop her crying in the night, and I had gathered them together when we installed it and told them that if any of it was unaccounted for, I would personally shop the one in charge.

The leader of her boys, Jog, who had been one of her many lovers before the cancer got the upper hand, had told me quietly that it wouldn't be necessary. It hadn't been so far. The stuff used tallied perfectly with the little computer chip.

Onion smiled at me, the secret smile she kept for great jokes, and she didn't introduce her visitor. I nodded at him, professional, wondering how I was going to get him to leave. Presumably this was another of her many past lovers, which would upset Jog again, the daft creature.

"Out," said Onion, less tactful than me. "Me and Anna have got business."

The Tattoo-man smiled and that was a bit of a shock too because it was a charming smile, with good teeth, and he had quite stunning blue eyes as well. Presumably before the tattoo he was quite tasty. I shuddered inwardly. Why do they do it to themselves? Why want to look ugly? I'd wanted to be pretty all my life, and had to settle for being presentable, square, but tidy. Nice hair. Good skin. Nice girl. Etc. He shut the door quietly behind him.

We did our business, some of it messy and personal. She was on her way out and her body was slowly disintegrating under her, and yet you couldn't tell how long it was going to take and every single second of it had to be lived first, by her. I have seen perfectly healthy middle aged women simply sit down and die after their husbands conk out and I have seen bodies so riddled with AIDS-related illnesses that they seem like a set of syndromes strung together with bone and still they lived on. My job was not to cure her, but simply to make sure she was comfortable and in the place she wanted to be. Quite a revolutionary concept, in its way. Even five years before we'd have got a court order and stuck her in hospital whether she wanted it or not. But since then the accountants had looked more carefully at the figures and realised that it was immensely cheaper for Onion and her ilk to be looked after *inna communidy* (as they put it, being believers in the magic of words and that buzzword *"communidy"* above all) than it was for her to tie up an intensive care bed for weeks and then be marked down as a negative statistic (ie. death) to be counted against them later on. Just occasionally the numbers add up to something better.

"Who's that?" I asked when we'd finished, as full of nosiness as anyone else.

"Oh that's an old friend, a very old friend, from way back." She giggled.

"Why'd he call you Lily?"

"What he always used to call me. To annoy me."

"He OK?"

"What?" She narrowed her eyes at me as I settled her back on the bed they'd rigged up to be adjustable.

"Looks a bit suspect to me," I said.

She snortled with giggles, partly from the new drugs coming in. "Oh, he's very suspect," she said. "Mad, bad, dangerous to know. But he's all right."

"Hmm."

I left it, tidied up, did paperwork for the drugs, more paperwork for other things, quick report form, another form.

Outside I found the Tattoo-man leaning against my car with his hands in his jacket pockets, obviously waiting for me. I nearly turned and ran because I really don't like it when people wait for me. You have to be so careful, even down in South Cornwall, a very long way past world's end.

Particularly you have to be careful with people who look like the Tattoo-man. I'm sorry, but you do. Especially when you're carrying a little treasure trove of drugs.

So I reached in my bag, fished out my keys and held them between my knuckles, locked the bag, and walked forward, heart thudding.

"Hi," I said noncommittally. "Can I help you?"

"Yes, I want to talk to you."

"I have got another appointment."

I saw a struggle there: he wasn't used to people not wanting to talk to him. He started to say something curt, then stopped himself and used the smile. I say "used". It was totally deliberate.

"I wanted to ask you about... Onion."

"Yes."

"All right. I know you can't tell me anything confidential. I just want to know if she... if she needs anything."

"Like what?"

"Like... I dunno." He raised his big shoulders helplessly. "Like somewhere better to stay than a bloody trailer."

"Do you think I haven't tried to convince her to go into a hospice? She won't do it. She says she loves it here and she wants to be die here. For what it's worth, she wants her ashes scattered here."

He stuck his fists deeper in his jacket, he stared at his boots and he took a deep hesitant breath.

"Electricity? Heat? Nurses?"

"Could you supply them?"

He heard my skepticism and looked up. Suddenly blue eyes drilled into mine. "Yes. I could."

Oh really, I thought, and how? By nicking them?

"All right. In due course she'll probably need a proper electrical supply. She's going to need a contract mobile, not the prepaid one she's got now. Maybe satellite TV. And eventually, she may well need round the clock professional nursing, which I doubt you'll get anybody to do in that caravan, as you so rightly imply."

He nodded once. "Anything else?"

"What's your interest, Mr... er..."

He smiled slowly and humorously, didn't fill in the gap I'd left. "Oh I think I'm one of her boys, Ms Clements."

He held out his hand, after a moment I shook it. His hand was dry, his grip firm. Something else worrying about it.

I left him there, chunka chunkaed away, struggling with extremely unworthy envy. Of course, I didn't envy Onion the thing that was killing her, though of course, something would eventually kill me. What I did envy very much was Onion's ability to attract men, Onion's ability to order them about, Onion's bland assumption that every man she met would fall at her feet and become her slave. And the infuriating thing was that they still did, even now she had lost the fragile beauty which had entranced Jog, they still did. The Tattoo-man wasn't the first lover from her past who had tried to come and see her, probably wouldn't be the last. He was definitely the most worrying. I quietly took down the number of his motorbike as I passed it, just in case.

Which was when I realised what had worried me about shaking hands with him. His hands were oily as bikers' hands usually were, but his nails were clean. In fact manicured.

I decided I would trust the Tattoo-man exactly as far as I could throw him, which was about eight feet.

# Chapter 2



*To do: Tuesday pm. Tescos: pizza bases, cheese, frosted Shreddies, Coke; is football kit clean?*

I defy you to find a mother of sons who hasn't, at least once, thought wistfully about boarding school, national service, the Foreign Legion. For herself, of course, as a rest cure. The delicate flowers who lope hairily around booming epithets about cool and brill and whatever other monosyllable is the last word at the moment, they would wither and die if not supplied with four large meals per day, satellite tv, xBox and a skateboard. Oh and plenty of leisure time.

When I came through the door, there of course was the soccer kit which had been festering since the last match and in which the socks were evolving into a new form of life probably banned by the Geneva convention against biochemical warfare. The smell of burnt toast wafted through the house. The TV was on and a fight was going on over the remote control. The washing I had put on the line before I left the house that morning was still there, although it had rained twice during the day.

I am, dear reader, as they say, married to a writer. You may have heard of him? James Stukely, writer of amusing little historical detective novels set in the English Civil War. (I use my maiden name for work purposes.) Oh, you get his books from the library, do you? Well that's nice. Did you know he gets about 0.0001 of a penny when you borrow one of his books? Yes, indeedy. As opposed to the munificent 50 p per paperback he might score if they're available and if they've earned out their advance and if the publishers remember to pay him. There were no Kindles back then, of course.

I met him when I was a student nurse in Oxford and he came into the Radcliffe Infirmary emergency room where I was working one night. He was pouring blood from his nose onto his frilly shirt front because he had been to a literary dining club dinner that night and got into a fight with one of his mates over the exact importance of Thomas Quincey, the opium eater, to Lewis Carroll's work. I kid you not. It could have had something to do with the strenuous quantities of wine, champagne, port and vodka the little cherubs had been drinking, of course. He was a literary lion at the time, Doing English at Oxford, because his first book had just been published ("an excoriating study of the dislocations of war in the quiet English countryside of the 17th century" *The Times*) and he had an entire advance on royalties to spend. £3,500 at the time, which was really quite a lot. Then. Funnily enough, that's what Trollope & Bender, his present publishers offered him on a two-book deal, recently. Not each; for both books.

He was always a bit moody during his twenties when he was trying to break into journalism and not doing very well. He found journalism rather boring. More moody in his thirties when I had the boys and couldn't work for a while, got himself a job selling advertising which he hated, and stopped the minute I could get back to work. That's when he started on the historical detective novels which specialise in extremely twisty plots with a religious aspect and have a Puritan protagonist called Job Gurney. Unfortunately, the ghostly Master Gurney and I have never got on very well. When Jim's in the throes of a book, I sometimes feel I'm married to two men at once.

I knocked on his study door where he has a bed and a very old computer that repeatedly swallows his efforts and which he will not back up regularly enough, and books lining the entire room from floor to ceiling. He's still trying to write the great novel, he's still churning out the detective novels once a year or so, and his publishers take him out to a Pizza Hut when he gets to London to see them.

The literary high-life. Poor old Bill, he says sometimes, of the friend he had the fight with, it must be terrible to have to work in a merchant bank when you have such creative talent as a writer. Poor old Bill has a pension fund the size of the rock of Gibraltar, a very nice house in the Home Counties, a lovely wife, and always, but always, buys one of Jim's books in hardback. For his wife. For Christmas.

After another knock on the study door, I got a hollow answer. "What?"

"Hi, Jim," I said brightly, "I'm back. Would you like some coffee?"

"Yeah, great." The miserable drone was there in his voice and my heart sank. When he's on form, Jim genuinely is fascinating and exotic and exciting to be with. On form happens about twice a year now, when the alcohol and royalty mix is exactly right.

So I went into the kitchen and found that every single surface was covered with dirty plates, dirty dishes, dirty knives and forks, dirty tea-towels, empty waffle packets, and dirty bits of bread. A neighbour's cat was busily licking the butter which some bright spark had left the lid off.

There was peanut butter wiped into the counter, the cooker, the toaster and the back door. How? And why?

I went into the living room where my two pizza-faced teenage boys were eating peanut butter toast and watching some soap full of very earnest Aussie girlies, not one of whom could have weighed more than seven stone after dipping in concrete. I watched them for a minute, acting away desperately with a script that had people regularly discussing their relationships as if the relationship was a sort of hairy animal that had just done a mess on the carpet. "I'm rilly worried about our relationship, Creteen. It's going nowhere. We niver seem to talk." "Ow Bruce, I'm rilly rilly sorry, I'm going eaht with Tosser."

"Good knockers," grunted one of my progeny. "Look."

"On the door?" I asked, trying for sarcasm, irony, those little conversation gambits.

"Nah mum," said the elder pizza-face, slurping coke, "Tits. You know."

"Dja see my kit?" said younger pizza face, also slurping coke. "I need it tomorrow."

"Oh do you?" I said. "Hello, hello mum, nice to see you, did you have a good day, yes, I did, thank you, Matthew, thank you Simon, and how was your day…"

Elder pizza-face tilted his face to the side, peering past me. "Come on mum, she's getting in the shower."

So I went and made coffee for the great writer, who was clattering away on his computer now I was home, and I checked the fridge to find the money-off spaghetti bolognese I'd been saving for us tonight had mysteriously disappeared, no doubt into a maw surrounded by pizza-face, and I carried the soccer kit at arm's length and slung it in the washing machine, where the socks growled and tried to claw their way out through the glass, honest, I promise. And I drank some wine, by myself, in the kitchen, after I'd loaded the dishwasher and set the delay button. Then I had another glass of wine.

And you may well ask why did I do all this? Why didn't I pound on the lazy author's door and tell him to get his arse out of there some time during the day and clear the mess? Why didn't I slap both pizza-faces and tell them to go upstairs and do their homework and stop leering at women? I certainly would ask you that if you'd just described such a cosy domestic scene.

And the answer is I didn't because I was too tired. It takes much less effort to just clear up and sort it all out than it does to nag and threaten them into doing it for themselves. I'd have had to explain where the dishwasher and washing machine were situated, describe the arcane techniques of putting in powder and switching on. And then I'd have had to sort out the mess when the soap powder exploded over the floor or the dishwasher seized up mid-cycle because all the badly-loaded bowls had fallen over. It's just too much effort. And I knew they deliberately acted helpless and sabotaged things so they wouldn't get asked again, I knew this. And still it worked.

This is why middle-aged mothers like I was then go to watch movies like *Lord of the Rings* or *King Alfred* or *Gladiator*, full of noble stoical men who fight and get knocked down and then get up again, about men who are competent, who don't run away or whine or hide, who keep their promises, whom you can trust. Mythical beasts, of course. Far easier to track down a unicorn.

So I sat in the kitchen, glugging red wine (I hate white), then belatedly remembered and took Jim his coffee. After the pizza-faces had lumbered out into the evening to see their mates (don't ask), we had scrambled eggs on toast and I asked him how the book was going.

"Bloody awful. I'm stuck again."

"Oh dear."

"Of course, it's got to be one of the Levellers, but which one?"

His voice was fretful and utterly self-absorbed. I loved Jim once, and still did then. He had never made it bad enough for me to make me take the decision to get out. I almost wished he'd beat me up because then it would have been simple. And I see women who are regularly used as punchbags and still stick around. He never hit one of the children, not even when they were little and it was still relatively safe. He used to be the quiet, gloomy type of drunk, not the dangerous, destructive kind. Which is why it was all such a surprise what the Prozac did to him. Of course, we know about it now, but not then. Hundreds of other spouses were as surprised as I was, and some weren't as lucky.

He was depressed because he had thought he was going to be a huge success, he had thought he was going to take out Martin Amis and completely crap all over Salman Rushdie, and win the Booker Prize and the Pulitzer Prize and the Nobel Prize for Literature, and he didn't. He genuinely is a good writer, I think.

I liked his books, I always read them and made (quite careful) comments. He thanked me in the prefaces.

But the fact is he was just a jobbing mid-list writer, earning, on average, less than an office cleaner, and it tormented him, he hated it. Every new *Harry Potter* was an insult to him. He sat in his room, drinking vodka and tonic and pecking away on his computer and sleeping and having a wank with the wank mags he thought I didn't know about and nipping off to the pub during the day when the coast was clear to play darts and drink. He was a local character, everyone in the village knew him. They hardly saw me because I was usually out by 8.30 and often not back till late. He used to look after the boys – very well, incidentally – but they were at school all day now and out most of the night too, leaving him loads of time to write, theoretically.

And there's the fact that divorce is a long, protracted and complicated business, very expensive in time and trouble. And money, which we'd never had much of.

Sometimes my patients told me to ditch him, luv, he's no good for you. But I felt sorry for him, it seemed wrong to kick a man when he's down and... Well, every so often I'd see him again as he was, and think I'd be mad to leave.

"…and the Fifth Monarchy men could be…"

The droning voice stopped abruptly in mid-sentence. He'd spotted me.

I'm afraid when he starts about his plots and who should have done it, I can't... I just find myself switching off.

"You're not listening, are you?" he said, putting his knife and fork down prissily.

"I'm sorry, I was thinking about Onion. Down at MiniWonders. Do you remember, I told you about…"

"Why should you listen? Nobody else is interested. Why should you be?"

"Well, maybe they're a bit distant from us…"

"Everything they said or thought was like a prophecy. They were the first truly modern thinkers. And everyone thinks they were just 17th century bible bashing nutcases."

"Well, er…"

"But you're right. It's boring. Now Animé – that's interesting. Levellers. Boring."

I recognised the symptoms. "Did the review not come out?"

"No. They had a very big urgent feature about the Animé graphic novel and literacy, so of course there wasn't room for the usual historical crime roundup."

"Oh dear.  Um. Are you going to Harrowed in Harrogate?" Big crimewriter's convention. Panel discussions. Formal dinner. Lots of writers, all complaining about publishers. A few fans, shocked that their heroes are so mercenary. A bit of quiet shagging, and a lot of noisy drinking. Fun if you like that sort of thing.

"No. Trollope & Bender won't sub the hotel or the fee."

"Bastards."

"You can understand their point of view," he said, dismal drone again. God, I hate that depressive tone of voice, the monotone that says: it's not even worth the effort to make my voice sound interesting, if I'm bored and miserable you can be too. "I mean, I don't sell very many, even the libraries are losing interest. I don't make much money for them, why should they sub me?"

"Well er…"

"Don't say it."

"Maybe modern crime…" Too late. Jim stood up, put on the corduroy jacket that came with the first royalty cheque.

"I write historical fiction because the past is important. It's like saying a person's childhood doesn't matter. It does matter. We have to keep it alive."

Man with a mission, misunderstood, miserable. Oh piss off, go and drone at them down the pub where you're the village intellectual.

He didn't, rather pointedly, slam the door as he went out.

So I cleared up the dishes, started the dishwasher, cleared the kitchen, left the washing on the line, fed the ancient rabbit, much loved three years ago, now completely discarded and not seeming to care very much, cleared pizza-face spoor from the sitting room, sat down to watch a sitcom repeat about a dry cleaning shop and fell asleep.

I woke at midnight, freezing, with a crick in my neck and the phone ringing. Sorry. That would be the landline phone, still attached to the wall.

It was the landlord of the Old Smugglers Inn, a brick-built low-level thing appended to a motel just outside the village, with a huge carpark and mass-produced fake Victoriana cluttering its brown and cream interior.

"Is that Mrs Stukeley."

"Er... yes?" I said cautiously, wondering if Matt or Si had been daft enough to pretend to be over 18 in a pub where every second regular had seen them trotting into primary school and could count.

"Thing is, Mrs Stukeley, I'm very sorry to trouble you so late, but what with the reverend's car and him waving that club, I'll have to call the police this time if you don't come fetch 'im."

"Who?"

"Jim. Mr Stukeley."

"Jim?"

"He's in a bad way, I'm sorry to have to tell you."

I really couldn't feel anything except weary irritation.

"Right."

And I got my keys and went out to the car, drove down the road and over the roundabout and into the vast car-park that had eaten two fields full of daffodil bulbs that no-one could sell because of competition from the Channel Islands. There was a small knot of interested spectators and Jim standing on a car with a big log of firewood in his hand.

"Wash me thoroughly from mine iniquity," he chanted, "cleanse me from my sin. Can anybody help the vicar with this simple question. Which Psalm is it? Eh? How about it, vicar?"

I watched the vicar, whose car Jim was standing on, shrink into himself. He was one of those pathologically nice Church of England gigglers, poor chap, and Jim had never liked him.

"Um... I really wish... um really, I think you should get down from there," he fluted, "You might slip and hurt yourself."

Jim snarled. "Tell me which psalm or I bust your fucking windscreen, you snivelling arse-licking happy-clappy wanker."

A younger me, or even an older me, might have found the whole thing funny. The me of that time just felt tired.

"What brought this on?" I asked one of the bar staff, standing poised with a mobile.

"About six pints, ten shorts and an argument about the modern Prayerbook."

"Bloody stupid," I muttered, "He doesn't even believe in God."

"He believes in the Book of Common Prayer," said the barman. "He said so. 'Course it didn't help that poor old Reverend Steve was being a bit too friendly with young Suzie."

I blinked at him, wondered what that had to do with anything.

"Who?"

"She's gone home," said the barman.

"Wash me thoroughly from my iniquity, cleanse me from my sin!" roared Jim, his bolt of wood poised and I thought of the dent in the finances mending the vicar's car would cause.

So I stepped forwards.

"It's the Fifty-first psalm," I told him, "And it's the neck-verse, the last thing you heard if you were going to be hanged."

Somebody clapped. Jim just stood there, mouth open. Well of course I know it, the whole plot of his last Job Gurney book had turned on someone not knowing the neck-verse.

"Right," said Jim, recovering fast from his shock and swaying dangerously. "And a good wife is a pearl beyond price, beyond diamonds and rubies."

"Thank you," I said gravely. He swayed some more, then belched, lifted the bolt of wood, blinked at it and put it down on the roof of the vicar's car. "But if you start quoting St Paul on matrimony, I'll leave you here."

I realised it pleased him immensely that I'd come, but wasn't sure why. He wasn't usually happy to see me. He bowed to all four quarters and got a sprinkle of ironic clapping, then jumped down.

The vicar rushed over and started furiously scrubbing scuff-marks off the top of his shiny Citroen with his hanky, which had a Snoopy on it.

Jim put his arm across my shoulders and leaned heavily.

"Once again thou hast saved me, Mistress Gurney," he said theatrically. "Swear thou wilt never leave me."

"Come on, let's go home."

"Swear."

"Come on."

He stopped just as we got to the car and he kissed me, quite nicely really, pity about the booze. Unfortunately I'd had to switch my libido off at the mains because it was so long since we'd last kissed.

"Thou art the best, most faithful of women," he slurred. "Really you are. Anybody die today?"

"No," I told him, "they didn't."

As I drove the quarter mile back home I watched the hectic gleam go out of his eyes, the slow folding up of his face, the dull whine come back into his voice. And slowly but surely it became my fault that he'd threatened to smash the vicar's precious windscreen.

I hadn't the energy to argue with him so I agreed and apologised and he went to his study muttering about the rape of the English language and prayerbooks written like municipal waste-disposal specifications.

It was all a load of bullshit about me being the best of wives, produced for his audience. He didn't even bother to say goodnight to me as he headed for his study, no doubt already lost again in the seventeenth century where he was so much happier. I checked the boys' rooms, and lo, both of them were in bed, both naked, one dribbling on his wank mag that he thought I didn't know about – lordy lordy, whyever would I find anything hidden under the mattress now?

I am a stranger in a strange land, I thought to myself, washed teeth, went to bed and dreamed prophetically about exploding motorbikes.

# Chapter 3


*Wednesday. Dress Mrs Golightly's ulcers, new patient, see Onion last thing, tkd.*

People ask in sepulchral voices how I could bear to do this job. When I had started about eight years before, it was at the cutting edge of terminal care "inna *communidy*" and I loved it. You were liberating people from the tyranny of hospital, you could help them to die in the way their grandparents had, with their families around them and all their bills paid, where they were important and not just an embarrassing failure for the hospital team. Now… there was starting to be the smell of cost-cutting about it. And I suppose I was burnt-out. So most of the time I managed by having a strict policy of compartmentalisation. I told myself I had to stay objective to do my job properly, which was true, but it left me wondering sometimes what I really thought of anything. Practicalities and body functions seemed all of the universe to me. When I was there, with a patient, I was, to the best of my ability, a hundred per cent there. When I was not, I didn't think about them. It may sound callous but the alternative was nervous breakdown and incompetence.

Just occasionally somebody will get under my skin, and then my work becomes very difficult. I'd seen a new patient that morning, a young architect who had two lovely kids, a furiously well-mannered wife and liver cancer that would probably wipe him out by Christmas. I knew that the two little boys would get to me because they were so like Matthew and Simon before they turned into horrible teenaged louts. You can never predict how children will take a looming death; the world we live in makes it much harder for them because in all the computer games and cartoon shows, death is only a temporary inconvenience and then you recover and go and fight again. Years ago, Simon had been devastated when our cat died: not at the time, but a week later when he wanted to dig up her body so Sooty could come back to life again, and I had to tell him she wouldn't. Ever. He had been haunted by monsters and dinosaurs for months afterwards.

Now of course, he'd turned into a monster himself and it took a real effort of will to remember how gorgeous he'd looked in a shirt and tie at a friend's wedding only two years back.

I went into the office to do paperwork and sort my diary out and write up a report. Slightly behind still, I went over to MiniWonders to see Onion before going on to what I normally called my exercise class. The rain was hissing down again, courtesy of the Gulf Stream, and a caravan that is in a beautiful place when it's sunny, is exposed to the howling rage of the Atlantic when it isn't. At least somebody had parked a small but solid camper van next to Onion's caravan where it took some of the force of the wind.

I locked the car, went to look over the cliff and saw that the surf was up and most of Onion's boys had their wetsuits on and were riding the waves. I don't believe in idealising floppy haired young men who beach bum their lives away, but Jog told me once that if he hadn't found surfing he would have topped himself because he would have had nothing bigger than himself in his life.

Jog's quite a philosopher. I wondered if he'd been the person who responded to the ad in the Big Issue.

I trudged towards the caravan, heard singing and a hissing spattering noise. Somebody was cooking which was worrying and he was singing as well. I recognised the voice and tensed up at once. Why was *he* still here?

The song came to an end, something about a gypsy rover as that sort of song usually is, and I heard Onion sigh.

"You should make an album."

"Maybe I will. Dedicated to you."

Boy, he's keen, I thought, cynically and unfairly.

So I knocked, went in and Onion was sitting in her managing director's chair, wrapped in one of her red rugs, watching the Tattoo-man cooking on the little primus stove, with a fire-blanket draped carefully over the oxygen apparatus behind her.

As I was about to read them the riot act for doing a fry-up in the same caravan as oxygen cylinders, this rather took the wind out of my sails.

Tattoo turned his horrific face to me and grinned as if he was reading my baleful thoughts. "Do you like morcilla sausage?" he asked, shaking the pan expertly.

"Love it. Do you think I got this shapely by sitting around nibbling lettuce leaves?" I said, automatic pilot as I clocked the fact that somebody had been cleaning up the caravan. Surely not him? Tattoo laughed at my feeble crack and cocked an eyebrow at me.

"Want some?"

It wasn't just a fry-up. Tattoo had made some sort of tapas dish: broad beans in olive oil with garlic, topped with black pudding. Obviously he was trying to fatten Onion up by the quickest method he could think of. It smelled fantastic. I checked my watch.

"I'd love some but I can't. I've got a class in less than an hour and if I eat that lot, I'll get indigestion. Maybe another time."

"Class?"

"Exercise class," I said, to avoid questions but Onion always liked to cause trouble.

"Martial arts," she said mischievously, "Anna does karate."

"No, I don't," I told her patiently, "it's taekwondo."

Tattoo looked interested. "Oh yeah?  Is that the one with the spin kicks and the jump kicks?"

"Eventually."

"Eh?"

"Eventually you get to do spin kicks and jump kicks. First you just learn how to punch and front kick properly."

"Can you break things?"

"Oh yes."

"Cool. I've always wanted to do that."

I watched him as he served Onion with her tapas, spreading some paper towel on her lap, putting a plank of wood across from the bed to the window ledge to act as a table. He arranged a little pile of beans and just two bits of black pudding on a big plate and gave her a knife and fork.

"Now eat," he said.

"I'm not hungry," said Onion, causing trouble as usual.

Tattoo gave her a long considering look. "Are you winding me up, darling?"

"Don't call me darling."

"Onion?"

She shrugged, delicately, looked at me covertly, then down at her plate. I thought she was hungry, she just didn't want to admit it.

Tattoo switched off the flame, poured the rest of the tapas into a bowl and put it in the miniature oven, then came and sat down on the bed next to Onion in her throne, crowding her. He still had the same faded black t-shirt on with some sort of skeletal bird printed on it.

"Now Onion," he said gently, "Is there something there you don't like?"

"N...no."

"You said you'd eat if I cooked for you, I've cooked it, now it's your part of the deal."

"I like it," she said, her thin blonde hair curtaining forward, "I'm just not hungry."

"Darling, I know you're playing funny games," said Tattoo. He leaned his bare muscular forearms on his knees and looked sideways and up at her. "Could we just skip the funny games? We've been through all that."

Standing ignored by the door, I suddenly thought that if Tattoo talked to me in that soft intense way, I'd eat every scrap.

"Not hungry," muttered Onion.

For a moment I thought he might shout or lose his temper. He just carried on looking at her for about thirty seconds, and then he stood. Something about it... I moved forward quickly.

But he did nothing except pick up the plate, open the oven, empty the food into the bowl, shut the oven, put the plate in the tiny sink.

"OK," he said. Just for a second I thought I saw the bewildered hurt of a much younger man in his face. But it closed up, he put on his jacket, went out into the rain. Suddenly the caravan was twice as big.

"Onion," I said disapprovingly, "Was that fair?"

She shrugged. I moved the plank and did things for her. She had an ugly looking tremor in her legs which were like sticks. I was sure she hadn't eaten anything since yesterday, if then, and she had no excuse because she wasn't getting chemotherapy any more.

"I don't know," I said, just to make noises and distract her from what I was doing, "If some big hunky bloke actually bothered to cook for me and make me something nice, I'd eat it if it killed me."

Something about her silence made me look closer and I found she was crying, which Onion never does, not ever, not even when she got her diagnosis.

I gave her a tissue, waited for her to get a grip, longing to know the story between her and Tattoo-man. Unfortunately, I knew Onion well enough to realise that asking her would be a certain way to make sure I never found out.

"All right," she whispered, "I'll have some."

So I got it out of the oven, put it back on the plate, put the makeshift tray back, gave her the knife and fork and she cut it all into tiny pieces and stirred it round and finally, she ate most of it. She drank water, mineral water I found under the sink, because alcohol argued with most of her drugs. I knew, once I'd safely gone, that Jog would come in and smoke a spliff with her which would do her more good than all those drugs put together, but you couldn't explain that to the Home Office and Customs & Excise back then. So I never allowed anybody to smoke blow in front of me, or anything else. Then I didn't know anything about it. The police would have liked me to tell them which ones smoked dope, but I'd have gone to jail first. I mean that. Some people did, so it wasn't impossible. I've thought about it since, and I'd honestly rather go to jail.

"How's Jog?" I asked, trying to find something neutral. The caravan was getting dark although it was a summer evening; more lovely rain of course. There was a big heavy battery torch there, brand new, I switched it on and lo, light.

"He's OK."

"And what's that guy's name? The biker?"

"Him? You'll have to ask him. I'm not sure what he's calling himself."

"*Calling* himself?"

She giggled, wrinkled her nose and nibbled down the last garlicky broad bean.

I cleared away, checked various things needing checking, filled in forms and asked if she needed help to get back in bed.

She shrugged, thought that Jog would do it. It was getting late, so I went out of the caravan and found Tattoo waiting for me. It didn't worry me so much this time. He didn't seem as bad as he looked. And it wasn't just a middle-aged mum getting horny for a young guy who could cook, believe me. Well it was a bit, I've told you how sexy competence is in a man. And he wasn't that young. As far as I could tell, he was at least ten years older than most of the twenty-something surfers who were caring for Onion, which said something interesting about how old Onion really was. She gave a different birth date each time I asked.

It took me a minute, but then I realised: he'd changed into sweatpants and trainers and a clean t-shirt, all new, by the way. The camper van must be his.

"Hi," he said, "That class of yours. Can I come?"

"What?"

"I told you, I want to learn something like that. Kung fu, taekwondo."

"Why?"

"I just do. Say I've got a professional interest."

"I don't think so."

Again, there was a tightening of his jaw. He wasn't used to being told no.

"Why not?"

"I don't know you. I don't trust you. You don't look…"

"Respectable?"

"That's not the problem." Knowing what I know about respectable people, I meant that. He didn't look very law-abiding, was my problem.

Jog was coming up the path, still in his wet suit in the rain, his board under his arm, his yellow mane flowing behind him, he looked like that comic book superhero, you know, the X-man from Atlantis. He has a bearded weather-beaten face that looks older than his chronological age but is in fact younger than his mental age. I like Jog, very much.

"Hi," I said.

"Yeah," said Jog. "How is she?"

He was speaking to Tattoo as well. "I cooked for her but I don't know if she…"

"She ate," I said, "as soon as you weren't watching."

Tattoo grinned wryly. "Same old… Onion. I thought she might."

Jog was watching Tattoo very seriously, almost examining him. Tattoo caught this and looked back. Well, I didn't trust Tattoo but I did trust Jog.

"Jog, what do you think. Er..." I couldn't call him Tattoo, which was my private name for him after all. "... He wants to come to my class. That cool?"

And I didn't care that Tattoo was standing there while I checked up on him. I wanted him to know that I do check.

Jog's expression suddenly reminded me of a poker player in a movie. "I think so," he said considering. "Yeah, why not?"

"You've never done time, never been convicted for any violent offence?" I asked Tattoo directly.

Tattoo blinked his blue eyes at me in surprise and then laughed outright. "Oh I get it," he said. "OK, I see your point. No, I categorically assure you, Ms Clements, I have never been convicted of anything except motoring offences and I have never been to jail."

It would have to do, I supposed.

Jog went towards the caravan to look in on Onion, and I went with him.

"Is there anything I should know about that guy?" I asked. "Is he a dealer, in a gang? Anything like that. What's his name?"

"He's not a dealer, he's not in a gang," said Jog judiciously, "And the tattoo – well, it's a bit of a youthful mistake, I think. Don't worry about it."

"Why won't anyone tell me his name?"

"Give him a lift in your car and...uh.. cross-examine him yourself, Anna," said Jog. "I don't think he'll do anything too bad."

He poked his head round Onion's door, said he'd be back to tuck her in, went to his tent and somehow slithered out of his wet suit and into dry bermudas and t-shirt in record time. I hate bermudas. Not even Jog can look dignified in them.

I went back to Tattoo. "Jog says I should give you a lift."

"That's kind." He was smoking, his hand cupped round the end to keep the rain off it. "If it's not too much trouble, could you bring me back. Gyro borrowed the Harley to do some shopping."

"It's not too much trouble, so long as you tell me your name."

"Alan," he said at once, "Alan Smithee."

And I still didn't get it. Jim might have, but why should I know stuff like that?

"Do you think the instructor'll be OK if I join in," said Tattoo as we chunka chunkaed up the hill towards Lyonesse Dance Palace. I still couldn't think of him as an Alan so I kept on with him as Tattoo. Bless the English language, you don't actually have to call anyone by name if you don't want to.

"Yeah, she'll be fine."

"Oh, it's a girl."

"Yup. That a problem?" It is for some male would-be martial artists, especially in things like karate and taekwondo, what are called the hard styles. Men often have the unjust suspicion that a black belt means less for a woman. Also there's the fact that your average lout has escaped from his mummy too recently to be able to take instruction from a female. I didn't mind their prejudice; as far as I was concerned, it was their problem and it kept the macho idiots out of the club.

"No. Mind if I smoke?"

"Not if I can have one."

"Very unhealthy habit, you know," he said as he lit up two and handed me one.

"Tell me about it."

"Yes, I suppose you would know. Why do you do it?"

"Because I'm addicted. It's my drug of choice. I do alcohol and chocolate too, but mostly I'm just a nicotine-head."

"Oh. Me too. Cheers."

"At least it's still legal," I said, thinking about Benjy's garden and the risks the surfers had taken to score for Onion.

Tattoo nodded, squinted at the rain on the windscreen. My driving seemed to make him nervous. He visibly winced as I drove up a lane where the brambles were scratching both sides of the car at once.

"Hey don't worry," I told him with sadistic glee, "At least I'm not overtaking a Harley on a blind corner."

He grinned at me. "So it was you. What did you call me?"

"Fucking organ-donor. It's what we called motorbike riders when I used to do emergency work."

He laughed until I went over the next tiny little hump-backed bridge. Well, maybe I did take it a bit fast.

"Not been to South Cornwall before?" I asked. You can always tell. The summer visitors are the ones with the white knuckles and the terrified expressions, driving at 10 mph down lanes the locals breeze through at fifty.

"Er… No. Got as far as Devon once."

"Oh. Up-country."

"It's pretty here," he said judiciously, "maybe a bit wet."

"And what do you do, Mr Smithee?" I asked.

Blue gaze sideways. "Do?"

"For a living? Where's the money come from? Jog said you're not a dealer."

He looked down at his hands. "I work in films," he said eventually, "I'm a grip, sometimes a wrangler. That's why I'm interested in doing martial arts, for stunts."

"Eventually."

"Oh yes, eventually. How long would it take to get a black belt?"

I sighed. If there's a worst question to put to a martial artist, that's it. "It depends. Some people take years and years and some people get it in three. Why?"

"Just wondered. Why do you do it?"

I thought about it while I stamped on the brakes for the radar trap and then negotiated the double roundabout, one of many since South Cornwall County Council are addicted to them. "Lots of reasons. For a start I'm a lot less unpleasant to my offspring when I'm training than when I'm not."

"Offspring?"

"Two boys, louts. Then there's my job. You know who gets attacked at work more than any other profession?"

"You're going to tell me nurses."

"Yes. I had a nasty experience a few years ago and went along to a class to try and increase my confidence. It worked. And then there's the... fascination of it. And the fact that while you're doing it you can't think of anything else, you concentrate. It blows off frustration, puts things in perspective... Nothing to beat it, really."

My mother, who had spent all her life obeying the Rules for Girls as laid down in the Fifties had been in despair over my karate, as she called it. Not only had god cursed her with a daughter who – as she often pointed out when I was a teenager – had much less elegance and poise than your average rhinoceros, said daughter was now doing some horrid aggressive thing that might give her muscles.

My mother lived in the Home Counties where she belonged to an embroidery circle and an art class and made my brother's life a misery. It is no coincidence that South Cornwall is further from London than Edinburgh.

Tattoo blew smoke and tapped his ash into the ashtray. "Hm," he said. "So you're an enthusiast, eh?"

"No." I grinned at him. "I'm a notorious martial arts bore. Ask any of my patients."

# Chapter 4

*Wednesday evening. Tae kwon do class, Lyonesse Leisure Palace.*

We got to the leisure centre, parked. I got my kit out of the back, locked everything carefully, left him at the entrance to the training hall and went to see the first dan black belt running the warm-up. I was about fifteen minutes late, so I nodded at Sid. We bowed to each other.

"He says his name's Alan," I said, pointing at Tattoo who had taken his trainers and socks off and was doing some self-conscious jogging on the spot, windmilling his arms. "He wants to have a go."

Sid looked at him, got the benefit of the facial decoration and sucked his teeth. He works in a garage, does Sid, and is an expert tooth-sucker. You can almost estimate the size of your bill from the length and vehemence of his tooth-suck when he looks under the bonnet. If Tattoo had been a car, his big-end would have gone.

"Jog says he's OK. I'll be out in a minute, you finish the warm up," I said to Sid, and rushed off to the pokey little toilet to change.

When I came out, Sid was out the front of the class, with Tattoo at the back, doing jumping jacks and bunny hops quite happily, and press-ups – like most men, he knew how, even if he was out of practice. No way was he going to do any on his fists, though. The little kids were fascinated by his face, but the thing I'd been worried about, that he wouldn't take the class seriously, no problem there. He was doing his level best with the odd stretching positions Sid was asking him to take up, and as I tell every class I ever take, that's all that matters.

I went up the front of the class and Sid called the class to attention and they all bowed to me. I bowed back.

All right. I admit it. I'd enjoyed not telling Tattoo that I'm the black belt instructor, it's my class. My mother isn't the only one who has funny reactions to women black belts. Quite a lot of men back off in exaggerated terror and ask if I beat my husband.

I'd been tempted. But I didn't. Speaking as someone who spends a lot of time learning how to do it properly, I believe that people shouldn't hit people. Well, not first, anyway. You're allowed to hit back.

"All right. Last chance to tell me about injuries and take your jewellery off," I said. No one moved. "Chunbi. Now we're going to do some leg techniques in linework, then we'll split up and practice patterns. Anybody who's got their pads can stay for the extra half-hour and do sparring."

Sid brightened at a sparring session, as did Markus, Kerry and Hans. Tattoo just caught his breath and gave me a reproachful stare. You have to keep an eye on the beginners at the back. Most of the time they're staggering about trying to copy the people in front of them. Tattoo had some notion of how to do a front kick, none whatever of how to do a side kick. I stood in front of him.

"Watch me," I said, lifting up my leg sideways and holding it there. He watched carefully, eyes narrowed. "Leg up this way, bend the other one slightly, chamber it, that means fold the kicking leg back, kick with the outer edge of your foot, pull it back, put it down."

He tried.

"Lower," I said. "It's more important to get the shape right than to get the height, height will come. Again. Use your glutes, not your thigh muscles. And again. Other foot. Again. OK. Bend both your knees, try and keep your bum in. That's good."

And it was. He was sweating and breathing hard, but he wasn't actually dying and he had good balance. He also clearly had what I think of as physical ept, a quality I don't have, being inept, but recognise when I see it. He could look at a movement or technique, get his body to do pretty much the same thing and then he could remember it. That's a much more complicated process than you might think. You could call it physical intelligence or sports ability and you're either born with it or not.

Even so, linework's a bit of a shock to the system when you're not used to it, so I let them relax for a minute before splitting them up to work on patterns.

Black belt always takes the most junior grades because they need the most instruction. I had Sid teaching the yellow and green belts and I had Kerry, who had a very new red belt and needed confidence building, take the blues and red tags.

So I faced four little kids, a couple of mums in track suits, a lad called Ike and Tattoo. We bowed. I knew Tattoo was also holding out on me, because he knew how to bow, he must have done something.

We ran through Sajo jirugi, four-directional punching, nos 1 and 2 which I won't bore you with. Then I worked on their punching techniques. A martial arts punch is completely different from a boxing punch because it comes from the hip not the shoulder. I like using the big punching pads because you get a feel for someone's power. Little kids have a surprising amount once they focus their attention. Adult women have problems with aggression in sparring, but don't mind punching pads, especially if you invite them to imagine their husband's face or their boss's face there. As for Tattoo...

Very solid, lots of dig, but a boxer's punch, not correct. I took him through it, moved his hands and feet to the right places. It was interesting. Martial arts are all contact sports. Generally, the simplest way of getting the techniques over is for the instructor to physically move the students' arms and legs until they're right. You want them to feel the right position in their muscles and sometimes people don't understand that. Men in particular often find it embarassing when a woman pulls their foot over to the correct placement. And Jim always said I only did taekwondo classes so I could cop a feel of the nice young lads who come along. We're still not a touchy feely society. Now to my surprise, Tattoo was fine with that aspect; for all the way he looked, when I shifted him about he didn't tense up, he went with it.

Then I told them about the Hard Look technique. This is sort of a joke, but it's also quite useful. When they're breathing hard and they need a bit of a rest, I do some stretching and then I line them up and tell them to give me a hard look. Then when they take their grading examinations, they know what to do with their faces while they're waiting to be asked theory questions. When in doubt, I tell them, Hard Look. Relax your mouth, tighten your jaw and the muscles round your eyes. Go and try it in a mirror, you'll be surprised.

The kids think it's hilarious. I get down at their level and I stare at them. They have to stare back without laughing. None of them can. The girls go cross-eyed. The mums think it's funny too. They stare back, usually they manage not to laugh until I've moved on. The lads feel embarassed but when they get into it, they're quite good. Tattoo was last.

"All right," I said. "I'll stare at you. And you give me a hard look."

"You sure about that?" I'll swear his eyes were dancing.

"You sure about that, *ma'am*," I told him. Taekwondo's quite militaristic.

"Ma'am."

"Yes. Go on. Frighten me."

"OK." He looked down for a second as I stared at him, then he looked up and .... Pow! Honest to god. It was almost like a physical blow. Blue eyes help, straight face helps, horrible tattoo helps, but it was still something special.

"Wow." I smiled, "You got a black belt in Hard Looks?"

"Yes," he said, with a little sideways cock of his head. "I do."

"I believe you."

And just for a second there, I lost track. Couldn't have been the smile or the blue eyes or the shoulders. No. No way.

I coughed. "OK, everybody, running on the spot, front kicks at my count…"

He had to stay for the sparring and I lent him some spare pads to have a go at some very gentle non-contact work. Again, he was good; a bit breathless, telegraphed his punches, but he got a nice sneaky kick in on me once and he was careful when he sparred with one of the other girls.

He'd brought a towel, and despite my warnings, went and braved the wonky Cornish showers. Sid and I waited, and heard him yowl when halfway through, the water suddenly went from hot to icy cold.

The sun had come out while we were doing the class, and it faded down to a very golden sunset as we got back into the car.

He was relaxed and happy, despite his shower. We drove back through the country lanes and he didn't even twitch when I had to stamp on the brakes for a tractor.

"Why didn't you tell me you were the instructor?" he asked as we did the double-roundabout dance with a summer visitor who was frightened about turning right.

"Dunno. Didn't feel like it."

"You're good.  I enjoyed it."

I smiled back at him. "Well, thank you. Still want to do spin kicks and jump kicks?"

He looked rueful. He'd fallen flat on his back when he tried bandae dollio chagi, the simplest of the spin kicks. Big people always have terrible trouble with them.

"Oh yes. I've got to."

"Why?"

"Business."

"Do you like working in films?"

Sideways gaze again. I was finding them disconcerting, especially after seeing his mastery of Hard Look Jirugi, as you might call it if you wanted to be a real martial arts nerd.

"I love it."

"Why? I heard it was really bitchy and difficult and stars throw tantrums."

"Well, is that from the press or is it from a witness?"

"Oh, magazine articles. I can do ignorant prejudice too, you know."

He smiled. "Are you going to ask if I've worked with anyone famous?"

"Of course I am."

"Mel. Al. Russell. Jodie."

"As in Gibson, Pacino, Crowe, Foster?"

"Uhuh. Jodie likes her coffee black, no sugar, Mel prefers latte plus two."

"Wow."

"It's less glamorous than it sounds. They're just actors."

"How'd you get into it?"

"Hereditary, I'm afraid. My mum was a wardrobe supervisor. Me, I'm just muscle."

"Who else have you worked with? Bud Anderson?"

"Once, a long time ago."

"James Kieran? Shaun Graham?"

"Yeah, Shaun Graham. On *King Alfred.*"

"Oh I saw that, that was brilliant. I loved the battle at the end. And the scenes with the Viking king – brilliant fight. And with Emma, it was so tender, and then so angry... Sorry.  I suppose it must all be very routine to you."

"No. It's always good to hear you haven't wasted sixteen weeks of your life."

"So what's he like?"

"Who?"

"Shaun Graham?"

Tattoo laughed. "Him? He's a prick. Big-headed drunken arsehole."

"Aw," I said ruefully, "Pam said he's probably gay."

Tattoo seemed to be having a coughing fit. "No, he's not gay. Definitely not. James Kieran is though."

"Oh everyone knows that. Even I do, and I'm famously sad because I never watch soaps and I don't read *Hello* and I've no idea who's in the top ten." But there had been a lot in the papers a few years back, some of it very nasty, about Kieran's partner, Andy, getting AIDS. That was before the AZT cocktail. Kieran had looked after Andy until the end and then given eyewatering amounts of cash to various AIDS charities in his memory. I'd respected him for that – it was well before AIDS was acceptable in Hollywood.

The Tattoo-man was looking out of the window where the sun was setting over the sea, making the brambles glow. I slowed right down because I knew what might be round the bend at this time. Sure enough...

"Shit!"

It is a bit disconcerting when a large mild black and white face comes and peers at you through the window. Hooves, tails, large square black and white back ends – they were going in from the field. The last survivors of BSE and foot-and-mouth, docketed, clipped, registered, less than three years old. Rescued in the nick of time by the Atkins diet. Most local farmers have stopped keeping dairy stock and beef stock because of the form-filling which they can't be doing with. Sometimes I think that the world is drowning in forms. Pity you can't eat them or drink them. One day we'll look round and wonder where all the food went.

I put the handbrake on and switched off the engine. "No point in worrying," I said, "They'll be through the gate in about ten minutes or so."

"No, that's OK. I'm happy. What you said about *King Alfred*. Did you really like it?"

"I loved it. It was as good as *Gladiator* or *Lord of the Rings*. Bowled me over. It had everything. Big hard-looking blokes stomping around waving swords, riding horses. Historical accuracy so my husband wouldn't whine too much – he's a historical novelist and you have never truly been bored if you haven't heard him complaining about the costumes and the use of Versailles in *The Man in the Iron Mask*... Reasonable script, lush music, mad plot, no irony, epic scale, no homages to Monty Python. It was great."

"Better than *Excalibur*?"

"Well, it didn't have Helen Mirren being sexy so the boys were sad, but yes, I thought so. And I'm very sorry to hear that Shaun Graham's a prick, because I thought he was lovely. The boys teased me for weeks afterwards and Jim got quite upset."

Tattoo was thoughtful as he watched the south end of northbound cows. "He easily upset, your husband?"

"Yes. Very. What did you do on the film?"

"Me? Well, a wrangler looks after horses, tries to stop them pissing and crapping during a shot – there's some magic ray given out by film cameras, that makes any horse near it decide to stale the instant the bloody thing's running."

The cows had finished their procession, so I started up the car, drove on still laughing. And I know what you're thinking, dear reader. You're thinking, eh up, what's going on here? And I can honestly tell you, nothing. Everything was switched off at the mains still. Well, I thought it was.

# Chapter 5



*To do: Wed eve: Tescos.*

We drove into the clifftop car park by the Taj Mahal, and found it was full. There was a van, an official looking car, and a couple of police officers, sitting in their own car watching.

Jog was standing in front of two heavyset men in suits and from the way his hands cut the air, I knew he was furious. Behind him were the other surfers, all standing about with their mouths open.

"What the fuck?" said Tattoo beside me. "Who're they?"

"I don't know."

"Shit. Oh shit."

I got out of the car, fully expecting him to follow, but he didn't.

I pushed through the large security men standing around. As I wasn't wearing any uniform, nobody made space for me.

"Excuse me," I said, marching forwards, in my best bossy nurse voice, "Would you mind telling me what's happening?"

"Keep out of it, my lover," said one of the two heavyset men, who was pushing a wad of papers into Jog's chest.

"You can't do this. You can't!" spluttered Jog.

"We are," said the other heavyset men, who I suddenly recognised.

"Hello Benton," I said to him. "How are you?"

He paused, looked, looked away, and then blushed. "Oh, hello Nurse Clements."

I couldn't ask him how his granny was because she'd died two months before. "How's your grandad?"

"Oh, getting along, getting along."

"What's happening here, Benton?"

"Um… we're… er… we're evicting some squatters."

"Who?"

"Vagrants."

I looked theatrically around. "Vagrants. What vagrants?"

Benton gestured at the surfer tents and the camper van and the caravan.

"Oh come off it," I sputtered. "They come every year just for the summer, they don't stay past September and they leave the place immaculate. Nobody minds them being here."

Benton stared at the ground and muttered.

"This legal then?" I demanded.

The other bailiff shoved the wad of papers at me. And it was in fact an eviction order, properly stamped and everything. All perfectly legal.

"Jog," I said, "why didn't you oppose it?"

"Uh…"

"Did you read the letter?"

Even Jog occasionally reads his mail. Occasionally. He looked at the ground, scraped his toe.

"It came when Onion was sick with those pills."

She had been very sick indeed, you could forgive him for not coping with official correspondance. Officials wouldn't of course, because that kind deal with their mail first thing in the morning, every morning no matter what. Not to do so is inconceivable to them.

I sighed.

"Look," I said to the bailiffs, "you can't evict these guys because they're looking after a very sick woman in that caravan."

"Why doesn't she go home if she's sick?" said the bailiff who wasn't Benton.

I gave him a Hard Look, well practised. "That is her home," I told him. "And you are?"

"Samuel T Tremayne. Bailiff."

"Well Mr Tremayne, I assume you're doing this on behalf of someone?"

"The new landlord. South Cornwall Property & Development."

"And the new landlord wouldn't like to cause anyone to die by his actions, would he? Or you, for that matter?"

"Who's going to die?" Tremayne had stuck his very large and smoothly shaven jaw out.

"The woman who lives in that caravan. She's extremely sick, she's got too many types of cancer to go into. She hasn't much longer to go and she wants to stay here, where it's beautiful. These young men are helping to look after her."

"Oh yeah," said Tremayne. "Well now I've heard everything."

"Would you believe a doctor?"

"I suppose…"

"Right."

I walked back to the car where Tattoo the Tosser was still cowering and shoved my mobile into his hand.

"What's happening?" he asked, not meeting my eyes. "Who are they?"

"Bailiffs. You're being evicted."

"What?"

"E-vict-ed. Onion as well. By South Cornwall Property & Development. If you want to put a stop to it, you go through my stored numbers and find Dr Gudgeon's home number, ring him and tell him Onion's being evicted and he's to get over here right now."

"Will he do it?"

"Bloody right he will," I growled. Steve Gudgeon is an old friend of mine, he knows me well enough to move his arse when I yell.

Tattoo started prodding the mobile and I marched back.

"All right," I said to Benton, "Would you like to come with me and meet the lady you're evicting? You too," I told Tremayne.

"Jog," I snapped over my shoulder, "go and make sure she's decent."

Delay, delay and more delay, that was the key. They'd brought muscle though the surfers weren't the kind who fought pitched battles anyway. But you could slow them down, and then get them into court and make applications and injunctions and get the press interested. You wouldn't win, they'd eventually be evicted. But you could spin it out for long enough.

Jog popped his head out and nodded. I led Benton and Tremayne forward, both of them looking nervous and uncomfortable in their cheap suits. I went up to the caravan, knocked on the door.

"Can we come in?"

There was a faint sound. I opened the door, ushered Tremayne in first. He went but only because he couldn't find any excuse not to. He was actually terrified. Most youngish healthy men are frightened of illness, you know, viscerally scared. It's what made AIDS such a cruel disease before the drug cocktail.

Onion knew about that too. She was draped on the bed, her breathing mask on. She had only her sheet over her, so they could see just how skeletal she was, except where the cancer had swollen her up. Her silvery hair spread over the pillow like a halo.

"Hi, Onion," I said to her cheefully. "This is Samuel T Tremayne who has a warrant to evict you from here."

She closed her eyes.

"And this is Benton," I said, ushering him in. "He wants to evict you too."

"We're only doing our job," quavered Tremayne. "That's all. It's a proper court order, we're just enforcing it."

"Of course you are," I said. Looking over his shoulder I could see that Tattoo the Tosser was still hiding out in my car, but Dr Gudgeon was driving up in his nippy little sports car. "Oh, look, there's the doctor."

"Her GP?"

"No," I said very sweetly. "Steve Gudgeon, Consultant in Oncology."

"Oh."

"He'll explain it all to you."

They backed out of the caravan and went unhappily to talk to him. I put my hand on Onion's delicate bones.

"Brilliant. Oscar worthy."

"Method acting," she creaked. "Did it work?"

"It will."

I came out, Jog went in, very hangdog because he'd let the eviction notice slide and he knew it. I went back to the car, where Tattoo the tosser was still talking on my mobile, I couldn't think why since Steve had arrived. He stopped as soon as he saw me, looked very uncomfortable.

"All right," I said. "I'll ask you once again. Who are you hiding from?"

"Not the police, OK?"

"Then who? Social services? Child Support? Customs? The Mafia?"

Small smile tucked in among the nasty blue lines which I was almost getting used to.

"Worse."

"Your wife?"

His eyelids flickered. "Not quite."

"I'm not impressed."

He said nothing, looked over to where the bailiffs were staring at the ground, worried men, while Steve explained the consequences of moving somebody as sick as Onion. He was laying it on with a trowel, but it was actually true. She physically could not take the strain of movement: her tissues were that fragile.

"What's happening?"

I wasn't really in a mood to talk to him because in fact when I had marched towards the bailiffs, I had really wished for some kind of sizeable trustworthy male back-up, and I was now feeling angry with myself for wishing that mythical beasts existed.

"Dr Gudgeon's explaining to them that they could make themselves responsible for Onion's premature death if they move her and because they don't want to get into trouble, they'll take the easy way out and they'll go back to the judge in the morning to seek guidance."

"And then what?"

"The judge will ask for reports and if he's feeling in a friendly mood, he'll delay execution of the warrant until Onion's dead. Then all the surfers will get kicked out but they won't mind."

"And if he isn't feeling friendly?"

"He'll tell them to proceed providing they have medical back up. An ambulance to take her to Treliske would do."

Tattoo blinked. We both knew Onion would never survive the seventy miles to Truro.

"OK. Name me a good lawyer round here."

I looked at him. "What are you going to do?"

"Get these guys a lawyer."

I was going to explain to him about legal aid and so on and how very much more difficult it was to get nowadays, but then I thought I'd let him find out for himself.

"Bertie Prince, of Prince, Tregorran & Stopes, he's a rottweiler. Or one of his partners, Charlotte Stopes."

"Got his number?"

"Office number, yes. You can leave a message. On my mobile. Go ahead, why don't you use it?"

"Thanks." Deadpan. He knew I was pissed off with him and he knew why, but he wasn't apologising, not giving an inch.

I walked back to the worried knot around Dr Gudgeon.

"We have to go back to the judge," said Benton, "We've got to. I don't want to risk it."

Tremayne was very unhappy, but it's hard to argue with a consultant in Oncology when he's giving you graphic details about what happens to a terminal cancer patient when she's disturbed.

And so, eventually, in the dark evening, the whole lot of them moved off.

"Dr Gudgeon," I said, "thank you for turning out."

"I do dislike this sneaky way of doing things," he sniffed. "Who was the chap who called me out?"

"One of Onion's old lovers."

"Oh." He sounded impressed. "Not a surfer."

"I don't know what he is, but he's definitely not a surfer."

"No. A bit too on the ball, really. No doubt they got the letter, but ignored it."

"It was during her abreaction."

"Well well. You're looking wonderful, Anna. Bit of excitement, eh? How's Jim?"

"Nearly finished his latest Job Gurney book." I always said that. Sometimes it was true.

"Oh splendid. I think they're excellent. Always look forward to them. So subtle. Will he sign a couple for me, do you think? Hardbacks?"

"He'd be delighted," I said and kissed Dr Gudgeon on the cheek because he's a sweetheart and there are many consultants who would have ripped me apart for calling them out at 9.45 pm on a summer's evening.

Dr Gudgeon had driven away, the boys were gathered round Onion to do her bidding. I looked at my car and saw that Tattoo the tosser had snuck away out of it. So I went over, found the mobile on the passenger seat and a tenner next to it.

Was I oversensitive? Did I misinterpret him? Maybe. I grabbed the money, went over to his camper van, banged on the door, no answer. So I pushed the money under the door, resisting the impulse to spit on it first. Then I rang Jim to explain what had happened. He was mad at me; he really hates it if I'm not there in the evening. Not that he wants to do anything, or really talk to me. He just likes me to be there. Then I drove home madly rejigging my entire schedule so I could go and talk to a judge.

# Chapter 6

*To do: Mrs Bosteagle. Court, Lyonesse. Robby. Onion. Get waffles, shoelaces, ask Jim for copies for Dr G.*

Once upon a time, I would wake Mat and Si with a kiss and tell them it was morning now, and they'd turn over in bed, the sweet smell of sleeping-child wafting up as I nuzzled their lovely soft cheeks and their little arms would come up and grip round my neck. All right, not often, more usually I'd be woken by Simon marching into the bedroom with his tedda at 5.30 am imperiously stating "It morning now. Where's my blekfuss. Tedda's hungwy."

Even Jim sometimes got them up and gave them breakfast, illicit cereal in front of the TV! Then I'd wake up slowly to the sound of cartoons shouting at each other and exploding dynamite, and really it was quite peaceful and pleasant.

Hormones are terrible things. Testosterone boots in and suddenly the soft and cuddly little brat becomes the rough, smelly, pustulent large brat, in thrall to its genitals, oafing around the place in search of acceptable grub. Mornings are no longer even a tiny bit tolerable, never mind the Himalayan heights of pleasant. There's me roaring up the stairs for the boys to get up and Jim huddled under his duvet exuding a black cloud of depression that actually seems to come through the door of his study and the oaves groaning into the bathroom where they leave foul odours of bodily functions. They shamble downstairs in shirts which I refuse to iron just to see them dumped on the floor and school ties loosely tied so they can be slipped on and off again like nooses...

My older friends, Pam for instance, tell me that they recover from it all and turn into strikingly handsome young men, but so far I have seen no symptoms of this transformation. I think she's lying. I think she sold her oaves and bought nice new ones with the money, that's what I think.

Eventually, exactly one minute before the bus is due at the bus-stop, they slurp down whatever noisome stuff they're eating and sprint out the door, always, but always leaving it open.

And I sit back and sigh and get myself some decent coffee and look at my diary and try to get my head together before I leave the house, smartly uniformed, on the ball, ready for anything. Jim is usually still asleep when I leave and to be honest, I don't know when he gets up, or even if he gets up at all. It's a real pity he can't be paid for sleeping.

I make myself eat something, meusli usually, because I know that if I don't I will be a foul-tempered witch by 11 oclock, will OD on petrol station chocolate and crisps and feel sick and headachy for the rest of the day.

This particular morning, I was in a bad mood anyway, no matter how much coffee I drank. I'd slept poorly because the famous compartmentalisation hadn't worked for Onion. I was worried about her, she had got thoroughly under my skin, even though if I'd met her when she was healthy, she would have smiled a very superior smile at this dumpy nurse-person and thoroughly patronised me. I suppose I have a soft spot for people with guts, which she had. Tattoo, or Alan, or whoever he was, I consigned to the outer darkness because he'd hidden in the car when it mattered.

I stopped off to buy a paper, *The Guardian*, which was far too high-minded to cover the sort of story I should have been reading that morning. I glanced at it, decided not to read yet another article by a bright-eyed and bushy-tailed little ex-journo mum-to-be about exactly which way her Branxton Hicks contractions pulsed when they hit her. You'll learn, girly, you'll learn, I thought, just like every old hag ever had.

I was looking forward to being an old hag. My family are very good at it. It's amazing we survived the seventeenth century really. Clucking and tutting at the wickedness of young folks today, it'll suit me.

So that's how I missed the gossip column stories. And I was in a hurry to meet my clients in the morning so I could get to Lyonesse to see what happened when the bailiffs went to get guidance from the judge in the afternoon.

Lyonesse has one small courtroom that doubles for the magistrates as well and it's in the old town lockup so it's one of the most picturesque courts in the country. Barristers who make it all the way down the line, often have themselves photographed in the looming entranceway.

The first person I met was the splendid Bertie Prince, tall, elegant, the kind of solicitor who would wear spats if he dared and who writes the rudest letters in Cornwall.

"Anna!" he said. "What have you been up to?"

"Trying to stop poor Onion getting turfed out of her caravan."

"I know that, what do you think I'm doing here. However did you manage it?"

"Manage what? I just had Dr Gudgeon…"

"Yes, yes, but what about this wonderfully timely *ex parte* injunction?"

"What?"

"It's all off. Nobody's going to get evicted. The receiver sold the place for a song to a property development company and the property company wanted vacant possession, but the entire site was bought as is early this morning, lock, stock and barrel, for double what they paid and the new owners have injuncted the eviction. Just like that. Please tell me you didn't machinate that?"

"Of course I didn't. I haven't won the lottery."

"Then it must be Onion's ancient swain as Jog darkly hints."

"Hmm. Could be."

"Pity he's not here. What's his name?"

"Alan Smithee. Claims to work in films, but I don't believe him."

And darling Bertie Prince laughed and laughed and the swine didn't tell me anything.

# Chapter 7



*Monday.  Gerry Goring at Treliske.  DO REPORTS.  Onion.  Tesco's.*

After that the Onion problem seemed to settle down for a few days and I had another problem with Gerry, the poor young architect, who tried to top himself by driving into a tree and succeeded only in writing off his Audi and knocking himself out because the silly twit had his seatbelt on.

I visited him in hospital to find him looking very sheepish and his wife tightlipped next to him. She left as I came in.

"Why didn't you tell me you were depressed?" I asked.

He blinked at me. "I'm not."

"Well you ought to be."

He smiled briefly. "What I mean is, I didn't do it because I'm depressed. It's just… What's the point of living on, when you know you're going to die?"

"We all know that," I said, sure that like many people, he probably hadn't yet worked out that death applied to him as well. "Or we should."

He stared at me.

"Everybody dies," I told him. "Hadn't you noticed?"

Silently, he shook his head. At least he was honest. Then he realised what he was saying and had the grace to smile.

"And by the way," I added, annoyed with myself that I hadn't told him before, "you might be able to get an early payout from your life insurance on your terminal diagnosis so you don't need to worry about the mortgage."

He stared at me and then laughed. He laughed a lot, which I took to be a good sign. His wife came in quickly, found him laughing and stared suspiciously at him, at me. Positive thinking OK, actual laughter – oh dear.

I left them to sort it out and drove like a maniac to get to Onion who was last on my list.

Where I found Tattoo bullying Benjy. Or at least that's what it look like from the car park. Benjy was sitting on the ground, curled up, with his arms over his head, while Tattoo stamped up and down, gesticulating. He loomed over Benji like a bald King Kong in leather jacket and jeans and looked like he was about to kick Benjy's head in. I screeched the car to a halt, jumped out, ran over.

"What's going on?"

"I just can't believe it, I can't fucking believe you could *do* that!"

"I'm sorry, man, I'm sorry, I didn't realise..." Benjy was actually crying while Tattoo paced to and fro with his fists up.

"*It doesn't care*," roared Tattoo. "Chemistry doesn't *care* whether you realised. Sorry isn't fucking good enough!"

"Excuse me, will you stop bullying Benjy and tell me what's happened?"

"*Bullying*? He's lucky I'm not beating the shit out of him!"

"But it's just like... air, man," Benjy sniffled.

"NO, IT'S FUCKING NOT! IT BURNS!"

"You're making my head hurt. I can't deal... No way. Way too heavy. Too much. She's... Oh no. No."

Benjy uncurled, ducked past me, through the bushes and down the cliff path like a rabbit.

Tattoo punched his palm with his fist, pulled out his cigarettes, put one in his mouth with shaking fingers, felt for his Zippo, then stopped, shook his head, put it away.

"Hey, it's probably OK out here," came Onion's slurred voice. I spun, to find she was lying on a pile of rugs and blankets out on the grass, a rug over her, her pallor made shocking by the sunlight.

"Would somebody tell me what's happened? If it's not too much trouble."

"Oh, it was all very silly," said Onion, amused. "Benjy was messing with the breathing mask, having little puffs which he likes, and he forgot to let the valve turn off."

"Inside her trailer. This was *inside* that bloody trailer," said Tattoo, jabbing at it with his finger, unlit fag looking comical on his bottom lip.

"How long?" I asked, looking at the caravan.

"The cylinder was pretty much empty," said Tattoo.

"It was cool," considered Onion. "Benjy was reading to me, we both felt fine. Then *he* came in, he was just going to light the stove and cook something when he heard the hissing and saw the valve."

I looked at Tattoo a lot more sympathetically.

"I had the matches in my hand," he said. "We were *this* close to kablooey." Thumb and forefinger were a milimetre apart. He risked lighting his fag and took a long drag on it.

Oxygen and air is an extremely flammable mixture, especially in a confined space. It's sort of what they use for space rockets. It's what killed the crew of Apollo 1 in a flash fire. Onion knew this because I'd told her.

"Jesus," I said. "But that's not supposed to be possible. Was it faulty?"

"Oh Benjy'd fixed the valve," said Onion lightly.

We both gaped at her. "Did you *want* to go up in flames?" I asked her. "With Benjy as a sort of burnt offering?"

"And me," Tattoo pointed out.

Onion shrugged her cavernous shoulderbones. "No, of course not. We just like it."

Jog appeared amongst the brambles, wanting to know what had put the wind up Benjy. Tattoo let me tell the tale. Jog looked severely at Onion, then more neutrally at Tattoo.

"How'd she get out?"

"I carried her," said Tattoo, smoking devoutly and staring at Onion. "Maybe I shouldn't have, eh, darling?"

She pouted and wouldn't meet his eye.

"If I hadn't wanted to sunbathe, I'd have told you," she said disdainfully.

Tattoo started to laugh, a cynical almost admiring sound.

"Christ, you haven't changed a bit, have you?"

"No," she said nastily. "What about you? Still drink like a fish?"

"All right," I put in quickly, seeing the light of battle in Tattoo's eyes. "What do you reckon, Jog? Can I still trust you guys with the oxygen cylinder or do I have to get her admitted?"

Onion looked scared at that, looked down, gripped the grass with almost transparent fingers.

"I'm not leaving," she said, "This is my home."

"If you blow it up, I lose my job. And why do you have to take other people with you?"

"To serve her in the fucking afterlife," shouted Tattoo. "Viking funeral, the works."

"I do want to go up in flames," she said. "I was talking to Benjy about it. I think that's very romantic. No worms either."

"Onion," I said. "You can always be cremated, but could you wait till you're dead, please?"

"And I'm not there," put in Tattoo. "Pretty please darling?"

Jog stepped up close to Tattoo and spoke very softly to him. Then he turned to me.

"Onion stays here, but Benjy's not looking after her any more. We'll double up from now on, I was planning that in any case. We've had a few lowlifes sniffing around after the stuff anyway. You know mate," he said conversationally to Tattoo, "you don't have to stay, you can go any time."

"You telling me to go?"

"No. I'm telling you to lighten up. I don't blame you for losing your temper, but you should lose it with the right one."

Just for a moment I thought Tattoo was going to argue with Jog, which would have been very interesting to see, but instead he tightened his lips and set off across the carpark to where his bike was parked.

Jog watched him go, eyes half shut, then turned to Onion.

"Don't you ever do that again," he said to her, quite quietly.

She didn't answer. Between us we checked the caravan and moved her back inside, where she could look through the window at the flowers and the rocks and the sea. Nobody said anything at all as I arranged for the empty cylinder to be collected and a new apparatus delivered.

When I drove away Tattoo was still there, standing by his bike and staring at the black rocks being hammered by the sea. I hadn't driven more than half a mile though when he roared past me, wrong side of the road, blind corner, leaning over as he accelerated out of sight.

# Chapter 8

*To do, Tuesday. Call Dr A re J.  Usuals. Tattoo? MS nr Penzance (why not their patient, check?) Tkd, Lyonesse LP.*

Jog rang me late that night asking if I'd seen the guy with the tattoo because he'd disappeared and his Harley was still parked down at the harbour carpark. Jim then got quite unpleasant about it, because he was being unpleasant about everything at the time.

He had got back a manuscript, with a ten page editing note that put him straight through the roof. Among other heinous crimes, the unfortunate little Sloane of an editor had suggested a love interest, she had corrected all Jim's "truly"'s to "forsooth" and she had wondered if it was right that they had clocks and telescopes all that time ago.

The truly awful thing about depression is that comfort is impossible because comfort is haughtily dismissed. I wouldn't wish it on my worst enemy. And yet as you watch someone churning away at the bottom of their pit, never missing an opportunity to try and drag you down with them, you start to want to kick their arse. You want to scream "Do something, anything, but stop whining," and cut off all food until they go out and earn it. But this you must never never do. Even thinking of it is bad. Somebody who is depressed isn't selfish, or self-obsessed or lazy or arrogant or a drunk, they're ill. They are.

Anyway, honesty just makes them worse. In fact, to be honest, everything just makes them worse. I just avoided him.

There was still no sign of Tattoo the next morning when I visited Onion. His camper van was still there which was worrying Jog as well as me. Nobody said anything, on the superstitious grounds that not saying it would stop anything bad from happening.

As it happened, I had to go over to the border with West Cornwall, practically to Penzance to visit a woman with MS, and I was heading back to Lyonesse in the afternoon when I spotted a familiar bald head, shaded with stubble, and that ferocious swirling blue mask as he stomped along the A30 cyclepath. He stuck his thumb out automatically, so I put the anchors on and waited for him to catch up.

Interesting attitude. Most would-be hitchhikers run up to the car, so you don't change your mind before they get there. Tattoo sauntered, opened the door, got in.

"Thanks for the..."

He saw who it was and would have got out again, only I'd already accelerated away.

I pulled a packet of fags out and chucked them in his lap, pushed the car lighter on. He lit up in silence, coughed horribly, relapsed into silence again.

He looked very very rough indeed and he'd lost his leather jacket. I had a sneaking suspicion I knew what had happened to him and yes, I'll admit it, I was sadistically pleased.

"There's a bottle of mineral water under the seat," I said. "Help yourself."

He found it and glugged down about a litre before taking breath.

"Thanks," he said, still not looking at me.

"Hungry?"

"What?"

"If I've missed lunch, I usually stop for something to eat at the next roundabout so I don't faint during my class."

"No, I'm not hungry."

"You can owe it to me." Bloodshot blue eyes narrowed suspiciously. I grinned. "I dunno, mate. I wouldn't want to poke around in your private life but if the last thing you remember last night involved doing something shady down Bostibern Street…"

Bullseye! His ears went pink.

"Not sure," he muttered.

"OK, were you… erm… *drinking* anywhere near Bostibern Street…"

He scowled, possibly at my sarcasm and then nodded.

"So you've experienced what's known round here as the Bostibern Street mystery tour and you'd better ring your credit card hotlines and mobile phone company."

He coughed, leaned back in the seat and glugged some more water, blinked at the windscreen. "I knew she'd got my money and my jacket, but…"

"If your bike keys were in your jacket you might want to call Jog and ask him to keep an eye on your Harley for you. My mobile's in the door-pocket."

He grabbed it.

"Yo Jog... Yeah, I'm fine. Anna gave me a lift. She says I've just experienced the Bostibern Steet Mystery Tour.... Yeah, har har.... No, just cash and my jacket. Yeah. The Harley?... Thanks, mate."

He finished, put the phone back, leaned back and shut his eyes, yawned, scratched his head, scratched his chin.

"Regular little tourist trap, eh?"

"Oh yes. During the big surfing events in August there's a procession of lads hiking sheepishly back from the moor. Does the local black economy no end of good."

He snorted. "Bit of a new experience."

"Coming round after a binge?"

"Waking up on a moor with a pony looking at me."

Bit of an admission there. "Oh you're lucky. They're quite rare." I swung onto the roundabout. "So you're sure you're not hungry?"

He finished the last of the mineral water and blinked at the bottle.

"I don't normally do this, but..."

"I expect you're good for it," I told him. "Come on, keep me company."

He smiled ruefully. "...In fact, I'm starving."

He was. He waded into the Big Trucker's All Day Blow Out Breakfast in a businesslike way and had polished off the last chip when I was only halfway through my more ladylike Cruisin' FishnChips. The waitress who brought the Diet Coke refills goggled at him until he winked at her and then she exploded with giggles and had to retreat in disorder to the kitchen.

"Do you know Lysette?" I asked, not very surprised.

His brow wrinkled with the effort of memory. "I think I was dancing with her and her mates last night some time."

"Before you ended up down Bostibern Street."

"Yeah." His eyes crinkled up. "No, it's gone. I can't remember why I went there."

"If you were dancing at the Cellar with Lysette, I don't know why you needed to."

"That's enough, she's a very nice girl. And less of the smug, please. I'm sort of on holiday. Waking up on a moor feeling crook is part of the fun."

I laughed because he was taking it so coolly, no cries of "call the police" and "oh god, I've been robbed."

"Jog'll put the word out for you," I told him. "I expect you'll get your jacket back, and the keys."

"But not the money."

"No. Most of it's probably already up the arm of whoever rolled you."

"Weird. You just don't expect that kind of thing round here."

"Wasn't any ten years ago, but it's all changed now. They say, Cornwall usually catches up with the last decade but one, in which case we're somewhere around the 80s and that sounds about right."

"Hmf."

"What'll you do for money?"

"Hadn't thought about it."

"You got any cards?"

"No, not with me. I suppose I could always busk."

"Very crowded profession round here, you'll need to audition for any of the good spots."

That did make him crack up with laughter although I was telling nothing but the truth.

"Or you could claim social security."

He stopped laughing, gave me one of his hard blue looks. "Never done that in my life. Anyway, there's no need. I'll sort it out."

I didn't fancy the rest of my chips, so I put down my knife and fork, leaned back and smiled at him. For a moment we just looked at each other and I found myself wondering why on earth I felt as if I'd known him for years.

"Won't this cause talk?" he asked, looking round at the other burger-eaters, while he absent-mindedly scoffed the chips I'd left.

"Let them. You're already pretty well-known."

"Oh?"

"Onion's funny-looking bloke with the tattoo."

He grinned. "OK. Get it over with."

"What?"

"The lecture."

"What lecture?"

"You're a nurse. You're supposed to tell me not to go out and get wasted in downtown Lyonesse..."

"Why would I do that?"

"It's your job, isn't it?"

"None of my business."

"Even the Bostibern Street Mystery Tour?" He was teasing me for some reason, trying to shock me.

"Look, so what if you got paralytically drunk last night and can't remember whether you had meaningless sex or not? You're old enough to know how you want to celebrate not going up in flames."

"Yeah, I like that. Celebrating not going up in flames. That's right." He paused, became suddenly serious. "Do you think she really wanted to do herself in?"

I thought about it. "Some people do," I said. "Not as many as you'd think, given their situation, but some of them do. Some of them just sort of give up internally and then it's very quick. Some can't seem to let go. You can't predict it.  I don't know. I don't think so. She doesn't strike me as the quitting kind."

"No. More the games-playing kind."

I smiled. "Testing you?"

"Maybe." The Coke was finished. No more on that subject, obviously.

I paid at the desk, kept the receipt, we drove off.

"You got time for me to get my spare key?"

Well, I could have gone home and coped with dirty washing, dirty plates, people wanting feeding, books being edited by idiots, agents never being there and so on, but funnily enough I didn't fancy it. So I drove him to MiniWonders where it turned out Jog somehow had retrieved the jacket and keys to the Harley and the Harley itself, but not, as predicted, the cash. Tattoo shrugged it off.

To my astonishment he then changed into his sweatpants and another t-shirt and came out to go to my class. I offered him a lift out of sheer admiration.

"How far did you walk today?"

"Dunno," he said. "Got a bit lost at one point. Several points. Nobody offered me a lift."

"Are you surprised?"

"No. I don't blame 'em. Anyway, I didn't mind. It was a nice walk."

I laughed in disbelief.

"No, seriously. It's beautiful round here, and quiet, except for the nutcase women in their Range Rovers and the occasional kamikazi cyclist, you've got all this incredible wildflower stuff growing in the hedges, birds, animals. I swear I saw ostriches in one field. And a rainbow earlier. Amazing. Haven't seen one of those in years. Walking along, no appointments, you've got time to think. I like going walkabout. At least it's still legal here; some cops picked me up in L.A. once when I was just peacefully walking home after a party."

"Must be the face," I said.

He looked at me carefully. "Yeah, expect so."

"Why'd you do it?"

"What?"

"The tattoo?"

"Oh. That. It was... well, it was an identity thing, I guess."

I drove up the hill to the Lyonesse leisure palace, shaking my head. He was right, the place was fabulously beautiful, almost outrageously lush and coloured. Why hadn't I noticed recently?

"I suppose we get so used to all the green and the flowers, we don't see it any more."

"Shame on you then."

"Of course, you've been lucky with the weather. Most of the time you can't see it because of the rain."

"I got rained on a bit. You know you can't have rainbows without rain." I didn't say anything. "Hey Anna."

"What?"

"Cheer up."

Was I down? I was shocked. I'm used to being the little ray of sunshine in so many people's lives, I'm usually the least depressed person in any given room. Certainly at home I sometimes felt I was the last forlorn bastion of happiness before doom and destruction closed in.

"Tattoo," I said, not realising I was letting out my private name for him. "You're not depressed, are you?"

"Hm? No. Why should I be? I'm a very lucky bloke."

"Why do you binge-drink then?"

Pause. Probably I'd gone too far. But I was curious.

"I'm sorry," I said when the silence had become quite uncomfortable. "That was rude. It's none of my business either."

"No," he said, not angrily, but thoughtfully. "It's not your business but you can always ask the question.  No law against asking."

"OK."

We parked, went to class.

He was tired, off form, a bit stiff, easily winded. Still, he gave me his full attention, did his best. He even used the wonky showers afterwards, which was truly brave of him, as well as considerate. I think he thought he'd got the timing between blasts of cold water worked out, but from the roar of bad language, he hadn't.

He came out, still complaining to the manager, "Have you got some law against proper showers here, I mean, is it beyond the mind of the Cornish to get some decent plumbing?"

The manager stuttered something about water pressure and drought.

"Drought!" Tattoo laughed heartily, waving his arm at the evening primroses standing sentinel around the carpark, "You call *this* a *drought*?"

I sussed him then, finally. He's Australian I thought, aha. Why it took me so long, I don't know. Well, I do know, he had a very neutral accent, very hard to place. That's why I'd thought it was Essex at first.

We drove back in companionable silence, sharing another bottle of fizzy water.

"Tattoo," I said for the second time and wondered why he grinned. "Are you an Aussie?"

"Yup. You've got me," he said. "Why?"

"How did you stop the eviction?"

"I've got friends with money."

"Must have a lot."

"Double the original price was still pretty cheap. They'll make money on the deal eventually, don't you worry about them."

"Why don't you call them and ask them to send you cash?"

Silence again. "Look Anna," he said gently, "I appreciate you're trying to help, but don't worry about it. Maybe I will, maybe I won't. It's my business, OK?"

"Sorry," I said, feeling the flush going up my neck and cheeks. "I know I'm bossy. It's a bad habit. Blame the job."

"S'OK. Now my turn for nosy questions. What do you do for fun?"

"Hm?"

"Apart from taekwondo which is kind of serious fun, what do you do to relax?"

I thought about it. "Sleep."

"No, I'm not getting through here. You work, you do martial arts, you sleep and... What else?"

"I don't. I haul the kids out of bed, clean up, put the washing out, kick them out of the house in the general direction of school, go to work, work all day, go home, cook, clean up, deal with laundry, go to bed."

"Weekends?"

"Clean rabbit hutch, shop, mow lawn, clean, cook, try to get boys away from TV or skateboards long enough to do homework, clear up, go to bed. Maybe I watch a bit of TV or read a book."

"Go to a pub, see a film, play, ballet?"

I laughed, not very happily. "Oh kulcha. Wot would the likes of me want wiv that, guv?"

"You're married, right?"

"Very."

"Where's hubby in all this?"

"He's a writer."

"Oh. What's he write?"

I told him, gave him the spiel about popular historical crime fiction, told him where to get copies, not that I thought he would. Told him about the more ambitious books, long ago.

"But he's not crippled, is he?"

"Not physically."

"Uhuh."

"Depressed," I said, trying and failing to keep my voice light, I didn't want him to hear the bitterness. "Very depressed. He drinks because he says it's the only way he can be creative."

"Uhuh. And you support him."

"I suppose so. Not very well. Not enough. I get very impatient... I'm sorry, this is boring."

"I'm not bored. Do you see me yawning?"

"I batter my girlfriends' ears with it, but it doesn't make anything any better, you just blow off a bit of steam and then get back to work. There's an awful lot of that and it's very tiring and stressful and so, when I've finished everything, what I really like to do is... sleep."

He looked as if he wanted to ask something else, but thought better of it.

I didn't say anything more as I took him back to MiniWonders. All right. I know I was being unspeakably dense but how was I to know? And I was angry. Not for any sensible reason, just envy that he could make the assumption that everyone did things for fun. Very occasionally I could prise Jim out of the house to go and see a movie, though usually before we got home, he'd have picked it apart and changed something shining and enthralling into quite a conventional little film with the usual themes of rescue and romance in it. There was no point trying to argue with him; very often, the more I liked a film the angrier he was with it.

I believe it was some Muslim philosopher who said, "You are depressed because you are too arrogant to praise."

Must stop this, I thought, I hate self-pity. It's the thing I most hate about Jim. His self-pity. And that in fact was why I liked Tattoo, for all my suspicions about him and his secretiveness. He didn't whine when things went wrong. Yes, he'd been understandably upset about nearly going up in flames, and so he'd gone and got comprehensively drunk. Somehow he'd ended up in Bostibern Street, probably doing something extremely sordid with one of the semi-amateur whores living there, where he'd passed out, been rolled, loaded into someone's van, driven out to the moor and dumped to sober up. Presumably they did this before they discovered that his wallet didn't contain any cards, so they didn't need the delaying tactic of making him walk back to civilisation. He'd come to, no doubt hungover, probably cold and damp, certainly penniless, and had then set off philosophically to hitch-hike home. Jim, who could quite easily have had a similar experience, I hoped minus the whore, would have been devastated with misery and the whining self-glorification of "Why me?" Go for a nice walk? Don't make me laugh. He'd have gone just as far as the nearest pub, reversed the charges, rung me and insisted on me coming to get him. By the time we'd got home, the whole thing would somehow have metamorphised into my fault, again.

No self-pity. There's a tip for you, boys. I'd always thought Tattoo was attractive, so long as I didn't look at his face. But for me, after competence, there's nothing sexier than a man who doesn't whine when he has reason to. Or doesn't whine, period. No whining, boys. Remember it.

# Chapter 9

*To do: Wed. REPORTS. Robby. Onion.*

Next time I looked in on Onion, I made sure I spoke to Jog. The man from Atlantis was sitting cross-legged at the opening of his tent and I sat down opposite him. Jog nodded at me seriously when he finished meditating.

What would be pretentious and embarrassing in anyone else, somehow comes out as utterly solid and sincere from Jog. He really does read philosophy too, second hand Penguin Classics of Plato's shorter books. He said it all started with reading *The Lion, the Witch and the Wardrobe* by C S Lewis when he was a kid, and wondering who Plato might be. The whole notion of Plato's Cave enchanted him; the idea that in this life we're like prisoners chained in a cave so we have to face forwards, with a fire behind us and people carrying objects passing in front of it so the shadows fall on the wall. We're forced to watch the shadows of real things flickering on the rock in front of us and we never realise that what we see are just distorted images and behind us is the exit to the open air and Reality itself. When someone tries to tell us about it, we think they're madmen and when it's time for us to break our chains and leave, we kick and scream with fear and fight to stay.

"It's incredible, isn't it?" Jog said when he relayed this to me. "Two and a half thousand years ago the guy invented the movies."

"What does Onion think of that story?"

Jog shook his head and smiled.

I'm sure that was why he liked the place and why he'd brought Onion there a couple of years before, because the MiniWonders were three-dimensional shadows, as he said. Onion liked it for quite other reasons, for the flowers and the sea and the surfers. She had camped out inside the Taj Mahal for a while.

I glanced over my shoulder at the primly suburban scaled-down version of the extravagant Taj Mahal, now almost drowned by the waves of brambles flooding around it, as if the jungle had been let in against it. Made me shiver for no reason, so I looked for something more familiar in the carpark.

Tattoo and the Harley were nowhere to be seen.

"Where's Tattoo gone?"

"Who?"

I gestured at the camper van and Jog's face lit up. "Hey, I like that," he said considering. "Yeah. Tattoo."

Uh oh, I thought, that does it. He's been surfer-baptised. He'll never shake the name now. Well, serve him right, the vandal, for ruining his own face.

"So where is he?"

"Tattoo's decided to sell the Harley."

"*What?*" The few genuine bikers I'd ever met would far rather have sold a kidney for transplant, than their bike. One or two would have sold their heart.

Jog smiled. "He said he's going to part-exchange for a scooter and keep the change."

"Blimey. Hasn't he got any credit cards?"

"Well he has, but he knows if he uses them, there's a record of the transaction and where it took place."

"But..." I shook my head. This was all adding up to a very worrying picture. "... is he on the run? Escaped from jail? Why's he so secretive?"

Jog smiled, started rolling a normal fag. "In a manner of speaking, he's on the run. Just a manner of speaking. I told you, he's not a criminal."

"Well, then what? A woman? He left his wife?"

"In a manner of speaking. Look, Anna, you want to know more, you ask him." That confirmed all my suspicions, though I wasn't sure which particular ones.

"Well, why's he here then?"

"I believe he came to get Onion out of his system."

"And has he?"

"Much to her horror, yes, he has. I think he's seen her for what she is. Finally."

"Which is?"

Long slow look from Jog. "She's a very beautiful, very neurotic, very shallow person who used to get her kicks from manipulating the people round her, especially men."

That was right on the money.

"She thinks her beauty is what gives her the right to be served but she's wrong."

"What then?" I'd thought that too. If you're beautiful or talented or weak, then people look after you. I'm none of those things, so I do the looking after. It's the way of the world.

"What I think is this," said Jog in full-on guru-mode. "Everybody has the right to serve and to be served. Depending on circumstances. It's a human right, nothing to do with what you are or who you are. Everyone needs looking after sometimes, when they're babies, when they're old, when they're sick, sometimes when they just need it. It's bad for you if you demand it when you don't need it, mind you, or if it's forced on you. But everyone also has the right to look after other people and that's the best thing, because that's actually good for you. It expands you, builds you up, makes you strong. Nobody should have a monopoly on one thing or the other. Monopolies unbalance things."

"So he's going home now?" Why did all this make me feel so grey and depressed?

"Not yet. Sure, he's got her out of his system, he doesn't love her any more, but he's here for the duration."

"What's the story there, Jog?"

He looked shifty. "I can't tell you, Anna, I'm sorry. Not that I know very much. Anyway, the important thing is that, surprisingly perhaps given who... well, he understands."

"But what about... whoever's after him?"

Jog smiled again. "It's cool, Anna. You worry too much. Tattoo's having a holiday, which he needs. He's surfing as well, you know, which he says he hasn't done for years."

"Any good?"

"Rotten."

Once again I had to fight down my envy that Tattoo could go surfing, something I'd never tried, that he could just loaf about, doing what he wanted. Every day of my life, for as far ahead as I could see, was packed full of things I had to do. Every hour was eaten up by appointments and housework and looking after people and trying to cheer up Jim. Tattoo's questions about what I did for fun had somehow brought it out into full relief. In fact, it had been so long since I'd done what I wanted to do, I wondered if I still knew what that was. And I had another appointment to get to so I stood up.

"Next time round, I want to be a man," I said to Jog, not expecting him to know what I was talking about. I don't really believe in reincarnation anyway, I think when the current switches off, we go out like a light.

"You need a holiday too," Jog said. "You look worn out."

"Har har."

"Seriously. You could hide out here if you wanted."

"Don't tempt me, Jog. Thanks all the same. The kids'd track me down and want burgers I expect."

Jog held up his hand in farewell. "Nobody has to do anything, you know," he said. "We choose and take the consequences."

"Bye Jog."

New Agery gets me down sometimes, even from Jog. I think he rather savours the sage man from Atlantis guru schtick. Pity things aren't really that simple.

But the next day, Jog was on the phone to me all his serenity gone.

"Benjy's gone missing."

I groaned and put down my out-of-date egg and cress sandwich - he'd got me between appointments, having lunch. "So's half his plants."

"Oh brother."

"Tattoo says, when you finish work, can you meet him at Lyonesse harbour, by the war memorial? He's very worried. He thinks it's his fault Benjy's gone AWOL."

"Probably is." I was very annoyed with him, particularly with his blithe assumption I would drop my plans for the evening so I could quarter the uglier part of Lyonesse with him. Not that I had any plans for the evening.

"He told me to tell you, pretty please, and if you can't make it, he's cool. He'll wait until 7.30 and then see what he can do by himself. But he'd appreciate it if someone who knows their way around could go with him."

"Jog, why don't you go with him?"

Silence. Jog's voice was tight. "I've tried, Anna, I don't know what's happened to Benjy. And Onion needs me here to look after her."

I sighed. That was true. "All right," I said. "I'll call you back if there's a problem."

I tried ringing home, got the message-machine and left one saying something had come up and I'd probably be very late, not to keep supper, don't forget the rabbit.

Mrs Tredurgan as always was mischievous. She sucked her tea through a straw, using her tissues to pat the drops that leaked out, and wrote notes because although she could still just about talk, very few people could understand her. I could, but she didn't like the noises she made. She knew all about Onion and Jog and Benjy and had been fascinated to hear about Tattoo, the mystery man as she put it.

"Where do you think Benjy's gone?" I asked her and she shrugged, scribbled.

"Wherever he feels safest."

I nodded, wondering where on earth that would be. Where had Benjy come from anyway? He'd seemed like a fixture, turning up every summer regular as clockwork, generally wasted. He was an extraordinarily good surfer, with an instinctive understanding of where the waves would be best, what he could do with them. He'd won at Newquay several times, flopping his brown hair out of his eyes shyly and unable to say much more than "Wow". He had fallen helplessly in love with Onion two years before, when she had been queening it around Lyonesse and Newquay on Jog's arm during her final remission. He had wooed her in the most chivalrous and old-fashioned way you could imagine, adoring her from afar and occasionally bringing her (illegally picked) wildflowers. On only one occasion, Jog had told me, Onion gave him a proper kiss and he had gone more red and bashful than a twelve year old. I suspected him of virginity.

Gerry the architect was having a stand up battle with his wife when I arrived, which they swiftly packed away for later, being nice middle-class people who don't fight. Her fingernails were bitten down to the quick, but she put out the middle-class barriers and I couldn't get past them. I could feel the rage steaming away inside her, behind the smiling mask and the coffee smell and I felt very sorry for Gerry indeed. And her. What had they ever done to deserve this? Being smug and conventional hardly merits a death-sentence.

And yes, of course I went down to Lyonesse at about 7.00 pm and parked there, facing out at the harbour full of pretty white yachts and dinghys with just a few rusty old fishing boats skulking down in one corner, being used for dolphin tours. The sharp cries and navy and white plumage of the yachties was everywhere in Lyonesse during the summer.

No sign of Tattoo, so I finished off my lunch sandwich and illegally fed the crusts to the seagulls, then I went into a yachtie pub called the Feathered Serpent, had half a shandy and changed out of uniform and into the tracks and trainers I always keep in the boot. The pub was filled full of the strange tanned practical people who sail their boats casually across the sea and only know the coast of any country. Mostly they were exchanging technical details about satellite navigation and a storm system down by the Azores. Being a person who feels sick looking at a reasonably well-painted seascape, I didn't feel like sticking around. So I was sitting on the steps of the war memorial, under the bravely waved bronze rifle of the young Cornishman, when Tattoo sauntered into view at exactly 7.30 pm. I was annoyed. He'd expected me to wait for him and even more annoyingly, I had.

"All right," I snapped bossily at him. "What's this about? Why do you want me here?"

"Don't fancy another Bostibern Street Mystery Tour," drawled Tattoo, offering me a fag and lighting one for himself. "Rough day?"

"Has anyone actually checked the police stations and hospitals yet?"

"Yup. This morning. And this afternoon."

"Maybe he's gone to Newquay early to do some surfing ready for the festival?"

"Well Jog rang the girl he usually stays with and she says, not only that she hasn't seen him yet, she also got a message on her machine from him talking about surfing on flames and Onion burning him."

"Oh shit."

"You know why he's got to be found, don't you? Quite apart from everything else, I mean?"

"Well he's not very stable and he tends to set fire to things if he's…"

"He's got the access code for Onion's drug pump."

"Oh." I was slipping on the paranoia front. I'd forgotten all about that. "And the information about what she's on, of course."

"Medical grade heroin. Cut down to street purity, you can make thousands."

"God." No wonder Jog had sounded tight-lipped. Gentle wasted Benjy might make some money simply selling the information, but far more likely he'd just give it away talking to somebody.

"Have you looked at the campsites?"

"Took a swing round them on the bike."

He nodded at an extremely dull-looking Honda, parked discreetly in the corner and I had to hide a smile because it was such a come-down.

"I can't believe you sold your Harley."

He grinned at me. "Me neither."

"Did you get a good price for it?"

"Well, Jog's brother gave me cash and the Honda but I still think he royally screwed me."

I snorted at that. Of course he did, Jog's a philosopher, but Newt his brother is a pure laissez faire capitalist red in tooth and claw type. They get on very well. Newt is the real owner of Jog's surf-board hire business and employs most of his friends when they need it.

"Never mind," said Tattoo, stepping on his fag end. "I'll get him back later. You coming?"

Some bits of Lyonesse are pretty and spruced up for tourists, petunia'd flower baskets hanging everywhere, with little cobblestoned pedestrian precincts and gift shops selling candle-holders and windchimes mass-produced in China and teashops selling mass-produced "home-made" clotted cream fudge in large heavy bars that somebody cuts up carefully and puts in a paper bag for that personal touch. If you got past the fish and chip shops and the yachtie pubs and seafood restaurants, you found whole streets mainly boarded up apart from the building societies and the charity shops. Bostibern Street curves round behind the road to the bus station and looks perfectly all right during the daytime, with its lock up garages and tatty houses and the two sad newsagents, a chippy and a shut video rental place in the middle. At night, that's where you go if you want to score.

I didn't want Benjy there, though he'd been one of the boys who went out like knights on a quest to get Onion what she needed before she had her pump. No doubt he'd been doing business there long before that.

We went up and down and through the tourist areas and the tatty areas, checking the spots where the tramps and the junkies gathered. Some of them were polite, some of them were rude, some of them simply incomprehensible. We didn't have any trouble with them at least partly because Tattoo would stand quietly next to me, simply radiating hard. He frightened me when I looked at him. Couldn't work out how he was doing it, either.

"Are you really as tough as you look?" I asked him as we passed down an alleyway.

"Nah. Soft as shite."

"What is it then?"

"Anybody crazy enough to do this to his face is crazy enough to do anything. That's what they reckon."

"Mm." No, that wasn't it.

He told me about a movie he'd worked on where the male lead was a complete jerk, scared of horses, scared of dogs, didn't like rats, horrified by spiders. And that was very unfortunate because it was a wilderness action adventure and he was supposed to be the tough hard injun scout who knew all about these things. Tattoo had me in hysterics mimicking the very careful bullshit-heavy discussions between the animal trainers and the male lead and the director.

Then he told me the name of the movie and I was staggered because I'd completely believed in the actor as a tough man of the wilderness. Tattoo wagged his finger triumphantly.

"You see. It's acting. It's what you do with your body, how you stand, little stuff like which way your feet point. That's all."

"I'm disappointed."

"Now the wierdest thing about it," Tattoo said, "is nobody can live with Bud Anderson at the poker table. He's terrifying. He's genuinely got no nerves at all, you can't tell anything from his face and he bluffs... Jesus, the bastard had me folding three tens against his pair of treys."

I grinned. I could hear the still-raw pain in his voice. So I told him about once making the mistake of playing three card brag against Mrs Tredurgan and some of her friends, the night before she had her first operation and how she very nearly had my car.

We found two people in Bostibern Street who thought they'd seen Benjy last night, but not since then. One of them said Benjy already seemed pretty out of it, talking wild talk about a serpent lady who tried to burn him, nobody knew what he'd been on.

"There's one good thing, you know," said Tattoo judiciously. He looked ludicrous, licking a small, prim frozen yoghurt cornet. "Anybody trying to steal the drugs would have to get past Onion and she'd probably end up adding them to her team of boys."

I laughed at the cynicism in his voice. "How does she do it?" I asked, trying not to sound too envious.

"She is utterly certain that she's the centre of the universe."

"Not unusual."

"Then she makes you believe it too."

"How?"

Tattoo thoughtfully watched a couple snogging next to a lamp post. "To tell the truth, I don't know."

"It isn't sexual - I'm sure Benjy's still a virgin."

"Mentally if not physically. No, you're right, it's not just sexual, it's... She climbs inside your head, tells you one time that you're the most brilliant wonderful man she's ever met, next moment, you're a piece of shit and she won't talk to you, won't tell you why. You never know where you are with her, but you keep thinking you can crack the mystery, you're the only one who can do it, none of the others can... And they're all dancing along thinking the same."

I looked at him, thinking, boy, she really got to you, didn't she?

"Yes she did," he said, and the hairs went up on my arms because I was sure I hadn't spoken. "She climbed inside my head, same as she climbed inside Benjy's - though I wasn't as crazy as him. But there was a time once when if she'd said, hey sh... shithead, fix the valve of this oxygen cylinder so we can sniff it, and see what happens when someone lights a match next to it, I'd have done it."

"You would?"

"Sure I would. You ever driven an XJ6 at 90 mph through country lanes at midnight in the middle of a snowstorm with all the lights off, so someone could see what it looked like?"

"Er... no."

"I have." He smiled at me.

"And now?"

"Now?" He shook his head, wiped his fingers and tossed the bit of napkin in the nearest bin.

"What broke the spell?"

He laughed softly, thought for a minute. "Recognition." There was something in the way he watched me, eyes half-lidded. I felt hot and awkward, looked away.

"I see." Though I didn't, in fact.

You know the only place we actually had any trouble at all? A yachtie pub. I went to use the bog, Tattoo wandered in to get a pack of cigs out of the machine, and I came out to find him hemmed in by large college boys in navy-blue pullovers who were claiming to find him offensive.

I pushed between them, "*Scuse* me!" went over to Tattoo who was starting to look cornered and angry, took his arm, nipped the new packet of Marlboro out of the hand of the nearest college boy, smiled sweetly, said "Thank you *so* much." and walked out with him.

Tattoo and I walked arm in arm in silence until we were safely back in a scruffy bit and then Tattoo shook his head.

"Fucking poms."

"It's the face. Like you said."

"One of them accused me of being a skinhead." He sounded insulted.

"Tut." We walked on for a bit, finding it comfortable, and Tattoo chuckled softly to himself and wouldn't explain why.

We even asked the bouncers at a couple of the nightclubs, although if you wanted to sentence Benjy to something he would really hate, you'd sentence him to do time in the average club.

It was getting late and I had to get home.

"One more place," I said, turning sharp right and heading up a little alleyway. Tattoo went ahead of me.

That's when I noticed that a College Boy had been following us. He was swaying and he had a very ugly expression on his face as he shoved past me.

"Hoy!" he shouted after Tattoo, "I know you, you cunt."

Tattoo turned and came back.

"Do you?" he rumbled. "Where from?"

"Cambridge? Outside Trinity? Remember kicking the shit out of me?"

Tattoo stopped, blinked and looked baffled.

"Never been near Cambridge in my life, mate. You've got the wrong guy."

"Oh yeah? I know that fucking tattoo, *matey*."

And the idiot lunged at Tattoo who went backwards, rolled to his feet and dodged another lunge.

"You've got the wrong fucking bloke!" Tattoo roared, to be answered by incoherent obscenity from College Boy and wildly flailing fists.

I heard the chink of glass, turned away from the fight to find another pullovered cretin trying to lurk past me in the darkness, an unbroken bottle in his paw, obviously too intent on hitting Tattoo with it to notice me standing right next to him.

Can't have that, I thought, coldly furious, so I axe-kicked his outstretched arm. I got him right on the pressure point, his hand went numb and the bottle dropped, rolled away. He goggled at me in horror.

"Fuck off," I told him and he turned and ran.

I was happy to stop interference but there was no way I was dumb enough to try and break up the fight still clumsily going on between the bins because that's when friends get punched in the face by the person they're trying to rescue. Anyway, having the immense advantage of being sober, Tattoo was coping perfectly well with College Boy. I saw Tattoo finally get a good grip on the pullover, heave up and pin him against the wall by a street light. He pulled back his fist ready for a good knockout punch.

"Wait!" I shouted, not really thinking he would. To my astonishment, he did.

They were both crowing for breath, but College Boy was looking dimly puzzled at Tattoo's decorated face, nose to nose with his.

"Hang on," he said accusingly. "He had a spiderweb. You're not him."

"That's RIGHT, you stupid prick," snarled Tattoo.

College Boy went limp, face a battered picture of social embarassment.

"Gosh, I'm frightfully sorry," he said and as Tattoo slowly lowered his fist and let go, he staggered away from the wall, shook himself, shook his head. "Mistaken identity, I'm afraid. Many apologies, old man. Good evening to you."

We watched him stagger away with our mouths hanging open.

Then Tattoo leaned against the wall and dissolved into helpless laughter. His amusement was so infectious, I calmed down and hooted as well.

"Jesus, this has been a bloody education and no mistake," he said, wiping his eyes with his sleeve. I saw blood on his knuckles and checked them as well as I could. It didn't look as if he'd broken them, just skinned them. He had a bit of a bruise on his chin and some grazes but nothing serious.

"You're well cool," he said to me. "I saw you stop the guy with the bottle." I smiled at him. "Thanks. And thanks for not joining in."

I shook my head. "I wouldn't insult you."

Suddenly he caught my face between his hands and kissed me on the lips. Just for a moment, I...

Well, I felt very uncomfortable, twenty-five years younger and completely bewildered by all the unaccustomed stuff happening internally which I didn't even recognise.

He let go at once, but he didn't apologise. I cleared my throat, took a deep breath to try and steady the thumping in my chest and went on to where the alley joined the very average-looking road. At the end was a larger building, once a school. I went up to the door, rang the bell, waited and listened to the dogs barking out the back.

When the door opened, I found Sandra peering past me into the darkness.

"He's in the back... Oh."

"Hi," I said.

"Anna, come in. Sorry, I thought you were the ambulance."

"What's up?"

"Who's that?"

"I call him Tattoo because he won't tell me his real name. He's a mate of Jog's and Onion's."

"Oh right. Come in then."

Sandra gave Tattoo the specialised kind of hard look that people who run hostels for the homeless have to have or they lose their badge. Skewered by it, Tattoo looked down sheepishly. "Had a bit of a fight over mistaken identity." he said, "No harm done."

Sandra looked at me and I nodded.

"Police?" she asked.

"No need," I said.

"OK." Her voice had the deep stewed sound only achieved by three packs of fags a day for twenty odd years and she wore a soft green angora jumper, slacks and a lot of bangles. Her bronze hair was excellently well cut, she had full make up and the council hated her guts because she used to run a string of nightclubs in the East End of London until she found God. Now she had a record for getting addicts off whatever stuff they were on five times better than anything run by the council. It worried me to see her worried.

In the kitchen which had stainless steel fittings mixed with rescued enamel and an enormous table that was partly split in two, there were two well-pierced youths making tea and a girl feeding a baby. Sandra waved at the sink and Tattoo meekly cleaned himself up, unintentionally frightening the youths. Then he stood in the corner by one of the fridges, watching.

"Sandra," I said, "we won't stay. We're looking for Benjy. Have you seen him?"

And from the way her face relaxed and then hardened, I knew she had and that this was not good news.

"He's why we called the ambulance. Come and see him."

We went into one of her smaller bedrooms, overwhelmed by a cheap wardrobe and an opened out sofabed, where we found Benjy lying on the bed talking very quietly to the ceiling and making no sense at all. His eyes were hectic, high as a kite, and his hands shook and there were plasters up his arms where he'd cut himself and burnt himself.

I sat down next to him. "Benjy," I said softly. "Benjy? What's wrong?"

"She did, she was the one, glass serpent lady you know, she tried to kill me. She did. And him. You know she did. I thought she... I thought she loved me..."

Tattoo let out a little soft grunt.

"Well, yes, she did, Benjy, I don't think she's quite right in the head at the moment. What about you? What've you taken?"

He looked at me slyly, put his finger to his lips.

"She wants fire so I'm all right... Must be careful. She's eaten me, you know. Barbecued."

We went out again, back to the kitchen where the baby had been taken to bed and the pierced youths had made themselves scarce.

"He's better than he was," said Sandra, sitting down at the table with a cup of teak brown tea and one of the Marlboros. "When we found him in the yard earlier he was trying to set light to himself."

"Do you have to get him admitted?" I asked. "He seems to be coming down."

"Daren't risk it. The council's looking at our funding at the moment and we're going broke again as it is, I've got to be absolutely by the book. Time was, I'd've waited till morning, seen how he was then. What was he talking about?"

"Onion pulled a dangerous stunt yesterday." I told her briefly what had happened and she looked at Tattoo assessingly.

"You're all right," she said to him.

"I think it was more of a shock for Benjy," Tattoo answered. "And I gave him a rough time too, shouted at him pretty good."

"I'm not surprised." She sighted along the barrel of her fag and sucked on it. "I've seen you somewhere, haven't I?"

"Have you?" Very noncommital voice.

"I know I have. I'm good with faces and names. Have to be. I'll get it in a minute."

She narrowed her eyes at him and Tattoo looked modestly at the floor. That was when the ambulance arrived for Benjy and a couple of cops having a look just in case. There was a flurry while they assessed him, thought he had an interesting cocktail in him, quite apart from what he might be growing for himself in his brain tissues, agreed to take him in. Did anyone want to come with him?

I looked around for Tattoo and found the bastard had disappeared again, quietly melted into the night. I couldn't go with Benjy and Sandra had to stay at the hostel. So Benjy went in alone, squirming on the stretcher, and crying softly into his hands about the serpent lady.

Once the cops had gone, I checked the sitting room again and the backyard where the dogs were wandering around howling and shagging each other, no sign of Tattoo.

"He's done it again." I fumed, "He's buggered off."

Sandra was smoking another of my fags, her eyes half shut and a secretive smile on her face.

"Do you blame him?"

"Yes, I do," I said. "Why the hell didn't he go in with Benjy? He's got nothing better to do with his time, has he?"

She blinked at me and her secretive smile got broader. "Oh. I see. You haven't spotted it."

"Spotted what? That he's very anxious not to meet anyone in authority who might ask him questions, like the police for instance. Yes, I've spotted that. He says he's not a criminal."

"Oh I think you can believe him. Well well." She shook her head, laughed throatily. "Well, well."

"What?"

"Don't you worry, he'll turn up again, Anna."

"Why is he never there when you want him?"

"Nature of the beast, luv. Come on. Finish your tea."

"Do you think Benjy'll be all right?"

"Yes, probably. So long as they don't give him any matches to play with. He won't remember much about it anyway. You could look in on him tomorrow, if you've got the time."

Time. I sighed. Time to be heading home and cope with my resident psycho. No that was unfair, he was just depressed. I finished up the tea which carved its tannin-soaked way down my neck, shared another fag, listened to the latest battle with the council who specialised in sending Sandra thank you letters for her wonderful work with the homeless and drug addicted of South Cornwall. Never any money.

"How do you do it, Sandra?" I asked her, blinking at the dregs of my tea, "or rather, how do you keep on doing it?"

"You'd be embarrassed if I told you."

"Try me. I'm not shy."

"OK. Remember, you asked for it. There's a medieval legend that every beggar child might be Jesus Christ in disguise."

"Oh."

"So I do it and keep doing it because I never know when I might meet Jesus in disguise. It's exciting."

She'd been right. I was embarrassed.

"He turned up yet?" I asked skeptically, then felt ashamed of myself. Who was I to sneer at somebody's faith, just because I haven't got any. "I'm sorry, I..."

"No, you don't understand." she smiled, unruffled, as she squashed her lipsticked fag end against the cut glass ashtray. "He turns up regularly, he's quite reliable. In fact, you'd be amazed how often."

What can you say to calm insanity?

"Er... right."

"In fact, from the point of view of funding, I suspect a miracle is due any minute." She laughed at my expression. "Told you! Look at you, you're all hot and bothered. Don't worry. When the time comes for me to be packed off to a loony bin, there's nobody I'd rather have do it than you, Anna."

I smiled back. "Not tonight. I'm too tired."

We talked about less embarrassing things like where she could get new supplies of freebie condoms to hand out. Finally, I left.

At the end of the road, a scary looking silhouette loomed out of somebody's driveway with a bright red coal of a cigarette near his face and I was just getting ready to kick his goolies and run like hell when he said, "Hi Anna."

Voice like poured velvet. I marched straight past.

"I'll see you back to the car."

"Hmf."

I didn't speak to him or look at him all the way back and he just walked along near me, hands in his pockets. However had I thought it comfortable to walk arm in arm with him? He was just another unreliable scuzzbag.

Back at my car, I got in.

"Thanks for the escort duty." I snapped.

"Don't mention it." It did not improve my mood that the scuzzbag's voice held unmistakeable traces of amusement in it.

# Chapter 10



I went home to face the usual accumulation of domestic squalor. Just as I washed up the second to last saucepan with burnt on baked beans, Jim wandered into the kitchen.

"Can I help?" he asked dolefully.

I managed to bite back ninety per cent of the things I thought of saying and answered, "No, I've nearly finished."

Then he made himself coffee, using the last remaining clean mug in the house, and getting in my way.

I went tight-lipped into his study and gathered up the six dirty mugs and five dirty plates there, wondering how he'd managed to get bright pink gunge on the sides of three of the mugs (honestly, I did).

When I came back he'd tipped some of his coffee into the sink where I was washing up the saucepans and he'd left a dirty teaspoon and an open milk carton and a ring of carelessly spilled instant coffee granules on the counter before sitting down at the freshly wiped kitchen table with his coffee.

Why are these things so enraging? If you look at them objectively, when you're not tired, not bored bored bored with always racing to keep up with the onrushing tide of filth, there's nothing so terribly offensive about a dirty teaspoon, an open milk carton and a ring of brown coffee on the counter you've just wiped.

We're abstract creatures. We see things in symbols. The actual effort involved in clearing teaspoon, putting away milk and wiping counter (again) was minuscule. It was the symbolic meaning. Scattering crap behind him was Jim's automatic way of making his mark, laying a trail, stating he was there. It said, I can't be bothered to clear up after myself. It also said, you've got nothing better to do with your time (apart from work and sleep), so you do it. It was contemptuous. Worse still, it was blindly contemptuous. He was so sunk in self-pity and selfishness, he didn't even realise how arrogant he was.

Why didn't I tell him? Well, because that would be nagging him, wouldn't it? After all, it was only a bloody teaspoon, a milk carton, a coffee ring. Why make such a fuss about it? It's not as if it's important. Not as if you're important, or your time is important. Typical woman, getting hysterical about a teaspoon.

Where's the exit? Where's the answer to the riddle? I don't know. I only know that whereas I'd been just able to contemplate talking nicely to Jim when he came in to offer to help (carefully timed, naturally, as I knew and he, seemingly, didn't), after the teaspoon insult, I couldn't.

In my experience, it isn't the big stuff that kills marriages, the infidelity, even the depression. Humans are quite good at dealing with big stuff. We all have far greater reserves than we ever think. But the constant baleful irritation of teaspoons and coffee rings... All the therapy in the world won't help that.

And then of course, once you start a tight-lipped silence, it's awfully hard to stop it. The thing becomes one of those big plastic novelty bubbles, getting bigger and bigger and filling up the room and refusing to burst until somebody says something at random, just to ease the pressure.

"Julian saw you at the Happy Trucker with some weirdo yesterday," said Jim suddenly. "Some hitch hiker."

I thought about this while I finished cleaning off the last of the baked beans. I hate baked beans. Almost as much as I hate ketchup.

"Yes," I said. "That was Tattoo. Or that's what I call him, because of this horrible tattoo all over his face. Really ugly."

"Julian said you seemed to be good friends."

Well, thank you Julian. I thought, wishing I could remember which of Jim's drinking buddies was Julian so I could thank him personally with a knuckle sandwich for shopping me.

"He's one of Onion's boys," I said.

"Oh? Like Jog?"

"Yes. He'd got rolled down Bostibern Street and dumped on the moor and I saw him and gave him a lift back. That all right with you?" I asked elaborately as I put the saucepan upside down on the draining rack.

Jim shrugged, his mouth going sourly sideways. "Why wouldn't it be?"

I sighed, emptied the plastic bowl, dried my hands. "I dunno, Jim. It's a mystery to me too."

"Where did you go tonight?"

"Well, of course," I snapped, "I had a really good orgy with every single one of Onion's boys, Jog included."

Jim's brown eyes blinked at me. Time was once when I thought they were very soulful. He was looking even more miserable than before, and I felt sorry for him. Don't ask me why.

"We went looking for Benjy who disappeared on account of nearly getting blown up in Onion's caravan by a wonky oxygen cylinder. We found him at Sandra's hostel..."

"Who's she?"

I nearly gave up right then. I'd come across Sandra a year before when dealing with one of her recovered junkies who had full-blown AIDS, and I greatly admired her. I'd talked about her at length to Jim.

"Runs a hostel for the homeless?"

"Oh. Social worker."

I sighed. Despite his socialism, Jim has the normal middle class hatred of social workers.

"Worse," I said. "She's a born-again-Christian."

Once again Jim blinked at me, probably suspecting sarcasm. Depression does that to you, it makes you blind to the nuances of speech, somehow.

"Anyway Benjy was there high as a kite and Sandra'd already called an ambulance, so I came home. That's all."

"Who's we?"

"Me and Tattoo."

More silence. "I thought you said he's a wierdo."

"No, you said that. He is very weird-looking and that's why he was useful because it meant we didn't have any trouble. Well, not much."

"I don't suppose I blame you, wanting to go out on the town with some young lad. I'm sure he's more fun than me."

Give me strength and patience, I thought, though I don't know who I thought was going to give me them, seeing I don't believe in God. I sighed and sat down opposite Jim at the kitchen table.

I could have tried kindness. No Jim, you're great to go out on the town with, really you are. But I'd been wrapping him in that kind of cotton wool for years and it didn't seem to have done much good to anyone. I kept hearing Tattoo's voice "Where's hubby in all this?" Well, where was he? In his study, of course. Sleeping, mostly.

"Well, yes, he is fun," I said, not realising until I heard my own voice just how chilly honesty can be. "He's quite relaxing, really. I don't have to watch every word I say for fear of offending him and spoiling the evening. He saw the funny side of him getting the Bostibern Street mystery tour, even though he'd been robbed. He's a scuzzbag, of course, totally unreliable, never there when you need him, the usual, but yes, he's fun."

Jim nodded, staring into space.

"What's he like in bed?" His mouth twisted. He wasn't joking.

I was this close to hitting him. This close. Against all my beliefs. And actually, if I had gone to bed with Tattoo that night or earlier, I would have been less angry, perhaps I'd even have been able to say laughingly, Better than you. But although I'd found Tattoo attractive right from the start, I hadn't done a damned thing about it, really, nothing.... All right, I'd chauffeured him around in my car and taught him taekwondo and I'd been willing to go on the hunt for Benjy with him, even though it wasn't strictly my problem, and all right, I hadn't exactly protested when he kissed me, but...

In retrospect I know why I was angry and I know why Jim asked the question. At the time, I didn't see it. And no matter how clear it may all be to you, gentle reader, it wasn't to me. Not at all.

"I don't know." That was all I said, dripping liquid nitrogen.

Once upon a time, I might have been able to add something joking like "Wish I did." and Jim might have been able to laugh and give me a kiss and say, "He's the loser" and stuff like that. But not that night. I was too tired. I stood up and started putting the mugs I'd found in his study into the dishwasher, just for something to do with my hands that didn't involve punching anyone in the nose.

Jim watched me, puppy-dog eyes and I didn't look at him. Suddenly he stood up, came over, put his hands on my shoulders and pushed me back and forth. It wasn't affectionate. He said something almost too soft to hear.

"Never leave me, Mistress Gurney. I need thee. Never leave me."

"I'm not going to leave you." I said wearily as I pulled away, not in the mood for seventeenth century fantasy, shut the door of the dishwasher and pushed the on-delay button. It had to wait for the washing machine to stop, you see. Details. All the details that add up and add up and crush you down with their multifarious dullness. "'Night."

Conscientiously, I gave him a kiss on the side of the head, had to give him a kiss goodnight, we were married for god's sake. Nothing there. I'd get more of a charge from kissing the bloody rabbit, not that I did. As for compared with Tattoo the scuzzbag... Better not think about that.

# Chapter 11

*To do: Benjy at Treliske. REPORTS. New patient; Tara Lupin.*

Next day I heard that Benjy was worse than anyone had thought and not responding to medication, but I didn't have time to see him. I did find a boring little Honda bike parked next to my car in Lyonesse carpark and went in search of its owner. I found him making a phonecall from one of the payphones near the entrance and again, I heard him before I saw him.

"Yeah, well, deal with it, Denise. Tell them I'm on holiday, tell them I'm drying out in Ireland, but keep them off my back."

Pause. He sounded different, less laid-back, more tense, more... complicated.

"Yes. Yes, I know. I'll be there."

Pause. Cradle phone on shoulder, light fag.

"No, I'm not smoking. For fuck's sake Denise, you're not my mother. Hold 'em off. Yeah. Thanks. Bye." Click.

Our eyes met, his narrowed.

"Girlfriend?" I didn't intend there to be an edge to my voice, but there was, damn it.

"No," he said curtly.

I shrugged and went back to my car. He followed me and leaned down to the window as I got in.

"How's Benjy?" he asked.

"Bad."

I started the car to drive away, and he reached in and switched off the ignition.

"Why the fuck are you so pissed with me?"

His voice was a dangerous growl. I rolled my eyes and did my best not to shout.

"I'm pissed with you because you're irresponsible. You throw your weight around and then you're amazed when a fragile kid gets damaged. You go looking for him, and that's good, but then you slink off into the dark the minute the ambulance and cops turn up. I hate bullies and I hate men who bugger off when things get tricky."

"And you think I'm both those things?"

I started to answer but then I stopped. Was I being fair to him? Or was I letting Jim's needling get to me? Suddenly all the puff went out of my anger.

"I'm sorry," I said wearily, not looking at him. "Probably I'm being unfair. Probably because I'm in a bad mood anyway and late for my next appointment and upset about Benjy and... and all the other stuff. And tired. Very very tired. So don't mind me. I don't care how you know Sandra..."

He scowled. "What did she say about me?"

"Nothing. But she obviously knows you which you never bothered to mention. Anyway. No doubt you had your reasons for buggering off last night which I don't know, so I can't judge, and in any case, I've got to go. So if you'll excuse me..."

I started the car again and drove off, wishing and wishing I wasn't so easy to manipulate. Would I have been so hostile to Tattoo without Jim's snide question about whether he was good in bed - how should I know?

And then, one night a day or two later, after a class where I taught Tattoo and we were carefully polite to each other, followed by a silent guilt-radiation session from Jim, Onion's panic button went off. I wasn't surprised. Jog had let me know she had pretty much stopped eating altogether.

So I got up, got dressed, looked at the diary to see what I was likely to have to move or get someone else to deal with. I tried ringing Onion's mobile, had to leave a message. I took some sandwiches, drank my emergency head-banger coffee and drank my emergency head-banger coke and drove off into the darkness.

It really is terribly dark in South Cornwall, they only have the luxury of streetlights at roundabouts and where lots of old people live. The trees shaded the road so I often didn't even have the nearly-full moon to help. I missed the turn off and had to reverse back up the narrow road - not the least of the things that made MiniWonders go bankrupt was the fact that many tourists couldn't find the place at all.

It was spooky going past Tower Bridge and the Sphinx in the silver darkness. A quiet night, but it so happened the surf was up, I could hear it pounding away in the north. I parked, got out, and found gathered there all the surfers who had looked after Onion so faithfully. Some of them were sitting round a little fire, cooking marshmallows. At  least they were keeping it well away from the now-drying undergrowth and flower display which hid the cannabis plants. The Taj Mahal caught the moonlight as if it was doing its very best to live up to the marble mausoleum on the other side of the world that had cast it as a solid shadow.

I went to the caravan, found Tattoo and Jog waiting outside as I expected. Jog had tears in his eyes, Tattoo - well, I couldn't be objective about him. But there was something contained and determined about him, as if, finally, he had come into his own.

"All right." he said, "thanks for coming." What was it about his voice, that tinge in it? Why did it always make the back of my neck prickle?

"How is she?"

"Go and look." said Jog.

I looked and I agreed with them. It wasn't going to be very long. And yet she was conscious, though she must have been in pain. This is one of the strange things about the morphine pump: once people have one, they use far less pain relief. She gripped my hand, she smiled, she even nodded but she couldn't talk. She wanted something.

I went out again, to where the boys waited. The moon was full, drowning the stars and I finally noticed they were all wearing wetsuits, even Tattoo. I looked around at them.

"What?" I asked.

"We're going to put her in the wheelchair," said Tattoo and when I started to protest about that, he lifted his hand so imperiously I shut up. "Then we're going to push her over to this place where it's concrete and the fencing is safe and you look after her, OK? Make sure she's comfortable. And Jog and the boys and me are going to surf for her."

There were all sorts of stupid things I could have said, like how dangerous it is to surf anywhere at night even with the moonlight and how she shouldn't even be in a wheelchair and how mad it was. And what sort of form-filling mail-opening arse-puckering piece of officialdom would I have been if I'd said them? I could see that the moon was bright enough, and the surf was up and the sea was on fire with phosphorescence and why would Onion have got involved with surfers in the first place if she hadn't loved to watch young men strut their stuff?

"OK." I said.

Jog just nodded, Tattoo smiled. His head was still shaved, he still looked terrifying, but that smile in the semi-darkness…

God, I thought, Jim's right, I am just a randy mum looking for a fresh young buck. And why not? came the quiet thought. It's been an awfully long time since Jim was on form.

Pay attention, I told myself. Jog and Tattoo went into the caravan and Tattoo picked her up and carried her out, while Jog carefully brought the drip and the breathing apparatus. The wheelchair was brand-new and had the very latest form-fit padding, I recognised the make. They settled her in it as comfortably as she could be, tucked her up with a blanket, they helped me wheel her and her encumbrances to the cliff edge, put the brake on and then they left us there.

They went down the well-trodden path to the beach, quietly, and you could see them dark against the green seafire as they went out to find the waves, and then they surfed. That was all. None of them did anything stupid, nobody went tubular, you could tell which was Jog by his yellow mane and Tattoo by his bald head and the way he kept falling off. The rest were just dark figures dancing with the waves, playing, giving their beautiful lady the purest, the most extravagant, the most perfect going-away present they could think of.

I have never seen anything so magnificent.

Usually the appropriate doesn't happen. Usually there's a time when a scriptwriter would end it, and it doesn't end, the lifestory carries on and on and on, into wastes of disappointment and middle age and the ugly insignificance of being old.

This time... I held her hand. She breathed with a sticky rattle and watched under half-shut bruised thin eyelids, a pleased smile under her breathing mask, as her boys surfed for her in the moonlight. Once I thought she was trying to talk, but then I understood. Even the weakest body fights. She sat and the sticky breath went slower and slower, catching occasionally, until I could only hear the sea and occasional distant shouts.

Me, I think she missed the best bit. When the sun came up behind us, they were still there, and from being black on green, they became touched with gold. Something inside my chest ached at the sight of it. Very briefly. After that they were only a bunch of young men. Surfing.

They came back up the path, dripping, some of them talking and laughing. I was tired so I was sitting cross-legged next to the wheelchair which was now empty except for some bony remnants. They paused when they saw it and then they came on hesitantly, stopped again.

"Is she...?"

I nodded. They all gathered together a few paces away, completely uncertain what to do. I'd disconnected the equipment already. Tattoo came forward with his usual sureness, but then he stopped. It was Jog who quietly picked her up and carried her back into her caravan and shut the door.

I went to sit in my car to phone the usual people. Tattoo came out to find me, once he was out of his wetsuit and into his rather staid jeans and t-shirt.

"You OK?" he asked.

"You?" I asked him, and he nodded. "Can I ask you something?"

"Depends what it is," he said warily.

"Did you think of that?"

He blinked and looked away.

"You did, didn't you. Somebody had to think of it and I don't think even Jog has the... imagination."

"Jog? Jog's a philosopher."

"All right." I took a deep breath. "I've misjudged you. I know you're lying somehow, you're running from something, but anyone who can think of that..." I shook my head. "I misjudged you, that's all."

He looked down at his hands, took a breath to speak, then stopped, smiled at me. "You watch," he said eventually. "I haven't started yet."

# Chapter 12



We dealt with the normal form-filling botheration and Tattoo disappeared as soon as the doctor arrived, puttered off in a hurry on his Honda. The police looked in but the boys had been expecting that and all the pot plants were hidden away where they were deniable. I went through the computer records on Onion's pump with extreme care and all was as  kosher as could be; it tallied down to the last nanogram.

The amount of equipment that had silted up there was too much to take back in my car, so Jog packed it in his van and went off to the hospital with it, just like that, including the wheelchair.

"Won't Tattoo want it?" I asked, "those things cost a bomb."

Jog smiled. "No, he's cool, he won't want it. But I'll get a receipt," he added, seeing my expression.

The undertaker arrived and did the necessary, leaving the surfers staring at each other, not knowing what to do with themselves now they didn't have Onion to look after. One of the youngest ones was sitting on the edge of the cliff unselfconsciously crying his eyes out. I went over to him, thinking of Benjy and how sad he would be to have missed it. But then, could he have coped with it at all?

"Are you..." OK was too inadequate and English is a very poor language in which to ask the question 'Are you about as bereft as you should be and no more?' The boy didn't look at me, so I left it. He didn't look much older than Matt.

I suppose I'm old enough, just about, to remember the days when men never cried, no matter what. Those days are gone which is probably a good thing. Many of the others were blowing their noses, often without benefit of a tissue, and shoving their arms up the sides of their faces. They may be permitted to cry nowadays, but they still haven't learned to do it attractively. Mind you, neither have I: in the days when I still knew how to do it, I generally produced industrial quantities of snot, my eyes went red and my face went blotchy. Eventually, I drove off.

I called in on Jim who was just pottering around the kitchen naked except for his socks and was not very pleased to see me. I was worried he might ask me what had happened but he didn't. He just muttered something about having to edit his manuscript properly and rushed back into his study, slamming the door. So I drank coffee, ate breakfast, checked on the boys, turfed out the one who was still snoring and told him I'd drive him to school personally as a great concession. He wasn't too pleased about this.

I found out why when we got to Trevair school. They welcomed him like a long-lost relative and it transpired that darling Simon was only to be seen at the place for register and the occasional art lesson. Darling Matthew much the same only worse. Simon turned into a pizza-faced deaf-mute when I asked him, quietly, calmly and at only the 120 decibel level where he was going every day, so we drove around for a while until I found the skateboard park and his brother, Matt, doing really quite accomplished something-or-others. He fell off when he saw me.

I admit it. I'm a sadist. "Oh hello Matt, what a lovely turn on your skateboard. Aren't you a clever boy."

He was mortified. He came knuckling towards me. "Mum, what're you doing here... aw... mum..."

"What are *you* doing here? As a matter of interest."

"I've got the morning off."

"No, I believe your physics teacher was eagerly hoping to see you. I asked her."

"You've been to the school? Aw, mum... *Why?*"

I had to hold my hands together very tight. "Is this new or is it longstanding?"

He just groaned. I went and picked up his skateboard, put it in the back of the car, locked the boot.

"Get in. I'm taking you back to school."

"Give me back my skateboard."

"Not yours. I paid for it. My skateboard. When you've got a job, you pay for your skateboard."

And the ugly lout actually dared to shove me out the way to get at his bloody skateboard.

So I decked him. It was a beautiful punch, got him right in the gut and he sat down and whooped. If he hadn't been my son I'd have kicked his balls in.

I know, I suppose I shouldn't have.

Still, it was a good punch. I got in the car, leaving them there, one sitting down whooping and holding his poor ickle tummy, the other with his jaw dropped over his nasty spotty adam's apple and their friends snickering.

"You hit him." said Simon, flabbergasted, "You hit him."

"He shoved me," I snarled. "You want some?"

Simon jumped back from the car as if it was red hot.

"Call social services, why don't you? Call the police. I don't care. And you're both grounded."

I drove off, got on the A30 and went all the way to Penzance, where I sat in the beach carpark and shook for an hour. Then I took the skateboard to the promenade and threw it in the sea. Then I rang Pam.

"Come round, darling," she said. "Of course you can moan at me."

It so happened her gorgeous red-haired son was there, just back from the incredibly short terms they have at University, where he was studying biochemistry. I sat at Pam's kitchen table, with its bunch of gypsophila and ferns so terribly stylish, and howled into the contents of two packs of Kleenex while Ken wandered back and forth making cups of tea.

"Oh darling," sighed Pam for the fortieth time, "I'm sure you haven't permanently damaged the creature. What was it I did to you, Ken?"

Ken looked thoughtful. "Slapped me really hard in the face. Did you really knock him down? Wow. Cool."

"I believe I burned your skateboard, didn't I?"

"No, that was Tim's. I wasn't into skateboards. With me it was... you know." And he went scarlet.

"Oh yes. Would you mind if I tell her?"

"God." Red hair and purple face, it wasn't nearly so attractive. I looked at him thoughtfully. What was it I'd heard? "Do you have to?"

"No darling, I don't have to, but it'll probably make her feel much better."

Ken came and sat down, his face burning, his ears burning, his neck burning.

"Oh she's a nurse, she'll think it's funny," he said, "I'll tell her."

"What? Not a baby?"

"Much worse," he said hollowly.

"What's worse?"

"Crabs."

I am very proud of the fact that owing to years of experience and training, despite being exhausted and thoroughly overwrought, I didn't howl with laughter.

"It was horrid, darling." Pam was wiping away an invisible tea drop from her shining pine kitchen table.

"Well," I said, my ribs aching, "at least he didn't catch anything else."

They exchanged a flicker of a glance so quickly that if I hadn't been so experienced I'd have missed it. I felt I wanted to keep Pam as a friend so I changed the subject.

"It's a sort of hormonal haze, isn't it." I said, thinking back to when I was fifteen, with enormous tits. Thanks to my mother I was convinced I was the ugliest thing in the universe, pathetically grateful for any attention from godlike boys and completely hopeless at dealing with them. It was a sort of miracle that despite all my efforts, I didn't manage to lose my virginity until it was at least legal, let alone get pregnant like the vicar's daughter. "I did so hope I could be understanding and not hysterical like my mother and now look what I've done."

Pam put her hand on mine. "Darling, there comes a time when understanding has to stop. You have to draw a line. You are far far too understanding of everyone."

I knew what she was saying. She'd been advising me to ditch Jim for years. Mind you she was ditched herself, after her husband met the new love of his life at the golf club, so she might not be objective. She does say now it's the best thing that ever happened to her.

"And you were upset about Onion," said Ken, unexpectedly.

"How did you know about her?"

He looked uncomfortable. "Oh she's like... like a legend. Everybody knows about Onion. They're organising something for her, you know, like a wake. Everybody's talking about it. Right there at the MiniWonders place."

I nodded, feeling extremely miffed that no one had said anything to me about it. But then when I looked at my mobile, there were three messages, one from Jim, one from Jog and one from Tattoo, the last two asking me to come to the party tomorrow, so I was mollified.

Pam admits she's a rapacious old bag and her ears pricked up when she heard about Tattoo.

"Who's that?"

"He's one of Onion's old lovers, but he's not one of the surfers. At least, he knows how to surf, but he's different. He's a bit older..." I described him, possibly at greater length and with more detail than was necessary.

"Snap him up darling, he sounds gorgous."

I felt my own ears do that prickling they do when you're blushing which was odd because I never blush. "He's not. I told you, he's got this horrible tattoo on his face. But he does have a nice voice."

Ken had escaped, I noticed, which he always did when his mother started about young men and who could blame him? I let Pam hear the message and she clucked approvingly.

"Mm. I like a bit of a rumble. Sounds familiar, you know. Are you going?"

I looked down, felt horribly inadequate. "I can't go. What would I wear?" I asked despairingly.

"Of course you can go. You must."

"Are you coming?"

"Lord no, darling, not my scene at all. Besides, I expect Ken will be there desperately trying to reconnect with one of his old girlfriends and he'd never forgive me if I turned up and spoiled it for him."

"Oh god." I hid my face in my hands. "I don't have time to find clothes. I have to go into the office. I've got to file a report."

"You look absolutely shattered. Why don't you stay the night here."

She was right. I didn't want to go home. I rang, but it was midday by then and of course, Jim was out and had forgotten to put on the answerphone.

So I drove home, picked up a bag with some clothes, toothbrush, recharger, left a note on the kitchen table saying that I was staying with a friend and they could call the mobile if they wanted to know anything and would Matt like to consider his position as a parasite because I'd had about enough of it. I didn't add that I was wondering what Jim, who was supposedly dealing with PTA stuff, had thought he was playing at because it came to me that of course, they were writing letters to him and so on, but he was ignoring them or Matt was getting to them first. I thought I heard something in Jim's study, maybe the neighbour's cat, but he'd locked the door when he went out. So I left all the dirty washing on the floor and the dirty plates and the rubbish bin overflowing and went to Pam's blessed sanctuary in the little annexe by her garage that she had built for her mother many years before.

"I've got a class tonight," I said, "Is that OK?"

She gave me a key to the annexe and one to her front door. "Mi casa, su casa." she said flamboyantly, not being at all Italian but enjoying gangster films.

Then I went to the office and did office things which was quite good really because it calmed me down.

The class was great. Sid had heard about Onion too and stood there, starting to suck his teeth and then stopping himself. "Um. Sorry," he muttered. Tattoo rode up late, so I made him warm up at the back before letting him join the class.

I've said he has the quality of being physically adept. That class he managed to do a proper bandae yop chagi, or reverse side kick, for the first time. He had his sajo jirugi off-pat, both of them. He could do the first three of the three-step self-defence sequences. I know your eyes are glazing over. What I'm trying to get over is that he had made more progress in ten days than I did in my first six months and I'd be lying if I told you it didn't piss me off.

But it would have to stop. Two weeks is the limit. I called him over after the end of the main class and before the later sparring session - I do it that way because I don't like the kids sparring until they're at least yellow tag level. Adults are OK, but kids get overexcited and injuries happen. To me, for instance. One little sweetheart had busted my lip when I invited him to try and hit me.

"Look, Tattoo," I said to him, "I have a problem."

"What is it?"

"Insurance."

His face fell like an elephant off a cliff. "What?"

"My class insurance covers the first two weeks for free. After that you have to get a licence, you have to give me your name and address and date of birth and stuff. I've been as tactful as I can..."

"Which I'm grateful for."

"But if I'm not covered for you if you get injured, then I'm not running a legal class."

He sighed. "Insurers are the kings of the earth, aren't they? Can't move a step without their say so."

"If you want to stay mysterious, you don't have to join this class, you could join Penzance or Camborne or find somewhere in London or wherever. I'm just telling you."

"OK."

We did some breaking as well as sparring. Now breaking is what you do at demonstrations where you get bits of wood and smash them and everyone goes ooh and ah and that's really hard. You also do it at your higher gradings and of course, you have to practice. Usually you use these boards made of heavy rubber, with a joint in the middle, which certainly break if you hit them just right and then you can fit them together again.

I like breaking. Everybody gets it wrong, including black belts. They think it's about power and strength, all the macho stuff. It is to a small extent. But mostly it's about technique and accuracy and speed. And, metaphorically, balls. Nobody says this, or they wrap it up in a lot of new agery about Ki, but really the fact is, if you are willing to hurt yourself when you hit or kick a board (and everything else is right), you don't hurt yourself and you do break it. If you hold back, if you're scared, then you don't break and you do hurt yourself. It's all very philosophical, zen even.

Of course if you're inaccurate then you hurt yourself no matter what you do because the thing won't break.

Well I set up the breaking horse that Sid had welded for me in the garage, and I showed them how with some easy breaks which for me are side kick and outer knife hand strike. I gave them the lecture about respecting the board, and the lecture about speed and accuracy and the one about ki. Everybody above blue tag had a go and most of them managed at least to bend the board.

Tattoo was on fire to try it. I told him no because he was a white belt and there were five grades for him to pass before he was supposed to try. And he really didn't like being told no. I explained why, I told him no again, and then while I was sorting people into sparring pairs, he went and had a go anyway with a side kick.

He failed of course, plus he bruised the side of his foot because he did actually have balls but no accuracy.

I had really had enough of people with testosterone poisoning. I grabbed him, sat him down on the bench and looked at his foot in silence.

"It's bruised." I said coldly. "It should be OK by the day after tomorrow but if it isn't you should get it x-rayed."

"Why didn't it work?"

I stood and looked down at him, with his foot on his knee where he was wiggling his toes.

Finally, he heard the silence and looked up. I think he was expecting me to shout. So I kept it quiet.

"I'm saying this once." I told him, "How *dare* you do that! You do not ever disobey me like that. This is my class. Taekwondo is a lot softer than it used to be, but it's still a dangerous sport. The only way we can keep the danger to a minimum is to have discipline. That means you do as I say, even when you disagree. You can argue with me afterwards, but you do it. And if I say, don't break, you don't know how yet, then don't break."

He was staring at me, very Hard Look jirugi.

"Listen." he growled, "I'm not one of your fucking kids. If I want to try it, I'll..."

"No," I hissed, putting my face right in his. "You're not. You're an adult. And if the kids see an adult take the piss out of me, then they'll take the piss and because they're kids they might actually damage themselves. You can take the piss out of me as much as you like outside class, do what you like, really, but in my class, you do as I say."

Still no give.

"Or?" he said softly.

"Or fuck off."

He fucked off.

I don't remember the sparring session. Afterwards I closed up the gymn, said goodbye to the caretaker, went out into the dark car park and found Tattoo sitting on his Honda next to my car. Oh boy, I thought, oh boy, do I not need this!

I very nearly didn't go to my car, I nearly went back into the Leisure Palace and called for a taxi. Remember Arnie Schwarzenegger on a motorbike as the Terminator? Tattoo was much less musclebound, balder, less friendly atmosphere.

I was tempted to pretend not to see him, ignore him, turn my back on him, get in my car really quickly and just drive. However, this was what I always told my self-defence groups not to do. You have to look, look them in the eye. At least then you know what they're up to. Never ever turn your back on someone, a man, you're not happy about.

I put my keys in my right hand, held my bag in my left, clocked the carpark to make sure nobody else was there, walked up to him.

"Well?" I said. I tried not to sound hostile, after all he might want to apologise. Actually I couldn't tell, what with the darkness and that tattoo and his helmet.

"See you at the party?" he said neutrally.

"Um ... OK."

Incandescent smile. "Great!"

Then he did the kick start and puttered off.

Pam was lovely. She had pasta ready for me five minutes after I came through the door and a hot shower that worked. There was no washing up to do, no clothes to get in off the line, no sympathy to be worked up for another terrible problem with Job Gurney's love life or lack of it, no senile rabbit to feed. Actually, there is no way to tell if a rabbit is senile because they are practically vegetation to start with. Never was a bestselling novel less accurate than *Watership Down*, which just goes to show.

I went to bed at about 11 pm, slept like a log and woke to birdsong from Pam's garden at exactly 7.00 am, feeling great.

# Chapter 13

*Tuesday. Onion's funeral, Lyonesse crematorium. Onion's wake, MiniWonders.*

Jog was complying with Onion's written request which was that she be cremated and her ashes scattered at the cliff edge. She left her caravan and contents to the boys to do what they wanted with. She had paid for the funeral in advance with the last remnants of her own money, one of the benefits of cancer being that you can do this and make sure you get the funeral you want. Not that you'll be able to watch it, unfortunately. Many of my patients don't seem to realise this. Onion didn't want anyone there except Jog and me, not even Tattoo. The boys went into Lyonesse and found a really nice black suit for Jog at an Oxfam shop, which fitted where it touched, and a black tie and Jog went to the crematorium in his van full of surf boards and fibreglass and wetsuits. I have a black suit of my own I keep for these occasions in the back of the car, and I ironed it and stuck it on and stood there while the fake organ music sounded. Jog read from *The Prophet* by Khalil Gibran, of course.

No, I'm sorry, I'd like to believe in God, but I don't. I wish I did.

Afterwards, Jog went to his van, sat there blatantly smoking a spliff which I had to be very careful not to see so I drove away first. Anyway, I was in a hurry to see all the people I'd missed the day before.

When I finished work, Pam led me triumphantly into her enormous bathroom, converted from one of the main bedrooms, with the bath like a pagan altar in the middle.

"Oh this is great," I whimpered gratefully. Pam has stratospherically expensive smelly bubblebath in a cut glass dispenser next to the bath and big thick fluffy towels. She gave me strict orders to wash my hair and use the conditioning treatment she had provided and leave it in for at least ten minutes, shave my bits, help myself to deodorant and put the dressing gown on afterwards.

"What are you going to wear?" she asked.

"Erm..." I didn't really want to tell her because I was suddenly worried she might disapprove – I waved vaguely at my bag which she pounced on and pulled out the black t-shirt and vaguely respectable jeans I'd brought. She rolled her eyes.

"I *thought* so," she said and marched off with them, looking determined.

I ran my bath, almost fell asleep in it, did everything as ordered and was just towelling my hair dry and wrapping the dressing gown when there was a knock on the door. Pam came in bearing a tray with bacardi and coke and some cold chicken and salad.

"Where are my clothes?"

"Well, darling, I heroically didn't put them in the bin where they belong," she said witheringly. "You can have them back tomorrow."

"But what am I..."

"You're going to eat while I do something about your hair and then you're going to brush your teeth and have a facial and then you're going to wear what I damn well tell you to."

"But..."

"Trust me!"

So I ate while she tutted over my neglected hair and trimmed it and then after trying various things opted for just leaving it loose over my shoulders. I usually wear it tied back in a ponytail so it doesn't get in my face.

"I wish I could have taken you into Hendra's in Truro and got somebody like Paul to cut it for you..."

"No point," I told her with my mouth full. "It's the most boring hair in the world."

"That's because you neglect it. Actually it may be dead straight but it's fabulously thick and black and just crying out for a nice blunt cut."

"Hmf."

"Now then."

I sat in the big armchair and she gave me a facial and then made me up which I never do mainly because I can't be bothered.

"Silk purses and sows ears come to mind," I muttered, sipping bacardi and coke as she havered over slate grey or charcoal grey eyeshadow.

"Oh shut up," she said, rather sharply, I thought. "Don't you know how good you look already? He'll drool, or he should."

Well, I had told her a bit more about Tattoo, after hardly any prodding, and she was agog with delight. I muttered something incoherent.

"It's about time, darling, really it is."

"Oh for God's sake, he probably won't give me the time of day."

She said something so obscene about what he could give me instead, that I went goggle-eyed and spoiled her careful mascaraing.

"Keep still."

"Don't be so rude."

"I can't believe you've ever had kids," she said, wielding a make-up remover wipe. "Are you sure you're not still a virgin?"

"I wish. Honestly, Pam, why can't you believe what I say, he's not interested."

"Are you?"

"No."

"Liar, liar, pants on fire."

Actually, never was a truer cliche, but I was carefully not allowing myself to notice.

"Listen, I'm not saying I'm not interested. I'm just not..."

"Not very enterprising."

"Not very ... er... single."

She stepped back, squinted and nodded, then started dabbing stuff on my cheek.

"Anna, sweetie, let me ask you. When was the last time Jim asked you to a party?" I said nothing. "Or invited you out? Or took you to a movie?"

"Well we've been married a while, we don't have much money..."

"He's depressed. I know. Now, when did he last show that he loves you? In any way."

I was silent for a while. "That's low."

"When did he raise a finger in the house, or cope with the boys or express gratitude at all the time he has to sleep... oh sorry, write?"

"He's depressed?"

"I'm not arguing with that. I'm just asking: what's he for?"

Then she handed me some clothes.

"Don't be daft," I said, looking at the labels. "They'll never fit me and anyway I can't wear shocking pink trousers…"

She sighed, rolled her eyes for about the fifth time and then put her hands on her hips.

"Right! That's it! I've had enough!" she shouted. "Now you listen to me, Anna Clements, and don't try and interrupt until I'm through. You will most definitely put those clothes on and they will most definitely fit you."

"But they're too small…"

"The t-shirt might be a teeny bit tight but that's a good thing, not bad, fer Chrissake! What the hell are you *doing* going around wearing baggy faded t-shirts when you've got a pair of tits the like of which some women pay thousands of pounds to acquire."

"Don't remind me…"

"Aaargh! *Listen* to me! You have a fantastic figure…"

"What about my gut and my…"

"Eight years ago, yes, you were a bit plump. Now – you've got fantastic tits, good hips and a bum like a peach. That's not me saying it, by the way, that's bloody Lloyd, damn him…"

Lloyd was her divorce lawyer who had comforted her – as he had many others before and since – after her divorce.

"Lloyd said that?"

"What he said, Anna, last Christmas, was "phew she's got a bum like a peach, do you think she'd…" and I hit him."

I knew my cheeks were going pink.

"Oh."

"If I didn't look so awful in white pyjamas, I might even start martial arts seeing what it's done for you. Sure  - you're probably heavier than the stupid idiots who make up height-weight tables say you should be but it's all toned muscle."

"Um…"

"You obviously haven't noticed this change the way any man with a half-awake cock notices and evidently nor has Jim, because he's an arsehole. You're still wandering around wearing tents and nursing that bloody silly chip on your shoulder…"

"I don't have a…"

"So you will put that bloody t-shirt on and then you will wear my nice cerise pink silk pants and I'll try and forgive you for bringing a pair of trainers."

I was gaping at her because her eyes were sparking with fury.

"You really think…"

"Gaaah! Just get dressed."

She marched out and slammed the door. I put on one tight black t-shirt with a princess-line neck and one pair of scarily pink silk trousers, feeling like Cinderella with a very aggressive fairy god-mother. The trainers didn't show too much. I peeped at the gilded triptych mirror and saw… Somebody different. Somebody new.

I was just looking for the scourer and bath cleaner when Pam put her head round the door.

"Don't you dare even think of cleaning that bloody bath, come on!"

So I followed her out feeling very timid and found Ken in her kitchen drinking a bottle of beer.

"What do you reckon, Ken?" Pam demanded.

Ken goggled at me and went red.

"Um… er…"

"MILF?" she said sweetly and Ken turned puce.

"Mu-um! Urgh… very nice, Anna. You look really great…" And he ran away.

"MILF?" I asked Pam.

"Go watch *American Pie*," she told me.

"Anyway," I said, apropos of nothing, "After the last few days I shouldn't think he'll want to speak to me again, so I'll just go to the party, have fun dancing, and come back."

Pam rolled her eyes yet again and then nodded tactfully. "Off you go," she said.

# Chapter 14

I know you'll laugh at me but when I drove up to MiniWonders, I honestly expected to find a sound system, a bonfire on the beach, lots of cider and Thunderbird (dreadful fortified wine, normally drunk by alkies and students). I was a bit worried about the drugs question, too, frankly, I didn't want to lose my job.

I didn't expect a marquee or two sound systems and a live local band or actual food on actual tables or fairy lights on all the moth-eaten old Wonders making them look gaudy and cheerful or bar staff or a laser show, or security guards on the carpark. I started feeling intimidated, but then I saw some of the surfer girlies, who had tactfully kept away from Onion's little court, and reflected that at least I was decent. Le tout South Cornwall was there, certainly the younger still-parasitical element.

The security guard who I happened to know was an off-duty cop waved me through with a smile and I parked, got out, locked up and looked around feeling very out of place. I was one of the enemy, really. The fact that I had pogo'd wildly to *Anarchy in the UK* is neither here nor there. In their terms, I was a wrinkly. So I goggled at everything for a while, wondering what I'd got myself into.

"Vulgar, isn't it?" said that beautiful voice right behind me and I turned to find Tattoo standing there in jeans and t-shirt, drink and fag in hand.

"How long have you been there?" I asked, full of suspicion.

He smiled lazily. "I was admiring the view."

That made me feel peculiar so I changed the subject.

"How did you know I was here?"

"Wonders of modern technology - had security watching out for you."

"Security," I said, shaking my head.

"To protect me, really. Anybody who isn't already drunk can come if they've heard about it, nobody's dealing, nobody's driving away who's drunk or stoned."

"What will you do with them?"

"I have hired Lyonesse Cabs for the evening and they'll do the honours."

"Blimey."

Smile, sideways blue gaze. When I'd told Pam about his eyes she'd gone all dreamy and sighed and said she'd always been a complete sucker for anyone with blue eyes. This was true, her ex and Lloyd the divorce lawyer had both had blue eyes.

"Go on say it."

"Say what? Oh all right. This must be costing you a fortune."

"Worth every penny, if I was counting, which I'm not."

"What's the new landlord going to say?"

"He's cool."

I looked at him and - yes, I know I'm slow - I knew who had bought the place.

"You're not Richard Branson in a rubber mask are you?"

He laughed, ushered me through to the second tent where food and booze was lined up being ladled into South Cornwall youth and I snaffled a prawns on toast thingy and a chicken leg. Ambrose the postman was there, very much on the pull, and I waved.

"You love the mystery," he said. "And when I have a party, even a small one, I do the thing properly." There it was again in the dark, that familiarity. Pam was right.

"What's Jog think about all this."

We'd come outside again and I was drinking the wine cup which was astonishingly good, because it didn't contain any Polish spirit or Thunderbird, and he pointed down onto the north cove beach where the bonfire was burning nicely and fifty more people milled around.

"He'll be up in a while," he said "Do you think I'd do this if he didn't like it?"

"No, I don't think so."

"Jog said, would you give them five minutes' warning if you're planning to go down to the beach?"

I grinned. "Of course."

His walkie-talkie went off and he turned away, saying he was coming. I looked at the disco tent (sorry, I know the very word disco dates me horribly, but what else do you call it?) which was heaving with people and lights and already spilling out. The DJ was someone Matt had wistfully wished to have at his fifteenth birthday party, until I found out what he charged. The dangerous cliff edges had been carefully roped off and security people were standing there as well. I still felt very unsure of myself, so I trotted along behind Tattoo as he went to deal with a police car full of officers standing around in the main carpark, looking disapproving and envious.

"Officer Tresco, isn't it? So glad you could come," said Tattoo, and he swept into them, smiling, shaking hands. I swear to you (all right, I know you'll believe me)that when he spoke to the police he had a public school accent. "Now, you've had a look round, is there anything you're not happy with?"

They looked about them a bit bewildered and Officer Tresco said that nobody had complained and things seemed well-organised and was there any charge for tickets?

"Of course not," said Tattoo genially. "It's a private party in memory of... er... Onion."

Ah, said Officer Tresco, a known miserable bastard, and could he buy a drink?

"No," said Tattoo even more genially, "But you can certainly have one free if you want."

Tresco was very sad.

"Now," said Tattoo. "If there's anything you gentlemen would like me to do or alter, just say the word."

Tresco allowed as how he felt no offence was being committed and as nobody round about had complained, he'd be getting along. And off they drove.

"You called them?"

"Just a sec." And he got a little voice recorder out of his pocket, listened for a second, nodded and put it away again. I goggled at him.

"And I thought I was paranoid."

"You are. I am. This is self-defence. You'll see. Now do you like to dance or are you one of the people who stand around the edges taking the piss?"

We were shouting now, because we were getting near the sound system again and the laser show which was making St Jude's tower look like a real wizard's citadel, evil sigils and all.

"I love to dance," I yelled. "I'm crap, but I love it. Promise you won't laugh."

He grinned, which a light caught sideways and made totally hideous because the tattoo looked like an evil alien disease from Dr Who - certainly not a spiderweb, unless the spider had been on LSD. He stamped out his fag, finished the drink, put it down on one of the tables on the grass. Then he caught my hand and swung me into the dancing.

It's true. I do love dancing. I don't care that teenagers think all senile old wrinklies over the age of 30 should be banned from dancing. I've never understood why anyone needs to take Ecstasy because just music and dancing put me in exactly the same happy state. I was already swinging my hips, and he did laugh at that, but then I was laughing too.

Remember physically ept? He's a wonderful dancer. Not because he's trained or anything, he just enjoys it and he's at ease with his body and he has none of that rhythmless self-consciousness of the average English male. Poor old Jim had it terribly. By the time Jim was drunk enough to have a go at the traditional English foot-wiping step, he was usually too rat-arsed to stand up. At Oxford I'd met a lovely gay man from New College who loved dancing as much as me and we used to go out together, but this was nothing like poor Phil, an early AIDS casualty.

You know peacocks when they spread their tails and rustle them, look at me, I'm such a beautiful healthy male? That's dancing, isn't it? Only both sexes display among humans. I sometimes imagine an alien David Attenborough whispering under a disco table, "And here the males demonstrate their fitness and strength while the females display their secondary sexual attributes. To good effect. Eventually some of them will find a mate and quite possibly copulate just outside in the area known as 'the bushes'..."

One of the nice things about martial arts training is how fit you get, and how supple. I can do anything I want on a dance floor, some of it pretty silly. Tattoo wolf-whistled and cheered when I did the splits at the end of something particularly vigorous. Cool girlies with their glittering bellybuttons couldn't do that. Hah! Most of the young things danced in same-sex groups so we were really showing our age.

I wandered outside when Tattoo got called away to approve the ejection of a couple of lads who'd been dealing in naughty pills, considered going down the cliff path to the beach party and then decided against. Although the path is perfectly safe in daylight I was nervous of it at night. Also I didn't want all the surfers and their girls having to hide their spliffs and pretend to be pleased to see me and then try and remember where they'd put them once I'd safely gone.

So I found myself picking my way amongst the overgrown paths. They were familiar and I suddenly remembered bringing Matt and Si here about eight years before, in the days when MiniWonders was only struggling, and how struck and enchanted the boys had been with it.

Wildly overgrown flowerbeds, the sad wrecked cages of the petting park, the little row of miniature houses where you could go in and play if you were small enough... That was definitely the high point for the boys. The houses were carefully scaled down to child-size, with half-size bunks and tables and chairs and painted wooden cookers and a wooden fireplace two foot high like in Snow White. Matt and Si had loved it, they'd leaped around busily making lunch, tea, breakfast and a birthday party and putting each other to bed. I'd come up with the wizard wheeze of being Snow White and going to sleep on two of the little beds, so I even managed an hour's kip before they started fighting over who was going to be the daddy.

The row of half-timbered small houses were all boarded up and there was a budleia growing through the roof and the sight made me sad. Well, more like drunkenly mawkish, so I turned around and went back, guided by the pulsing music and the wizard's citadel.

I went past the Taj Mahal looking very Indian restaurantish with its fairy lights blazing and almost bumped into Tattoo on the path.

"Hey Anna," he said. "Come and look at this."

He took my hand and led me round the back of the Taj, where the large garden shed that formed its core had a half-door that still worked, usually padlocked but now open.

He bent double, went in.

"Come on," he said. "It's amazing."

I hesitated because... well, you know by now how paranoid I am. It was very dark and I still didn't know that much about Tattoo and... I was being a moron.

I swallowed, scurried in. It was quite big inside, no problem standing up, smelled of damp, mould, black as pitch, occasional little random glows where the fairy lights were near a hole, sort of glittery, smell of candlewax and something not quite animal. For a moment I thought I heard breathing, but the sound system was too close.

"OK," said Tattoo's voice. "Stay still."

There was the flick and chung of his zippo and the hissing as he turned the flame right up and held it high and I gasped. I was in a house of jewels.

It was painted white on the outside but on the inside someone had artexed the walls in sections and stuck on... Not jewels, no. Broken glass bottles, brown ones, green ones, blue ones, white... There was red glass as well and yellow and I remembered a time about eighteen months before when no traffic light, no car's rear lights were safe.

In one corner, on the left, partly hidden by an enormous fruiting body of the dry rot fungus, were brown and green jungles of glass, then waves of ocean and sky and on the right it became a jagged sea of fire where the brakelights came into their own, interspersed with broken mirrors. The ceiling was all white glass and mirrors.

"It's fantastic," I breathed. "Who did it?"

"Benjy. He showed me the day before Onion pulled her stunt. He did it for her when she was living in here, before Jog got her the caravan so she had windows to look out of. It really needs more light, spotlights maybe. Here, I brought this."

The zippo flame moved back to the door, there was a scrape and a clatter and the big torch that had lit Onion's caravan shone out, making the whole place gleam and glitter and flash, showing the colours better but also the sharp edges sticking straight into the air. You had the disoriented feeling of being in someone's head during a wild acid trip.

Then the light shone into a dark corner and onto a pair of pale white buttocks, rather plump and well-shaped, though the girl was hiding her head in the pile of sleeping bags they were lying on while the boy, almost buried underneath her, peered, very aggrieved, over her smooth bare shoulder.

"Hey. Turn that light off," he said, quite politely in the circumstances. "We were here first."

Tattoo switched off the torch. "Sorry mate," he said, strangulated. "I didn't realise anybody was…"

"And would you terribly mind shutting the little door behind you?" asked the girl, slightly muffled but very cut-glass tones. "Please?"

"Right," said Tattoo and we groped our way out of Benjy's artwork.

Tattoo laughed all the way back to the marquee, shaking his head. I laughed too, though not quite so much because after all, I may be slow but I'm not daft. I looked at him sidelong as we came to the dancefloor and found a bold knowing blue stare waiting for me. He knew that I knew what he'd been up to and he wasn't even slightly abashed. He gestured courteously for me to go ahead and then stepped up behind me before I could spot that they'd simmered the lights down, changed the music to what oldies like me call smoochy. He put his arms round me and turned me to face him. Did I say, unhand me, you scoundrel? Don't be silly. I'm unenterprising, not mad.

Yes, of course they played *Lady in Red*, very naff. It had been a long time since Jim was on form and it seemed somebody had snuck round to the back of my head and switched my libido back on again and if there's anything sexier than a man who can dance holding you tight, I don't want to meet it because I'll only rip its clothes off.

I'm not entirely sure how long we danced or what to or anything really. You stop going dancing or clubbing when you turn into that boring drudge, a mum, and you think the person who did it is dead, but she's not, she's just lying in wait to snare somebody large with a beautiful voice and go dancing with him. What was the feeling under my ribs, I wondered vaguely as I snuggled into him, was the chicken leg disagreeing with me, and then I recognised it as being the unfamiliar and peculiar sensation of happiness. It worried me that I hadn't recognised it at first.

Then something in the tone of his body changed, went tense and at the same time I heard a familiar moan.

"Uuuuh."

I turned, looked, stopped and there was Matt, swaying, eyes crossed, totally out of it while Simon, also swaying, also eyes crossed but slightly more compos mentis, tried to drag him away.

"Whah you *doing?*"

Well at least I'd shocked him, I thought as I started coming down from my high.

"What does it look like she's doing?" growled Tattoo.

Somewhere under a table I hallucinated the alien David Attenborough whispering, "And sometimes the covert rivalry for mates comes out in the open as the competing males enter the ritualistic state of aggro."

I let go of my lovely alpha male and marched forward.

"What the hell are *you* doing?" I snapped. "I told you, you're grounded. When did that ever include going to parties?"

Matt rocked sideways, "Mu-um!"

"Come on, Matt," whispered Simon, "Quick."

"I'll call security," said Tattoo, getting out his phone.

"No, it's OK. These, god help me, are my two sons."

Tattoo looked at them and then at me, quite shocked. "No shit?"

The drink and whatever other chemicals were blasting my son's brain decided to get him into trouble properly. "Why you dancing with my mum, huh? Huh? Who th'fuck are you?"

Tattoo looked as if he was finding this quite funny, for the moment.

"Matt, we gotta go," hissed Simon. "C'mon."

"Don' wanna come on. Wanna talk to him. Wha' you doin' snogging my mum, huh? Wha'bout my dad? Urk."

And yes, gentle reader, that is when he was sick all over himself, the floor, my feet, with a few spatters for good measure even reaching as far as Tattoo who had spotted it coming before the experienced nurse and started shifting away. Luckily by some miracle Pam's pink silk pants escaped.

"Fuck," said Tattoo.

"I'm sorry," I said, miserably. "I'll fetch a mop."

"Anna," said Tattoo, "you will stay right there." Mobile, quiet words. Two security guards materialised, got hold of my sons. A third minion turned up with a mop and bucket.

"Don't hurt them," I said to the guards, a bit dramatically. Possibly I was slightly the worse for wear too.

"Get them out," said Tattoo. "Let them finish chundering..." Simon looked as if he was on the verge of it himself. "... put them in a taxi and either send them to Treliske or home."

"Home," I said, giving my address. "I'll follow you in my car... No, wait... I'll take them in mine."

Tattoo caught my arm. "How much have you had to drink?" he asked seriously.

"I dunno, about three."

"Must have been before I saw you, because you've had about five good slugs of the punch that I've seen."

"I'm not drunk."

"Sweetheart, the cops will be sitting in battalions on every road, lane and footpath in a radius of two miles from this place, in the hopes of filling their Christmas quotas of drunk-driving convictions before September. Could you pass a breathlyser?"

I did stop and think. "No." I said. "All right, I'll go with them in the taxi. Make sure they're all right."

Tattoo looked thoroughly thwarted which was nothing to how I felt. I was raging, miserably frustrated, embarrassed, humiliated, furious...

Nothing to be done about it because I am in fact their mother and I had to make sure they got home all right and lay on their sides in the recovery position to go to sleep and all that. I had to. I wasn't about to lose nine months of pregnancy, twelve hours of labour, eight stitches, six months of breast feeding, fifteen years unremitting toil to a simple thing like inhalation of vomit.

But I was unbelievably disappointed. It was nice that Tattoo looked displeased as well, but I supposed that in the morning he'd recover and feel thoroughly embarassed. Or he might well recover very much quicker than that and wake up with some Cornish wench ministering to him. They'd been gyrating around him assiduously enough while we danced. I'd even caught a glimpse of the ever-willing Lysette.

He nodded at the security men, and I went with them, watching with distaste as my sons heaved their guts up a couple more times. The taxis waiting there all had plastic covers on their seats, I noticed, so I supposed I wasn't the only mother wishing that each generation didn't have to discover for itself how truly horrible it is being completely rat-arsed.

We piled the boys in the back, I sat in the front, told the taxi driver where to go. He was watching me covertly.

"Quite a do, eh." he said. "Some big film company?"

"Something like that."

"Is it true Mel Gibson's there?"

"No. It isn't."

He got the message and shut up while the boys groaned and snortled in the back.

We got to the village, parked, I removed the boys from the back by their floppy hair, offered the driver money which he steadfastly refused, saying it was all taken care of, not to worry, hope the boys recover. Then he drove back to the headland above Lyonesse where the lighthouse glowed and flashed blue and a faint thumping drifted down.

I was very determined not to kick the little turds, nor abuse them in any way. I was sure there'd be psycho-drivel in plenty from Jim about traumatising Matt with a punch. So I went to where they lay side by side in the bushes, preparing to go to sleep for the night, bent and got a good handful of hair with each hand.

"Baldness beckons," I said. "Up, or I'll pull you up."

"Ahuuugh mu-um."

I pulled them backwards into the house, having kicked the front door open, backwards up the stairs and into the bathroom. I have dealt with drunks for many many years. Too many. I ran the shower, stripped them both, put them one by one into it to get the worst off, threw them towels as a great concession. Luckily I didn't need to change my own clothes, I looked at them for signs of serious alcohol poisoning, saw none and they'd pumped their own stomachs pretty effectively. I shoved Matt into his bedroom, waded through the clothes, CDs, burger wrappers, newspapers, wank mags, shoes, sports equipment, skateboard mags and tissues to the bed, shoved him on it and put him in the recovery position with the duvet over him.

I went back for Simon to find he'd drunk some water, peed, and got himself into his bed. He'd even had the courtesy to hide the mags he'd borrowed from Matt. And he was lying there, crying.

I tried very very hard not to melt.

"I'm not going to talk to you now," I said. "I'm too angry and you're too drunk. I'll do it another day. Maybe. Thanks for wrecking my evening. Maybe I can do the same for you sometime."

He sobbed heartbrokenly and I couldn't stand it any more. So I sat down next to him and stroked his damp forehead, said shh, it was all right really, and when he'd calmed down a bit I gave him a kiss on the cheek where there was a space between spots.

# Chapter 15

I thought wistfully of Pam's lovely clean tidy sweet-smelling annexe but my car was up at MiniWonders and she lived ten miles away.

So I went downstairs again to get myself some water from the kitchen and carefully put all the vomity stuff in the washing machine. I walked right past the spoor, stuffed the machine, put in the soap, switched on, got water, drank, turned to go back upstairs and stopped dead.

It wasn't just that the domestic detritus had been hidden, mostly, in the sink under a couple of tea towels and the table wiped. It was on the table. You may think me very naive, but when I saw two plates with the remains of steak on them, two bowls with ice cream, two glasses and an empty winebottle and one of the glasses - a classic, an oldie but a goodie, folks - with a lipstick print... . I couldn't think what they might be doing there. Well, I suppose I am arrogant. Or naive. Or stupid. The lipstick was the exact same colour as the gunk I'd vaguely noticed on Jim's coffee mugs a few days before.

That was when there was a soft knock on the door. I went out into the hall in a daze, recognised the shape through the glass and nearly didn't open the door at all.

"Hi. I realised you'd need a lift to get your car back, so I..." he started and stopped. "What is it? The boys all right?"

My mouth opened and shut like a goldfish's. I didn't know what to say. I don't know what he thought, he just pushed past me, glanced up the stairs, went into the kitchen and he stopped too. I really wished he hadn't. I didn't want anyone to see before I could sort it out in my own mind.

"Ah," he said.

I had to know, had to find out. I went to Jim's study, found nobody there. Phew I thought, false alarm, maybe he had some dart-playing friend... No. Knickers under the desk, instantly identifiable as not-mine because too-small.

So I went upstairs to the master bedroom at the other end of the corridor from Matt and Si's rooms, and opened the door and... Second pair of buttocks that evening, male this time.

It's cruel, really. Evolution made us so undignified. I noted that Jim had finally found someone who'd let him fall asleep his favourite way and I noted that he had quite a few hairs growing down his back and his legs were skinny. Lack of exercise, you know. He snored with alcoholic firmness. She seemed quite nice, soft pink little mouth dribbling slightly in sleep (same colour lipstick etc), nice curly dark hair with those little coloured springy things glittering in them. What you could see of her. I think she worked at the pub. Oh yes. Suzie.

I took in the scene for a long long time. Tattoo finally put his hand on my shoulder, half-turned me. He looked me in the eye, took a breath to speak. I was seized with a wierd and enormous feeling right under my ribs where the happy feeling had been earlier, something that made my lungs feel tight and my throat sore. I put my finger on my lips, went to my little desk, got a permanent marker out of the drawer, went over to the bed and very carefully wrote YOU ARSEHOLE on Jim's bum. He snortled and wiggled it lasciviously, squeezed a tit. Then I wrote PTO on his forehead, and signed his leg.

Then I got two dressing gown cords and tied their wrists together, right to left, left to right, and then I put the duvet over the two of them so they wouldn't get too chilly.

By this time Tattoo had his hand over his mouth and nose and his shoulders were shaking. I went out, leaving the light on.

And then I went out the front door, closed it behind me, quite softly.

We carefully waited until we were in Tattoo's car - hired, new smelling, rather good, not that I know cars. Then we cracked up.

"You're a genius," hooted Tattoo. "Honest to god, you're a genius. I thought you were going to punch him in the bollocks or something, I really did. But that... that's much better. Oh I wish I could put a camera in with a movement sensor to get them when they wake up."

"We could wait and watch," I giggled. "He'll wake up pretty soon because he'll need to pee."

"Do you want to?"

I thought about it seriously. Then suddenly all the laughter went out of me and I thought what an idiot I was. Who was I to judge?

"No," I said. "Not really. Not really."

He was lighting two fags again, offering me one, and I took it and sucked carcinogens gratefully. He started the car without more ado and drove off into the night.

"Where do you want to go?"

"Are you OK to drive?"

"Oh yes. I don't get drunk at my own party."

I sighed. "I don't feel in a party mood any more."

"Nor me."

"Why not?"

He shrugged. "Some people turned up I didn't want to see. I knew they would eventually, I was just hoping they wouldn't hit the place until the morning."

"Who?"

He shook his head. "Come on," he said. "I'm driving at random here and these little twisty lanes three feet across still scare the shit out of me."

So I told him the way to Pam's place, and then when he very politely saw me to the annexe door, I looked at him and thought a bit, and I asked myself whether this was on the rebound, and myself said, who gives a shit?, and then I wondered what he'd say and myself was waving her fists in the air...

"You're in a state." he said gently. "Do you want me to go?"

"No. Yes. No."

He put his hands on my shoulders and kissed me chastely on the forehead. "You could..." he breathed in that deep voice of his, "You could offer me coffee."

"I... I don't know if there's any here."

"Your friend has provided coffee," he said.

"How do you know?"

"Because I can see a double futon through the window."

"Oh. Um. Let's see?"

I stumbled across the threshold and he steadied me, smiled slowly, looked around.

In the kitchenette were two cupboards, both with post-it notes on them: one said "4:1" and the other said "4:2!". I looked at them stupidly, wondering what they meant. Ages? Time?

Tattoo opened the one that said 4:2 and found: two mugs, a cafetiere ready primed with fresh ground coffee, milk, sugar. He took the tray out and found at the back a half bottle of calvados and a small white envelope. He opened it, his brow wrinkled and then he gave a shout of laughter and put it back.

"What?" I said, pushing past to grab the envelope, and found it had a pack of condoms in it.

All right, I'm a nurse, so why did I go as beetroot as one of my sons would have. Tattoo was already foraging nosily in the cupboard which said 4:1. In it was a big bottle of brandy and a very large box of Belgian chocolates. And some Kleenex.

"I like your friend." he said, eating one of the chocolates and switching the kettle on. "She has style."

"She's been telling me to ditch Jim for years."

"That was Jim... er..."

"In an alcoholic post-coital slump, yes."

"Your... er..."

"Yes, my husband. Father of my two repulsive truanting sons."

"They seemed all right to me, for... what? Sixteen?"

"Fifteen and a half and fourteen."

"Well, it's almost compulsory to do that stuff at that age. They'll be in such agonies of embarassment tomorrow, I almost feel sorry for them."

"Maybe they won't be so morally snotty after they see their dad..."

"Oh nobody's got doubler standards than boys that age. They've probably been covering for him and blackmailing him about the bunking off school."

I thought about it and sighed.

"Probably."

He poured hot water, stirred, managed to push down the filter without causing a volcano, brought the tray over to the futon, turning the lights down with his elbow on the way. Then he sat there looking at me.

"Are you going to come here and have some coffee or are you going to stand there and hog all the chocolates?"

I picked up the box, brought it over and sat down... I'm sorry, I can hardly bear to write this, but I kicked off my shoes and then I genuinely did sit down on the floor opposite him. I don't know why either.

I didn't let him get me with his hard blue look, I let him pour me some black coffee with sugar and drank it demurely, not looking at him. What was my problem? Dear reader, one of my problems was that I was wearing an elderly but comfy sports bra so that I could dance without knocking myself out with a tit, and a very faded and ancient, but comfy, pair of knickers. If Pam had known she would have disowned me. Another was that I had not slept with anyone else since I met and fell for Jim, though plenty before, of course, I am a nurse, after all. Medics mostly. Another was that I...

I didn't know what to do. Yet again, I felt as awkward as I had when I was a teenager desperate to lose It, clumsily pawing any boy who so much as glanced titwards or getting clumsily pawed... I looked at him and I thought, god, I like the way he sits and what do his shoulders look like naked, does he have hair on his chest..? The face thing didn't matter any more, nor the daft mystery he'd created. Oh yes, dear reader, I wanted to shag him so much. And yes, I would have been easy meat in Benjy's jewelled Taj. But I was so churned up with it all, I just couldn't move.

"Fuck this for a game of soldiers," he growled, put his coffee mug down, knelt on the floor where I was sitting cross-legged, put his hands on my shoulders and kissed me on the mouth, very delicately and then again, much less delicately. "If you want me to stop, punch me or something."

Of course I didn't bloody punch him. He tasted lovely, coffee, a little bit of booze, a bit of fags... So strange, actually to taste somebody, play games with your tongue.

You know the Madonna song, *Like a vir-er-ergin...* No way was I a virgin - not, believe me, after two normal deliveries of strappingly healthy baby boys. Nor was I inexperienced but it had been a  while since Jim had been interested and even then I generally had to be very careful what I did or said or face accusations of being frigid/too frantic and too aggressive/too passive depending on his mood at the time.

But this was definitely the first time I had been seduced by a grown-up. Not some frantic adolescent on penis-driven autopilot nor a beery medic who was clock-watching because the football started in fifteen minutes, nor yet a husband with a routine. This was a man who was certainly not new to exploring unfamiliar bodies, who was willing to take his time, who was... how can I put this without being ridiculous, dear reader? ...interested?

Not that he was any better than Jim at undoing the multiple hooks of my bra. Also I didn't really want him to see the ghastly thing, so I did the trick of taking my bra off under my t-shirt and hid it under a cushion and he gasped flatteringly and said he'd been hoping they were really real. Then he spent a very satisfyingly long time getting my t-shirt off and exploring exactly how big they were with the sort of leisurely attention to detail and imagination that had me ripping clumsily at his clothes... Pink silk is stronger than you'd think and luckily the disgraceful knickers came off in a tangle with the trousers. His shoulders were just as good naked as I'd suspected - muscular but not gym-perfect - and he had enough chest hair to tickle my nose and I'm afraid I just couldn't wait any longer so I hauled him down on top of me. Bless his heart, he was the one who remembered, though I was the one who had to run giggling over to the kitchenette to paw in a cupboard for a little white envelope. And it was gloriously greedy and unstylish, nothing like that boring self-conscious ersatz stuff that Hollywood peddles as sex, in which nobody ever yells or squeals or farts or makes undignified grunting sounds because their autonomic nervous system just took over.

Also nobody in Hollywood nowadays lies next to each other, tired, sweaty and completely relaxed, smoking unPC post-coital fags. I stared at the smoke and wondered how on earth this had happened and suddenly found tears dripping out of my eyes. And I wasn't even sad, I was happy. But it felt like something had cracked and it hurt, as if my poor small constricted little heart just couldn't cope with three comes in a row. At least three, I wasn't exactly capable of counting at the time.

Tattoo gently caught the tears with his finger, kissed my eyes. "Shh." he said.

"I'm not sad," I told him anxiously.

"Shh. I know. Now I want you to let me do something kinky."

Well, you see, in Hollywood sex, the man never never but never lies on the woman's shoulder, which Tattoo wanted to do, because then, as he said, he could cup one magnificent tit in his hand and watch the other nipple unpinking at close range while he dozed off.

We fell asleep like that.

# Chapter 16

*To do: Wed. See Mrs Tredurgan, Gerry, Robby, meet Matt & Si's Head of Yr for Chat.*

And I woke up thinking, Mel Gibson?

No, definitely not Mel Gibson. He wasn't nearly small enough or skinny enough or (sorry Mel) old enough. Russell Crowe? No (pity).

I looked down at the baldness and the blue lines and tried mentally to add the beard, Anglo-Saxon crown and sexily haunted look he'd worn as *King Alfred*.

Then I went out to the bathroom, found a nice bathrobe, white, hanging next to another one, blue, put it on and stirred around in the cabinet, found some surgical spirit and cotton wool.

I worked away at just one patch, on his cheek, and sure enough the blue lines came off. I did a bit more, sure he'd wake up from the coldness, the sting, but he didn't. He's a very sound sleeper, by the way. And bit by bit I turned him from Tattoo the putative biker/drug-dealer into Shaun Graham, film megastar, Aussie hellraiser, recently gone missing, rumoured to be drying out at a special clinic in Ireland.

I was genuinely finding it difficult to breathe. I was sort of gasping with it, but what? Anger? Excitement that I'd actually laid Shaun Graham? Fury that he'd so comprehensively taken me for a mug? Desperate horrible embarrassment (had he noticed that bra?).

I hadn't finished when his hand came up and caught my wrist. The surgical spirit went on the floor, he sat up and kissed me on the lips. I kissed him back and then I pulled away, scrunched up in a ball and put my hands over my face.

He sighed.

"Oh bollocks," he said, very heartfelt, got up and wandered out to the bathroom where Shaun Graham, the actual Shaun Graham, Oscar winner, did what everybody does in the morning, exactly the same way as half the population, including forgetting to put the seat back down again, and yet it was a surprise to me. Then he saw his reflection in the mirror, still a few blue swirls on it under the stubble.

"Fuck fuck, fuckity fuck fuck, fuck fuck," he said as he came back, coughing, lighting a fag and offering me one which I took with hands that shook so much he nipped it out of my fingers, lit it and put it in my mouth for me.

You think it would take a lot more plastic surgery than just a fake facial tattoo and an all-over head shave to fool you? I tell you, these things go by the context. You see who you expect to see where you expect to see him. Tattoo from Onion's past made more sense than Shaun Graham in South Cornwall, for Chrissake. And all right, I suppose I'd been in denial.

"You... you're Shaun Graham," I told him, inanely. This apparently is normal. Everyone tells him who he is.

"Yup."

"It was the p...press," I said. "Th...they were the ones you were hiding from."

"Yup," he said.

"And... and Onion?"

"Once upon a time there was a magically beautiful and fascinating model called Lily Bates, who took up with a very young and callow struggling actor, cooking tapas not too far from Earl's Court, only the stupid arsehole decided he would rather shag a famous actress and dumped her. I'm sure that's not why it happened the way it did, no doubt she thought good riddance at the time, but she got into coke and heroin and all the usual and disappeared from view."

"Ah." I burbled wisely. "Hence Onion. Related to lilies but smelly."

"Then a while back I heard rumours, put an advert in the paper, Jog rang me on the special line, and I wanted to see her, but I knew I couldn't do the Whatever-Happened-to-Lily-Bates, Where-Is-She-Now? features to her, so..." He circled his fingers at his face.

"So you did... all this to yourself." I shook my head. "I can't believe I didn't recognise you.  I can't believe... I can't believe this. It's too wierd. I just can't."

He cocked his head to one side, gave me blue look number two, half-closed lids.

"Anna," he drawled, "I'm a very good actor. Why wouldn't I fool you?"

The arrogance of it was scary.

"What about Jog?"

"He knows, though I don't think he's that interested. The other boys don't – yet. I got Sandra on the phone before she called anybody and she was cool. Expensive but cool. If anyone else spotted me, they haven't said anything." He picked up what was left of the surgical spirit, went back into the bathroom and expertly got the rest of the fake tattoo off.

I wrinkled my nose and started laughing. I suppose, I did sound a bit unhinged. Well you would be too, gentle reader, believe me. Oh, you're cooller than that, are you? Lucky you.

"What?" he said, a little suspicious, smiling round the bathroom door at me. Without his tattoo it was a devastating smile. He's not that splendiferously handsome, by the way, he isn't Pierce Brosnan or Brad Pitt or anything like that. In fact, without what's behind it, his face would be quite plain. It's the whole package, eyes, voice, smile, brain, shoulders, height, never mind the incipient gut I'd spotted the first time I met him, who am I to criticise someone with a gut for god's sake?

Actually I'd always fancied Daniel Day Lewis more, really. Remember him running through the forest in *Last of the Mohicans*? Cor.

"It'll put the crowning infamy on Jim. Shaun Graham seeing his arse."

Shaun Graham splashed his face with water, dried it, puffed his cheeks out, lit another fag off the one he was putting out and smoked it devotedly.

"It's so weird," he said conversationally, and you could hear that Aussie tang. He'd said chunder. Oh god, my son had puked on Shaun Graham. "You're one of millions of struggling actors, everybody despises you, you're trying to get a break and you scratch around and you scratch around and you're desperate, going bust, and then, through an old flame, you get some part in a movie you think you can do something with if you're careful, and then you think O fuck it, why be careful? So you steal the picture off the so-called star, but luckily he's getting divorced at the time so he doesn't keep such a tight grip on the cut and you manage not to end up on the cutting room floor, and people actually see it and some of them say, he's good, he can act. So you do more movies and none of them really gets you into the A list. And then you get another hot script, but it's boring and here's one you think might really be fun to do so you say no to the boring one and you do the fun one, and the boring one takes $40 million first weekend and the fun one goes straight to video and the bank want their money back and you think, can I afford a bullet to top myself? And then... And then you get a sidekick part in a wierd little film that does a steady $15 million a week for week after week after week. You get offered a big historical turkey after everybody else turned it down, only it turns out not to be a turkey on the fifth rewrite and then... boom! Queues round cinemas. Oscars. Plenty of other actors out there, just as good as you, or almost, but you're the one with the scripts piling up and people who wouldn't even take your calls two years ago, ringing you up and saying, Shaun you've just gotta meet with this director, he lervs your work..."

"Sounds terrible," I put in, deadpan.

He raised his eyebrows. "Did I say that? No. It's fucking great. It's money and fame and success and everything you wanted, and you get to do stuff you like and find interesting and it takes cash in bucketfuls and this time you've got a pretty serious fee and the money just rolls in."

I laughed enviously.

"Do you think I didn't enjoy myself, nicking time on your phone to get onto my business manager in New York and tell him to pull his finger out of his arse and buy MiniWonders? I loved it. Do you think I don't enjoy throwing parties, even little ones in South Cornwall? Properly? I knew the hacks'd get to me eventually, especially once I started using my cards, so I thought I'd go out with a bit of a splash, plus celebrate Lily Bates properly who won't even get an obituary. But I did it because I like to. It's fun."

He was pacing up and down, punctuating with his fag.

"Except... you get rarefied. You get separated from people. One minute, you're just another unemployed actor, taking shit from businessmen in tapas bars. Next minute you're being treated like some sort of god. You never meet people who just talk to you, they're always worried about what you'll think of them. If you want them to teach you something, like taekwondo for instance, they're terrified to tell you that you're doing it wrong. Believe me, it's great to get away from that. That's mind-numbing. That truly makes you crazy."

"Jim calls it the two-headed writer effect."

"Does he?"

"Yes, he used to say if you tell people what you do before they've got to know you, then you never ever get to know them or even have a sensible conversation because they're afraid of you, they're worried you'll put them in a book and they want to ask where you get your ideas and how long it takes to write a book and would you mind just looking at their 900 page handwritten manuscript about heroic badgers who fight with swords."

He laughed. "Too right. Would you have said a word to me if I'd been Shaun Graham, movie star?" And he came over and kissed me.

I couldn't believe this was happening. To me. The one they used to call "Barrel" at the teaching hospital? "I might have got up the courage to ask for your autograph." In bed, I am not at all shy, as you might have noticed. But now I felt hot and uncomfortable and very tentative. I sort of pecked him back and he looked at me gravely.

"What's so different, Anna?"

"But... but... you must meet such beautiful women?"

"Sure I do," he said. "So skinny you're scared you might break them, so hungry you can't eat in front of them or they'll cry, so desperate to please you they'll do anything, anything at all, except relax enough so you can enjoy them enjoying it."

"But I'm not beauti…"

"Oh for Chrissake, Anna, I've been having x-rated fantasies about you ever since I first saw you.  Half the surfer kids have the hots for you and you don't even notice…"

"Well, nurse uniform…"

"Does nothing for me, mate. But luscious juicy tits and that tight little arse of yours…" He kissed me again, not at all chastely. "And you know what really does it?" I shook my head. "You look like you might really enjoy fucking and then… It turns out you do! Magic."

I could feel myself flushing. He couldn't have said anything nicer. And I do enjoy it. I always have. Enjoyed it before Jim, enjoyed it with Jim, enjoyed it pregnant (not lactating which pushes an off switch somewhere inside you), enjoyed it desperately in the back of the car because there was nowhere else we could hide where little boys wouldn't find us and demand cornflakes.

Enjoyed it with Tattoo – No. Shaun Graham. Oh shit.

He sat there, naked, smoking, and I sat there, bathrobe provided by Pam falling open. Men can lie, of course, but not with their dicks. And Tatt... Sh... his dick was saying he wanted to enjoy me enjoying it again. And it's the sexiest sight in the universe, isn't it? Well, I think it is.

Sorry. You're going to have to use your imagination. Remember, nothing Hollywood, leave out the soft lighting and pretend that a squashed Belgian chocolate gets involved.

# Chapter 17

*To do: Reports, Tesco. Dry cleaning?*

After we'd both showered, I found that the stupendously stylish Pam had supplied croissants as well as plenty of coffee, all in the fridge, with some bacon as well. Tattoo...Shaun looked at it all and sighed.

"I'm supposed to be dropping fifteen pounds for the next picture."

"What? Why?"

"Script calls for some nudity and the director wants me with a six-pack."

"Why?"

He smiled, eyes hooded. "So ladies like you can get your cookies."

"You mean rapacious old bags like me. And anyway, I much prefer you without a sixpack."

He looked down. "Haven't got one, have I?" He rolled his stomach muscles which looked so daft I snickered. So he lay down on the floor and started doing sit ups - the wrong ones, the kind that destroy your back, so of course I had to tell him this and demonstrate the right ones and he told me I was a bossy little girl with enormous tits and gave them each a suck and we were just about to do it again when I saw the clock and nearly destroyed Shaun Graham, Oscar winner, by leaping away and running to the wardrobe.

"I've got to get to work," I gasped. "I'll be late and I have to see Mrs Tredurgan this morning..."

He picked himself up, rubbed himself reproachfully and started to get dressed.

There was a timid knock on the door, so I went to get it and found Pam there and in an instant I knew exactly what he'd been talking about and that in fact nothing was going to be the same again. She was holding a wad of newspapers, all tabloids, but the thing that suddenly depressed me was that she was dressed as for an important cocktail party and fully made up. Pam is always elegant, but would she have bothered with more than mascara and lippy for me or me and some ordinary bloke? No, of course not.

The trouble with women friends, as Phil used to say, is that they can read minds. Pam looked at me and I looked at her and she knew she'd dropped a brick. She smiled ruefully.

"I won't come in, darling, though I'm dying to. But you may want to take a look at these..."

And she piled the tabloids into my arms, kissed me on the cheek and trotted off down the path.

Behind me Tat... Shaun's voice - how in the name of god had I not recognised it?

"Are you the friend with the post-it notes?" He was just behind me, smiling, casually naked to the waist, barefoot. At least he had his jeans on, the bad man. Pam screeched to a halt, turned, blushed and twittered.

"Um... er... yes." she squeaked. "Um.. hi?"

"Just wanted to say thank you, it was cool."

"Um... er... well... nothing really..."

I was watching her in disbelief, was this the Pam who had told the mayor of Lyonesse to his face that he was a conniving little pimp? And I knew I would have been far far worse. Faced with the shock of the actual Shaun Graham's actual manly chest in those circumstances, I'd have turned into a silent, beetroot-coloured klutz. All things considered she was coping quite well.

"And I'm not expecting any visitors or phone calls so if anyone asks for me, could you tell them you've never met me in your life?"

"Um... er... yes."

He gave her a complicit wink which destroyed her completely, moved back into the sitting room, and she sort of came out of it.

"Oh god, oh god," she said. "What am I doing?"

"I'd be worse," I said sympathetically.

"Oh godohgodohgod," she muttered as she practically ran back to the main house.

I looked at the top tabloid. Evidently the football hooligans had let us down. In the absence of a good riot, or plane crash, there on the front cover was a blurry picture of Tattoo, with the horrible facial decoration enhanced and the banner headline "GOTCHA SHAUN!"

I scanned the article which made it clear that the journalist who wrote it had arrived just after I left, had been turfed off by security and had got his very profitable picture with a long lens. Shaun Graham was back from Ireland, had fallen off the wagon, got himself tattooed and shaved for a bet, had thrown a party nobody knew why at the back end of nobody knew where and had disappeared again.

He sat down on the futon, lit a fag and went through the whole pile of them, mostly me-toos. I made myself go and get coffee and breakfast, though I wasn't hungry any more. I just know how bad I get if I don't. I brought him some coffee which he thanked me for abstractedly and sipped while he scanned.

"I'm sorry, Anna, I truly am," he said. "You'd better collect your messages and ring your office to tell them you won't be in."

"Why not?"

"Do you think Mrs Trewotsit would thank you if you turned up at her place with a braying pack of journos in tow?"

I shuddered. Mouth cancer has awfully ugly consequences.

"But why would they know about me?"

He did that patient squidging of his eyes which men do when they're trying not to ask you why you're such an idiot.

"I believe we did bump into each other on the dancefloor a couple of times."

"Well but why..."

"Somebody's got photos because somebody's always going around with a camera and right now they're developing them and putting them up for auction, if they know anything, or getting them ripped off if they don't. By tomorrow... Oh brother." (Youngsters, this was before the arrival of the smartphone, by the way.)

I started to cry. Which I never do.

He tried to put his arms round me, but I shook him off because I was so angry and he went and got the Kleenex and chocs, what were left of them, instead. Then he sat there, forearms on his knees, watching me and looking tired.

"I'm sorry."

I tried to stop because I know how dire I look after I've cried, but I couldn't.

"I think you could have told me, why didn't you bloody tell me, then I'd have... Oh god."

"It'll blow over, you know."

"You don't understand," I wailed. "I look terrible in photos. Horrible."

He had the sense not to argue. I got my mobile to ring the office and found three messages, one from Jog saying, "Yo, Tattoo, shit's hit the fan, be seeing you", one from somebody called Denise asking me to get a message to Shaun to ring in, and one from Jim saying, "You bitch, you fucking bitch."

Well at least that cheered me up. A bit. The snot fountain had eased slightly, but I then found I was shaking for no reason at all. After all, there was Jim to think about too. I felt sick.

So I rang the office, got a message machine and left a message, a very long one with updates on everybody for the next few days. Because I knew I couldn't go to work. It wasn't just the thing with... Tattoo. It was the thing with Jim as well. I wouldn't be able to think straight, wouldn't be able to give even 50% to anybody. Crying? Good god, I never ever cry. Never.

"Can I?" asked ... the man I'd been having sex with, holding his hand out for the phone. Me. That was me, having sex with somebody other than my husband for the first time since we met. Fucking around, in fact. Unbelievable. And not just that, which was frightening enough, but with... him.

I really wasn't ready for it.

I gave him the mobile and sat and watched while he leaned back on the sofa bed and talked. Suddenly he was Mr Filmstar. He spoke to one person and drawled that he'd be there, stop panicking, and of course he hadn't bloody had a tattoo done, didn't fancy that much pain, it was fake, but he had shaved his head and if it hadn't grown back enough by the time Naismith wanted him for the movie, well, he'd just have to wear a wig. Brilliant work on the catering, DJ and marquee, by the way, he owed her. Yes, he'd talk to Denise.

"Refuse all requests for today, draw up a list of non-offenders, usual rules. I'll do a press session for them tomorrow or the day after. It's possible there's a pic of me dancing with someone doing the rounds, and if you can track it down, put in a bid for it."

I shut my eyes in horror. Oh god, what if somebody had snapped me when I was doing the splits?

Then he finished. Smiled at me. I didn't smile back. Anger was burning its way up my spine; seeing him in filmstar mode brought it home somehow. The selfishness of what he'd done.

"You know," I said thoughtfully. "It's throwing the party that sticks in my craw."

Head on one side. It struck me that morning stubble on the top of your head is very unattractive. Of course most cancer sufferers are delighted with it because it means their body is starting to come back from poison-hell.

"You could have gone back to London quietly, or wherever, leaving me none the wiser, or you could have told me before we got so far or... You knew throwing the party would bring them down on you, there was no way you could do it without tipping them off, especially after all the stories about Ireland."

He blinked. "You mean, you honestly didn't suspect?"

I shook my head.

"I must be good," he said complacently, and then caught my expression. "I'm sorry, I didn't mean... I mean, I thought you'd rumbled me but you were playing along with the game, being tactful like you said. After the class, I was just waiting for you to say something about it."

"That's why you were in the car park?"

"Yeah. Also, it goes against the grain to let a woman wander out into a carpark at night on her own."

I laughed softly. "You scared the shit out of me. You looked like the Terminator."

"Jesus, I'm sorry. I never thought of that."

"No, it's OK, just me being paranoid."

"I thought you were going to say, Shaun Graham get out of my life, or I'll see you fry before I come to any party of yours, so when you said you'd come I was so pleased, I thought... Well, I thought it was OK."

"I thought you were angry about me telling you off."

"I was at the time, but I'd calmed down by then."

"Well," I said sadly, climbing out of the nurse's uniform, and into the jeans and t-shirt that Pam had confiscated a hundred years ago last night. It seemed all wrong. Surely this should be a slinky satin number. "I think you overestimated my savvy there. I deal with people who are dying, not... not journalists. And I just don't expect to meet any film stars."

I wandered out to the kitchenette, looked around for something to eat, no chocolate, we'd eaten it all, bacon, couldn't be bothered to fry it... I didn't know what to do with myself. Suddenly, I had a day off from work and nothing at all planned.

So I wandered back, spotted that the bed was unmade and so I shifted himself off it, stripped it and we folded it over back into a sofa, put the sheets in one drawer and the duvet in the other, and then sat down on it. I was still feeling sick.

Shaun... I still couldn't think of him as that... himself went to the kitchenette, poured something into a glass and brought it to me, had something half as big himself.

It was Calvados, which I love and hardly ever dare to buy, which Pam knew of course.

I sipped a bit, though I was brought up by a woman who devoutly believed that the world would  drift from its moorings and crash into the moon if you drank before 11.00am, sharp. Didn't matter how much after that, of course.

It wasn't the drink. It was the sad crunched up feeling under my ribs where the happiness had sat so nicely the night before. I didn't cry again. I just had that familiar grey ancient feeling and said, "What am I going to do? Everybody's going to know, they're all going to ask questions, they're..."

"You could sell the story to the press," said himself judiciously, standing up, sipping his bloody drink.

"What?"

"Probably get £20,000 for an 'I shagged Shaun Graham' story, complete with juicy details."

Only years of training stopped me sidekicking him into the wall. I stood up, threw the Calvados at him, but not the glass because I knew it was one of Pam's best ones.

"How fucking *dare* you!" I roared. "How dare you talk to me like that? Do you think I'm a fucking tart? Do you think I'd actually..."

He put his palms out defensively. "Whoa, whoa, I'm  sorry. I didn't mean..."

"What the fuck did you mean?" I put the glass down in case I did throw it at him after all. I was frightened by my own anger: this wasn't me, usually I was much more patient.

"I meant... I meant... if you've got the press after you, the best way to stop it is to blow them off. You give them the story, on your terms, in your way and you negotiate enough money from it so it's worth while."

"Why…" I was shaking with rage now. "Why… do you think I want money for shagging you?"

"Money for the story, not…"

"What's the difference? Do excuse me, I'm not used to the sophisticated ways of movie stars, Mr Graham, please explain to poor provincial little me how it's different to get money for an I-shagged-Shaun-fucking-Graham story from ten quid for a blow job, twenty quid for a fuck and fifty for no condom down Bostibern fucking Street?"

"It isn't, it isn't, I'm sorry, I'm an arsehole, I'm a dick, I'm really sorry. Listen, Anna, please will you believe me, I absolutely did not mean to insult you."

He's a good actor, but he looked sincere. Grey ancientness started replacing red rage. "But why didn't you think I'd be insulted?" Jesus, was that my voice with the tremulous little-girl wail in it? "I haven't said anything about you… you making me fancy you and… and everything and knowing it was going to ruin my life."

"I don't know. I didn't think." he said sadly to the Calvados. "Well, I thought it'd make you laugh."

I flopped back down again, pulled my knees up.

"I suppose you play games like that in your world."

"It happens all the time." There was weariness in his voice.

"Would you ever speak to me again? If someone ever did that to me, I wouldn't just not speak to them, I'd…"

"Beat them to pulp." He was trying to jolly me along.

"No. You know I'd never do that."

"How do I know that?"

"Because if I did, I'd have kicked you when you… said what you said."

He sat down next to me, very properly, sideways on, no octupussing his arms along the back.

"I'm glad you didn't. I really hate domestic violence."

I watched him, that serious mobile face. It was true what he had said, it hadn't just been the tattoo and the baldness, it had been the way he moved and how he frowned, everything was different. He still felt dangerous but more intelligent. And more... something else. Something slippery. Less straightforward, more complicated. As if Tattoo was inside Shaun, but not the other way round.

"I'm not feisty, you know." I said and he smiled, a little puzzled. "Feisty means a woman who's small and cute enough that when she gets aggressive, it doesn't matter." He laughed cautiously. "And I'm not small or cute."

"I like that line. I'm stealing it."

"I want royalties."

"Have your people call my people to sort the contract."

I knew it was a joke but it still put a chill down my neck, because generally speaking I am the people, or even the people's people. Not the one telling the people to do something.

"Er... Shaun."

"Yes Anna."

"Please remember I'm just ordinary."

"No, you're not. Not feisty, not ordinary. Believe me. And do you think I always had all this...this stuff? I told you I didn't."

"I know you didn't once, but right from the start you must have been ferociously ambitious, hard-working, willing to take risks. Talent isn't enough, you know. I'm married to a very talented writer, but he's lazy and he stays where he's comfortable. You have to..." I made a gesture. "...push the envelope, you know? Like they say in those self-help books. And you must have looked at success and stardom and ...been immensely hungry for them."

He contemplated me with those vivid eyes of his. "You're very wise."

"Yes, I am." I said, not complacently, "I have to be to do what I do. And I've never ever wanted success and celebrity and so on. I've been married to someone who yearns after them and won't do the necessary, but I've never ever wanted them for myself. That's what I mean by ordinary. I mean no ambition."

He smiled, shook his head.

"So I was doing what I was happy doing, terminal care, martial arts, I was even successful at them, a nurse's pay is crap but never mind, I'm not expensive to run. And you come along and act like a sort of bomb in the middle of it all. So I was already angry when you made that crack about selling my story and that's why I didn't find it funny."

He took my hand, unclenched the fingers very gently and kissed each one.

"Anna," he said softly. "The choices are these: you stay in South Cornwall, I go back to London which I have to anyway today because I'm supposed to be at a bloody premiere in Leicester Square this evening. I run the best damage control I can from London and you sit here under siege until they get bored and give up or until your resistance cracks. They'll be onto your husband and sons too, until they get their story, so lord only knows what stuff's going to go into the record. It's honestly better to get your side of it in."

I shuddered again at some of the things Jim could come up with. And he would. Oh he would. The publicity would be too much temptation for him. Jim Stukely, writer of the Job Gurney historical crime series (TV optioned) told us today about the terrible pain his wife's infidelity with the famous movie star Shaun Graham has caused him, especially in his graffiti'd backside...

"Alternatively, you could come to London with me, come to the premiere if you like and we'll sort the stories from London where I can make sure you're protected. Also, if you're in London, after the initial flurry, they may lay off hubby and kids in the boondocks to concentrate on you."

"Oh god." Both options seemed equally terrible. "But the tabloids will say I'm fat and ugly."

"What?"

"Well, I am by their standards."

Tattoo shook his head in despair. "I just don't understand," he said. "Who passed the law that said you're not a beautiful woman unless you look like a stick insect? I think you've got a gorgeous body and... Oh shit, I have this conversation with every woman."

I had to smile. "Every woman?"

"Every bloody one. Thin ones, thinner ones, anorexic ones, they all say the same and then when I tell them I think they're beautiful, they look at me as if I must be hallucinating. And now you too."

"Well, which do you prefer, thin ones or ones like me?"

He spread his arms wide. "Sure there's a physical type I like. It's female. I don't do it with blokes. But apart from that..."

"You're not choosy?"

"I'm choosy, I just don't specialise."

I giggled. "You say this stuff to all the women you meet or just all the women you take to bed?"

"No, just the women I take to bed." Deadpan, he did it very well. "Give me a break, why would I take a woman to bed if I didn't think she was gorgeous? At least?"

"To celebrate not going up in flames."

He started to answer, got the reference, stopped dead, thought about it.

"Anna, there's a place for meaningless sex and you know when you've had it."

"Do you?"

"Yes, you do. You can't wait to get away for a start."

"Hmm."

"Don't you believe me?"

"Yes," I said thoughtfully. "The willy does not lie."

He tickled me which I really find objectionable and told him so until my mouth got too full of his tongue.

But I pushed him away. I needed to make an important decision as objectively as I could.

"What would you like me to do?" I asked. "Seriously? Not thinking about my welfare or my feelings or anything, just you, purely selfishly."

He paused in what he was doing, looked me in the eyes. "Me, selfish? *Moi?* All right. Selfishly, I would like you to come with me to London. Not that that will make it easier in any way, in fact it will probably make everything much more complicated and difficult, especially for you, but because I want you to. Mainly so I can fuck you again."

Well, he was making such a hamfisted struggle of it, I took my bra off myself.

# Chapter 18

So that, gentle reader, is how Anna Stukely, nee Clements, terminal care worker, 2nd dan black belt in Taekwondo, ended up in a BMW, frantically shouting directions while (the actual) Shaun Graham white-knuckled and swore his way through the back lanes of South Cornwall. Finally I broke.

"Tattoo, what are we doing?"

"We're avoiding the A30 until we get to Penzance because I'll bet the bastards will have somebody keeping an eye on it for them. And I forgot to get tinted windows when I booked the car."

"This isn't Stalinist Russia."

"No. At least they won't shoot at us with anything except long lens cameras. I could ask for a police escort, I suppose, but I don't want to. The heliport's shut for some reason. And the earliest we could get a slot at Newquay airport for the jet was this evening."

I shook my head in wonder, police escort, heliport, 'the jet'.

"OK," I said. "Stop the car. Can I drive this, or is it just you?"

"I'm fine."

"Listen. I drive all over Cornwall all the time, I know it like the back of my hand and I'm used to it. Or are you one of those sad blokes who's scared your willy'll drop off if a girly drives you?"

Bam. He braked.

"OK, OK, ballbreaker. You are hereby appointed my driver."

"Right."

"Anybody ever mentioned your attitude-problem?"

"Fuck off."

We swapped, I adjusted the seat and the mirror, sorted out which was what on a dashboard that looked like it belonged on the *USS Enterprise* and we set off. I do know all the rat runs and sometimes I have to move. I wouldn't call myself a very good driver, since I've had a couple of crashes in my time, but when I want to motor through the little lanes, I can.

Tattoo went a bit quiet and only screamed softly once when I slalomed past a tractor and a Range Rover coming the other way. I drove until we got past Truro and onto the big roundabout there with its giant-sized flowerbed of windmills.

"OK," he said. "Me now."

I was happy to swap since I don't like motorway driving much. Tattoo got on the duel carriageway and put his foot down.

After a few minutes I said, "Do you want to lose your licence?"

"Don't care," he grunted. "I'm in a hurry."

Lyonesse to London takes about five to six hours. That's without children, without stopping except to pee, get petrol, coffee and junk food, swap drivers.

Now you really can't do a road movie in England because it's too small and there are too many cars and the scenery is cosy and changes all the time - hopeless. But there's a reason why people make road movies and that's because there's nothing more like a marriage than driving somewhere with somebody. Remember *Thelma and Louise*? I sort of liked it, because I liked the Susan Sarandon character but the other one annoyed me so much it almost wrecked the movie for me. I hate ditzy women. I hate them because they have this strategic incompetence and I hate them because they get away with it - notice, you never ever see a ditzy woman who isn't small and cute or tall and blonde. Or any combination of those. If you aren't s and c, t and b, ditziness is completely impossible to run because the men who become helpless slaves of the ditzes, just look at you in annoyance and ask why you're not concentrating.

So my feeling is that ditzies get an easy ride and the rest of us have to work twice as hard because of them and also of course, sea green envy plays a part. Do you think, if I *was* small and cute, I'd hesitate to run the ditzy line? Of course not.

Incidentally, dear reader, there is a reason for this diatribe. You'll see.

Somewhere around the Eden Project turnoff I decided that if I had to call him Shaun, I'd never be able to talk to him like a human being, so as Shaun was his real name, I resurrected Tattoo. He thought that was amusing but it did help.

"Shall I really get my face tattooed?"

"God, no!" I yelled. "I thought it was horrible."

"Interesting, though. People's reactions. Like the yachties and that dickhead in the alley. And the first time I went to the pub with Jog and Monty and the guys, I nearly got in a fight with some locals."

"There's South Cornwall for you. The Oxfam shops have only just stopped selling flared jeans. Besides, wouldn't a tattoo like that destroy your career?"

"Probably. If the crap scripts don't do it first."

"This is something Jim gets aereated about. He can't understand why people put money up for something that's obviously crap."

"Don't blame him. Like this next job. Called Bone Crack.. Harry Naismith directing. Two cops moonlighting as security guards, find a shipment of... oh I dunno, drugs or arms or something... and..."

"One of them's a maverick and one of them's conventional and it turns out there's corruption in high places and they have 48 hours to solve the crime and the police chief is black."

"Yup."

"Is this what the spin kicks are for?"

"Yup."

"They have you doing spin kicks and jumps?"

"In the fights. Yeah. My character's supposed to be into kung fu or taekwondo or whatever."

"Oh for god's sake."

"It's about the only thing in it that's interesting."

"Well, yes, but someone your size and shape would be mad to use spin kicks or jumps in a fight, a real one, not a choreographed one."

"Why?"

"Because you're big and strong. It's all in the physics. Big people take longer to go round than little people, so they're vulnerable for longer, they telegraph it more, they're off balance just that bit longer. If you and me were sparring in a competition and you tried a spin kick, I could guarantee to score."

"Oh."

"Now spins and jumps are right for Buffy the Vampire Slayer because she's small - her technique's lovely, by the way..."

"Yeah, she is."

"I was talking about her technique."

"So was I."

"What?"

"Got you."

I sighed. "Sorry, I didn't mean to be a martial arts bore. You are allowed to tell me when your eyes are glazing over, you know, especially when you're driving."

"No, I'm interested."

"Well... a spin kick's good for somebody who's small and fast-moving, but not very powerful because they build up the speed to make up for it. And, like, why would someone your height bother with a jump kick - except to cover ground? Jumps are for shorties who want to kick somebody in the face. That's what I think, anyway. Somebody else would probably say something different."

"So what is right for someone with my build?"

"In a real fight? What you did instinctively, go in fast and hard, use your hands, maybe back kick anyone coming up behind. Really simple stuff you can't get wrong, that works."

He nodded thoughtfully. "You ever been in a real fight? Apart from last week."

"That wasn't a fight. My guy ran away after I axe kicked him. You were doing all the work."

"Have you?"

"As an adult?" My stomach did that automatic squeezing together it does when you remember something very very bad. "Well yes, a couple."

"Really?"

"First time was horrible, I got... Well, it was the husband of a client, cancer, and he decided that I wasn't doing enough to help her... I actually think he used to thump her himself until she got sick and then he was just riven with guilt, so he took it out on me because he was used to taking it out on women. And he grabbed the front of my dress and banged me up against a wall and just... Well, it was awful."

He looked at me seriously. "How awful?"

"A week in hospital and two weeks at home awful."

"Fucking bastard. Where is he now?"

"I think he's out of jail this year, but he's not in South Cornwall any more. It's all right. The judge gave him extra because I'm a nurse - he said so - and the cops... er... well, they said they had to use a lot of force to restrain him because he went crazy when they arrested him, and I quote."

"Did he...er..."

"No, he didn't rape me." I said drily, "Just beat the shit out of me."

"Sorry...I..."

"It's funny, everybody wonders, as if that's the only reason a man would hurt a woman."

"Other reasons being?"

"Power. Because he's terrified of women. Because he can't think how to say what he feels so he says it with his fists. Because he can."

Short, thoughtful silence.

"So was that why you took up taekwondo?"

"Yes. That was eight years ago. I did a self-defence course first, and liked it, and the guy recommended this class he taught which happened to be taekwondo, and I enjoyed it so much I just kept at it. And the next time somebody took a swing at me, I didn't freeze up like the first time, and I managed to kick his kneecap hard enough to get away. Sort of sealed it really."

"Hmm."

"What are you thinking?"

He smiled. "None of your business."

We had a fight about the M4 somewhere round Exeter. He wanted to make for Bristol and take the M4, then the M25, then the A40 and get into the West End that way. I thought that was crazy, having done the trip so many times to see my mother when she was ill, and said so which seemed to surprise him. We stopped for petrol and he showed me on the map, acting as if I needed telling that the thick blue lines were motorways where you could go faster and the red lines were just dual carriageways where you couldn't go so fast (no GPS then, youngsters, and a map is sort of like Google Maps but on paper. And it doesn't move.)

I told him I'd made the trek times without number while adjudicating World War Three between Matt and Si in the back of the car (I couldn't leave them with Jim when he was working on A Book, which he generally said he was). I said that the M4 was a mistake because motorways were all very well when you could actually go fast, but what if there were lots of inconvenient other cars in the way and there would be? Etc.

He growled that it was his bloody car and we'd take the M4.

I said he'd be sorry, and went into a sulk.

We got on the M5 to Bristol and ground to a halt. Turned on the radio to find multiple pile-up had jammed it, plus there were roadworks on the M4 plus there was some sort of pop festival near Bristol...

I waited, arms folded, nose in the air while we inched along at about two miles per hour.

"All right. How did you know?" Tattoo said.

"I *must* be psychic. Couldn't be because I live here and it's always like this in summer, could it?"

"OK then, oh great road guru, which is the true path to salvation?"

"Dunno about that, guv, but if I was going up to the Smoke, I'd take the A303, M3, M25..."

We finally managed to get off at Taunton, joined the A303 which has a narrow bit down by Honiton, but after that is really quite civilized as A roads go. Tatttoo drove until we were on dual carriageway again and then leaned across and gave me a kiss on the cheek.

"What's that for?" I had to resist the temptation to hold him and kiss him properly, because after all, we would have died. Sex at 85 mph, very bad for the health.

"Not saying I told you so."

"I'm thinking it." I wasn't. I was thinking, Jim would still have been sulking over being wrong.

I dozed off for a while and woke up to find he'd switched the radio off and was singing Whisky In the Jar so I joined in with the "mush a ring rubadoo" or whatever the chorus actually is, and we carolled along vying with each other to find chronic old folksongs we'd misspent our youths learning the guitar chords for. I think it's something about Salisbury Plain that does it to you, there's probably a folk-culture ray emanating along ley-lines from Stonehenge. The voice that had first seduced me was a baritone and its owner even sang me the corniest of corny Riddle Song (if you're not sad enough to know what that is, then you'll just have to take my word for it). I went all mushy inside.

I haven't mentioned the word love, have I? I suppose it's because I'm superstitious and also because plain lust is a lot easier to understand. Love is way too heavy and meaningful and relationshippy and generally too abused by being used as a substitute for religion. I actually didn't want anything to do with it. Lust was fine by me. I felt like I was bunking off school again to go to see a matinee of *A Fistful of Dollars* with gorgeous Rick-from-the-sixth-form in the hopes that he'd do something about It. He didn't, not because he didn't want to, but because I got so bored with him telling me about his football team over hamburgers afterwards, and the blow by blow rendition of their latest game, that I fell asleep and for some reason this annoyed him, so he left me to pay the bill.

I sighed and gave thanks that however loutish their behaviour, at least neither Matthew nor Simon could get pregnant. Crabs... well, crabs I could cope with. Or any of the other STDs. Except not AIDS, please god. Or herpes. Or warts. Come to think of it, had Jim bothered to tell them about condoms? Could I do it? God, no. They'd run like the wind. Surely they knew? What else was I paying taxes for?

And I'd fallen in love with Jim all those years ago, hadn't I? I really had, all the symptoms, everything. We'd been unable to keep our hands off each other in that seedy nurse's residence bedsit in Oxford. We'd spent hours talking and laughing. And that hadn't ended too happily, had it? A bang-up wedding, kids followed by years of steadily worsening disaffection. What was I doing, getting mushy under my ribs for somebody else? Being a rapacious old bag was one thing, the L-word something quite different. So I sang him that Burl Ives song (did I mention how sad I was?), the relevant bit of which goes "love is bonny a little while when it is new, but love grows old and waxeth cold and fades away like evening dew."

I suppose it was a bit near the knuckle.

We drove in silence for a bit.

"Anna," said Tattoo seriously. "Promise me one thing."

"What?"

"Promise first."

"Certainly not."

"Never tell anyone I sang you the Riddle Song."

I did my best impersonation of Sid sucking his teeth. "Dunno. I've heard the Sun might pay good money for that."

He tried to tickle me again and I shrieked when we had to swerve to avoid a juggernaut. Why is lust so dangerous?

# Chapter 19

In order to avoid incriminating anyone, I will not specify exactly how long we spent on the M3 and M25, nor what happened in relation to the hard shoulder and the slip road. When the traffic solidified, despite us going against the normal flow, and the time was cracking on past 5 o'clock, Tattoo stopped tapping the wheel and used my phone again. The upshot was, if we could get ourselves as far as the Shepherd's Bush roundabout, the organisation would do the rest.

"Who?" I asked.

"The film company who want me at the premiere," said Tattoo, leaning back and switching on the radio which announced immediately that missing film star Shaun Gr...urx. He turned it off so hard my eyes watered.

"Well, as my good ol' pappy would say, leastways there ain't no wars startin' today," drawled Shaun the hillbilly, lighting up a fag and smiling sweetly at the woman who was staring fixedly at him from the car next to us in the jam.

I hunkered down in the car seat and tried not to get more paranoid than I already was. The trip had been fine, but now... what?

"You coming?"

"Where?"

"To the premiere?"

"Er... For what film?"

"Um... Bud Anderson directs Bud Anderson in *Fool For Love*, a bitter sweet something or other of comedy, spills and action..."

"You don't know."

"Can't remember."

"Why do you have to go?"

"I'm here, I'm hot and Bud is supposed to be my partner in my next job, so make nicey-nice for him."

"Who's the maverick cop?"

"He is, I'm the straight one."

"Planning to nick the film off him?"

The grin I got from him was pure arrogance. "No Anna, I really rate Bud as an actor and a person and I..."

I tickled him, right in the gut he was supposed to lose but wasn't going to at the rate he was chomping crisps, so it was lucky about the traffic jam really.

And then we had to stop the pushy-shovy games because the traffic suddenly got moving again at a dizzying 5 mph.

"What I don't understand is why you're doing it at all if it bores you?"

"Money."

Unanswerable, really. I wondered just how much but didn't dare ask.

"My idea is this," he said as we inched through Perivale. "I've hired you as my personal trainer for the martial arts I'm going to need for the movie. It's all quite normal, I've done it before. I get the company to put you on the payroll as such and cover your own hotel room. That way we can start to defuse the press because a personal trainer is way less interesting than a lover."

I looked at him steadily for a while. He was keeping his eyes chastely on the road, not that there was any need since the road was full of cars inching forwards at walking speed.

"You've just thought about her, haven't you?" I said. I had too. Tattoo could be enigmatic, but everyone knows something about Shaun Graham's complicated not-very-private life. Even me.

For a moment, I could see in his eyes that he was going to say, "Who?" but didn't dare.

"Um... yes." he said eventually.

"So have I. I knew there was some niggling little problem."

"Well, you're married," he pointed out.

This was certainly true, though probably not for long, and I wasn't actually throwing stones, just wondering how delicate the glass house I was about to live in might be.

"Are you?"

"Have been, not any more. Never again. It's too complicated."

He meant expensive. There had been some kind of recent messy divorce, with all the sums normally bandied about multiplied by 100. Again, it's the sort of thing people who have time to read women's magazines would know more about.

"So she's just your girlfriend."

He made a little sort of groaning noise in his throat.

"Are you going to dump her? For me?"

He looked very unhappy, hunted and trapped simultaneously, if you follow me.

"See why I was angry before?" I said quietly, "See? You come sashaying in, blow up my life, and sashay back to your girlfriend who is the Highest Paid Actress in the History of the Universe, or something."

He blinked. "Do you want to go back to Cornwall? I can organise a car or whatever you want."

I thought seriously about this. Why had I done this mad thing of driving off with an AWOL filmstar? Was I running to, or running from?

Running from. Every time I thought about it I felt crumpled inside at the thought of going back to Jim, anywhere near Jim. Of course, now the evidence was right in my face, of course I realised he'd been shagging little Miss Pink Lipstick for weeks, months, maybe years. I'd been complacent and again, in denial. Jim's prick had been off-colour because it was tired and shagged-out, not just because he was depressed.

And yet I could have forgiven him that. Yes, really. It was the other stuff. Especially the dishonesty. All the things Pam had been pointing out and I'd been making excuses for. Because I'd now been with a man who didn't constantly drain me of strength and happiness, who didn't act like a metaphorical vampire, and it was such a relief, such a pleasure. Like coming out of an overheated stuffy house and going for a walk in woodlands.

Nobody's perfect and Shaun Graham was a well-known pussy-hound, famous for it. In fact, so famous, I'd assumed it was mostly legend. However, thinking about the way he'd moved in on me...

"No," I said. "I came because I wanted to come with you, because I was promised shagging mainly. My life is already blown up and actually, I think it needed blowing up badly. Now I want a... an adventure. With shagging."

He laughed.

"Don't make fun of me, I mean it. Stop that. Concentrate on driving. Now you don't want me to come with you to this bloody do, you'd shit yourself if I said yes because you know you're supposed to have skinny and blonde or brunette and feisty on your arm, and not only am I not it, there is no way I could find the right thing to wear in the time... and... anyway I hate that kind of stuff. That's not a party for me. For that you need... um... her. But working for the film company as your martial arts trainer... hmnm. Being your bit on the side of your bit on the side. Hmf. Not very dignified, is it?"

He didn't say anything, just lit yet another fag, so I smoked the one still lit in the overflowing ashtray.

I tilted my head back and considered everything. He had made precisely zero promises, I had followed a mad impulse despite being twenty years older than the age when mad impulses are routinely followed...

Well, if the end of the universe came, I could always go back to mum.

No. Never. However, I could certainly use some money.

"All right," I said. "I'll go with the deal. I'm your martial arts trainer, who you met while I was nursing Onion or Lily Bates or whoever she was. You invited me to come with you, I said yes.

Everyone will tap their noses and look knowing, but I don't care. Officially I will be part of your entourage - that's what filmstars have, isn't it? - and Nadia Shan Sen can look down her beautifully moulded nose at me."

"Nose job."

"I know that, everybody knows that, it's the standard one you get after a nose job, practically every young starlet you see has it. Now what are you going to pay your trainer?"

"What do you want?"

"Oh no. I don't know what kind of stupid money Shaun Graham's personal trainer should ask for."

"Fifty an hour."

"Hm." I said, "I'll make sure I mention it if I meet any other stars."

"OK, a hundred fifty."

"Hmm. I will call my people, to wit, Bertie Prince, to draw up a contract and he'll fax it so we can sign it."

"Don't you trust me?"

"Nope. My dad told me once, never trust anyone who says trust me."

"I never."

"A lawyer boyfriend of mine once said I needed to chop off the last four words and then it would be a perfect maxim."

He smiled.

"Also Bertie Prince has told me he makes most of his money out of people who liked and trusted each other too much to need a contract, suing each other into bankruptcy. Husbands and wives, for example."

He smiled less.

"As for the hotel room... Well, I dunno. I've got to sleep somewhere and your bed might be a bit crowded what with the tabloids and Nadia in it as well."

I could tell from the faraway look in his eyes that he was actually giving this latter concept serious consideration. So I leaned over and whispered in his ear. "She'd never go for it. And where would the man from the News of the World put his chips? A separate hotel room is fine.”

We'd reached what the boys used to call the Sheep roundabout, and the phone went off. Tattoo listened, said “Yup.” and cut the connection. Then quite ceremonially, he stopped the car and gave me a smoky lingering kiss on the lips. I felt naked, exposed, was everyone watching?

Tattoo stopped, tipped my chin with his fingers.

“Anna,” he rumbled. “Pay attention, it's still me.”

Well no, it isn't, I thought, it's more than Tattoo. You're Shaun Graham. I stared at him, at the famous eyes, the famous mouth, considering.

“It's a job,” he whispered. “Only a job.”

No, I thought, it isn't, as a culture we pay you huge amounts of money to embody our collective dreams and nightmares and we pay you so much because only a few people can do that and many of them are destroyed by it.

Suddenly it felt quite miraculous that I, me, I could touch him and hold him. I put my arms around him, held tight and he was real, he was solid, he had a couple of spots under his ear and he smelled of man and oh god, I wanted to fuck him right there and then.

He wanted to as well, his mouth found mine and we dived into each other, completely lost track of time. Cracks were opening up all over me, each one hurting with that itchy relief of a scab coming off.

PARP PARP PAAAARP.

What was that? Oh yes, we were jamming up the whole of the Sheep roundabout. A woman leaned furiously on her horn behind us, Shaun stuck a finger in the air and finished the kiss. Then he slid the car into the scrum of traffic.

Talk about entourage, there were two BMWs waiting at the side of the road. There were people lined up, all expensively suited. A driver. Somebody else in a suit. A girl, skinny, in a cerise suit with nothing under the buttoned jacket, flawlessly made-up.

I was sure this was the fabled Denise. Suddenly my stomach went into freefall. I felt crumpled, hot, sweaty, awkward, out of place.

He parked illegally behind the cars. Then Tattoo reached in the pocket of his leather jacket, pulled out his statutory pair of Raybans, or whatever (I'd be lying if I said I knew anything about brand names) and something happened inside him. Seconds before he was indeed just a man. Yes, sexy, yes, charming, all that. I could hardly keep my hands off him. In fact I hadn't, hence the problem with the slip road. But now he was something else, radiating *noli me tangere*. He was no better groomed than I was, in fact much worse, what with the all-over stubbly effect and the t-shirt and jeans and boots and leather jacket, and nobody's that fragrant after they've been sitting in a car all day and eating junk. But. Shaun Graham got out of the car and smiled, went forward, and made all of them look overdressed and fussy just by the way he walked, the way his shoulders tilted, the way he smiled. And his stubbly head looked quite staggeringly horrible and all his people were staring at it aghast which made him laugh an easy Mr Filmstar laugh.

My mouth went dry. Partly it was lust for him but also it was fear. I felt cornered. I didn't want to get out of the car, I didn't want to move, they'd see I had sweaty bits in my t-shirt under my arms despite the air conditioning. Oh godohgodohgod....

He was talking to them. He was gesturing back at me. He smiled, waved me over. I couldn't move. Froze. Get me back to Lyonesse, I thought, I can't... I shut my eyes.

"Anna," said a beautiful voice, vaguely familiar. "Are you going to take root there?"

"Yes," I gasped.

"You're the meanest hardest martial arts expert in the country and I found you. When you get out of the car, move slow, relaxed, don't hurry. And don't smile. Hard look, remember? It's a class and every one of the bastards kicked a board when you told 'em not to."

I had to smile at him and he grinned back.

So I got out of the car, slowly, as he said, and walked over to the entourage, completely forgetting the little bag I'd packed - which was perfect, of course, because a people was already getting both bags out of the boot and it would have spoiled the effect if I'd scrambled around looking for it or even, heaven forfend, carried my own bag.

"Anna, this is Denise and Arthur and Yori and over there is Steve. And this is Anna Clements."

Don't smile, hard look. Nod. Wish I had Raybans too.

"I kidnapped her."

Just for a moment I looked into Denise's eyes. She was inspecting me. Was I a squeeze? It was like a think-bubble over her head in a cartoon. Shaun's known for it, is this a new one?

She looked at me, up and down, faded t-shirt, style-free jeans, dismissed the whole idea. Never happen, said the think-bubble.

Oh yeah? retorted my think-bubble, what do you know about it? You're probably one of the skinny girls who cries if he eats in front of you and is so desperate to please, you bore him. Ha ha.

I gave her Hard Look jirugi.

"So you're helping Shaun with his stunts?"

"Yup." I said.

"You're a black belt in taekwondo?"

"Yup."

"You won't mind if we check your qualifications, for insurance purposes, of course."

I didn't blame her for that, I don't look anything like Buffy after all.

"Be my guest."

Shaun Graham got in the front car, we were in the second car like the family at a funeral, and then we set off at a truly amazing speed, considering the traffic. I was sitting next to Denise who smiled with one side of her mouth.

"How's he doing?" she asked, smoked glass making her look quite odd, the wrong colour. "Do you think he'll be ready in time?"

"When's that?"

"About three weeks from now. Principal photography starts then."

I thought about physical ept and being able to teach one to one. "Yup." I said, hard look.

"Assuming your qualifications and insurance check out, what will you need?"

"To teach Shaun Graham?"

"Yes."

I hadn't thought about it. "What have you got?"

"We'll get it. Just give me the list."

"OK, I'll need a gymn or dojo, ideally with both hard floor and mats. Punching pads, sparring equipment - hand and foot pads for him and me. A breaking board if he needs to learn how to break. And I need to know what kind of techniques he's going to have to do."

"They're not established yet. The fight arranger hasn't arrived."

"Isn't it in the script?"

She smiled patronisingly. "The script's still being rewritten."

I nodded. "That's OK, in fact it's better, because then I can make sure that what he's doing is suitable for him."

"Why?"

"So he doesn't pull a hamstring or snap an achilles tendon."

"Ah. Speaking of which, do you have a First Aid Certificate?"

"I'm a fully qualified nurse."

"Oh. Right."

"Where are they filming?"

"Elstree mainly."

I nodded as if I had any idea where it was - well, I did vaguely remember something about film studios there.

"So Ms Clements." said Denise, smoothing her cerise skirt over her tanned legs. "Where has he been for the last few weeks?"

"Not in Ireland. Nor drying out."

"I know that, I made up that story." She looked at the tinted London flashing past. "Why did he shave his head?"

"So no one would recognise him. Same for his face."

"Mm. And South Cornwall? Why there?"

I didn't really like being pumped, no matter how politely. "I'm sorry," I said. "You're going to have to ask him about that."

Perfectly lipsticked lips were delicately bitten by very nicely capped teeth, leaving just a smidgeon of red on one of the incisors. She looked out of the window again. Her phone went and she diverted the call automatically.

"Ms Clements," she said. "My job is essentially damage control. The press are having a feeding frenzy at the moment because of this party and the pic of Shaun with his face painted. So I really need to know. Who was he with?"

"At least you're not asking if he was on a binge," I said, remembering the stuff about drying out. And Tattoo stomping back from the Bostibern Street mystery tour.

"I know he wasn't. Or not recently. But he was up to something and I must know what if I'm to do my job."

"Look, umm... Denise. I don't think I can tell you without checking with... er... Shaun Graham. One of the things he was doing was training at my class three times a week, so he's already laid a good foundation. But that's all I can say at the moment."

Tiny little bite on the cherry coloured lip again. I'm used to being confidential. People always want to know as much as possible about my patients, everyone, family, friends, children, as if knowledge is by itself a defence against the void.

Her phone went off again and this time she answered it. Under the foundation, her cheeks went pink.

"For you," she said, handing it over.

"...and don't fucking divert me."

"Hello."

"Oh... Anna. What have you told her?"

I didn't like the way he said that.

"Why do you assume I'll tell her anything without checking with you first?" I asked coldly.

"Because she's very good at pumping people."

"I'm used to being pumped. I've told her you were at my class and that's it. Until I get the go ahead from you, that's all I'll say."

And I pressed the end-call button. Denise actually gasped.

I smiled at her. "See?" I said gently. "Aren't you glad I'm discreet, now?"

The phone went again. I answered it.

"You hung up on me."

"Yes."

He was getting angry. But so was I.

"Don't you think it's a bit rude?"

"Don't you think it's a bit rude to assume I'm a moronic blabbermouth?" I asked him.

Silence. Denise had her mouth hanging open.

"I'll say sorry if you say sorry." I could hear he had a smile in his voice now.

"Sorry I hung up," I said and Denise shut her mouth.

"Sorry I assumed you were a moronic blabbermouth."

"Now I'm going to ring my lawyer to sort out the contract."

Again silence. "OK." And this time he hung up.

I grinned at Denise. "OK?" She nodded. I rang Bertie Prince's number, got his secretary who said he was in a meeting, asked him to call back.

Two minutes later Bertie was on the line.

"I've just told Jim I can't act for him since I know you too well. Do you want me to act for you?" he asked without preamble.

My heart went thunk. I had this sudden vision of my life, full of things, the boys, all packed in a car heading over a cliff. Blown up, kaboom. No special effects. Not computer generated. Real.

"Oh yes," I said breathily. "Very much so."

Denise was looking out of the window again, earwigging frantically.

"Irretrievable breakdown?" said Bertie. "That's what he's running."

"I can't really talk now. But it sounds about right. Listen, Bertie, I want you to do something else for me." And I told him roughly what it was and there was a very long silence at the other end.

"So what Jim claims the boys say is true."

"Sort of." Thank you, lads, for shopping me. I'll remember that.

"Great Scott!"

I smiled fondly at the phone. Only Bertie Prince would actually say "Great Scott!" like that. I was longing to have a good old gossip with him, but no way, not with Denise around.

"Can you do it?"

"Of course I can, though it might complicate legal aid. Give me a fax number and you'll have it in a couple of hours."

One of the things I like about Bertie is he can pull his solicitorial finger out when he needs to move.

I passed him the fax number Denise gave me. "Best of British luck to you," said Bertie as he hung up.

I gave the phone back to Denise who noted down my martial arts credentials and then started making calls and I watched her as she made them, wondering what it must be like to vibrate constantly with tension. She smiled at the air, she talked in a sprightly fashion, and the message in each case was, yes, he's back, of course, he's OK, nope, no problems there, everything's fine. And the tattoo was fake. Yes, of course it was. He's already taken it off. Don't worry, he'd never do anything *that* crazy.

That was when I started to wonder again if all the stories I'd heard about Shaun Graham were in fact the overblown lies I'd naturally assumed they were.

# Chapter 20

*To do: Wed pm.  Ring Judy Curzon, Pam, boys.*

Just before we got to the hotel, Denise got a call that tightened her tension by about three notches.

"Nadia Shan Sen is on her way from Heathrow."

"Ah," I said neutrally.

"She will naturally want to know where he was."

"Will she?"

"What will you tell her?"

I suddenly felt very sorry for her, cerise suit, perfect figure and all. "Denise," I leaned forward, touched her tightly crossed knee. "She's going to have to ask Shaun."

Off went the phone. Denise passed it to me.

"Nadia's on her way," said himself, Shaun, Tattoo, couldn't really work it out. "Now she'll want to talk to you." No, this was Shaun, I thought.

"I can't imagine why. I'm only a lowly personal trainer."

The laugh that came from the phone was remarkably unpleasant. "I don't think she'd be very happy to hear about Onion."

"Mm. You want me to keep quiet about it, I'll keep quiet," I said, "But I think you're making a mistake. She's going to find out eventually because somebody will dig up the story."

"My decision."

"Certainly, your decision. And when it all blows up in your face, I will not say I told you so."

Click went the phone. I gave it back to Denise, thinking that I'd come away with the wrong man. There was I thinking it was Tattoo, when really it was this media monster.

We came to a special back door into the hotel that looked like a goods entrance but actually had a very plush reception just inside. I'd seen luxury before - well, of course I had, everybody's seen *Pretty Woman* - but I'd had no particular yen for it, perhaps because my mum has longed after it with religious fervour all her life.

We had to wait for the Filmstar and I watched through the tinted glass as Shaun Graham pointed his shoulders and hurried in, disappeared. Something was different about him and I realised that he'd shaved in the car, though not his head which still had the nasty dirty-looking three day stubble on it. Well, it was six-fifteen and he was supposed to be in Leicester Square by seven-thirty.

I put on Hardass Martial Artist face which he'd given me at the Sheep roundabout, and made it into reception where Denise sorted out all the forms and suchlike and I signed in my maiden name which I use most of the time anyway. People often go on about carpets in luxury hotels and how deep they are, but it's the quiet they give you that's really expensive. It smelled quietly pleasant and cool. Nobody was in a hurry. Everything was neutral shades of pink and grey.

We were just about to go up, when there was a flurry and movement among all the cool flunkies, and in came a knot of dark-suited people, and in their centre a tiny woman with ivory skin and long black lashes, brilliant pink lipstick, black eyeshadow, a pink silk suit (and oh, Denise was wishing she hadn't worn the cerise, which clashed) and a lowering cloud of fury all round her beautifully cut helmet of black hair.

Naturally we waited for her to register, because she was the princess and we were only the plebs. I watched her with interest because after all, you don't often see the Highest Paid Actress Ever in the flesh (or bone), and she was tiny. Maybe five foot two, and skinny. Did she weigh six and a half stone? I doubted it.

Shaun's official girlfriend, the one who had busted up his just-out-of-college marriage. Rich, famous, infinitely chic. No, dear reader, of course I wasn't jealous. Why would I be jealous? Sea-green with envy, certainly…

Suddenly I had a mental image of them shagging and wondered how she wasn't crushed because Shaun Graham is a big lad and with the gut, probably over fourteen stone (or two hundred pounds, if you're American). Surely it had to be with her on top. And it made me want to giggle. And then punch her in her cute little face. Oh all *right*. I was jealous. Satisfied?

Quiet muttering around her and she came marching over to me, trailed by two very hard looking women in shades as well as by all the men. Oh cool, I thought, she has female bodyguards.

"You are Anna Clements." she stated. Her voice was sharp, nothing like the way she sounds in her films, and strongly New York. She's half-Vietnamese immigrant after all.

I looked at her. Hardass Martial Artist, I thought. "Yes ma'am," I said and stood at ease, as you do when you're beginning a class. There's a very military side to most martial arts, especially taekwondo which was started by a Korean general (don't be afraid, I won't tell you who).

She gave me the exact same suspicious look as Denise, up, down, is she? No way, never. Her face relaxed slightly, very slightly. Bitchily I wondered if it could ever relax completely on account of plastic surgery and botox. Bitchily I thought, ha ha, think you've got him tamed, eh?

"Where has he been?"

"In South Cornwall."

Her flawless ivory brow wrinkled very slightly. "Where?"

"South west, about 330 miles away. Down in the toe of England."

"What was he doing there?"

I sighed. "You'll have to ask him yourself, ma'am."

Her extraordinary almond eyes narrowed. "I'm asking you, honey."

"Yes ma'am."

She waited, eyes boring into me. I remembered why they were so famously extraordinary - they were grey, not brown. Quite pale. Most odd in that face and quite mesmerising. And I waited too. I have been bullied by experts, including hospital consultants; being a student nurse is a bit like being in the army, certainly it was when I did it. They're much softer now, of course, nobody would tolerate the kind of nonsense I put up with.

Denise was trembling beside me. Suits were looking at me. The force of personality in Nadia Shan Sen was impressive; you might say she had great *ki*. I wondered what it was like when she and Shaun fought. Frightening, probably. In fact, I would bet she won all the fights. Unfairly, of course. (Hah!)

Why didn't she frighten me? Well, she did, a bit, but I was getting better at hiding that I'm frightened and having no ambition is a wonderful thing too. In fact, I was quite resigned to this tiny force of nature having Shaun send me packing back to South Cornwall. After all, he hadn't signed any contract yet, and probably wasn't going to. And while driving up to London with Tattoo in the car was great, I wasn't at all certain that Shaun was anybody I wanted to be with, let alone shag.

"Are you going to tell me, Ms Clements?"

"No ma'am."

"Why not?"

"Because Mr Graham asked me not to."

"Why?"

I thought about it. "Are you asking my opinion, ma'am?"

"Yes, I am."

"In my opinion, he doesn't think you'll understand but I think you would."

Ridiculously heavy lashes dropped slightly.

"So tell me."

I smiled slightly. "Ms Shan Sen, how would you react if somebody you wanted to hire as a personal trainer went blabbing to Mr Graham about things you'd asked her to keep confidential?"

And she smiled back. It was an extraordinarily beautiful smile. Perfect pearl-like teeth. Made mine feel quite yellow.

"What do you teach?"

"Taekwondo. Spin kicks, jump kicks."

That cleared up something that had been puzzling her. She looked mischievous and held up a pretty pink silk clutch bag that could have held a phone and a lipstick and maybe, with a struggle, a tissue.

"Could you kick that?"

"Yes, I could."

"Do it then."

I didn't even stretch, because after all I had plenty of adrenalin in my body. In fact it was quite nice to use some of it. I just kicked it out of her hand, dollio chagi. One of her guards caught it, not terribly impressed. Denise swallowed and opened her eyes.

"Oh," Nadia said and then, patronisingly, "Very good."

"Thank you ma'am."

A woman from her entourage, complete with headset, whispered in her ear. She nodded munificently at me and swept away without a further word. I thought Denise was about to collapse next to me and I looked at her quickly. She was holding the reception desk. In fact, she looked quite grey and her lips were white. I took her arm and sat her down in one of the pink and grey velvet seats.

"Feeling dizzy, sick?"

She nodded, gulped and her eyes did the slight skittering they do when somebody's about to pass out.

I put her head down to her knees and held it there. "Push up against my hand. Relax. Push up again." Blood to the brain, that's what you need. "When did you last eat?"

"Oh... um...This morning."

A flunky in grey was handing her a glass of water.

"Dry toast and coffee, no doubt."

"I had a grape too."

"A grape. Would you mind fetching some fruit?" I said to the flunky. There's no point trying to get anorexic people to eat sandwiches, they just fuss, cut them in bits, arrange them in daisy wheels, hide them under forks, eat two pieces the size of postage stamps and then throw them up later. I'd learned this with Demelza Perkins who had been diagnosed with everything under the sun except the anorexia/bulimia nervosa she actually had. That's South Cornwall for you. Her lovely old GP, Dr Tregorran had been genuinely astonished to find this sophisticated London illness turning up amongst his patients. Her parents had been trying to cope with the thought of their darling dying of cancer or something and they thought it was a miracle when I revealed to them that all she had to do was stop upchucking everything she ate. Took two years of struggle before she did, of course.

A very nicely arranged platter of fruit arrived and after some coaxing, Denise managed to choke down some more grapes and a tangerine and a slice of mango. How can anyone eat just one slice of mango? All or nothing for me, preferably all. I snaffled a banana, much shocking everyone - didn't I know bananas have 80 calories?

A little colour came back to her face under the foundation. I sat in the pink and grey velvet chair next to her.

"You know I'm a nurse," I said. "And I just want to ask you this. Would you expect your car to go if you never put enough petrol in it?"

She blinked in puzzlement at me. Something starving yourself always does: it makes you stupid because your brain needs more fuel than anything else.

"Er... no."

"Eventually, the petrol tank would be empty and it would stop. Right?"

"Er... yes."

"Why do you expect your body to carry on without fuel?"

She didn't answer, nor did I expect her to.

"Are you feeling better?" I asked. She nodded and became superefficient again and we all swept up to the room that had been booked for me, which was probably nothing like as glamorous as the one Shaun and Nadia were no doubt tearing up between them right then, but was excellent as far as I was concerned. I love hotels anyway, even polyester motel-rooms, because none of it is my responsibility. If I leave towels on the floor, somebody will pick them up. It's like having a mummy again.

She looked round critically, uncertain. "Will this be all right?"

"Perfect," I said. "But Shaun's nicked my mobile and I need to ring home." She waved at the phone. "Who's paying?"

"Oh, the film company, of course. Put everything on the room number," she said. "Don't worry."

"Well, I'm new to this personal trainer lark," I said. "He just came to my class and wanted me to carry on teaching him, you know?" My dad always said, when you're telling a lie, make sure it's as close to the truth as possible. "So do tell me if I'm about to make some stupid mistake. If I've already made it, don't tell me."

She smiled, the first real one I'd seen from her. "You were very kind to me, thank you," she said. "I'm sorry I..."

"It's OK."

Tiny bite of her lip and she nodded, off she went, already calling somebody as she trotted.

Of course, I checked out the room, had a shower, left the towel on the floor, lay on the bed, watched the tv, got up, unpacked what I had, wandered around, looked at the stuff about where to go, switched the TV off, switched it on again, channel hopped.

Celebrity newsflash. He's back! Limos pulling up in Leicester Square, photo flashes, cheering crowds, mainly women... There he was! Very expensive-looking black suit and stylishly ordinary t-shirt, black fedora at rakish angle. He stopped, turned, there she was in something elaborate of emerald silk that looked like a butterfly, getting out of the limo gracefully, putting her hand on his arm gracefully, fluttering her eyelashes as she aimed an adoring look up into his face. He used his smile on her, then on the crowd, flash flash flash. Somebody in the crowd shouted,

"What happened to you, Shaun?"

Smile, smile, lifted his hat so they got the benefit of the ghastly stubble, laughed at the whoop, and Nadia laughed too in a way that made me feel quite sorry for Shaun.

I watched them go into the cinema and thought how thoroughly grateful I was not to be anywhere near the place, how very much better Nadia looked on his arm, as exotic and decorative as an orchid. The bitch.

Then I went down and had steak all by myself in the restaurant, nobody wanting to know where the ketchup was (behind the stereo in the living room, where you left it, Matt) and no clearing up afterwards. Lovely.

Did I ring home? No. I looked at the phone a lot though.

# Chapter 21


*To do: Thurs.  Go to Rigby & Peller?*

Next morning, room service at 8.00 and at 9.00 on the dot, there was Denise clutching a fax. This was purest luxury - long sleep in, not cooking breakfast, not having to wake kids - bliss. I resolutely didn't think what might be happening at our house, or not, more likely, everybody just snoring away like babies. They'd have to wake up some time because otherwise the socks would come and get them. You could do a really good disaster movie about neglected socks biologically mutating into people-strangling predators - get some daffy actress to play the brainy scientist and a has-been soap star to play the brawny sock specialist who has followed their strange habits for years, the way they pair at first but then one disappears leaving the other bereft... Where Do They Go? Good title. Could be as frightening as, say, *Tremors.*

I invited her in, checked the fax and found Bertie had been as good as his word. And there at the bottom, Shaun Graham and some apparatchik from the film company had already signed. So I signed it. Denise got my bank account details and asked if I could come and look at the hotel gymn, so we wandered down and of course it was full of torture machines and treadmills.

"No, what I need is somewhere to move. A dance studio for instance."

Her face cleared, she made a note. The Taekwondo federation I belong to had confirmed my qualifications, and added some nice things about medals at competitions.

Their insurance company and the film company's insurance company were doing some complicated deal even as we spoke.

I'd already contacted Penzance club to ask if they could get Harry, a black belt, to take the class in Lyonesse for me while I was away.

Judy Curzon, my boss, had been very sniffy the night before when I called her at home. Leaving out everything important, I told her I'd just broken up with my husband and I simply had to take two weeks off, at least, so I could sort myself out. I managed to choke back all my apologies and dropped some hints about the levels of stress I'd been under contributing to the break-up and mentioned that I had six weeks of holiday stacked up including some from the year before... She broke. She tried some emotional blackmail, which being rested and six hours away I could recognise for what it was, and then she gave up. Tried Pam, got a message machine, left a message about tents and then wiped it in favour of a more easily understandable message explaining what I'd done and giving the hotel name and address and my room number. I didn't bother to ring Jim. Didn't see the point, really. I would have liked to talk to the boys but I... well, all right, I admit it, I was scared.

After Denise had gone, I wrote a list of my long-term patients with their phone numbers so I could explain to them personally. Yes, children, back then we kept important phone numbers in our brains not our phones.

There was a knock on my door. I said come in, expecting Denise, but it turned out to be Shaun Graham erupting into the place. Or Tattoo. He kissed me on the cheek, flung himself into an armchair and groaned loudly.

I blinked at him, wondering which it was. His head still looked ugly. He looked tired and hungover, which I discovered when I kissed him again that he definitely was. So I found some mineral water in the fridge, poured it out, gave it to him and ordered him to drink. Ninety per cent of the misery of hangovers is dehydration as you really ought to know by now, dear reader.

"She's gone shopping," he said. "Tell me, Anna, why do women shop?"

"I don't know," I said truthfully. "It's always been a mystery to me. I hate it."

"What, even for clothes?"

"Especially for clothes."

He came over from the armchair, kissed my forehead ceremoniously, went back. It was quite an asexual kiss and I wondered if she'd tired him out already.

"You're a wonderful woman," he said. "I heard about you and… um… her meeting downstairs yesterday."

"I'm protected by being totally unchic," I said thoughtfully. "Nobody can believe you'd ever want to shag me, so they accept the martial artist story. It's almost embarassingly easy."

"Shows how little they know. Jesus, am I sick of chic," he said. "The press haven't caught up with you yet either."

"Did you tell her why you were down at the back end of the back end of beyond?"

His nostrils flared and he looked away. "No."

"Why not?"

"I didn't want to."

"She'll be convinced you've got some tart down there."

"She is."

"If you don't like her, why stick around?"

He didn't answer, only got that mulish expression round his mouth that Jim always wore when I asked him why he didn't get a job.

"I'm sorry, Tattoo, but I really want to know: why don't you want to tell her about Onion?"

The mobile face struggled for a moment, then relaxed a little.

"It's private." He leaned his forearms on his knees, looked at his hands, opened them, curled them, turned them over. "If I tell her about it, she'll have to know every detail. She'll cross-examine me about where and when we met, what Lily was wearing…"

"If you can remember."

"Actually, I can. And where we went for dinner and what plays we saw and what parties and who we met and how often we fucked and which positions and then who I dumped her for and why and what was wrong with her and then why I wanted to know where she was and what I did and who Jog is and... It's voracious, like a secret policeman or something. She wants every single detail laid out in front of her and then she... It's funny, it's as if she can't help it, as if it's compulsive... She picks off every important moment and shows you why it isn't important, why it didn't matter."

"Ah," I said, recognising the pattern. "So for instance, if you tell her about surfing for Onion, she'll wonder why you did it when Onion probably couldn't see very much by then and what was the point and wasn't it silly and dangerous..."

"Yes. Exactly that." He looked up at me. "You don't think that it was silly and..."

"Dangerous? Certainly it was a bit dangerous, but that was part of the point, wasn't it? I thought it was... Magnificent. Truly magnificent. A perfect present."

He smiled properly for the first time. Then he gulped some more fizzy water and burped. I tutted.

"You wouldn't do that in front of Nadia. Or Onion."

"God no."

"Behave, then."

"This training thing."

"Yes."

"It's not just a scam. I really do want you to get me ready for this job. They'll have a stuntman for anything the insurance company won't let me do that can't be computer generated and the stuntman could fill in for the fights, but it's just better if you really do the thing. Can you do what you said you could?"

"Yes, if you give me your full co-operation."

"You've got it."

"I want your undivided attention two hours in the morning, minimum, preferably two in the afternoon as well. If we don't get a session in the afternoon, I want you to swim at some time because that'll counteract the fags."

He offered me one and we lit up, looking anxiously for sprinkler systems first. But they were smoking rooms. Back then, hotels still had them. Denise was good at attention to detail.

"Nadia keeps telling me to quit."

"Of course she does. That way you never will. Me, I don't care. You'll be able to afford the very best oncology or cardiology when you need it."

He cocked his head and gave me one of his blue looks. Number 3, enigmatic.

"What if Nadia shows up? She was saying she'd like to kick as high as you did."

"She probably can already. She's welcome but she'll soon get bored. I'm not going to be doing anything exciting at first, just working on your basic techniques and your flexibility. Nothing wrong with you having different partners to spar with, though I wouldn't be happy about her doing anything too aggressive."

"Why? Because she's frightening enough already?"

"Well yes, but also because I'd be worried about her popping a silicon tit."

He mimed being kicked in the goolies. "Oaugh. Let me guess, you don't like her."

"Wouldn't you love us to have a catfight over you?"

"Yes, I would. In bikinis. That come off easily. With mud. Can I have mud too?"

I tipped the rest of the mineral water down his back and when he tried to grab me, I dropped him on the bed and wrestled him until he won.

No, she hadn't tired him out – seemed pretty fresh, in fact, as I thought smugly afterwards. You're wondering how I could bear to share him? It was the whole situation – it was so totally weird, I couldn't really believe in it. And so when I was in bed with Tattoo I didn't think about him being in bed with Nadia because that was that filmstar, wasn't it?

Then he had to go off to meet the gentlemen of the press. Despite my ministrations, this was the famous occasion when

Shaun Graham, Oscar Winner, Aussie hell-raiser etc. blah blah, beat all previous (impressive) records for rude monosyllabic unco-operativeness and a final bad-tempered walk out.

Denise was in despair.

"You know what he said to the woman from *The Guardian*? He asked her if she realised how boring she and her paper were. He said the average beach-bum is harder-working and more interesting than any hack journalist. Why does he do it? It's part of his job to get talked about in the press, so why does he deliberately annoy them? It's bad enough when they're on your side."

I'd found her in the bar that afternoon, drinking a spritzer and tearing a matchbook into 32 very precise pieces. She was trying to write a press release about where Shaun had been on his unplanned break and not getting very far.

"I don't suppose you could help me..?"

I shook my head.

"He wasn't in trouble, was he? With the police, I mean?"

"No."

"Or drunk?"

I shook my head again.

"Must have been a woman, then."

I smiled at her. "Stop trying to pump me, Denise."

"I just dread what they're going to write about him for tomorrow."

"Why?"

"Because I'll get the blame."

She saved what she'd written, banged her laptop shut, glugged the spritzer and shrugged. She looked very tired and sad and my heart went out to her.

"I'm sure you won't," I said, ineffectually.

"You don't understand. But it's all right. You will."

She trotted off, digging for her mobile as she went.

# Chapter 22

*To do: Fri. Rigby & Peller. Ring Mrs Tredurgan, Robby's parents, Gerry.*

Next morning, Shaun Graham reaped the whirlwind as Denise had predicted. *The Sun* did a nice little number called 20 things you should know about Shaun, which included his weight and waistline measurement (both wrong), how many people he'd punched (impressive, if true) and his normal daily alcohol consumption - respectable but far outclassed by the average writer, as I knew only too well. *The Star* ran a piece alleging that on his way back from drying out in Ireland, Shaun had gone to a rave in South Cornwall (how? why?) where there had been UNDERAGE DRINKING. The *Daily Mail* did a jokey piece called "SHORN!" alleging that he'd set his hair alight while drunk. A bimbo who worked at a TV company earned herself a fat cheque from the *Mirror* by describing his activities with her in the back of a car at a time when I knew for a fact he'd been at a taekwondo class in South Cornwall. The newspaper which had run the original picture and the copy about the party ran a follow up which dripped with greedy disappointment that there had been no drunk-driving arrests after the party, no drug busts and not even any fights. The police allowed as how there had been no complaints. The DJ gave an interview saying nothing. The hacks discovered after strenuous research that the party was a local custom to celebrate the onion harvest (honest). A short editorial welcomed the fact that old traditions were still being upheld, albeit in modern form with lasers and hip hop. There were a few catty little pieces in the gossip columns about Shaun's strained relations with Nadia and a truly bitchy review of a dire old movie of his that was being repeated on TV that week. Even the *Telegraph* weighed in with a very pompous would-be-funny article about the pampered lifestyle of those modern princelings, movie-stars, and how one had even installed a female "personal trainer" supposedly to help him get ready for a movie which everyone was predicting would be a disaster. It was a miracle of lawyer-sanitised innuendo and the only one to get anywhere near the truth. At least *The Guardian* was loftily quiet on the subject.

It was interesting because it seemed South Cornwall had collectively behaved true to form and put up a dense defence of "oo-arr" rusticity against the gangs of hacks who'd bravely ventured all the way down the A30 and into cow-pat country. Those who bothered to file copy must have given the South Cornwall tourist board a nervous breakdown. Some of them had had to sleep in their cars because what with Newquay full of surfers and the summer season, there was apparently no room at the inn. More likely the respectable B&B proprieters of South Cornwall had objected to their manners. A few of them had had car-crashes in bramble choked country lanes. One found the goddess Hecate and a commune of organic farmers, fell in love with the place, stayed and later made a fortune writing New Age nostalgie de boue articles from her country fastness. As for the rest of them, they busily interviewed locals and got a lot of: "Well, bless moy soul, did that there feller turn out to be some big star, what's 'e loike, eh? oo-arr. No, never erd of him. Arr. Good parrrty though. Arr, well oi'll 'av another point of scrumpy, thank 'ee very much. Naw, can't say as Oi seed him there moyself, zee. arr." Etc.

I was deeply touched that despite all the people who'd seen me and Tattoo dancing our arses off at Onion's wake, the great Cornish tradition of omerta against busybodies such as excisemen and journalists held good, and not one single person so much as mentioned it.

Jim hadn't contacted any newspapers either, which was a profound relief to me although not so surprising in view of what his story would consist of.

Shaun turned up while Denise and I were leafing through them over breakfast in the private dining room (dry toast etc for her, bacon and egg for me), Denise making notes, me sniggering as I read between the lines.

"Sounds like he pissed them off royally," I said apropos of a particularly unkind piece of sneeralism and she gazed past me transfixed. I turned and there he was, eyes bloodshot, unshaven, advancing on us like a thundercloud.

He slumped into the spare chair, poured what was left in my coffee pot into a spare cup and slurped it down. Then he scowled at me.

"What are you so bloody happy about?" he snarled, grabbed the newspaper out of Denise's hands, spat words at her. "This is a fucking disaster, you useless cow." She wilted.

I looked at him and was suddenly hit with the most awful deja vu of my life. Oh my Christ, I thought, it's Jim. He's somehow managed to get some magic spell off the Internet and he's taken up residence in Tattoo's body, a la *Being John Malkovich* (which, if you haven't seen, you must, really you must).

I suppose I stared at him for far too long.

"What?" he demanded. "Piss off," he added to a waitress who dared to ask what he wanted for breakfast.

I waved the waitress back and told her to bring more coffee, a large bottle of mineral water, two Ibuprofen, a glass of fresh orange juice and some toast. She scurried off, looking terrified. Denise was expending every ounce of acting ability on playing the part of the upholstery of her chair.

Nobody is at their best when their liver is coping with alcohol-poisoning. But this was the second morning in a row that I'd seen Shaun seriously hungover. In some ways you could say it was a good sign, because your real alcoholic never gets them, he's always anaesthetised against the pain by the new intake. Did you know that European livers make large quantities of a special enzyme called alcohol dehydrogenase to deal with alcohol that many other races don't have? Now how did that evolve, you may well ask?

I just looked at him. It was the first time I'd seen him act the complete celebrity arsehole. Eventually he looked away, picked up another paper and continued reading.

Waitress came scurrying back with the order, murmuring that the toast would be along in a minute.

"I'm not hungry."

I nodded firmly at her to bring it anyway. I poured out a large glass of mineral water, waited until he reached for another newspaper and put it in his hand.

"What?"

I pointed. "Painkillers. Take. Water. Drink."

Looking more like a sulky boy than I cared to see, he gulped down the pills and the water, and I solemnly put the next newspaper into his hand.

The toast arrived.

"If I put butter on your toast, will you eat it?" I asked.

"What? No. I told you I'm not fucking hungry."

"And I don't fucking care," I hissed at him. "You and I have a private class at 9.30 and if you're like this when we do it, you'll probably die."

"I'll be all right."

"No, you won't. You'll be better than that because you will have drunk plenty of water and you will have eaten at least a slice of toast. Would you prefer honey or jam?"

Truly ferocious scowl.

"You're not my fucking wife."

"No, which is good because I'd divorce your sorry petulant ass. I'm the personal trainer you hired, remember? Do you want to train this morning or not, bearing in mind you've only got about three weeks? Your choice."

I held his glowering blue eyes with mine, sort of a Hard Look jirugi wrestling match, and I must have held him to a draw because eventually he growled, "Yes, I want to train."

"Good," I told him. "Honey or jam? Or Marmite?"

Shooting me an ugly scowl which said, I'll get even later, he smeared honey, munched down two slices and drank another glass of water and some more coffee.

Leaving him to finish with the papers, I went off to the loo and came back to find him shouting at Denise.

"... didn't you even send the bloody press release out?"

"W... well, it was very short and... and... th... there wasn't any new information in it... so they..."

"I don't know what I fucking pay you for, I really don't."

"S... sorry."

"Silly bitch."

I folded my arms and watched him until he felt the stare and looked up. The Ibuprofen should have been kicking in by then and he should have been feeling better. This wasn't bad hangover. This was having fun. It was an extremely nasty sight.

What made me so angry was that I'd been on the receiving end of exactly the same kind of thing from Jim, for many years. I remembered it clearly. I had been a lot more bullyable at the beginning of our marriage and Jim had been loftily certain of himself. The subjects had been different, the contempt had been the same. God, I hate bullies. Unfortunately they're often very attractive charismatic people as well. Likeable, even. Large, powerful personalities who don't understand how big they are. If you're strong, it's very easy to get into the habit of using your strength whenever you feel like it and you can always find good excuses for the damage you cause. This is what the comic-book cliche leaves out, why bullies are often so successful. And yes, Jim had had charisma. I'd forgotten it in the wobbly pile of self-pity he'd turned into, but all sorts of scenes were coming back to me.

"Shall we go now?" I asked softly. I could look back at the painfully uncertain young wife I had been and wish I'd dealt with Jim completely differently right from the start. I wasn't about to make the same mistakes with Shaun.

"When I've finished dealing with the press cuttings."

I waited for him, standing deliberately close enough to make him feel uncomfortable. He ostentatiously leafed through every one of his pile of disastrous press reports. He didn't even laugh at the bit about the onion harvest. Denise sat hunched over, arms wrapped around her, looking like she expected to be hit. I didn't think he'd actually do that, certainly not in public, but then Jim had done plenty of damage to my nerves and self-esteem using no more than clever words and the bludgeon of his personality.

Eventually, Shaun put the papers down and looked up at me. I knew perfectly well he hadn't really been reading them properly. I tilted my chin.

Sudden decision. He stood up, dropped the last paper on top of the pile, took the mineral water bottle and headed for the door. I went with him.

"Give me five minutes to get my bag," he said.

"Send a flunky," I told him, not wanting him in range of the minibar.

"Anna," he growled.

"We'll talk at the dance centre," I told him coldly. "Send a flunky."

Frost should have been forming on the old gold slub-silk curtains by the time the sports kit got to the lobby. I retrieved my own bag from the porter and we went out and round the corner to the dance centre that had been block-booked for the morning. In that time two girls asked for his autograph and one madman tried to take his picture. He gave the autographs, adding a full-on megawattage smile because the girls were pretty, and stuck two fingers up at the photographer.

We changed in the respective changing rooms and went into the dance centre room, laid out exactly as I'd requested. I fielded the anxious proprieter, checked that she'd provided the various punching pads and protective equipment I'd asked for, told her that if any journo or photographer was ever seen in the place except by invitation, I wouldn't be responsible for the consequences and shooed her away before Shaun arrived.

He sauntered in, ancient baggy tracks, team singlet from some bunch of Aussie rugby players, feet bare, arms folded.

His voice was tuned to earthquake level. "What the *fucking hell* gives you the right...?"

"Do you want to talk or do you want to train?" I demanded.

"Talk."

"You'll have to keep up then," I said and started off running round the room. It had mirrors all around, typical dance studio for self-obsessed image-worshipping constant-dieting lycra-wearing bimbos and I did my best not to see my tits bouncing. I wouldn't normally do the same kind of fitness training as I put my students through because if you're going to instruct you have to be able to talk, but on this occasion I had a plan and I needed to be warm. It was a bit risky, but I felt it was necessary. If I was going to be able to work with the man, let alone sleep with him ever again, we had to sort some things out.

Of course, there was no way he was going to talk once we'd got running because you don't smoke thirty fags a day and get boozed up every night and keep the wind you had as a fit young thing of 20. I had him stretching, doing the usual fitness stuff and then we went straight into linework and practising his kicks. Really, they were excellent. If anything they'd got better for having a few days off.

Then I got him onto the focus pads, building precision kicking which I thought he'd need, let him do some punching as well. He had loads of power even though he was dripping and panting by then, so to rest him, I got him to hold a big focus pad for me and knocked him backwards a few times. I am truly very strong. Not as strong or fast as a fully trained-up man of Shaun's build, but strong enough. And despite my own bad habits, I was still fitter than he was then by some way.

Then I had him put all the protective kit on, hand pads, foot pads, shin pads, helmet, gumshield, put my own on.

"You warm enough?" I asked. He snorted and shook sweat off the end of his nose, gave me the sort of look the Viking King had got from King Alfred. It was scary. "OK, we're going to spar. Medium contact only. Attention, bow. Begin."

I blitzed at him with my fists, powered him right across the gym while he was still surprised, had him dodging me in the corner before he started to come back at me. As soon as his fists started whistling past my head, I backed off and put some kicks in, light contact, but he felt them and that annoyed him more. I could tell he was going to lose his temper. Which was perfectly fine by me. I wanted him to.

Yes, I know what I was doing was dangerous and yes, I certainly could have been badly hurt (and so could he, I'd like to point out) but I felt it was worth the risk. There was something I wanted to show him.

And no, this was not kinkiness. I can't describe the thrill I get from sparring, but it isn't sexual. It's something much more visceral and primitive, ugly even, elimination rather than seduction.

So for the first time I fought him as I might in a competition, which was very unfair because he wasn't nearly as skillful as me. Skillful enough to get some good kicks in, but I was getting enough in on him that I didn't mind he wasn't watching the contact at all. All right, I confess, neither was I, or not as much as I should have been. In fact, it was a disgraceful exhibition on my part for which I would undoubtedly have been disqualified at any properly conducted competition.

And I'd be lying if I told you I didn't enjoy it. Especially when I got him with a side kick in the floating ribs for the third time.

Finally, his temper went kablooey. It was obvious the instant he lost it because everything he was doing went haywire, his punches were wild, his kicks were rotten and I knew he couldn't see me properly because he had a red mist going over his eyes.

He very nearly knocked me out even so, physical ept again, but the next time he tried it, I sidestepped, arm-locked him and dumped him on his face, put the lock on properly.

"Don't make me have to break your collarbone," I gasped at him. "Stay still."

"Fucking cunt, let go."

"Fucking prick, lie still."

Eventually the pain in his arm and shoulder got through to the rational bits of his brain and woke them up. I felt the tiny give as he stopped fighting the lock. I didn't take it off though, I wanted to talk to him.

"All right, are you listening?"

"Bitch."

"That's OK, I can wait. Incidentally, if you're interested, you made it easy for me because you lost your temper."

"Listen, you fat cunt, you can stuff your..."

I admit it, I did nearly kick him in the face. I'm proud of the fact that I didn't. But maybe I twisted his arm a bit hard. At least he shut up.

"Right. Now, for your consideration. Is what I'm doing to you now, fair?"

"This some fucking power trip?"

"Yes. Is it fair? Are we equally matched?" No answer. I knew he was thinking, but not what about. The way I had him pinned face-down on the floor, I couldn't see his expression. I could feel him though, which is often more instructive. "Speaking dispassionately, pretend I'm a bloke for a second if it makes it easier, would you say that the way I fought you and dumped you was fair?"

"OK," he said, and now his voice was hardening. He was one very angry man. "It wasn't fair. Shall I cry now? I can, you know?"

"Speaking dispassionately, why wasn't it fair?"

"Because you know more about taekwondo." he said. "Is that what you want to hear?"

"It's a start. And I'm fitter. So I bullied you, because I can. Give you three months of training at your present rate of progress and you ought to be able to beat the shit out of me. I'll give you a rematch then, if you like."

Silence.

"This morning I watched you bullying Denise. The fact that the press have had a happy day of taking the piss out of you and making up lies about you is entirely your own fault and you know it. It's not hers, she's been doing her best. But you took your temper out on her when she can't fight back and that is fucking despicable. And you've done it before because she's terrified of you and that is even more fucking despicable. Does it give you a thrill when you humiliate people who work for you, hm?"

"Jesus. Is that all it is? She knows the game, she's used to it... Ow."

"Don't give me that. I don't care what the game is. I am never going to watch you bullying somebody like that again. Never. You do not use your power to frighten and humiliate people who can't bite back. You can slug it out with directors and producers and co-stars as I understand you do and that's your look out. But when you bite pieces out of people weaker than you, that's a shit's trick. Only wankers and arseholes do that. If you don't like the way she does her job then train her or fire her. But don't you ever call her a useless cow or a silly bitch because of a disaster that you caused."

"You queer for her or something?"

If he'd calmed down enough to sneer, I could let him go. So I untwisted his arm and stepped back smartly. He got up, shook himself.

"No, I'm not gay. I wish I was." Shit, my voice was shaking. "Then I'd never have fallen for you or gone to bed with just another big bully. Big fucking bruiser who picks on little people..."

My eyes were fuzzing, my nose prickling. Oh god, no.

"Sex change, maybe? Don't say I've been fucking an ex-bloke?" That hurt. He was circling his shoulder, rubbing the joint and I hoped it was really sore.

"Don't you wish. No, you've just been beaten by a woman and I hope it rankles. I'm not teaching you a martial art, so you can use it to throw your weight around even more. I expect you'll find some macho moron who'll be impressed enough to do it, but you're not learning it from me. You can fuck off."

I had to get out before he spotted I was bloody crying again, like a baby. I turned, marched out as fast as I could, cursing the way I seemed to be falling apart. Got cold water on my face, changed quickly, went back to the hotel. I was going to go straight up to my room to pack, when Denise stopped me in the lobby.

"Anna, we had a call from some boy calling himself Matt who... Good god, what happened to your face?"

I looked in the nearest pink mirror and saw a big graze on my cheekbone where I'd obviously managed to walk into one of Shaun Graham's flailing fists. It was puffing up but I hadn't even felt it. Obviously, I hadn't been as calm when I fought as I'd liked to think. Now I thought about it, I could feel some very sore spots that were probably going to be flamboyant bruises too. I wondered what Shaun would look like and had to stop myself right away.

"Oh, he got me. It was my fault, I let it through." This is what I always say. Denise looked scared. "What about Matt?"

"Do you know him?"

"I used to. He's my eldest son."

"He's at Paddington station."

"*What?*" This was truly all I needed. "What's he doing at Paddington?"

"I'm sorry, I d...didn't realise..."

"Oh shit. What's happened now? It's OK, Denise, I didn't tell you. All right. It's probably no bad thing anyway. This arrangement with Graham isn't going to work out, nobody's fault but mine. If I haven't already been fired, I've quit. I'll go and meet him."

"I could send a car for him."

"That's kind.  I'll go in it, might as well."

So I sat in the back of a chauffeur driven car, trying to phone my own home, getting no answer. At last I thought of Pam.

"How's it going?" she breathed, which made me feel terribly sad. Tattoo had been great. Why the hell did he have to turn into Shaun bloody Graham, Oscar Fucking Winner.

"Not too well," I said. "I don't think I'm cut out to be a filmstar's moll."

"Oh dear. I'm sorry. Well, is he at least good in bed."

"Yes," I said, seriously. "He is."

"That's something. You'll be wanting to know about Matt."

"Uhuh."

"I told him where you were because he's had some kind of fight with Jim last night which sounded serious."

"Why didn't he just phone?"

"You'll see. I loaned him ticket money for a sleeper, you can pay me back whenever. I really think he needs to see you."

"I was planning to come back pretty soon anyway," I said. "I miss the boys. And it hasn't really worked out with... himself."

"Hmm. My feeling is you need more time away. Really."

"I dunno, Pam," I said. "I can't just leave them as well."

"Of course not. But don't let Jim use them against you."

It hadn't even crossed my mind that he would. For all his faults, he'd always loved his boys. Or so I thought.

# Chapter 23

Once at Paddington I asked the driver to wait for me and he said he hadn't got anything else to do. Then I went in search of Matt.

Couldn't find him of course, it's an enormous station and he didn't have the sense to be standing anywhere obvious like next to the Paddington Bear concessionary stall or the bronze monument to Paddington Bear or the huge clock. I had him tannoyed twice before he came rushing up to where I was biting my nails next to the bear.

Like me he'd been in a fight recently, and unlike me, he'd got the worst of it. He had a black eye, a puffy nose and a bust lip.

I could not believe it. I couldn't. I hugged him tight, careful of the sore spots, then I held his face between my hands and kissed his poor bruises.

"Mum, don't cry."

I never cry. I swallowed mightily, blew my nose. "Right," I said. "Just wait while I get a ticket and then I'm coming home with you. So I can discuss this with your father."

"Oh god, no mum. You'll kill him."

"Yes."

"No, listen mum. Listen. It wasn't all his fault."

"I don't care. I've had enough. I've just pounded one bully, now I'm going to go home and pound another one."

"Mum, listen, calm down. You can't kill dad. Not without hearing what happened. You've got to listen. Come on, have a coffee. Come and get a coffee. There's a coffee place over there, it's really nice, please mum, please."

In retrospect it was quite funny how he coaxed me over to a little coffee bar in the corner of the main concourse, sat me down, got me a cappucino and a sandwich. Of course, the waitresses were juicy Eastern European girls in very tight skirts, so it made sense he'd been there instead of waiting by Paddington Bear.

I sat and vibrated with fury. I thought I'd been angry with Shaun Graham, but actually, I hadn't felt anger like this since discussing with the mother of one of Simon's classmates the fact that her son was a rancid bullying little toerag. She was very shocked at my language.

"All right," I said, trying not to overbreathe as he blinked anxiously at me. "Tell me."

Matt was no more coherent than any other nearly-sixteen year old. It took a long time. Nor was I at all sure I'd understood what had happened. As near as I could sort it out, they had argued about something. Not very important. Matt denied he could remember what it was.

Both of them lost their tempers, being on edge and everything. Matt had yelled that he wasn't surprised mum left you, miserable twat, always hiding in your room, never doing anything...

"I said he was a crap father. He said he wasn't even sure he was my father, seeing you're such a tart."

So far so predictable. I waited for the punchline.

"So, is he?"

"What?"

"Is he my father?"

I shook my head irritably. "Good god, is that what this is about?"

"Well, I said if he wasn't my father, it was OK to hit him, and so I hit him."

"Oh."

"Yes. He was sort of defending himself."

"Well... Fair enough." Looking at Matt, thinking about my own nasty temper (yes, I know, I know) I started to revise my plans. In my book, you're allowed to hit people back. Matt's clumsy but he's quite tall, yes, like Jim and he's not a little boy any more. If Matt started it…

"So, am I?"

"What?"

"Mum, pay attention. Is he my father?"

"Oh for fuck's sake! Of course he is," I roared, making all the other people at the coffee bar do that instant English thing, where they so pointedly don't turn and stare at you. Except the waitresses of course, who goggled freely.

"Mu-um."

"You've been watching too many bloody soap operas. What do you think? Darth Vader's your dad? Shaun bloody Graham?" Just saying his name jolted me under my breastbone, as if there was a bruise.

"Mu-um!"

"I've been married to your father for twenty years and in that time I've slept with precisely one man, to wit, your father. Until the other night. When, if you're aware of it, I found your father rather artistically draped over…"

Matt had gone beetroot-coloured. "*Mum*! Shh!"

He had a point. I dropped my voice. "… his girlfriend. Now that wasn't why I slept with Shaun bloody Graham. I slept with him because I fancied him and really liked him… No, that's not quite true… More than liked, you know? As just a regular bloke, he was great, not just great, fucking brilliant, best man I ever met, he made me feel as if I was your age again, Matt, and when you're a boring old mum and have been for bloody centuries, that's… that's…"

Matt was in agonies. I supposed it was because teenagers can't cope with their own emotional lives, let alone their parents' emotional lives. He was staring past my head, eyes like saucers.

"You wouldn't understand," I said sadly. "Anyway, he turned into Mr Fucking Filmstar at the Sheep roundabout and I've just told him what an arsehole he is, so he'll never talk to me again." And I took a swig of coffee.

"Mu-um...."

Just as it finally occurred to me to wonder what exactly was transfixing Matt so much, the Voice rumbled into my ears.

"Mind if I join you."

I looked at Shaun Graham coolly and said, "No, not at all."

Actually, I didn't. That's what I wish I'd done. What I really did was go "Awuugh!" because the coffee was hot and it had suddenly gone up my nose and then I had the most revolting coughing and sneezing fit I have ever seen in ten years of caring for the elderly and terminally ill.

Matt hid his face. Somebody kindly handed me a wad of tissues, which just made it worse. I was pounded on the back and that helped. A glass of water was pressed into my hand.

At last I could breathe. There was coffee all down the front of my clothes. My face was bright red. Talk about a mucus fountain. Shaun Graham was sitting in the spare chair, watching me and Matt was queuing at the counter again.

"I sent him off for a salad roll and a coffee for me." he said. "And another cup for you, since you've spit in this one. By the way, I'm not firing you and I hope you don't quit."

"Uhhh." I said. I had hiccups.

"Did you mean what you just said?"

"Um...."

"No, it's OK. Don't answer that. I know I wasn't supposed to hear it."

"Uh..."

"What happened to your kid? I take it you didn't do that to him and I know I didn't."

"No," I wheezed tartly. "His dad."

"Oh yeah?"

"Though from the sound of it, Matt threw the first punch."

Shaun... Tattoo nodded, smiling reminiscently. "Sounds pretty normal."

"What?"

"I got myself into a fight with my old man around then. I think it's sort of traditional."

"How can you say that?"

"Oh come on. Two bulls on the same patch? It's why boarding schools were invented."

Matt came back with a salad roll and two cappucinos which he miraculously managed not to tip into anyone's lap, doing better than I'd have done. He sat down and tried to stop himself gawping.

I thought about that, and wondered what had started the Matt-Jim argument. "Have you met… your dad's girlfriend?" I asked innocently, modern mum to the life. "I mean properly, when she had clothes on."

Matt went puce. "Her name's Suzie," he mumbled.

Tattoo caught my eye as he engulfed the roll and I swallowed a very improper giggle. Bullseye.

"Look Matt," I said. "Why are you here?"

"Dad wants you back."

"Mm."

"He sort of sent me, you see."

"Before or after you had the fight?" Tattoo asked curiously.

"After," said Matt, looking resentful. "We were upset. We both said sorry, shook hands. He said it wouldn't have happened if he hadn't of been so unhappy. He wants you back, mum, desperately. He really wants you back, he really misses you, he says he's sorry about Susie and everything…"

"Oh god," I said, wishing Tattoo hadn't heard this grovelling. "Is this from you or him, really? Truly?"

"Him." said Matt, "Him, really. He's just… he's just gone to pieces. He sits there crying and saying he can't bear to think of never seeing you again and doing that weird thee-thou stuff from his books."

"Why?" put in Tattoo. "She's only here for a few weeks."

"What?"

"Didn't your mum say? She's helping me out with some martial arts moves for a film. She's training me."

Matt's mouth fell open. "Wow. Cool!"

"We were training this morning and I got clumsy. That's why she's a bit banged up."

"Is she? Oh yeah. Her cheek. You should have seen her after last year's national finals. Somebody kicked her in the head, she looked awful."

"I won the bout," I pointed out coldly.

"You didn't get a medal though," said Matt innocently.

"That's because I was disqualified for excessive force."

Tattoo burst into laughter. "That happen often?" he asked with fake innocence.

I tried to scowl at him because I didn't want to be charmed. "Yeah," I said.

"So you've only left for a couple of weeks," said Matt hopefully. "Is that right? Not forever."

"I dunno, Matt," I said. "I'll have to think about it. But yes, this job in London is only for a short time. I will be back in South Cornwall after that."

Matt stared hard at Tattoo. "And you're not sleeping with my mum?"

Tattoo stared right back. "None of your business, boy."

"I think as long as your dad thinks he can do as he likes, I can too," I put in.

To my surprise, Matt nodded. "That's fair," he said. "That's what I said to dad, but he doesn't see it that way. Keeps calling you the Whore of Babylon."

"Maybe you could explain it to him," I said to Matt. "Or maybe not. Try not to fight him again, Matt, it's not respectful. Now, what are your plans?"

"Huh?"

"You came to talk to me, we've talked, what do you plan to do now?"

"Uh..."

"Where are you staying tonight?" Tattoo asked kindly.

"Oh, I dunno. I thought I'd go to a youth hostel."

"In summer? Without booking?" I was about to tear him to shreds, horrified at my little boy roaming London on his own.

"You could come back to the hotel we're at," said Tattoo casually, and I shot a suspicious look at him.

Matt went pink again. "Oh no, I couldn't possibly, I'd..."

"They'll fit you in somehow. Come on. I'm supposed to be in a meeting in an hour."

And Tattoo somehow chivvied us into following along in his wake to the taxi and pick-up area, where he called the car over on his mobile.

"Wow cool," said Matt predictably when he saw it and then he sat in the back on the white leather seat, peering through the smoky windows muttering "Cool." to himself whenever he saw a good pair of tits that hadn't seen him.

Tattoo sat in the front next to the driver, so we could have some privacy, he said. It was so he wouldn't have to sit next to me, I thought darkly. Also he was making calls. Was he meditating some horrible Mr Filmstar revenge, I wondered in my usual paranoid way? Would the cops be waiting to arrest me for assault?

Back at the hotel I slunk upstairs to change out of my coffee-drenched clothes and have a shower which I badly needed since I hadn't had one at the dance centre, while Tattoo handed Matt to Denise to sort out. I was just thinking that I was really going to have to break down and go to a launderette or even buy some more clothes when I remembered that hotels have laundries and nearly cheered at the thought.

Matt knocked on the door and shambled in looking stunned. "Oh Mum! You know who's here, don't you? Her. Nadia Shan Sen. She was going out shopping. Denise introduced me. To Nadia Shan Sen."

"Yes," I said drily. "She's...er... Shaun's girlfriend."

"Oh. Like wow. Wow. Lucky guy."

"Try not to dribble, Matt."

"Yeah, but I thought... Oh."

"Oh is right."

Matt blinked, bobbed his adam's apple in that unattractive way adolescent boys have, and fingered one of his better whiteheads. "She smiled at me. She gave me her autograph."

"That was nice."

"Don't you mind? About... um... her."

I gave this due consideration. "I don't know." I told him as honestly as I could, which wasn't very. "The whole situation is so weird, I really don't know. But I suppose, if I can do what I like, so can he."

"Oh."

"On the other hand, I'm quite certain that Ms Shan Sen would mind very much indeed if she had any idea what's going on, so do you think you could try to be tactful?"

"What?" Matt was lost in an adolescent dreamworld. "Um... oh, right. Right. No, I won't say a word." This gave me no confidence at all.

"Maybe you'd better go and stay with grandma."

"Ow mu-um. Do I..."

"All right. Keep your mouth shut. Try not to put your foot in it. Behave. Otherwise, grandma's."

He nodded frantically.

I finished packing my dirty clothes in the receptacle-provided and looked up to find he was flicking through the channels on the TV, mind not on the job to judge by his vacant expression.

"Mum."

"Yes Matt."

"She's really tiny, isn't she?"

"Who?"

"Nadia Shan Sen."

"Er... yes."

"I mean smaller than she is in her films, even like *Snow on the Mountain*."

"Yes."

"Do you reckon I could pick her up? I mean, lift her."

There is a famous shower scene in *Snow on the Mountain* and I gave him my best patented old-fashioned mother stare. He didn't notice.

Sometimes I don't feel I'm even the same species as women like Nadia Shan Sen. It's not just that our builds are so different, or that I probably weigh more than twice what she does. It's in the head. Take elegance. I can look at women who do the elegance thing, never mind Nadia, take Pam, and I admire it, I can enjoy it as an artistic achievement. But it isn't something I want. It isn't even something I can imagine involving me. I don't understand how you do it. And this isn't just me having a chip on my shoulder about my body, though I do have chips on my shoulder, a whole plateful as Jim told me once. It's as if I'm tone deaf to glamour. I could study Vogue and Harpers and mags like that for a three year university course and still not understand.

But there again, sometimes I don't even feel like the same species as my own sons. So probably I'm an alien from outer space and I don't know it. What's that Hollywood cult the sci-fi writer invented? Scientology? That's it. I'm a Thetan. I-am-a-The-tan-ex-ter-min-ate! Ex-ter-min-ate!

Matt found the girls-running-around-wearing-bikinis show he really loved, and settled down for some ogling.

"School?" I asked him.

"Finished."

"Oh yes. Any revision?"

"Yeah, yeah."

"Where's your bag?"

He looked up at me, puzzled. "Huh?"

"Overnight bag? Toothbrush? Fresh underpants?"

"Uhhh..."

I switched the TV off. "Come on. We're going shopping."

We hit Marks & Spencer, we hit something unspeakably dire called Cool City where Matt set his heart on a hideous pair of trousers that stopped at knee-level - why, god, why? Baden-Powell looked awful in them and so does everybody else  - and so I punished him by taking him with me to Rigby & Peller. He skulked outside with the doorman, horrified at the general pink-and-frillyness, while I spent eye-watering amounts on proper bras and a swimsuit. Then we went to Boots and got toothbrush, antipong device (Extra Strength For Problem Perspiration) and his essential anti-spot battery of creams and nostrums. None of them work, but they comfort the agony of being a pizza-face with the illusion of purposeful action.

# Chapter 24

We got back to find Shaun Graham stamping through the lobby looking foul-tempered once more. As I hate shopping and had had enough of Matt going "Mu-um!" at me every time I opened my mouth, I was ready to fight him all over again.

Matt looked at the grouchy two of us and flabbergasted me by producing a pearl of wisdom.

"Hey mum, is there a swimming pool in this hotel?"

"Yes Matt," I simmered. "Why do you think I bought a swimsuit?"

"Why don't you go swimming? You're always horrible after you've been shopping and swimming cheers you up."

I goggled at him.

"Good idea, Matt," said Shaun to him. "You coming?"

Matt went pink. "Um... No, thanks, um... I thought I'd go watch the telly in my room."

He grabbed his shopping bags and ran to the lift. I looked thoughtfully at Shaun.

"Meeting OK?"

"Buncha cretins." He pronounced it the American way, Cretan. "Unlike your son. I'll meet you down there."

The very lush aquamarine private pool with adjoining jacuzzis and exercise bikes was next to the gymn full of torture machines I'd rejected and it had that special water system that doesn't need chlorine so it even smelled pleasant.

By the time I'd got the price tags off the swimsuit and poured myself into it, Tattoo was in the pool swimming peacefully up and down, ducking under like a fish.

When I walked in, wondering if maybe I should have got a size bigger and perhaps black rather than bright red, Tattoo ducked underwater and popped up right in front of me dolphin-fashion, whooping and applauding and wolf-whistling.

I gave him the sternest look I could and he meanly splashed water all over me and my new swimsuit, swam off too quick for me to retaliate.

I slid into the pool, perfect temperature, started a slow breast-stroke. I'm not at all a good swimmer. I like it but I was never any good at any identifiable sport at school and my front crawl is more of a slow drown with windmills. Tattoo did two laps for my half a lap and started swimming round me as I paddled doggedly on, laughing at me and making *Jaws* shark-music noises.

"Don't duck me," I warned him. "I panic and get violent." So he goosed me instead and when I flailed water at him, he turned on his back and floated away, waving.

"Catch me," he taunted.

Well, dear reader, I tried. I got him once by pretending to ignore him and suckering him in too close, but the rest of the time, no chance. We finished up wrestling in the shallow end until he noticed some more of my bruises which were coming up by then and stopped still.

"Shit, did I do that?"

"Must have done," I said. "I can't remember fighting anybody else today."

He tutted and kissed them better, very nicely. Then he pointed at his own battle scars and so I kissed him better too. Extremely curative things, kisses.

All right, I suppose it was inevitable, and you saw it coming, as it were, but no, we didn't, not there. Have you ever actually tried it in a swimming pool? Hopeless. No lubrication. Too cold. Puts paid to all the romantic *From Here to Eternity* nonsense. Yuk! Think of all that abrasive sand.

Also one-piece swimsuit. It's possible, mind you. In the jacuzzi. Oh you knew that. Well, good for you.

The other bad thing about swimming pools and jacuzzis and so on, is no post-coital fags and you can't doze off afterwards or you'll drown.

We towelled each other down and when we'd dressed, as both of us react to swimming by feeling as if we're starving to death, we went in search of afternoon tea. They'd almost stopped serving it, but made an exception when Shaun Graham asked nicely and we sat in a private chintzed off smoking corner amid the murmuring civilization of Americans being just as British as they possibly could, and laid into thin cucumber sandwiches and scones and tea.

"Well," he said thoughtfully.

"I'm not apologising for this morning," I told him chippily.

"No. Nor am I," he said, blue stare at full wattage. "Or not to you, anyway. As a matter of interest. Was it just me in the dance centre, or was it your husband as well?"

I looked at the chintz carpet, and could feel flush going up my face. "Yes," I said softly. "People at school, Jim, older boyfriends, doctors when I was training, some patients, the guy who beat me up. You're right, it wasn't only you."

Tattoo nodded thoughtfully. "Like Beetle in *Stalky & Co.*"

"Who?"

"It's a book by Kipling. *Jungle Book* Kipling? Not the Disney one, the original?"

"Oh yes. "If you can keep your head when all around are losing theirs and blaming it on you...."

"That's the one."

"They had *If* on the wall of the nurse's residence when I was training, with 'man' crossed out and 'nurse' written in."

Tattoo smiled. "You should read it. *Stalky & Co*, I mean. It's about Kipling's own time at a boarding school, very very weird book, 'cos what he's describing is a horrific sadistic dump for unwanted kids, but he makes it so funny. But there's a bit where him and his mates trick some bullies into letting themselves be tied up and then they... Well, in the book itself they torture them.

You never see it in modern TV adaptations because we'd be too shocked."

"Sounds lovely."

"Seriously. It's one of the nastiest scenes in English literature, and I'm not excluding the King Lear eyeballs bit. And the worst of it is when Beetle, that's what Kipling calls himself in the story, sort of quiet bookish type, who was really badly bullied when he was a kid, completely loses control and even shocks his mates."

I studied the carpet again.

"I didn't do that to you."

"No. But you wanted to. I could feel it."

I didn't answer. Had I scared him? I'd certainly scared myself.

"I'm sorry I called you a fat cunt. But I don't think I'm as bad as you made out."

I blinked at the carpet. "Maybe I am hypersensitive to.... I used to get it at school, constantly. Not physical. With girls it's always verbal, little digs and needles and smart comments and looks. I was the one who got physical, I was always in trouble for fighting. During nurse-training, I was always the fat sweaty one who dropped things or lost things or forgot things and then they'd just weigh into me, literally. Skinny pretty ditzies who made exactly the same mistakes didn't get half the sarcastic sneering I did. The only time I got a social life was when the skinny pretties wanted a nice contrast for a double date. Jim used to bully me when we were first married and I didn't even realise what he was up to."

I paused, because really, what I needed was a therapist and I'd rather have Tattoo as a lover. Just so long as he didn't go turning into Shaun Graham again. He was shaking his head at me, looking at me in wonder.

"You were never ugly," he said positively. "S'not possible. Somebody must've convinced you..." he began.

He stopped and stood up suddenly and I looked over my shoulder. Nadia Shan Sen was crossing the drawing room, couture to her fingernails, followed by a minion carrying bags.

Everybody watched her, she walked through a wake of people's stares, which she accepted as her rightful tribute.

I honestly felt that what we'd been doing down by the swimming pool was printed in dayglo pink on our chests: say linked male and female symbols, one labelled Shaun, the other Anna. But it wasn't of course. I stood up too, feeling maybe I should be respectful.

"Shaun, darling. What have you been doing? How was the meeting?"

He kissed her, with unnecessary thoroughness, I thought, and it crossed my mind that here was the pasha of our times, thoroughly enjoying his harem, and probably still quietly plotting in the fetid Y-chromosome-ruled swamps of his hindbrain some clever ways and means of getting Nadia and me in bed with him as a threesome.

Looked at dispassionately, it was quite funny. I expect. Ha, I thought, ha. Bitch.

"You've been swimming?" said Nadia, sitting gracefully on the edge of the chintzy sofa, knees together, tightly to the side, just the way my mother tried and failed to get me to sit down when I was young.

Shaun was ordering earl grey tea for her.

"I beat him up at the dance centre this morning," I said. "So he was working on his aerobic fitness in the pool this afternoon."

Her brow wrinkled slightly, probably as much as it could. She'd forgotten who I was.

"His kicking's improving wonderfully," I said, to help her out. "But he needs to practise his falls and rolls."

Yes, that did the trick. The brow cleared. She nodded. "Shaun is very quick to learn. The swordmaster on *King Alfred* said so."

"I'm sure he did," I said. "I envy someone who can pick up physical moves so fast."

Shaun smiled complacently at this. "It's mostly getting out of your own way."

"I know," I told him.

"You'll be ready, won't you, Shaun?" said Nadia. "He has to rescue me in one scene."

"Hm. Oh yeah. Ready for anything." And he did a half-smile and looked depressed. Nadia turned to him and began showing him and telling him what she'd bought, every single item of which, including the eyeshadow, cost what I might consider spending on a car. And he was good, he looked, he admired, he even asked questions. Very well trained, I was impressed. It occurred to me that Shaun was expending quite a lot of his acting abilities on Nadia Shan Sen and when he ordered his first double whisky and soda, I suddenly decided I really didn't want to watch them together any more. It spoiled the essential Tattoo/Shaun compartmentalisation, frankly.

"If you'll excuse me, I've got to go and make sure my son's not enjoying the porn channels too much," I said to her. "I'll see you tomorrow, T... Shaun?"

"It's Saturday."

"The centre opens at 10.30," I told him brightly and he knew perfectly well what I was on about. "You've only got me for a few weeks," I added. "So make the most of me."

I took Matt to see a movie with Bud Anderson in it, can't remember the title, though it had a shower scene in it too and then we went to Chinatown to eat chinese and Matt was as open-mouthed as a kid at the gates and the Chinese writing and the supermarkets open so late.

Over beef in black bean sauce I apologised for hitting him in the gut and he said it was OK, the bruise was almost gone.

"Where did you hide my skateboard?" he asked.

I coughed. "In the sea."

"Oh mu-um."

"Matt, you could soon get a job and earn enough to buy a new one."

"I can't believe you did that."

I shrugged, trying hard not to get angry. I must learn to control my temper. I used to be quite patient once, back when I never cried and never felt very much, back before Shaun Graham happened.

"Get a job, Matt. You're old enough."

"What, in Burger King?"

"Certainly in Burger King. McDonalds. A fish & chip shop. I don't mind. Anywhere."

"Do you know what they pay down there?"

"Very little I should imagine. But it mounts up if you're not paying tax. Get a job, Matt."

Matt spooned up rice and then finished mine, hollow legs. No doubt he was planning another couple of inches of growth just in time to have no school uniform wearable in September.

"I wish you'd come home, mum."

"When I'm ready."

Despite the tension over the skateboard, it was a pleasant evening. It almost made me believe Pam's promise about the transformation of oaves.

# Chapter 25

*To do: Sat. TKD Tattoo. Put Matt on the train. RING LONGTERM PATIENTS*

In the morning I let Matt do what adolescent boys do best, namely sleep. I met Tattoo at the dance centre. We trained carefully and sedately. He was only mildly hungover, but we both ached badly from our activities the day before. We kissed, but we didn't shag because we both had too many tender spots and Tattoo said he didn't feel like it. Personally I blamed Nadia. Those bloody compartments were hard work to keep in place, I can tell you.

In the afternoon Nadia wanted to go shopping with him before he took her out to the Mirabelle, so I kindly let him off our afternoon session, even though he begged me not to. I took Matt to Paddington and put him on the train, told him to tell Simon to get in touch if he wanted a jaunt to London as well. Then I went and queued at the Leicester Square ticket booth. In the evening I went all on my own to see a very peculiar production of *Othello* in which everybody was black, except Othello. It had got rave reviews.

I can't tell you how lovely it is to do exactly as you want. When you've been part of a couple for so long, it's exciting just to make the decision for yourself whether you'll have a pretheatre Thai supper or Italian or Vietnamese or whatever. I'd spent an hour in Waterstones choosing the latest middle-brow novel which I read while I ate and after I'd seen the play, I wandered the long way back to the hotel, relaxed and happy. No, when I'm not carrying a valuable drugs bag around, I don't worry nearly so much. London felt safer than South Cornwall because it was so full of people. As for muggers - they should worry about me.

It was about 2 am when I got there and as I wasn't planning any training the next day, I went into the bar to get a nightcap.

"Hi Anna."

I'd known he was there, as soon as I walked in, sitting quietly in a corner reading a book, shirt open, jacket probably costing more than my yearly salary chucked down in a crumpled heap beside him.

"Hi yourself."

I got my drink, cocked an eye at him. He certainly wasn't sober, but he wasn't exactly drunk either, he'd reached the point of equilibrium or come back to it. We looked at each other and it was one of those moments when you know what each other is thinking; not that I believe in anything psychic, it's probably to do with body language. I thought, he looks lonely, and he knew I was thinking it.

I came over and sat down opposite him.

"What are you reading?"

"Latest bestseller, possible movie option."

"Oh. Lucky writer." A movie option was Jim's holy grail and he was about as successful at finding it as King Arthur's knights had been. "That one? I was reading it earlier."

"What did you think?"

"OK. I thought the guy was a bit of a jerk."

He grinned. "I haven't got to that bit yet." The grin faded. "I'm probably not going to." And he lifted up his jacket and produced an early edition *News of the World* which had him splashed all over the front along with a girl I vaguely recognised.

My stomach swooped for a second until I realised that it wasn't me, because I'm not blonde. There was Tattoo, bald, face patterned, dancing with Lysette at the Cellar in Lyonesse.

"SHAUN'S NEW GAL?" yodelled the headline. Inside was a five page spread about Shaun's country jaunt with more nightclub pics. They must have had a team of hacks working night and day on it because it was a marvellous example of tabloid creativity: he'd been surfing and a surfer chick claimed he'd groped her; apparently he'd been berry picking, which sounded unlikely to me; he'd done all the nightclubs in Lyonesse, some of whose bouncers had obviously been telling tall tales of disorderly filmstar conduct firmly handled by them. And of course, Lysette had told her story of the night, which for all the breathless massage of the tabloid hackette who'd interviewed her, was very innocuous. Shaun had been rowdy, he'd been drunk, he'd smoked a lot, he'd danced a lot, they'd had a lovely snog, and then he'd gone off in search of more entertainment.

"He was really sweet and nice," burbled the prose, "but he never let on who he really was. I wish we could have got to know each other better."

I'll bet, I thought.

Hey Shaun! squawked the foot of the page, you've still got her number, give her a call!

"Really sweet and nice, eh?" I said. "And you've lost her number, you bad man."

"No, I haven't."

"And she's kicking herself that you didn't...."

"Too right, I didn't. Her boyfriend and his mates turned up and I didn't fancy my chances."

"Not Reg the Rock?"

"That his name, is it? Good name."

"So that's why you went off down Bostibern Street.

He leaned his head back and shut his eyes. "Yeah, that's right. It's coming back to me now..." The eyes opened wide and there was a moment of silence. I waited for it. "Oh fuck."

I don't know about you, but to me there's nothing more hilarious than self-pitying male dismay at the trouble their wicked Y-chromosome gets them into when they drink too much. Yes, even if it was someone I was shagging. Maybe it was working in a clap clinic in my youth. I bit back my giggles. "How much did you spend?"

"Ten quid."

I did a Sid-tooth-suck. "I'm glad. If it was fifty, I'd be taking us both to an STD clinic as fast as possible."

"How do you know the rates?"

"Who do you think deals with the working girls when they get AIDS?"

"Shit. Oh shit." He'd shut his eyes again, head back on the banquette.

"Don't panic. A blow-job's the third safest kind of sex there is."

"Third?"

I grinned at him. You can take the nurse out of the clap clinic, but you can't take....

"Think about it."

He thought. "So what's the second?"

"Not open to you, sorry." He frowned in puzzlement. "Lesbian sex. Followed by oral, hetero with condom, hetero without and then anal penetrative, with and then without."

He looked at me gravely for a few moments. "One of the things I really like about you, Anna," he said seriously, "is that I never know what the fuck you're going to say next."

I had to resist the impulse to kiss him. I also had to censor the next four things I thought of to say, on account of the barman and the fact we were in a public place and so on. Poor bunny, I thought, doesn't Nadia like it, then?

"You're probably OK," I said, "though it might be smart to get yourself checked."

Shaun sighed. He picked up the paper, dropped it down again.

"This is nothing to what'll hit the fan when the tart who rolled me realises who I am."

I tried my hardest not to smile smugly. Whatever would Denise say? Suddenly I knew what she'd say. "You know, you could use this, head them off at the pass and get some revenge."

"Urrr," he rubbed his hand over his eyes. "How?"

"Ring the *Sun*... No, don't explode, let me finish. Do what you told me to do once, remember? Blow them off by giving them the story on your own terms..."

"You chucked Calvados at me for saying it, I seem to remember."

"I was overwrought. OK. So you have Denise ring the *Sun*. Say you'll give them an exclusive about your night out in Lyonesse. Tell them that at the end of the evening you got mugged and anyone who rings them with any further story about you is almost certainly the one who did it. You haven't bothered the police with it before now because you felt it was your own fault for getting drunk and lost in a town you don't know and anyway, you couldn't remember anything about whoever did it because you think your drink was spiked. Bostibern Street Mystery Tour, all that. But now, with the *Sun*'s help, etc."

He stared at me for a long time. "Yeah. That could work. I just hate co-operating with the bastards."

I gave him a stern look. "Come on, you know it's part of your job."

He suddenly leaned forward. "Do you have any idea how boring it is doing interview after interview, every single one asking the same boring questions? You lose the will to live."

"How you must suffer," I murmured sarcastically.

He wasn't listening. "What I really don't understand is why everybody's so... so fucking interested."

I couldn't answer that. I'd always assumed that, linked as it was with enormous wealth, fame must be fun. I would never have believed I could feel sorry for Shaun Graham, living in the goldfish bowl he'd worked so hard to climb into.

"God knows I'll be for it with Nadia tomorrow."

"Naughty Shaun to dance with another woman."

"Oh yes, and naughty Shaun to dance with a pretty young girl wearing a top from New Look, a cheap knock-off skirt that's too tight and white sandals."

"Ooh, naughty naughty Shaun."

"Stop it."

"Tattoo," I said. "Lighten up. This takes them off the scent as far as I'm concerned and Onion too. This is good, not bad."

He lit up, offered me one and the bartender came over to say that the bar was due to close and would either of us like anything else.

I said no, Shaun said yes, we drank in silence for a while, and he watched me in a way which made me feel very nervous.

"What?" I said, too aggressively. He smiled.

"How was your evening?"

So I told him about the weird *Othello* and how nice it had been to be free and not having to accommodate anyone else and how much London had changed since I lived there, how lively it was, and civilized despite the beggars. And I told him about the King's Cross tarts I used to deal with when I was working at an STD clinic and the stories they told me and how shocked I used to get at the way their pimps treated them.

We didn't kiss goodnight when we headed for our respective beds, because that would have been silly.

# Chapter 26



*Sunday.*  *RING LONGTERM PATIENTS.*

I slept late, luxuriating still in not having to do anything in the morning except get myself going, had brunch, got two Sunday papers and actually read them, all of them, finished the book without improving my opinion of the protagonist, and finally rang round my patients to explain.

Mrs Tredurgan asked right off if I'd run away with Onion's drug-dealer and I told her I had, which made her laugh and then I told her who it really was. I wasn't worried she'd tell the tabloids because that wasn't her style and anyway they wouldn't have understood her at all. She was lovely: said she could quite see why I needed a break and I should have had one long before this, I worked too hard, and it was well past time I dumped my layabout husband.

This was pretty much a theme with all of them except Gerry, though I didn't tell anyone apart from Mrs T the name of the man who had been the immediate cause of the break-up. Gerry said he felt sorry for my husband because his wife had just left him as well.

I was not particularly shocked. I asked how he was coping and he said he was surprised, but he felt a lot better. I didn't say any of what I thought about it or her - not my place.

"How's Gina doing?" I asked – Gina's the girl who fills in for me when I'm away.

"She's lovely," he said warmly. "Don't worry about me."

Robbie was sad because he'd had to go into hospital again, and I hadn't been there to see him through and I told him if I'd known he was planning anything that drastic, I'd have changed my own plans to fit in, which made him laugh.

It's amazing how enough sleep, no black hole husband draining you, and getting to decide where you want to go for your pre-theatre supper can make you see things differently. A week or two before I would have been prostrate with guilt; now I just felt... Well, maybe a little miffed because it had turned out, of course, that they hadn't really needed me that much. Thinking you're indispensable is the carer's sin, as a wise old lady who had once been a nurse herself had told me. "Don't give yourself airs and graces." she'd told me quite brusquely when I'd dared to apologise to her for having flu. "I managed without you before and I will again." Then she'd relented and smiled slyly at me. "Of course, I am pleased to see you, especially as my back needs a rub." Hers was the last time I'd cried at a funeral.

Denise came hunting me when I was having tea in the tearoom in the afternoon, listening to a comfortable American lady in beige telling me how she liked to fill a container with antiques to ship back to California every time she made the trip, because her ex-husband who had turned out to be gay had a shop opposite hers and she had better things than he did....

Denise was looking shell-shocked.

"What have you done to him?" she demanded.

It was on the tip of my tongue to boast that I'd beaten him up for being horrid to her, but luckily it occurred to me that one reason why Shaun had been so forgiving about the way I'd humiliated him was because nobody had seen it.

"Why?"

"He's... he's being reasonable. He actually scheduled an exclusive with the *Sun* about his trip to South Cornwall. I spent an hour doing meditation and positive thinking this morning so I wouldn't get upset when he shouted at me about the *News of the World* and he didn't even shout." She flushed and looked absurdly pleased. "And he... he apologised for the other morning."

I thought carefully for something tactful to say. "Well, you know," I said finally. "I'm much more pleasant to my children when I'm training. I think doing violent things for a couple of hours every morning burns off your spare aggro."

She nodded. "Maybe. Nadia wants to join you for a few sessions, is that OK?"

"Fine by me, though she'll have to check with Shaun."

"She was asking me questions about you."

"Oh? What sort?"

"How old you are, where you come from, who you are."

"Well tell her."

"I don't know myself."

"I'm originally from London, but I live in South Cornwall, I'm a nurse-practitioner specialising in terminal care in the community, I am a second dan black belt in taekwondo, I'm married and I have two teenage sons. OK?"

Denise nodded. "How did you come to meet Shaun?"

"I didn't know who he was when he came to my class in Lyonesse." I said carefully. "But he liked the way I taught."

Denise nodded. "I'll do a quick info sheet about you, if I may, just in case anybody else asks."

I didn't really want her to, but considering how I'd lectured Shaun, I couldn't really say no.

Shaun himself didn't appear at all that day, though from some of the anxious expressions of the hotel staff and the fact that Shaun and Nadia changed to a different suite of rooms, something must have been going on.

My mother rang the mobile, for no particular reason except for the psychic link which meant that she knew something was up. I put her off with vagueness and then claimed to have someone beeping me.

Afternoon nap, bliss! Wandered through Soho, ate pastry, looked at pigeon eroded statue of Charles II, checked out martial arts emporiums and laughed at all the daft weapons they sell to macho idiots. I can't tell you how much I'm against people carrying things to defend themselves with. Some of the worst slashings and knifings I saw in A&E when I was young were the direct result of people who didn't know how to knife-fight waving a blade at someone who did.

I'd been spending rather briskly and nobody had paid me yet for my filmstar instruction, so I had a pizza and went back to the hotel, where I found what I recognised as yet another filmstar entourage milling about in the lobby. Denise trotted past looking marginally less tense and when she saw me, she came over and sat down.

"Whatever you did to him, it's still working. He was an absolute pussycat with the old harpy from the *Sun*, had her eating out of his hand, practically." I lifted my eyebrows at the excitement in the lobby. "Bud Anderson," she said, waving at the people. "Came to see them. Probably to comfort Nadia over the *News of the World* story."

"Really? Wow." I was as celebrity struck as any of them, remembering Bud Anderson granite jawed and unshakeable in that movie where America saves the world from the bad bug-eyed aliens, Bud Anderson as the canny injun scout guiding the lost backpackers through the wilderness... I laughed, remembering Tattoo on the subject.

Sudden influx of people, and I sat back and watched as all the flunkies suddenly turned towards the men coming down from the mezzanine, loud talk and there was Shaun and this short middle-aged man talking and laughing away.

"That's Bud Anderson?" I gasped to Denise and she nodded, looking very amused. "But he's tiny."

"Shh." she said, "Go on, Shaun wants to introduce you."

And yes, he was waving at me.

"Oh god, no."

"Do it," she hissed.

I went reluctantly over and shook hands with a wide, ugly, balding person who was introduced to me as Bud Anderson.

"Hey, I've been hearing all about you, honey," boomed Bud Anderson. "Shaun says you're one dangerous lady."

"Only when she gets mad." put in Shaun.

"Um..."

"You can get as mad as you like with me," said Bud, not at all accidentally patting my bum. "D'ja want a part in the movie?"

"No thanks." I said, retreating into frightfully British.

Bud Anderson took my arm confidingly. "OK now," he said in a whisper you could have heard in Lyonesse. "You can tell me. What was he really doing down in Cornwall."

Shaun was lighting a fag and looking at his watch, they were obviously waiting for Nadia. He had clearly dropped me straight in it, probably for entertainment. Possibly revenge. Perhaps he was just bored.

I looked down at the terrible disappointment that was Bud Anderson. "You'll never believe me."

"Try me."

"Shaun," I said, just to warn him. "You sure about this."

He shrugged, looked at his watch again.

"OK," I said to Bud Anderson. "As you're his friend, I'll tell you." I put on my sickliest voice, "Actually he was helping me care for a lady with terminal cancer. In a trailer."

There was a moment of silence during which I glared straight back at Tattoo who was glaring at me and then Bud Anderson's belly-laugh filled the whole hotel.

"Oh boy. Oh that's rich. Oh that's a good one."

"See?"

"Ha ha ha. *Shaun*! Caring for a.... Ha ha ha. Was that the one he was dancing with all over the papers, huh?"

"Not quite."

"No, Lysette was the one with the enormous boyfriend," put in Shaun smoothly. "What's his name, Anna?"

"Reg the Rock," I told him.

"Hey, why didn't you kick his ass for Shaun?"

I looked puzzled. "I wasn't there. And anyway, you'd need an axe to take Reg the Rock."

More belly laugh. The lift stopped, doors opened and Nadia plus her two hard-looking people came out of it. She stalked straight past Shaun, delicate nose in the air, and put her arm in Bud Anderson's who managed to lean over her, looking avuncular. Luckily, she was short enough for him to do it.

Shaun brushed past me.

"Watch it," he growled.

Maybe I'd been a bit cheeky. Suddenly I lost all my pretend confidence.

"Sorry," I muttered, hoping my face didn't look hot.

"Hey, Annie, why don't you come with us?" said Bud Anderson, over his shoulder. "We can talk stunts for the movie."

"Me?"

"You," said Shaun, pouncing on this with an evil look. "Have you eaten?"

"Um... yes, I have. I had a pizza. But I..."

Nadia looked very shocked at the word pizza. She never turned a hair at fuck but pizza...

"I'm not really dressed for..."

"Come on," said Shaun. "We're going to Maria's, nobody cares what you wear there."

"But I don't want to," I said between my teeth. "And what about... her?"

"*I* want you to," he said, also between his teeth. "I'm being flaunted at and there's no point me trying to chat up Nadia's girls because they're gay."

"But..."

"Plus I owe you a meal."

"How... what for?"

He'd got my hand firmly and courteously under his arm and I was being swept out to the door. I looked back over my shoulder at Denise who waved encouragingly at me.

"Don't you remember, the Trucker's Big Blowout Breakfast?"

"Oh yes." I tried to escape, but he wouldn't let me. And you really can't use armlocks and break-looses in a luxury hotel lobby. "How about you buy me a cocktail and we call it quits."

"Flirt with me."

"I think that's very dangerous."

He grinned recklessly and his eyes were unnaturally bright. "Gee, do you suppose it is? Better not then."

Nadia was making a tremendous fuss about getting into the car, Bud Anderson was being solicitous.

"I've had about as much as I can take from her," Shaun whispered. "I've had it backwards, forwards, sideways, diagonally and right in the nuts from her and you're my only hope of keeping out of jail for assault."

He was being ridiculously dramatic.

"Rubbish," I sniffed, "you'd never hit her."

"I might hit somebody else."

"Don't go then."

He sighed. "Get in."

I narrowed my eyes at him.

"Please Anna," he said, and of course I melted.

We sat sedately next to each other in the back of the second car and I thought how ridiculous it was to be upset that I hadn't even got any lipstick. I didn't have any with me - I wasn't expecting to do anything or go anywhere. What was Maria's anyway? I had on a big loose casual shirt over a t-shirt and a pair of jeans that were so totally out of fashion they were the latest thing in Lyonesse. Pam would probably have hit me. And I'd left my bag sitting next to Denise when Shaun called me over: I hoped she'd look after it for me. I wasn't sure what Nadia was wearing but I thought it was white and combined casual with knockout chic.

"This is a really bad idea," I said to Shaun, feeling sick and not just because of the squooshy suspension. "Really bad. This is not my scene, man."

"Fake it then," said Shaun unsympathetically.

"You're the actor, not me."

"Learn."

The car stopped. Shaun got out and the chauffeur opened the door for me and I scrambled out and nearly fell over the kerb which was rather near.

My impressions of Maria's are vague because it was extremely dark - *X-Files* dark, in fact, huge, with a lot of steel girders covered in fake rust and unnecessarily rough-hewn wood. Stuffed animals peered from behind chains and buckets. I spotted a beaver, two badgers and ferret and a number of rats wearing bandannas.

We were shown to a table on a restored weighbridge, slightly separated from the hoi polloi and screened by cargo-nets and chains - but still there was a stir as the diners spotted who had arrived and argued with each other over whether it really was and tried to crane their necks without being too obvious about it. Shaun was very much being Mr Filmstar and Bud Anderson loved it.

Three girls in checked shirts and very tight dungarees brought us menus on clipboards and I found I could have anything I wanted so long as it was some species of outrageously costly (pure organic Aberdeen Angus beef) burger. Such a disappointment. As for the meal itself...

Dear reader, do you remember how they used to do it in Seventies movies when split-screen had just been invented and you'd sometimes have the phone conversation on one side with next to it, what really happened? Well, when I told Pam about the Night I had Dinner With Shaun And Bud And Nadia, you're going to have to run something similar for yourself.

Pam: So what did you eat?

Me: Oh just a salad, I told you, I was stuffed full of pizza.

Actual scene:

Bud: Don't tell me you're trying to lose weight?

Me: Um, no.
Nadia (superior smile): Really?  How... self-confident of you.

Phone conversation:
Pam: What did you talk about?
Me: Oh, shopping.

Actual scene:
Nadia: Did you go shopping?
Me: No, that was yesterday.
Nadia: Where did you go yesterday?
Me: Um... Marks & Sparks.
Nadia (slight brow-wrinkle): Marks and who?

Phone conversation:
Pam: You must have talked about something else.
Me: Yes, Bud Anderson told me about the stunts he does.

Actual scene:
Bud: So there I was hanging off the side of this mountain and one of the pitons broke. Well, I could see one a little way away but there was a 400 foot drop and I just...
Me: (stunned silence)
Bud (a little later): ... and the rattlesnake struck at the horse which made the goddamn beast rear up and I nearly fell on my ass, but I just managed to hang on and got it calmed down and they liked the shot so much they kept it...
Me: But I thought... Oh. Gosh.
Bud: Can you ride horseback?
Me: A bit. I went through the pony-loving stage when I was about ten but we lived in London so I never...
Bud: It's a great hobby. That feeling of oneness with an animal. Nothing to beat it. I ride a lot when I'm at my ranch in the States.

Me (working hard not to catch Shaun's eye): That must be lovely.

Phone conversation:
Pam: You must have talked about something else.
Me: Bud told me all about his martial arts training with a Japanese karate master.
Pam: Oh brother, you poor lamb.
Me: Yes, I think so.
Pam: What was Shaun doing in all this?
Me: He was watching. I think he liked the show he'd arranged.
Pam: What did you drink?
Me: Too many cocktails.
Pam: Uh oh.
Me; Uh oh is right.
Pam: Who did you fight?
Me: Excuse me, I'm not a maniac, I didn't fight anyone.
Pam: Well, you are a very ugly drunk.
Me: Thank you so much. I did get Nadia one time though.
Pam: Go on then.
Me: Well, she was telling me how good breast surgery had got and how they hardly leave any scars at all and how some Californian surgeons even do abdominal liposuction.
Pam: Uh oh. So you slugged her?
Me: No, I bloody didn't. Will you stop that? So I said I didn't fancy all the expense and pain and luckily nobody cares what a nurse looks like.
Pam: Uhuh.
Me: So I said, she seemed to know a lot about plastic surgery and maybe she could recommend someone who could do reconstructive surgery on an old lady with cancer of the mouth.
Pam: (unseemly hooting and cheering)
Me: So Shaun said he really didn't understand why everybody was desperate to stop the clock, which you can't stop anyway. And I said how people who've had too many facelifts get this

terribly stretched skin which you can't even stitch because it tears so easily.

Pam: Mm. Lovely.

Me: So I said I was never going to have a face lift even if I could afford it which I couldn't. And she said... shut up Pam, stop giggling, you'll like this, I'm really proud of it. She said, maybe I'd think differently when I was past the age of 40 and I said, I am, I'm 43 and she went all stiff and blank and Shaun said, you are? And I said, of course I am, you've seen my sons.

Pam: Oh dear.

Me: What do you mean, oh dear? I thought that was good.

Pam: Well, she'll hate your guts forever, darling, but I think that's what she was after all along.

Me: She was?

Pam: Yes, to put... er... Tattoo off you.

Me: Oh. No, I'm sure she doesn't think...

Pam: She's just taking precautions. He's in his mid-thirties, isn't he?

Me: How old do you think *she* is?

Pam: A couple of years younger than you, according to the websites.

Me: Well, why on earth is she so hostile?

Pam: Instinct. And of course, you've never had plastic surgery.

Me: But she's beautiful.

Pam: She's never been anything except beautiful. Old age is terrifying for her. What did you say next?

Me: Nothing much. Bud Anderson asked what was my secret elixir of youth and I said, probably subcutaneous fat because it fills up the wrinkles plus a very healthy grandma and also I thought getting older and losing my looks wasn't such a shock for me because I've never been pretty and you don't miss what you've never had.

Pam: Now that was a good one even if it's not true. How did she react to that?

Me: What? But that's true?

Pam: Honestly, Anna, you're hopeless. Hopeless.

Me: Well, Nadia didn't say much but Shaun told the story about his Bostibern Street mystery tour and it was very very funny, even Nadia laughed a bit. I had Death by Chocolate just to annoy her, which was probably a bad idea.

It was a very very very bad idea, which I didn't tell Pam because I was so embarassed about it. I hadn't even had that much to drink, it was the squooshy suspension. Honest. The car was sliding through the one way systems on the way back, and Bud Anderson had his hand on my leg while he told me about doing it with his girlfriend on horseback one time and how about a game of strip poker? I wasn't even annoyed, I just felt horribly carsick.

"I'm sorry," I gasped. "I've got to get out..."

I rattled the handle of the door which wouldn't work and I was terrified of vomiting all over everything and I was upset anyway because... well, all right, possibly I did improve the conversations for Pam's benefit, though I didn't invent anything, and while once I might have been excited at the prospect of sharing a car with *the* Bud Anderson (so Shaun and Nadia could make it up in the other one), the reality was octopus-like and unsnubbable.

"Hey Annie, what's wrong?"

I gulped, tilted my head back, removed the hand that was making its way busily up to my crotch.

"I'm car sick."

"Why don't you lie down here for a bit?" said Bud patting the seat and leering with fake solicitude and I could see he was getting ready for a snog-dive at my mouth.

"Look, I'm sorry... I'm just not... I'm married and... anyway, I'm sorry, I feel carsick..."

"There's the part in my movie..."

"Don't want it." I resisted the urge to break his fingers as I removed them from my bra-strap.

"Aw, come on, don't be like that..."

He was diving for my lips...aargh...yuk... Bloody superannuated teenager. Also he'd smoked a cigar.

There's a little place, just at the base of the neck under the voicebox which is a pressure point. It's the tracheotomy point, by the way. If you put your finger in it and push quite gently, the other person has to move because you're pressing on his trachea.

I did this and got some breathing space.

"Bud," I said, full-on nurse voice, "Get off. I'm feeling carsick and..." My stomach heaved as the car swooshed round a corner. "Do you really want me to puke in your lap?"

I banged on the partition and the door. "Let me out before I'm sick!"

"Hey, not so dramatic. OK, OK."

The chauffeur was slowing down, he released the door and I had it open and practically fell out.

Then I was sick in the gutter like a student after a party and felt much better once I'd got rid of Death by Chocolate and a couple of those bloody cocktails. Forty-three years old, mother of two and I'd made no progress. So humiliating. At least Matt and Si had the excuse of being adolescents.

Bud Anderson let out a disgusted "Jesus!", shut the door and the car drove off into the night, leaving me stranded.

# Chapter 27

I stopped spitting, wiped my face with a scrunched tissue from my pocket, waited until my head had stopped whirling and then said fuck about fifty times. It wasn't enough. Now fuck has become an ordinary item of conversation, we need something stronger really. Devaluation of swearwords. Serious social problem.

I was surrounded by the enormous slabbed mausoleums of modern commerce, about five miles from where I wanted to be. It was dark, unidentifiably late, the few cars were motoring ecstatically through the empty streets. I saw a taxi with its light on, almost hailed it, realised I only had about two pounds fifty in my pocket and no bag, let it go past and then remembered that I could have got it to go to the hotel anyway and sorted something out with reception to pay the driver. Too late, it was gone.

So I started walking westwards in the hope of spotting a night bus or a tube station, feeling more and more tense. I found myself walking down a wide empty street where every shop or office doorway seemed full of homeless people, sitting around in sleeping bags and cardboard boxes, smoking rollies and staring at me. Right on cue, an animal howled in the distance.

It probably is the guilty reaction of someone who still has a home, who has been staying at a luxury hotel, but my paranoia immediately expanded into a thing like a large dog padding along behind me, whispering evil stuff about all the worst muggings and beatings I'd dealt with. I walked faster and tried to look dangerous.

And then I saw him. He came out of an alleyway right under a streetlight and I gasped and stopped dead because I thought it was Tattoo come to fetch me - only Shaun had taken the thing off his face and this lad, his was permanent. His was a spiderweb not a Maori war-pattern. Also he had nose studs and ear studs and eyebrow studs, a metal detector's nightmare.

He turned his uglified face to me, our eyes met.

"You gotta mobile?"

"What?"

"Mobile. Gotta mobile?"

He didn't look drugged up, but he was hard to understand because of the tongue stud.

My knees were starting to shake and I began to think about where I was going to kick him first and which direction I was going to run in.

"Sorry," I said. "I haven't got anything."

His webbed face contracted, he put it in his love-hate hands and started to cry.

"Oh God. Oh God. What do I do?"

Sandra would have known what to do. Sandra dealt with this kind of thing every day. I took a deep breath, tried to think like Sandra.

"What's wrong?" I asked. "Is there... is there anything I can do."

"I need an ambulance."

I looked at him closely. Horribly dirty tracks, odd trainers, ripped t-shirt, smelly, but no visible blood or broken bones.

"Why? You look..."

"Not me!" he howled. "Yarrow."

"Who?"

"She's sick. She's dying. Get an ambulance."

"Where?"

He grabbed my hand in his cold grubby fists and pulled me down the alleyway, past the slippery boxes and bags of rubbish and into a cave made of boxes where a girl was on all fours, grunting and groaning, and in a way I'd known it had to be that or a drug overdose. At least it wasn't an overdose.

"It's all right," I said, sighing. "It's all right."

"It's coming, right?" said web-face, "She's having it?"

"Of course I'm fucking having it!" screamed the girl. "I'm dying, Jesus. I'm gonna die. Awwwuuuuuuu."

I don't know what it is, I know I wasn't any too sober myself, but click, in snapped the Nurse Module.

I grabbed the boy and shook him. "Listen," I said, "You do need an ambulance, you're right, but she's not dying. She's not going to die. You understand?"

He panted open-mouthed at me. "Yerss."

"What's your name?"

"Jesus."

"Your name?"

"It's his name," shrieked Yarrow. "His mum's a religious nutcase."

I had to gulp and swallow several times so as not to fall apart into hysterical laughter.

"OK... um... Jesus. You go out and find a phone box that's working. You dial 999. You tell the ambulance to come to the phone box, then you lead it back here. Tell them your girlfriend is in labour. Don't tell them your name. Got that?"

Yes, children, back then calling 999 was that complicated without a mobile.

"Awwwuuuuuuugh!" yodelled the girl as her belly heaved. Oh brother, I thought, two minutes between contractions. Great. Just lovely. Please find an ambulance before second stage, please.

"Tell them it's one minute between contractions and she's in an alley."

He nodded, turned and ran. I heard voices outside, thought for a minute and took my casual shirt off, rolled it up and put it on one of the cleaner boxes.

Yarrow was wearing her elasticated peasant-skirt rolled up to her waist and a grubby t shirt. The silly girl still had her knickers on, so I took them off, thought about an internal examination, but my hands were dirty and so were the surroundings. When she stopped howling I put my hand on her shoulder and said,

"Listen, Yarrow. I'm a nurse. I've delivered dozens of babies. I've had two myself. I know what to do, it's going to be OK."

Her tear-stained, snot-stained, pierced white face turned to me and her forehead crinkled.

"It's going to be OK," I repeated.

"It hurts," she whimpered. "Can you give me something..."

I sighed again. "I know it hurts, but I can't because I don't have anything. They'll give you some stuff at hospital."

She nodded and frowned. "But it hurts now."

"I know."

"Make it stop hurting."

"I can't."

What's she been on, I wondered, heroin, crack? Is she HIV positive? Poor poor kid.

"But what can I do?"

Worst pain there is, except perhaps for passing a kidney stone, no escape.

"You have to go through it," I said to her. "All I can say is, the pain won't kill you. It's just pain. It isn't damage."

Her brow wrinkled more as she maybe took this in, but then she looked down at her belly.

"It's starting again, oh no, oh no, awwuuuu.... Awwwwuuuuaargh."

It didn't look like she was bearing down yet, which was good. I longed to find out how much her cervix was dilated, but didn't dare. I held her shoulders, supported her - hands and knees is as good a position as any, certainly better than the stranded-beetle lithotomy position that makes life so much easier for midwives. I've always felt that toddlers are right, the tummy button is a much more sensible place.

The yodelling died down and I tried clearing away the dirtiest bits of cardboard, replacing them with clean bits. There was a sleeping bag pushed in the corner which was sodden and sticky with her waters. Footsteps behind me.

"Will I boil some water for ye, missus?" said a gruff Scottish voice.

I turned to find a small hairy man in filthy polyester trousers and an anorak, blinking down at me.

"I need something to clean my hands with," I said. "I should do an internal examination."

"It's hard for the puir lassie," he said, listening to her gasping. "Ah mind my missus allus greeted. Would she like a nipoff of mine?"

He offered a bottle of cider, but Yarrow shook her head.

"And ye've nae things for the bairn," said the Scot. "Och, it's shocking."

"All I really need is something to clean my hands with. Vodka maybe?"

"Ay, ye do. Ye bide there, Yarrow, I'll see tae it." He ran unsteadily back up the alley.

I had no idea how he was going to boil water, but didn't have time to ask. Maybe he'd even bring me vodka, which would be fine. Yarrow suddenly reared up and grabbed me.

"I've got to go to the toilet. I've got to. Oh God..."

Oh God is right. I hoped, I really hoped it was just her bowels emptying, but it didn't look like it. I held onto her shoulders again, shouted.

"Yarrow, pant blow, like this, whoo whoo whoo. Like that. Do it. And don't push."

She tried, writhing as the contraction went through her.

There was a distant crash, another crash and screel of metal and the tinny clamour of alarms. Pause while Yarrow twisted under my hands and went whoo whoo desperately. Then the sound of running feet.

The Scot rushed towards us, his arms full of things. Dropped them in front of me. Anti-bacterial wipes. A big cot blanket. A babygro (small). A teddy (large). Paracetamol (many). Dettox spray. Nappies (toddler size). More wipes. A kettle.

"What the hell..."

"Ah robbed the chemist," said the Scot casually. "I'll go wait for the cops now."

"You're a star, McKenna," whispered Yarrow.

"Ay, Ah know. See ye, missus. Ye do yer best."

I don't fucking believe this, I thought to myself as I ripped open packets, I really don't. I sprayed Dettox spray around. I used wipes on her legs and on my hands. A rat, with no bandanna, poked its head up and I squirted Dettox right in its inquisitive little whiskers which made it scuttle away sneezing. Then I carefully had a feel inside Yarrow, which made her squawk because it's very uncomfortable. Her cervix was ten centimeters dilated, fully open and ready to rumble.

"I gotta shit again," she screamed. "Oh shit!"

I sat her bum on the teddy with her back against the wall, legs bent up like a frog's, wide apart, and wished I could see a bit more.

I didn't know when the ambulance would come and there was no medical reason why she shouldn't push. Plenty of social and hygienic reasons, but her body and the baby were ready now. My own stomach was busy freefalling for the centre of the earth. The stakes are so high with babies, it's terrifying; terminal care might be harrowing, but it's not frightening. It's quite safe: to put it brutally, if you mess up you probably haven't destroyed an entire future life. Caution said I should make her wait for the ambulance. But she was ready NOW. And the baby could run out of oxygen if I made them wait.

I swallowed, took a deep breath. OK, let's rock and roll!

"Listen!" I roared. "You're not shitting. You're having a baby. Different muscles. Wait for the urge, then push with it, front not back."

"It hurts," she wailed. "It hurts."

"Of course it fucking hurts," I snarled. "Do you think babies come free?"

She stared at me. Nothing shocks the young so much as officialdom swearing.

"Give me something."

"No."

In came the pain again, made my own stomach clench with memory to see her, it's like a tidal wave, and then that mighty primeval imperative to push down.

"Go!" I shouted. "Don't yell. Push."

She did. She had to really, but she stopped wailing, shut her mouth and pushed. I held her up, mopped her, told her she was a good girl, a brave girl, waited and in came the sea of life again and she pushed again.

I really hate those American movies where women have their babies by immaculate parturition, just a few well-mannered oohs and aahs and out it comes, nice and clean and three months old. ER gets it a bit better, but you simply can't show the real thing on TV because it's too loud and it takes too long and it's such fucking hard and unpleasant work. It's everything civilization dislikes and works to obliterate and hide; the incontrovertible proof that we are animals.

Special animals with big heads which is what causes so much trouble. Dogs and cats don't suffer nearly as much. The baby's head crowned, and I supported it, tried to keep the perineum from tearing, eased it very carefully. "Wait," I told her. "Pant." She did, harsh noises through clenched teeth. That teddy would never be the same again. The damp little patch of hair was clear, another contraction coming.

"Go!" I shouted and she pushed again, mightily. "Go through it, go." I had no forceps if the baby stuck, nothing, no monitor, couldn't even see what colour it had because of the orange streetlight glare, oh shit, oh God, let it be OK. When the baby's head crowns, they call it the crown of thorns because that's what it feels like you're sitting on. Yarrow's face was streaming with tears and sweat and her eyes shut with the effort that turned her puce... "Go, push more." She did, dug deep, pushed again.

And out it came as she heaved and pushed, top of the head, face, all smeared with blood and gunk, making the half-turn easily, eyes open and looking at me gravely.

"One more push," I said and she heaved and out popped the rest, slithered like a seal all covered with gunk and I nearly dropped it, girl, quite small, healthy-looking cord, still pulsing, no need to cut it yet. Cleared the baby's mouth with my finger and she breathed with that shocked air of surprise at what a nasty thing it is to do, began a nice healthy see-saw wail.

"Oh look," panted Yarrow in amazement, crying over her deflated belly. "Look, look at the baby."

Quick squint to make sure Yarrow wasn't bleeding too much, no, it was fine, that strange warm metallic earthy smell of birth all around us. Somebody was ripping open the cot-blanket pack next to me, handed me the blanket and I wrapped the baby up in it, swaddle style, put it in her arms.

"Is it over?" she asked.

Over? I thought to myself, you silly little girl, of course it's not over, you've got twenty years ahead of you. Then I smiled. "That bit's over," I said. "Well, you've got the afterbirth to come, but there's no hurry, it'll take a while to detach. And it won't hurt. Just cuddle the baby. Would you like to try her with your breast?"

She looked surprised and then thoughtful. "Um. OK." She wasn't wearing a bra, just pulled up her t-shirt and then looked confused, so I showed her how to point her nipple and the baby got latched on right the first time.

"Aren't you clever?" I cooed at the baby. "Cleverclogs. There. Just stay like that."

Suddenly, kneeling on filthy cardboard, up to my armpits in gunk and blood, looking at a baby about whom the only thing you could say was that she was definitely going to die one day... It was like a voice in my head and what it boomed at me was: "You're finished with this now."

I know that one reason why doctors and nurses are looked on in such a peculiar way in our society is because we are the gate-keepers: we're there when you're born and we're there when you die, usually. I'd specialised in gate-keeping, at the other end. And now I was finished. I'd ended on the highest note I could, really, nothing like the wonder of a healthy baby for cheering you up, no matter how dire its general prospects. There's an importance that comes from gate-keeping and that had drawn me more than I liked to admit. There's the urge to control, the urge to make sure it all works out, the urge to care, to be the cure for the world's ills. I'd done my best, I'd been good at it, but somebody else was going to have to do it now. I was going to do something else. I was going to do what I wanted to do and enjoy the mildly pointless, but very interesting bit in between, where the shadows flicker on the wall.

It takes a long time to say in words what I saw in one second as I looked at the small baby girl suckling her pitifully young mother. "I was brave, wasn't I?" she said to me.

"Yes," I told her. "You were brilliantly brave. Heroic. You saved your baby's life."

She beamed at me proudly. She had been brave. Some girls in her appalling situation might have just keeled over and refused to push, but she'd tried her hardest. A tribe somewhere, I forget where, has a legend that every mother has to go down to the Underworld and battle with Death for her baby. The mother doesn't always win, sometimes Death wins, but on this occasion, victory, damn it, victory! Yarrow had won.

I turned and found webfaced Jesus squatting next to me with his mouth wide open.

He was crying unselfconsciously.

"Look Jesus," said Yarrow. "Isn't she beautiful?"

Of course she wasn't. She had the normal newborn baby's squashed bruised purple and furious face. Jesus put out a filthy finger and gently touched her cheek.

"Yer," he said unconvincingly. "Yeah, she is."

I looked at his concealing spiderweb and wondered if he'd ever been to Cambridge and if so had he ever duffed up some snotty student there. I thought of Sandra telling me how often Jesus turned up among the homeless and treasured the thought of telling her about this one.

"Um... Jesus," I asked. "Can I just ask you."

"Hm?"

"Why did you do that to yourself?" I indicated his face.

He looked at me as if I was an idiot. "So no one would know who I was."

"Yes, but..."

"I'm not Jesus, you see," he said confidentially. "My mum called me that when she was alive, but I'm not. So I did it so people wouldn't make mistakes. I'm somebody else, really."

"Right." The logic was there. Hard to put your finger on the flaw in it. "So... er... who are you?"

"Well, I thought Barry might be a nice name."

"Yes, it is."

He gave me a shy sideways grin. "Or Damien?"

I was a bit slow. "What?" He nudged me gently and I cracked up. Yarrow laughed too.

"He always says that," she told me proudly.

The baby had let go of her nipple to stare at us. Yarrow tried to get her back on.

"No, it's all right," I told her. "When they're so little they can't suck for more than a minute at a time."

"My arse is killing me. I want to sit down."

I didn't want her doing that on the filthy pavement.

"Hang on," I said. "Wait for the ambulance."

"All right. Here you are, Jeez. You hold her a minute while I get decent."

She plumped the baby-parcel into his arms and he clutched his? daughter in the typical new father is-she-made-of-glass? manner while Yarrow sorted out her t-shirt and skirt as much as she could.

Never mind her arse, my knees were killing me. I used a lot of wipes to try and get the gunk off my jeans, retrieved my shirt from the cardboard box.

Yarrow took back the baby and scowled up at someone who turned out to be a policeman.

"McKenna said you were here," said the policeman. "And her. Everything OK, Nurse?"

"Where's the ambulance?"

"Outside."

"Wheel 'em in," I said, heartfelt relief, trembling slightly myself. "The afterbirth's not detached yet."

We came out of the alley so the paramedics could go in and put her on a stretcher and take her somewhere warm and clean where people could look after her and patronise her and have meetings about her and decide what she needed for her own good. I waved at web-face as the paramedics there-we-goed her into the van.

"If you're the father, Barry, you ride with her."

He gulped and climbed in behind her.

I went with the policemen to their station where I cleaned up and made a statement about what had happened and heard a bit more about McKenna and also Jesus. I tried to make it clear in my statement that McKenna had been trying to help in a crisis and said I'd testify for him in court if necessary. The cops laughed and said they didn't think McKenna would like that since he was worried enough that people might think he'd gone soft.

They gave me a lift back to the hotel eventually, only they dropped me outside the main door not the special celebrity door. The doorman wasn't going to let someone looking like me jump out of a cop car and come into his hotel, so I told him my room number and two minutes later Shaun Graham banged through the glass door and the doorman wilted into a heap of apologies. I said thank you for the lift to the cops who were simply dying of curiosity now. Finally, they drove off and Shaun led me inside and through to the special super duper celebrity bit. For a moment I felt completely disoriented.

"Where have you been? Are you OK? Why the cops?" he demanded.

"You wouldn't believe me," I said, shaking my head because the whole incident with Jesus and Yarrow had suddenly turned into something I could quite easily believe had been a dream. Except for the thing inside which had said, "Finished now." That was still quite clear. No more gate-keeping for me, no more looking after strangers, no more doing what people expected of me, no more...

"Why did you make a break for it like that? Did Bud..."

Thud. Back to reality. My reality, anyway. There isn't one that's any realer than another, you know.

"I was carsick," I said. "I always get carsick when I sit in the back of swooshy cars. I'm used to driving myself. And I think Death by Chocolate was well-named."

"Are you sure Bud didn't upset you?"

"Well, he was copping a quick feel but he didn't upset me, no."

"He was *what?*"

"As you must have known he would, he was trying for a shag and he was very cross when he not only didn't get one, but I chundered in the gutter in front of him."

Shaun scowled. "He was trying to..."

"Fuck me, yes, he was. Of course he was. It's obviously what he does..."

"Bastard!"

"Shaun." I said softly, feeling he was overdoing it a bit. "Shall we make a big scene and have it all out in the open about us, or shall we just quietly go and get a drink before I go to bed?"

He snorted. "I've already done the big scene."

"Oh dear."

"I can't believe he just drove off like that. Leaving you there."

"It was fine. I needed fresh air, I got it, there was a... an... incident and as a result, I got a lift home. No problem."

"Yes problem. Don't you even realise when you've been treated badly? He had no right to dump you like that."

"I was being sick."

"So what?"

"Well, what would you have done?"

"At the very fucking least I'd have got you a taxi. At least."

Suddenly I had the alarming sensation of my eyes prickling, because I was being too cynical. Shaun genuinely was outraged on my behalf, not because he was shagging me, but because I'd been badly treated. And I had. I wouldn't have done that to Bud in those circumstances. But why hadn't I thought that before?

I headed for the bar, got a brandy to cut through all the fat I'd eaten that day and he got one as well. We sat primly opposite each other and the barman wiped up nonexistent spots behind us.

"I'm sorry I made you go out tonight," he said. "I know it wasn't much fun for you."

"Well, it worked," I told him. "At least you're not in jail for assault."

He laughed, put up his finger and thumb a millimetre apart. "This close," he said. "I was this close to punching Bud out."

"Pity I missed it. Has he gone?"

"Oh yes. Did he really try it on with you?"

"Yes," I said. "And don't give me that shocked look, you knew he would. It's quite reassuring really. At least you haven't been talking about me to Bud Anderson."

"Do you think I'm a total shit?"

"No, I think you're male. Stop being pompous."

Shaun grinned suddenly and tried not to laugh. "All right. OK. But not to Bud because it would be slower to use a megaphone."

"Good."

"Did he get anywhere?"

I eyed him and wondered about kicking him. "No, he didn't. Which you know as well." And don't think I don't know that your wicked Y-chromosome was involved in setting the whole thing up just to see if I'd let Bud have his lecherous way with me. I thought it, didn't say it.

"I never reckoned he'd just dump you in the middle of nowhere like that." It was getting a bit eerie, the way we were reading each other's minds all of a sudden.

"What did you think?"

He leered wickedly. "I thought *you* might punch him."

I sighed. "Well you reckoned without my wonky inner ear and reaction to working suspension systems. And you were a very bad man to set up a fight between me and Bud Anderson."

"So what happened?"

"I was sick, I was dumped, I walked, I got paranoid and I... Well, I met a man with a cobweb on his face called Jesus who may or may not have been to Cambridge one time and a Scotsman called McKenna who decided for reasons too complicated to go into that he wanted to rob a chemist's shop and the cops eventually gave me a lift back here."

"That's not all that happened."

"No, it isn't," I said, lifting my chin at him. There was a strange moment when two silences locked shoulders and pushed. But the whole surreal thing with Yarrow and her baby and what I thought about it, that was all too fresh to talk about. I still had wet patches on the knees of my jeans where I'd scrubbed off the grime and gore from the alley, and looking around at the pale wood and last year's chrome of the bar, my head felt light with the wierdness of it. I needed to think it over.

Shaun nodded very slightly, lifted his glass to me and we both drank smooth brandy. Who was it said, "I've been rich and I've been poor. Rich is better." That sounds very cynical. Of course it was outrageous that a kid could give birth in an alley like that, of course it was. I didn't know how she'd wound up there, or who had made her pregnant or how old she was or anything. At least the baby didn't look too bad, I didn't think she was a crack-baby or already addicted to heroin. Even with the Welfare State as tattered and patched as it is, that baby might be Yarrow's passport to somewhere decent(ish) to live. I could follow her up, track down the right people, be the interested middle class voice on the phone that sometimes got things moving. I could and would do that. Some gut instinct was telling me that Yarrow might well be all right in the long run. Not because of anything to do with me, mind, but because I thought she might have found something flinty inside herself when she needed it and once you've found it, you've got it forever.

Suddenly I felt happy. Not sure why. Something very heavy was melting away from between my shoulderblades. Maybe it was thanks to the brandy. Maybe it was my new understanding.

"Nadia's spotted something," I said as the thought occurred to me.

"Probably. But she's more worried about Lysette."

I sipped and looked him over. His hair was now visible and he only looked as if he'd just got out of jail. Suedehead effect. Brown.

"She doesn't know you at all, does she?" I said.

"What do you mean?"

I shook my head, not sure myself. "I'm knackered," I told him. "And we've got training in the morning. Night night."

# Chapter 28



I know I'm a martial arts bore. Somehow it's considered quite stylish to be a tennis bore or a football bore, but very uncool to be a martial arts bore. So I won't go too much into what we did in our training sessions at the dance centre - it was very chaste and quite dull, really. When you're building up fitness and muscle memory and flexibility, the most effective thing you can do is repetitions, so that's what we did. First we warmed up, then we did some stretching, then we did linework and kicking combinations and I taught him some patterns - sequences of movement like dances - then we did some strength and fitness stuff, more stretching. The first day he had no energy because he was following some damned stupid diet suggested by Nadia, so I told him I was going home if he didn't eat properly and unless he'd been living in a hole in the ground for the past ten years, he knew perfectly well what to avoid.

"Everything I like," he said gloomily, scratching his head which was itching him terribly. I went down into sideways splits and he looked crestfallen at how high he was off the ground.

"Don't worry about how far you go compared to me, just compare it to last week when you couldn't even put your palms on the ground."

We did a lot of kicking and you know, when he wasn't hungover and grumpy, he was a dream to teach. It wasn't just the physical eptness. He was willing, he was focussed, he kept going when he was tired. You could see why he'd got where he was, or some of the reason anyway. And I was getting better too: I could feel my flexibility increasing and my kicks were getting better, more precise. I was enjoying myself immensely and getting paid for it.

And the showers even worked.

So we had a wheatgerm and tofu snack for lunch at the back of the little cafe, and Tattoo put on a baseball cap and turned himself into this shy, gawky guy with a giggle, so no one noticed. It was amazing. He handed me a big sheaf of paper, got out a paperback and said I should just read it.

Well, I couldn't. It was a screenplay which means it was laid out strangely and since a screenplay is only the skeleton of a film, it was very thin, somehow. Also it was too boring. I flipped to the end and saw the Shaun Graham character dies saving his buddy in a very unlikely and hackneyed way. His dying speech brought tears of mirth to my eyes. All the good lines were for the Bud Anderson character.

"Gawd," I said. "Were you drunk when you signed for this?"

"I don't remember. I must have been." He sighed again, stirred the wheatgerm and tofu, glugged some peach flavoured water and made a face. "Nadia's in it."

"She isn't."

"Yes, she's the love interest. Look."

Sure enough, I'd missed the completely irrelevant and unnecessary love-interest which wore very wonderful clothes because it was a model. Who had vital information. Or something. Both cops fall in love with her, the straight cop rescues her, but it's the maverick cop who seduces her. And then she dies dramatically.

"You don't even get the girl!"

"Nope."

"You must have been drunk. Any way out of it?"

"I've tried. No go, too expensive. I signed before *King Alfred* happened, and back then it looked good. I've fired the agent who cocked up the contract, we're working on the script, but that's all I can do."

"Doesn't it matter that you nearly had a fight with Bud Anderson?"

"God no, they're used to that kind of thing. Everybody nearly has a fight with Bud Anderson. No, pre-production's nearly finished and they've brought in another writer to tighten up the dialogue."

"What dialogue?"

"They want the two characters to crack wise together."

"Those *Lethal Weapons* have had a devastating effect on action films, haven't they? Just once I'd like to see a non-maverick non-wisecracking cop. You know? Someone boring who does what he's told and keeps records and obeys the rules?"

He laughed, trying to hide the tofu under a pile of lentils. "That's way too radical."

"You want me to injure you so they have to get someone else?"

He grinned. "Don't tempt me."

I stole his tofu because I love tofu.

I rang Pam who told me that everyone was speculating wildly and the latest was that I'd run off to the Bahamas with the treasure Onion had hidden under her bed. She had successfully kept quiet about Shaun Graham although it was killing her and I owed her at least a blow by blow account. As it were. So I gave her edited highlights as above. She claimed that Matt and Si had been seen at the skateboarding park, that Jim hadn't been seen much at all and my car was still at MiniWonders and did I want it towed to her place? I'd forgotten all about it and said yes please.

I went into nurse-practitioner mode, rang the cops, found out the hospital where Yarrow had gone, rang the social work department and patiently worked my way through the usual ranks of idiots until I found a human being to whom I told all of the story I knew. She sucked her teeth exactly like Sid, got my mobile number and promised she'd do her best but she couldn't promise that Yarrow would let her help. I told her I knew that and her best would be all I'd ask. I fought off the urge to do the woman's job for her by ringing round the agencies, and went back to work with Shaun.

We could have one of those sequence of quick cuts that indicates the passage of time here, if you like, gentle reader. Just a few days.

Then Nadia turned up at an afternoon session, both her bodyguards in tow and changed into dayglo fluorescent pink lycra, the kind of colour that gives you a migraine if you look at it too long. Tattoo made the internal change to Shaun and I retreated to Hardass Martial Artist. Both the bodyguards, Lulu and Lisa, had studied something, kung fu and aikido probably, so they knew what they were up to, except they were so much in love they wouldn't spar with anybody else and certainly not with me. They were rather beautiful to watch, though impossible to talk to.

Nadia clearly did a great deal of aerobics and probably a spot of weight-training as well. She was like whipcord, very flexible and almost comically slow to learn because she wasn't concentrating. She was watching me and Shaun like a hawk and being as rude as she dared to me. I probably wasn't teaching very well either because the tension was telling on me and I was watching her and Shaun like a hawk.

You may think that Shaun was all over the place. No, he wasn't. He was better than ever. He liked the tension and he was enjoying the unexpressed catfight. I was very annoyed with him. After all, he was having it all his way, wasn't he? One beautiful and decorative woman to display in public and buy clothes for and shag. One moderately sane and well-padded woman to work out with and shag. Perfect for the modern pasha.

How sane was I for going along with it? Why on earth did I stand for it? Was I just reverting to type with exactly the same kind of talented drunken bully I'd loved before? Only successful this time? Was that what turned me on? Being treated badly by a star? I had to ask, didn't I? None of us can pretend to be psychologically naive nowadays.

And watching him with Nadia, I felt sorry for her not him. Because she bored him. You can be a very good actress and still quite stupid because the quality you need for acting has very little to do with what we call intelligence and everything to do with emotion and expressiveness and that physical ept thing. I couldn't say how good Nadia was because she always chose her parts very carefully so she played more or less the same person. Her beauty had got her where she was, and her ability to rule people. But she was really quite dumb. She had no sense of humour, she didn't know anything about the past or the world outside movie gossip and clothes, and while she was decorative to look at, her voice soon put you on edge.

So he was bored. Physically fascinated, but mentally bored. She sashayed around the dance centre, admiring her lycra'd self, high-kicking like a can-can dancer while I tried to get her to connect with a pad instead of pointing her delicate little toes. Shaun watched her the way men do when they're exercising that legendary spatial ability of theirs in order to undress somebody in their minds. But when they'd try to have a conversation, it always turned into a movie-people gossip or a what-shall-I-wear saga and I could almost hear the click as he switched off.

The Bostibern Street mystery tour story ran in the *Sun* on a Wednesday after a woman rang them claiming to have given Shaun Graham the time of his life (as she put it) and wanting to sell her story. She was quietly arrested by police who found in her possession a very strange collection of credit cards, jewellery, pens and wallets, one of them the Gucci alligator skin item owned by Shaun. Not to mention drugs. Since she had previous as long as your arm nobody was very interested when she claimed to have been looking after them for a friend.

The story was great: Shaun looked ruefully sexy in the photos. In breathless tabloidese, interspersed with those funny paragraph spacers - Suffer! - Skint! Pony! Hitch! - he explained what he'd done after Lysette's boyfriend suggested how badly his health would suffer if he didn't leave The Cellar. He couldn't remember much, he'd gone drinking downtown… and he'd woken up, skint and jacketless on the moor with a pony looking at him and had to hitch-hike home. He hadn't made a fuss because he'd felt it was his fault and anyway, he was having a holiday from celebrity, as he put it. And it was a nice walk. He said some things about wildflowers and rainbows that must have made the South Cornwall Tourist board go all pink and bashful. I noticed that there was no mention of any kind of sexual behaviour at all – no, Shaun was the poor innocent lamb to the slaughter.

There was another picture of him with his head bald and his famous tattoo: "How Shaun Fooled the World!" They had computer-generated pictures of Tom Cruise, Mel Gibson, Leonardo diCaprio and somebody I'd never heard of, complete with tattoos and slapheads in case they wanted to try it. They had a picture of the wild moor where he'd been dumped (and narrowly missed getting eaten by the Beast of the Moor, according to one old lady who had seen it that very night). They had a picture of the tart who'd rung them with her face blanked out but every tattoo easily visible so I knew Shaun had been with Gaby and so did everyone in South Cornwall with the right contacts. If reputation means anything, she probably had given him a very acceptable blow-job. Luckily for Shaun, Nadia wouldn't know about her reputation.

They had a picture of the kind of rare pony that might have been looking at him. They also had a gloriously pompous second leader about film stars who got themselves into trouble when they went out without their minders and how at least one had shown himself to be a public spirited sort of chap who co-operated with the police, despite previous bad behaviour... I suppose tabloid editors would be in favour of stern treatment for anyone who robs drunks.

According to Denise, every satirical show on air was beseeching him to appear, only to be firmly turned down. *Have I Got News For You?* featured an Odd One Out round which included Arthur Miller and the famous wild pony, and concerned people who had looked at sleeping filmstars and lived to tell the tale. An Irish comic with a new ultra-trendy (not-quite-Graham-Norton) show had his head shaved and tried wandering round London with a facial tattoo but nobody paid him any attention.

"By next week me and the fucking pony will have had an affair," Shaun predicted to Denise but he was reasonably happy with the way it turned out. Denise took the opportunity to organise a photocall about Shaun And Nadia Training Together since there was a rapidly growing audience of excited girls outside the dance centre every day. Since no one was interested in me, I didn't appear in any of the pics, but Shaun and Nadia were there in almost every newspaper, high-kicking together. Denise fielded two requests for interviews from me and turned them down. I found myself running a second session for the bodyguards and chauffeurs of the combined entourages, all of whom had clauses in their contracts requiring them to keep up their training in self-defence techniques. *Hello!* published an interview with Nadia about being so in love, and I knew the break up wouldn't be long in coming.

And yes, dear reader, I was perfectly well-aware of the fact that I was treating Nadia exactly the same way Susie of the pink lippy had treated me, and I could see the fun in it too. They must have been dying of giggles that time when I went back for a bag of clothes and thought there was a cat in Jim's study. There's nothing so childish as having an affair - check out the jacuzzi incident. The only places we didn't make out were Shaun's actual suite and the dance centre; the suite because I was superstitious and the dance centre because there were girls boosting each other up road signs so they could try and peek in through the second floor windows. The proprieter was distraught and the local police weren't too happy either. Apparently, some fan had posted the location on the Internet and women were flying in to London so they could come and gawk.

Shaun got more and more tense about it until the day came when we had to call security to come so he could get out. He paced up and down like a lion in a trap while some enterprising girls who had hired a double-decker sight-seeing bus cooeed at him from the top deck.

"What the fuck do they want?" he demanded. "What are they after?"

"You're a top-level alpha male primate. Naturally, they're after what's in your high quality genes," I said seriously, not having thought it through.

He stopped and stared at me. "*I know that.*"

"I meant high quality DNA..."

We were still helpless with laughter when the cavalry arrived. Unfortunately one of the girls had a long lens and got a picture of us laughing which went into a FORLORN FOR SHAUN website with the headline, "Who she?"

After we'd fought our way into the car for the hundred yard trip back to the hotel, Shaun leaned back and said bitterly that he'd always thought it would be great to have so many girls after him.

"I don't know why they're so rough," I said, looking at a nasty scratch on my arm.

"They're frightened somebody else will get me. And you know what? It's not even me they're after, it's King bloody Alfred, who doesn't exist, who I made up. They're in love with him, not me. I sometimes wonder if they'd rip me open to try and find King Alfred inside."

I stared at him. "Christ," I said. "That's awful."

"Go on, admit it. You're the same. You told me how much you liked him."

"Well, I did. And I'm not saying I'd kick King Alfred out of my bed on a cold night, so long as he takes his chainmail longjohns off, but you're real."

He leaned over and kissed me on the cheek.

The hotel rallied round (to the tune of heroic amounts of money) and cleared and equipped one of their convention rooms for us and we carried on. Some of the hotel staff started coming to the open sessions in the afternoon and Denise insisted that I charge at least £10 per person which seemed like highway robbery to me after Cornwall.

The fight arranger, known to everyone simply as Harris, had arrived and turned out to be a short solid man with enormous knuckles who spoke in that half-cockney snarl of the lifelong soldier. He'd been told what to do by the director, they all had a meeting to which I was not invited, he talked it over with Shaun in the gym who repeated what I'd said about spins and jumps (with attribution), while I stood modestly by holding a punching pad.

"Quaite raight," Harris said, glancing at me. "However not at all what Mistah Naismith was talking about," and you got the feeling he was only swallowing a clipped half-contemptuous "sah!" with great effort. "Very well. Let's have a look at you."

Shaun had put together a series of routines, a hand-technique set, kicking combinations and some set-sparring with throws and self-defence. Then we free-sparred. Harris watched, very nearly standing to attention with an invisible swagger-stick, eyes narrowed critically.

We came to a stop and bowed to each other.

"Hm," said Harris, picked up a glove and launched himself at Shaun. "Knife attack!" he yelled.

Shaun caught the hand, swung his shoulder under it and just stopped in time to avoid breaking Harris's arm.

"Hm," said Harris and swung a punch at Shaun, who grinned, blocked it and punched back. Harris caught him and threw him. Shaun rolled with it, bounced up in guarding stance and I stood between them.

"Pads," I said to Harris. "Please."

"Hm?" said Harris. "Oh. Quaight raight." He put them on, the two of them squared up.

It was perfectly safe because Harris was far too good for Shaun to get anywhere near him with a fist. However, his tradition was evidently karate and ju-jitsu, so Shaun took a couple of very nice points with a side kick, back kick combo.

I'll admit it. I enjoyed watching the two of them. Harris reminded me of the contained ferocity and muscle of a Staffordshire terrier (though not their boneheaded stupidity) while Shaun... Shaun had a mesmerising power and grace of movement. He could turn it on and off like a tap; it was there when he performed and that's what he was doing for the first time. For me. Harris was a hundred times better as a martial artist, but I watched Shaun because he's beautiful.

All right. Perhaps I'm a tiny bit biased.

They stopped when Shaun was breathless and Harris didn't seem to have broken a sweat yet.

"Hm. Normally, I'd take on the trainer too," he said half to me and half to Shaun. Shaun grinned.

"Fine by me," he said.

I stood up, bowed. "You ever fought a woman?"

"No. Wasn't actually planning to this time..."

Since I still had my pads on, I walked straight up to him and punched him on the chin. Really, I shouldn't have pulled it because he came after me like a tiger.

There's something very exhilarating about sparring with someone that much better than you, if he knows what he's doing and he's got good control. Harris came for me with his karate hand techniques, I knocked him backwards with my feet and he started catching my legs and tipping me over that way. He had blindingly fast hands. So I blitzed him and he got me fair and square with a perfect side kick.

"Jesus," I coughed. "I walked into that one."

"Hm," he said, and came after me again.

By the time we finished, I had at least caused him to sweat a little, though he wasn't breathing noticeably hard. I was dripping and panting and Shaun was cheering both of us on with a satirical running commentary in the style of a cable sports channel. We shook hands and I thanked Harris for a most instructive pasting.

"Hm," said Harris. "We'll have two versions of each fight, one pretty, one realistic. Then Naismith can choose. Ah, would you knife attack overarm, half-speed..."

Thus I became a villain while the two of them worked out what sort of things they could do and built up a vocabulary of fighting sequences. I found it exhausting and sometimes very painful when I landed badly or walked into someone's fist or foot. And fascinating and engrossing and the most fun I'd had outside a bed for years and years.

After one particularly ferocious session when I'd been a villain with a gun and a villain (backing Harris) with a knife and then just a villain creeping up behind, in fact I'd villained for all I was worth, I'd showered and changed and come back down to find Shaun had disappeared to go to a meeting but Harris still lurked in the hotel bar, nursing a pint.

"Ah," he said, which is what he tended to call me. "Fancy a drink?"

I smiled at him, wondering what was up, and said mine was a bitter shandy and could he make it a pint to save time because I was dying of thirst.

He got the drinks and  brought them over to the little table where I'd sat down.

"Cheers," he said as he took a pull and I knocked my pint down in one. "Ah, I hear you're a nurse?"

I told him what I did and he half-interrogated me about it and how I'd got into martial arts and what I thought about them. He was terribly shocked by the story about the patient's husband.

"Thing is," said Harris, finally struggling to the point. "How are you at teaching women and children?"

"Pretty good, I think," I said, fighting the urge to ask what this was all about. "They seem to keep coming back to my classes. Why do you ask?" Some fights you lose.

Harris went and got more beer and sat down, looking very determined.

"Thing is," he snarled. "got a job starting next month. Been worrying me. Big job, movie, some stuntwork and preparing of actors. Thing is: it's a sort of tribe of space explorers, *Lost in Space* crossed with *Star Trek* apparently, and the two gels and four children are supposed to learn some martial arts. Now I have no trouble with male leads, can just about cope with women, but have to say children... Not. No children of my own, you see. Never came up."

"Oh."

"You available next month?"

"Um... I don't know, to be honest." I spoke slowly, thinking about the voice booming in my head that I'd finished with gate-keeping, I'd done that. What else could I do? Well... "I might be."

"Raight," said Harris, deep breath. "If you did happen to be available next month, I wonder if you'd consider working with me on the movie? Preparing actors, actresses, kids, stunts, so forth. Hm?"

I was staggered, despite knowing he was building up to something.

Just for once, I managed not to choke on what I was drinking or blurt that it was nothing really. "That's a tremendous compliment," I said. "Thank you. I'll have to think about it very carefully. It's a bit of a shock really."

"Quaight understand," said Harris. "Can't just drop what you're doing, have to think about it of course. Thing is..." He coughed and looked round shiftily. "You're good. Done a bloody fine job with Graham and don't think I haven't spotted what's going on, because I have, but that's not why. You've got his respect and that's not easy with a bloke like him. Very impressive." He put his business card on the table and stood up. "Got to go now. If you're free September, October on, give me a bell."

And he made a strategic withdrawal or, as the US Army in *M.A.S.H* would call it, a bug-out. I watched him go, shook my head and blinked at the bubbles chasing each other on the top of my shandy. It was a thought. It really was a thought.

I went off to see *Les Miserables*, still shaking my head. I came out still shaking it, but this time in wonder at why the thing had been such a success. Must be the set. Can't be the music, it's only got two tunes.

Next day I went back to work with Harris and Shaun and a new stuntman who was understudying the main villain, a languid Brit actor who did not do any of his own stunts on principle. Harris now addressed me as "Clements" as opposed to "Ah" which I took as the sincerest of compliments and a real promotion.

There was still that curious feeling of suspension, as you often get in August, with half the world on holiday and the other half wishing it was and aliens giving interviews in the *Sunday Sport*.

The script went through its rewrite and numerous script-editing meetings and got worse.

And every night I had mysterious silent calls to my mobile from my home. I talked to Matt and Si who didn't know anything about them. They said that Susie had moved in and had already swapped the sofa and the armchairs around. But the silent calls continued.

# Chapter 29



*To do:  Tkd Tat and Harris, am & pm.*

Then Shaun turned up for a private afternoon session, completely rat-arsed. I told him to piss off and sober up. He fell on my neck and burbled something incoherent at me, so I manhandled him back to the top floor, didn't have a card for his suite and he couldn't find his, nor could I find any entourage when I needed a people badly, and so I took him down again to my room, made him drink a pint of water and dropped him on the bed in the recovery position. There I left him to sober up, left a message for Denise and Harris to tell them what had happened, went out for a walk.

I got back to my room, late afternoon, with a box of chocolates from the nearest Godiva shop, my own drug of choice, and found Shaun watching sport on the TV. He looked at me sidelong as I came in, put the chocs down, washed my hands, sat in an armchair and looked right back at him. He often had wine and a few shorts at lunchtime, but never before had I seen him drunk enough to be incapable in the afternoon.

"Sorry," he said, which was meaningless.

"No, you're not. You knew exactly what you were doing," I said curtly.

"I've got a headache."

"Good."

"Don't I get any..."

"Cossetting? Sympathy? Sorry, mate, wrong woman. I used to find highly talented men who drink too much very sexy but not any more. I've not only done that and got the t-shirt, it's been washed so often the pattern's gone. I'm bored with it."

He pretended to be interested in the cricket. I resisted the impulse to get him paracetamol and water; he wasn't crippled and he had far too many people running round looking after him. And yes, I was clocking the parallels with Jim. Again. Was I obsessing about it? Yes.

"She wants to get married."

It would be silly to ask who. "Just say no." I said, trying not to look sour, and he didn't get the reference which meant he really wasn't concentrating.

"She wants us all to go out to dinner tonight, make an announcement."

"Oh?"

"You too. She's insisting."

I thought that might well be a euphemism for a full blown, foot stomping, carpet beating tantrum.

"Tattoo?" I said. "Why are you so pussy-whipped?"

It was a very masculine thing to say and it shocked him for a moment. Then he gave a sad little laugh.

"Always have been. Why stop now?"

"She will make you miserable. She already bores you. She'll probably help you complete your transformation into a proper drunk. She'll get you into more films that bore the arse off you because you're not using your abilities properly. I hope she's an absolutely fabulous fuck because otherwise it doesn't make sense."

His brow wrinkled as he gave this consideration while his liver busily broke the alcohol into shorter chains, including formaldehyde, and his brain frantically pumped neurotransmitters around to try and even up the mess the stuff was making.

"I used to think she was."

"Uh oh."

"But then I fucked you."

I smiled at him. "What a lovely thing to say," I told him. "Do you think if you butter me up enough I'll fetch you the painkillers and water you're too lazy to move your arse to get?"

Just occasionally, his blue eyes gave me the same electric charge as they had the first time I got him to give me a hard look. Even bloodshot in a puffy face.

"I mean it. Will you marry me, Anna?"

"Certainly not. One, I'm still theoretically married to Jim. Two, you are supposed to be getting engaged to Nadia Shan Sen who's far more suitable. Three, as the old lady said, you only push a pea up your nose once."

"Eh?"

"One of my patients. When I asked her why she hadn't got married again when her husband died, she said, oh well, you only push a pea up your nose once."

His eyelids crinkled with puzzlement. Brain too busy with the neurotransmitters probably. As I still wasn't moving bathroomwards, despite how pitiful he was, he heaved himself up, staggered gently to get the pills and water and came back.

"Drink four glasses of water," I said bossily.

"No. I won't," said Tattoo. "Pea? Nose? Is this some sexual kink or other?"

"She meant it's easier to get married than get out of it; easier to push the pea up, than get it out again. Metyfor."

Forehead cleared. He was smiling again.

"Come to dinner. Please."

"No, I don't want to, really."

"It won't be like last time. No Bud Anderson, Denise will be there and Jimmy Kieran." Jimmy Kieran is gorgeous, allegedly charming and firmly gay as men like that often are, alas. He hadn't had a big blockbuster hit for some years but was probably too rich to care.

"No," I told Shaun.

It wasn't exactly disenchantment. It was that thing over whether he was Shaun or Tattoo. Training he was still Tattoo –

focussed, hard-working, getting quite dangerous now. Drunk he was Shaun and drunk he reminded me so much of Jim without the depression. And Shaun was still shagging someone who wasn't me and I… All right. I fucking hated it. So maybe the holiday was over and it was time to get back to reality.

"I still feel I owe you a meal."

"Don't be daft."

"It's not just Nadia. I want you to come."

"Look…"

"Please, please, don't leave me alone with her."

"I can't come. What can I possibly wear?"

"Is *that* the problem? Right." He hauled out his mobile.

Ten minutes later, Denise was vibrating at the door. She had some kind of company credit card and Shaun told her where we were planning to go for dinner, waving down my feeble protests. We had about an hour and a half before the shops closed.

Do you know what I feel when I go shopping for clothes with someone holding a functionally unlimited budget? Miserable. It is a fact never believed by the more normally endowed majority of women who lerve to shop that when you have big breasts nothing fashionable ever fits or looks right on you. Nothing. Sure, you might see something you'd like to wear but you know that 99 times out of a hundred it will never ever fit you. Entire swathes of outfit-types, entire brand names are simply closed to you. The one in a hundred times you do find something that fits, they'll only have it in a fetching combination of ochre and purple which makes you look as if you're in the terminal stages of hepatitis. And in every shop you enter and ask if they've got anything your size, the sneer on the face of the stick insect you're talking to makes you either want to go and hide in a hole and howl, or hit them right in the middle of their pert little mass-produced nose.

Chippy? *Moi?* Why would I be chippy?

By this time, Denise and I were getting on quite well as fellow members of the Shaun Graham entourage, almost friends. She was in a blue suit today. I'd counted and I was sure she had seven, colour-coded. Or maybe 14 so one lot could be dry-cleaned while she wore the other lot. I don't know how chic people do these things.

I glowered at her as she trotted out the back door, looking as if she actually liked this part of her job. From being able to deal with Tattoo as an adult, I instantly reverted to a sulky mishapen teenager, getting dragged around the boutiques by my mother. Evolution in reverse is an ugly sight.

We trotted past those ineffably cool shops with blonde floors and hardly any visible clothes, where the stick insects stand on guard to repel barrels. Denise paused, looked at me.

"Where do you usually shop?" she asked.

"Evans," I said, naming the shame.

Her brow wrinkled. I don't think she'd actually heard of it. Larger sizes, you know.

"Is there anything you like?"

"No," I growled. "I hate all of these places."

"You *don't* like shopping?"

"Hate it, loathe it, despise it, want to be sick," I said. Well, I didn't, actually, I'm happy to relate, what I really said was "No." That's just what I wanted to say.

Her face looked so like my mother's when I used to say the same to her that it made me want to laugh. It was the... the puzzlement. The face of a chocolate-eater when they meet someone who hates the stuff.

"We can get you anything, you know," she said. "Shaun's very generous, he's given me a good budget. He said he felt bad because he hasn't done this before."

I felt like crying because really this was completely wasted on me. Talk about feeding strawberries to pigs, silk purse, sows ear, pearls before swine... All piggy metaphors, you note. I am the original pig in the story.

"What's wrong, Anna?"

"Look, Denise, this isn't going to work. You can't get me anything, because most of it won't fit and there isn't time to have something made. There's no point trying any of this stuff on..." with one arm I dismissed all of the blonde clothes-less clothes shops "... because none of it will fit. Short of breast surgery and a corset, it never will. Let's just get a kaftan or something and go and have a coffee instead."

Her mouth was open, teeth fastening on the side of her cherry lips again and she shut it. I admired the way she could get her streaked honey blonde hair up into a pleat and make it stay there, and the way she could wear these lovely sharp suits and look feminine in them. Because in order to look feminine in suits like that, even pink ones, you have to be very small and petite. And she never ever got coffee on herself or ripped anything.

"Kaftan?" she repeated. "Oh I don't think so."

"I don't want to go, I feel ill. This is dumb. I'm a personal trainer, not a bloody film star."

She was thinking, head on one side. "Who wants you there, Shaun or Nadia?"

"I gather, Nadia. And Shaun."

She frowned. "Hmm. No choice then."

Out popped the mobile, prod, prod.

"Hermione," she said. "I've got an emergency for you."

Still a mishapen sulky teenager, I was inveigled into a cab and we went to a place so frighteningly expensive that I'm afraid even to mention the name. If Al-Fayed could have bought it, he would.

We were met by the doorman, whisked upstairs to a private area. You've seen the shopping scene in *Pretty Woman*, where they go to the really nice place and everybody cossets her and looks after her and she has a lovely time. It was a bit like that, only for me Denise played Richard Gere (very well, I thought) and we met Hermione.

Hermione is a personal shopper, but when I saw her, I knew why Denise had the job she did. She was almost the same shape as me, with the balcony - just fifteen years older and very much better dressed. Less aerobically fit, though I says it myself.

Her eyes narrowed as she saw me and then she smiled.

"Denise," she said. "How lovely of you to bring her to me."

Denise looked smug. I struggled to expunge the sulky mishapen teenager.

"Ms Clements," she said softly, coming close and smiling. It was quite a tucked in, mischeivous smile. "I know exactly what you're thinking. You're thinking the whole thing is totally hopeless, nothing will ever fit and why are we wasting our time?"

The piggy they wanted to designer dress grunted. Then I pulled myself together a bit and said politely, "I'm sure it'll be OK."

"I love my job, Ms Clements, and I particularly love it when I can get to work on someone like you."

"A challenge?"

She gave me what you could only call an old-fashioned look.

"Any fool can make someone like Nadia Shan Sen look beautiful because she is beautiful. She can wear a sack and make the sack look as if it cost £20,000. It takes skill to make someone who isn't conventionally beautiful look as good as they probably do naked."

I blinked.

"In fact you probably look a lot better when you're naked because I'm sure you have far fewer scars to hide than... many people."

I had to smile. Well, we all like a little bit of a bitch, don't we?

"So, Ms Clements, bear with me while I use my skills. Walk over there."

I walked over there, trying not to see myself in the mirrors by unfocussing my eyes.

"Walk back."

I did.

"Jog on the spot."

I raised my eyebrows and did.

"You're the martial artist, aren't you?"

I smiled. "Yes."

"Thought so. You carry yourself well and you move well. Also, you have a decent bra. Rigby & Peller?"

I nodded. A magazine article had sent me through their hallowed portals many years before and I'd never bought a bra anywhere else since.

"Excellent. Normally, with a client of your shape I start with the foundations but we can skip that. Now then."

She cross-examined Denise over where we were going while she measured me in a dozen different places, in centimetres. She cross-examined me on what I normally wore and it was so long since I'd actually had any reason to dress up that I had to dredge up memories of what I'd worn in my student nurse days when I'd been equally top-heavy but had less of a gut.

Mind you, training with Tattoo every day was doing wonders for my tum – which had been a bit flabby thanks to two kids and too much sitting in a car. The grandmother who'd died marble-less at 100 had told me when I was little that we were good peasant stock, bred to work in the fields for 12 hours a day, and we needed to move around as much as possible. My mother shushed her in horror but she was right.

Hermione spent ten minutes talking on the phone to her minions and then she offered me coffee and we chatted about the trials and tribulations of being completely the wrong shape for the fashion industry until said minions brought in what she'd asked for.

Gentle reader, if you can afford it, get yourself a personal shopper. Everything they brought either fitted or (cunning touch) was too big. Everything looked at least plausible on me. There was a red thing that Hermione gently talked me out of and we settled (sorry, she settled) on a classic black washed-silk trouser suit which was so ineffably well-cut that it made me drop another ten pounds instantly and cost such earth-shattering amounts that Denise refused point-blank to let me hear how much. Under the jacket went a sort of subtle black top with glittery bits and cunning little boned bits. I looked in the mirror and for the first time since ugliness descended in my teens, I saw someone who looked almost good. Hermione smiled with satisfaction so maybe she saw something I didn't.

"There," she said. "You see what's possible?"

Then she got me shoes and a little bag and then I was quietly hustled downstairs for a blindingly fast wash and cut in the salon. I stammered what Pam had said about a blunt cut for my hair and they did something skilfully simple that looked amazing, even to me. Then a girl made me up. It was the fairy god-mother effect again only without Pam shouting at me.

And then I was hustled, with my clothes tissue-wrapped in a loudly understated carrier bag with little strings, not handles, down to the street and out into a waiting taxi. Hotel, quick pit wash, careful not to damage hair, clothes on, I might damage them by sweating, deodorant, clothes back on, ohgodohgod what do I do now? Daren't eat any chocolate, might get sticky.

I grabbed a little bottle of vodka out of the untouched minibar and glugged half of it down, choked, nearly upchucked, managed to find tissues, ohgodohgod mascara! Caught the choke before it sullied the Clothes, got myself breathing again. When will I bloody learn to drink in a ladylike fashion? Sipped the vodka this time.

For all its faults, alcohol is a very good drug for panic. Denise arrived, immaculate and very subfusc. It was not her job to be glamorous and so she wasn't. Her colour was a bit better and I hoped she was easing up on her diet. I didn't mention it though. I do at least try not to boss people around all the time, even if I don't succeed.

The car took us to a restaurant so very chic it had no entrance. Well it did, sort of, but you had to know where it was. Upstairs there was an enormous space which included stained glass and wood but also the emptiness that says modern, up to the minute. No doubt eventually, chintz and clutter will come back in and that will date me. But no, I don't think so. When very few people had things, clutter was chic. Now everybody has things, it's much more chic to be empty - viz. the clothes-less clothes shops.

At the lift I screeched to a halt. I hadn't felt so sick with fright since I took my black belt examination. I was sure I was sweating into the Clothes and my stomach felt like a concrete mixer and...

Denise put her hand on my arm. "OK?"

"No, I'm very far from OK," I muttered, quoting wildly. "Look, I can't do this, I'm a provincial nurse who thinks a takeaway chinese is cool. This is just not me."

Denise turned to me, quite seriously. "Nobody is forcing you."

On the other hand, there was the matter of Face. The Chinese have a word for it, the English language doesn't. That doesn't mean it isn't important - it's just one of those things so important to us that we daren't mention it. We think the Orientals are rather unsubtle for doing so, in fact. Jim had explained it all to me one evening, and it certainly made a few things clear about hospital consultants.

Also does Hardass Martial Artist turn and run from a restaurant because she's frightened? Don't think so.

"All right," I said, still gulping. "Tell me how you do it."

Denise smiled. "OK. What I do is, I imagine the one I'm most scared of, sitting on the toilet. Because whoever it is, he still has to do that."

Brilliant, of course. I should have known that, being a nurse. And I was sure that Nadia would be very dainty about it too. Perhaps she'd be like my mother, rustling the loopaper so you couldn't hear the sounds.

"Secondly, you have to act the part of someone who feels comfortable in these situations. Nobody really is, not to start with."

I looked at her properly. "Yes, I see." If she knew all this, why did she vibrate with tension all the time?

It was essentially what Tattoo/Shaun had told me to do at the roundabout when I was panicking before. It was also what darling Zach, the black belt who trained me, had told me. And there had been countless times (stitching first wound, delivering first baby) when in the absence of actually knowing what to do, I'd simply acted the part of a competent nurse. In fact, everyone does it, don't they? No wonder we're fascinated by actors and acting.

OK, put on Hardass Martial Artist, mark II, restaurants, for use in. It did feel better. The Clothes were helping too. I smiled back at Denise. "Thank you so much. You've really..."

"Shh," she said, and let me go first.

# Chapter 30

Well, Hardass Martial Artist stalked across the floor to the small group at the table by the smoked window, followed by Denise, and Hardass Martial Artist was greeted by Shaun Graham and James Kieran who both looked fabulous despite being slobbily dressed in suits and casually open-necked shirts - my mum would have reared back her neck in horror at it, especially when, as she would certainly sepulchrally have said, they could afford ties.

The suits and open-necked shirts were very expensive, of course. Armani or something. And they politely stood up for us and Shaun… Tattoo gave me one of those leisurely up-and-down I'm-undressing-you-mentally looks. Then he smiled, slow and sexy and just for me.

Denise joined us and so did another suited person who turned out to be Clive, Shaun's new agent. Suit and t-shirt, the new uniform. And everybody was acting away like mad, even Shaun who had been comfortably at home tucking into the Truckers' Big Blow-Out All Day Breakfast, but here looked subtly fake.

At centre stage of the round table sat Nadia Shan Sen, perfect and doll-like, in crimson taffeta, as haute as couture could be, very skillfully slashed and frayed in interesting and subtle places, very much at home. She tilted her head and smiled at me so sweetly I could have gagged.

"Oh Anna," she cooed. "You needn't have worried. You look wonderful."

And suddenly, I knew I did. Shaun had told me with that satisfied smile, god knows Pam had told me and so had Hermione and maybe they weren't just being kind, maybe it was even true.

The best moment for me in a competition comes after we've done our bows to the judges and each other, and I face my opponent and look at her. There's a kind of settling inside you, a moment of complete focus when everything else disappears, your marriage, your depressed husband, your louts, your dying patients, everything. It doesn't really matter whether you win or lose, that moment is what you do it for. Or I do.

Focus. "Thank you," I cooed back. "But really, you should praise Denise who got me sorted out. And of course, Shaun, who paid for it."

And I smiled at him and gave him full-contact Hard Look jirugi because I had the feeling he might have been easier to persuade about this whole thing than he'd given out, that we were there to entertain him. Again.

"Where's the mud, Shaun?" I asked him quietly, a few minutes later when Nadia was being helpless about the enormous menu with no prices marked on it and James Kieran was helping her. I caught him while he was drinking his vodka & orange and I'm delighted to say it went down the wrong way.

I looked at the menu which was some kind of stupendously fusionish psycho-Pacific cuisine. Personally, I suspect they put lists of every kind of edible thing into a computer and randomise them. Were wichity grubs on it? Not sure.

I closed it, smiled at Denise. "I'll have what you're having," I said. "Hope there's lots of it."

She looked scared and then smiled back."I'm not sure," she said. "What do you think about prawn toast and seaweed?"

Believe me, there were no such things on that menu which would have curled up and faded for shame at the thought.

"Oh yeah," I said. "And sweet'n'sour pork and beef in black bean sauce..."

We giggled like schoolgirls. Nadia's pale eyes were upon us, not sure what we were laughing at, only when Shaun laughed, she did too. I felt sorry for her again, until she started her complicated menu game about what she was going to eat and how this would be too much and that would be too red meat and the other would be starch at the wrong time.

Finally we got the ordering done, James Kieran chose the wine after an argument over Aussie vinyards and Clive the Agent began a movie-star gossip conversation which my mother would have happily handed over several teeth and an arm to listen to - what an awful thought. I decided Hardass Martial Artists probably stay mysteriously silent especially when they have absolutely nothing to contribute to talk about why Kate thingummy likes being tied up and how John somebody-else-stellar is seriously into feet, the smellier the better.

Nadia could talk about this sort of thing till the cows came home (though only shampooed and ribboned cows, with groomed tails and strategic corks) and she certainly did while she picked over the gloriously strange grub. Denise and I ate heartily, me because I always do (unless I've loaded up on pizza earlier) and her because I suspected that, if only for this evening, she had rediscovered the delights of food. Nadia had heard rumours that an impossibly big-name star was going bust and while she pretended discretion and James Kieran tried to winkle more out of her, Shaun listened with his head cocked on one side and a most peculiar expression on his face.

Clive asked me if I'd ever thought of getting representation to find more personal training work and when I told him I knew about agents but I didn't realise they did that sort of thing, he gave me a standard selling line about what he and his company could do for me. I was surprised, but Shaun put in that Harris had taken to me, and since Harris hated everybody, especially women, this was considered a miracle.

"Harris asked me if I'd like to work with him on another movie," I said idly.

"He *what?*" Shaun put his knife and fork down. "Why didn't you tell me?"

I shrugged. "I'm still thinking about it."

"Do you have any idea how unheard of that is?"

"No," I told him. Clive put his card in my hand and murmured that he'd definitely be in touch. "I suppose I am a good teacher," I said complacently. "It's because I'm physically inept."

"I'm sorry," Denise asked. "What did you just say?"

"I am. I'm not as bad as I used to be, but I've never learnt any physical move the way Shaun does by watching it, copying it and remembering it. I have to take it apart and put it back together again and practise it over and over before I can get it right and so when it comes to teaching, I know exactly how it's constructed. Somebody who's really got talent picks it all up so easily and naturally he can't understand how anyone finds it difficult."

"That's Harris," put in James Kieran. "You can see him boiling inside when you don't get what he's on about immediately."

"He's very good though," said Shaun. "I watched him years ago working with Bud Anderson."

James laughed. "How did they get on?"

"Harris took one look at Bud, challenged him to a boxing match, and beat him. After which Bud was a pussycat."

I was busy unwrapping a little parcel with a mysterious prawn in it and so I didn't get the full benefit of the way Shaun said this.

"Was that the wilderness adventure where he was a wise injun scout?" I asked idly.

"That's right."

Nadia's brow wrinkled. She'd hidden her prawn under a fork and had just eaten the little sliver of lime peel that had tied up the parcel.

"I didn't know you were in that movie?"

Shaun smiled gently at her. "I wasn't in it. I was working on it. I was one of the peons holding horses and scooping up cattle shit and catching escaped rattlesnakes."

"Oh." Pause for thought. "Bud never said anything..."

"He doesn't know. He's never recognised me from it. Even though I lost most of my wages to him at poker."

"Oh."

"So you did tell the truth about that," I said. "That your job was to stop horses peeing on camera."

"Certainly. Very difficult and technical work, believe me."

"When did you tell her that?" asked Nadia.

"I was cross-examining him about what he did and he said he worked in films and that he was a...grip and a wrangler."

"And I was a very good one until I decided I wanted to bust through the wall to where the real money was and went and learned acting."

"He also told me that he'd worked with this guy Shaun Graham and the man was a big-headed arsehole."

Everybody laughed, except Nadia.

"Why were you cross-examining him?" asked Nadia, nibbling on a sliver of pickled ginger.

"He wanted to join my class and I didn't like the look of him, what with the all-over shave and the horrible swirly face, and he was trying to convince me he wasn't a drug-dealer or a football hooligan or a skinhead."

Another laugh and I drank some more.

"I wish I could understand why you would do all that, Shaun," said Nadia. "Making yourself ugly."

"I told you, darling, I wanted a holiday."

"Mmm. We could have gone to Mauritius, remember?"

"You were busy in Paris."

"You could have come."

"So I could."

"And why South Cornwall? Who goes there?" She lifted her long delicate hands helplessly.

Little cubes made of mysterious jelly arrived which Nadia refused to have anything to do with.

"Were you visiting someone?" she asked Shaun who was speculating wildly with Jimmy about what the jelly might be made of.

"No," he lied. "I threw a dart at the map."

Right there and then I could understand some of Nadia's suspicion because Shaun was such a good liar. Of course he was, it was his job. But it's unsettling to know that the man can fool you so easily. Generally it's supposed to be the other way round.

Nadia caught sight of Denise laughing at one of Clive the Agent's jokes as she noshed down a jelly square, and her delicate face suddenly became pointed.

"Well, Denise, how is the nutrition program going?"

Denise looked round and sort of closed in on herself.

"I've stopped. It wasn't agreeing with me."

"Oh dear. It's supposed to be very effective if you follow it properly."

"Well I did and I nearly fainted, so I tapered off."

"Just because you fainted?" said Nadia severely. "You only have to go and lie down for a bit."

Which is perfectly fine if you have time to do that and I could see Denise thinking so, but not daring to say so.

Shaun and James rather blatantly started up a conversation about football which successfully put us down. There was sorbet next, I think it was mint or perhaps basil. I don't know. Gorgeous anyway. Nadia didn't touch hers. Poor love, I thought, is today a fasting day?

More showbiz gossip happened between Nadia and Clive. I listened while I packed away the next course, which she skipped. Next course and she came back to me, nibbling with her tiny pearl-like teeth at the words.

"So you're really a nurse."

"Yes. Martial arts is my hobby."

"Do you really have a black belt?"

Are you calling me a liar, lady?

"Yes she does," said Denise. "Second dan. We checked very carefully. She's won some tournaments as well."

Nadia gave her a beautifully modulated, 'who asked you, peon?' look. "Some?"

"A few. I'm a better teacher than I am a competitor."

"And where do you nurse?"

"South Cornwall."

"No, I meant which hospital."

"Terminal care, in the community."

Shaun's blue glare cracked past Denise and into me and I realised I'd got a little careless. But while I could be discreet, I wasn't going to lie for him.

"Oh. What does that mean?"

"I nurse people who are going to die soon."

Clive had his head cocked, listening. James Kieran was listening too. He hadn't paid me much attention, but he reminded me so much of darling Phil all those years ago that I didn't mind. I was starting to enjoy myself. Was this increasing confidence or just very nice wine? Was I starting to burble? Possibly, I didn't care.

"Oh. But aren't they in hospital?"

Just the very question my mother had asked in precisely the same tone of voice. The unspoken end to the sentence was "where they'd be tidier."

"No need. The doctors aren't going to cure them, all they need is nursing and TLC and if the family situation is right, it's far better for them to die at home where it's familiar rather than alone in hospital. Better for the hospitals too, since they don't tie the beds up which could be used to cure somebody curable."

"I see. Do you like it?"

I gave this question careful thought. "I do, mostly. Of course it's very stressful sometimes and that's why I've needed a break."

"Working me like a dog," put in Shaun.

"But what's the point of it?" asked Nadia. "If they're going to die, why not let them die?"

She had no idea how outrageous the question was. James Kieran shut his eyes for a moment and I suddenly knew he was trying not to strangle her, remembering his lover who died of AIDS before the AZT cocktail therapy came in.

"Well, in a way I suppose that is what we do..." I began slowly, wondering how to get through the monumental self-absorption, the total lack of empathy that could let someone ask such a thing.

"Hey honey," said Shaun brightly, in the manner of a breakfast cereal advert. "You know it wouldn't be nice to have people dying in agony, screaming with pain, stinking in their own wastes. Would it? So somebody has to look after them."

She knew she'd been slapped in the face, metaphorically speaking, I'm not sure she knew why. James Kieran coughed into his chest. Shaun and Nadia glared at each other.

"That's not what I meant," Nadia said, speaking very precisely. "Of course they should be made comfortable. But why not offer them... er... a way out."

"You mean euthanasia," said Shaun. His glare had turned to an intent, quite neutral gaze, examining her as if she were a new species.

"Yes, euthanasia. I saw a TV program about it once. It seems very sensible."

Shaun put his hand gently on hers. "What if they don't want to go, darling?"

"Hm?"

"What if they know they're dying but they don't want to die, no matter how bad it gets, they want to live as long as they possibly can. What about that?"

James Kieran was staring at Shaun as if at someone completely new. Nadia avoided Shaun's eyes, a tiny stain of pink on her smooth cheeks. "Well, really, I suppose there'd be some like that who wouldn't see sense, but most of them would want to... Well, they'd want a way out, the sensible ones, they'd want a decent quality of life. Why tolerate the intolerable? Surely you agree, Anna?"

Stop digging, I thought and then unworthily, no, keep on digging you ugly-minded little doll.

"Considering what people go through, I'm always astonished at how few of them even ask." I said gravely.

"Perhaps they're embarrassed..."

Shaun laughed. "What, when you've just put a suppositary up them? I doubt it, sweetie."

"Shall we talk about something else? More pleasant?"

"No, let's not. Let's talk about you. How about if you had a terminal illness?"

"I very much hope I never get one." said Nadia firmly.

"But you will, Nadia," said Shaun softly, eyes burning blue. "Everyone does. If they don't top themselves or crash a car or something."

James Kieran moved suddenly and then stopped still. Clive was staring: I could almost see the gossip machine whirling full of speculation. Denise was looking at me thoughtfully for some reason.

Nadia suddenly reached out and finished her wine, slowly nibbled a little bit of mysterious vegetable matter off a stick. "I don't understand. Why are we talking about horrible things? I thought this would be a fun evening and we're all serious and gloomy."

"OK, maybe not you. What if someone you loved had a terminal illness, what would you do?"

Astonishingly Nadia's eyes glittered immediately with tears. "Oh my God." she whispered. "Shaun, you don't... you're not..."

"No, I haven't got anything wrong with me," said Shaun impatiently. "I'm speaking hypothetically. Just try and imagine it. What would you do?"

Magically the crystal tears disappeared without causing any kind of snot fountain. I decided that someone who could do that couldn't really be human.

"You frightened me. I thought that might be why you'd gone off like..."

"Well it wasn't. What would you do?"

Delicate hands to delicate face, a perfect picture of the Woman Facing Her Loved One's Potential Demise.

"I would be terribly upset, terribly."

"I'm not interested in how you'd play the part. I want to know what you would do?"

Shrug of red-taffata'd shoulders. "I don't know. Who knows? I don't like to think of it. So undignified, ugly, messy... I would have to consider my position very carefully."

Shaun smiled cynically as if he had at last got the answer to something which had been puzzling him. "Thank you for your honesty." he said, with grave courtesy, and she seemed frightened by it.

"Well, I would stick by you, darling." she said. "Of course I would. But I might have to put my career on hold for a bit, that kind of thing." She sipped the miso soup which had appeared and then she drained it, picked out the bits of tofu with a spoon.

"The worms crawl in, the worms crawl out,

The worms play pinochle on your snout."

That was James Kieran. Everyone looked at him and he shrugged wrily. "Andy used to sing it in the shower," he said helplessly. "It just came to me."

"Ugh," said Nadia, putting her spoon down.

There was a toffee-textured silence. Shaun was looking at Nadia with a kind of pitying distaste, while she applied herself again to eating the glorious concoction in front of her.

I broke first and started burbling about how sometimes you did get miracles, like that Demelza Perkins who everyone thought had some mysterious metabolic disease but it turned out she was just bulimic, or Mrs Wendron who had leukaemia and went to a faith healer and got better and...

Clive took up the gambit and started on about how it was a pity Chris died because the new computerised neural reconnections were looking very promising... Nadia told a quietly bitchy story about one of the *Superman* movies and Shaun laughed at it and poured her some more wine and she began to explain how radical and exciting some of the outfits she'd seen in Paris were.

But I knew she was very upset because suddenly her plate was clean. And the next course came and that plate was clean too.

James Kieran asked quietly if I'd ever nursed anyone with AIDS and I told him about Phil and the various others, two of whom had been family men, never out of the closet in all their little South Cornish lives, who'd caught it off a rent boy on a London business trip. One wife still had no idea what had killed her husband because he'd gone so quickly.

James was knowledgeable and obviously still bereft, so many years after the death. I found myself on the receiving end of some things he'd probably wish he hadn't told me in public, but it was all right because Nadia was ignoring me in favour of Clive and the occasional little dig at Denise.

Shaun wasn't saying very much, and he was still giving me the blue-eyed stare, quite considering, which made me uncomfortable.

"But listen," I said after James came back to the same point for the third time. "It doesn't make sense because it doesn't make sense. Of course it was a terrible injustice for your partner to die when all these scumbags are still alive. What makes you think there's justice in the world? Evidence?"

He's an intelligent man, and he started to answer, then stopped and thought. "Well, *I* deserve what I've got," he said candidly and I laughed at him.

To be honest, it's around that point that the whole thing starts getting misty thanks to wine. I was enjoying myself, much to my surprise, mainly because James was lovely company and so was Shaun when he roused out of his thoughts enough to join in. Nadia cleared plate after plate and then had ice cream for pudding and I knew exactly what she was up to. I was too full for pudding, which was very sad indeed. I managed only half of it, which was a small miracle of greed, but how could you turn down chocolate and almond praline mousse and spun sugar? No, me neither.

And then, just before the coffees and little clever biscuity things arrived, she got up and went off to the Ladies, carrying her bag.

I needed to go too but I thought I'd let her vomit in peace. She spent a while in there, so it must have been a hard session.

"Why's she taking so long?" Shaun asked me, looking worried.

"She has to brush her teeth." I said.

"Oh."

Nadia came back, make-up retouched, with that faintly spacey, quite complacent look they usually have, sat down and drank her coffee. She didn't have any of the biscuity things. No, I don't think it was coke, her eyes didn't look like that. There were little spot haemorrhages under the skin which she'd covered up and her salivary glands were swollen. Unmistakeable.

"Are you all right?" I asked her after a while, because she was whiter than ever. She looked at me quite blankly and I got the smell of wetwipes and peppermint.

"Of course I am." But she wasn't, she looked sweaty and sick and she gripped the table as if she thought it might fly away. Deliberately making yourself puke after a big meal plays merry hell with your electrolytes, especially if you've been starving yourself. I reached over and felt her pulse which was thin and fast. Her wrist was like a bird's, the skin a little papery. The silly woman was probably dehydrated as well.

I snaffled a waiter, told him to bring half a banana, a piece of cheese and a large glass of mineral water for Ms Shan Sen.

She knew as well as I did what foods replace the electrolytes - banana for potassium and a few slow-release sugars to soak up the insulin, cheese for the sodium and calcium. Water for the dehydration. "I'm a nurse, Ms Shan Sen," I said very quietly. "You'll feel better for it. You don't want to pass out or have a heart attack, do you?"

She glared. I glugged the rest of my wine, got up and went to the loo myself so she wouldn't feel I was watching her. There were goldfish in the transparent cisterns. Not real ones, of course. The smell was just noticeable if you were looking for it. Such a waste of food-art. Poor little doll.

When I came back the banana and cheese had come and gone and Shaun was proposing a club, James was seconding him and Nadia was insisting, not surprisingly, that she was too exhausted and had to go to bed. Mr Agent wasn't sure because he was pretty tired and jetlagged. Denise quite fancied the idea of a club, and by this time I was thoroughly drunk and wanted to dance with Tattoo again no matter how mad it was.

Nadia Shan Sen is one of those women who become quite luminescent with rage. It had been building up all through the evening and now Shaun had not only failed to announce what she had confidently expected him to announce, he was actually going to carry on enjoying himself whether she wanted to or not. I thought he had been cruel to her: expecting someone like her to think intelligently about death was a bit like wanting philosophy from a butterfly. Very few people nowadays think intelligently about death; the world doesn't encourage it and as Nadia had pointed out, it's a gloomy subject.

She stood, glowing with fury, quite ethereally beautiful, said a frosty goodbye to everyone and told the maitre d' to ask her car to come round. Shaun went with her as she titupped across the blonde floor, leaning over her, talking quietly, persuasively, trying to get her to come too. She hissed something at him, looking feral, and slapped him very hard across the face, twice.

Everybody stopped in mid-sentence to watch. Shaun folded his arms.

"Darling," he growled. "Can we behave?"

Undeniably patronising, especially when it was his fault she was upset. "I wouldn't marry you if you were the last man in the world," snapped Nadia.

Shaun smiled. "Who said anything about marriage? Not me."

She reached up and hit him again, this time with her nails curved and left three red lines across his cheek.

I half-stood, drunkenly prepared to come to his rescue, but Denise put her hand on my arm and I sat down quickly. Not quickly enough. Both James and Clive the Agent looked at me in astonishment and then James grinned.

Nadia was flouncing away unsteadily, maitre d' and waiters flocking round her. Shaun took a deep breath, came back to the table and sat down. Denise produced a handbag mirror and tissue and he went off to the gents to deal with the blood and stop shaking. He'd probably done worse cuts to himself when he was learning to shave as a teenager, but nobody likes being slapped around.

"It's for the best, you know," said James to me, knowingly. "I'm amazed it lasted this long."

I looked as blank as I could. He tutted at me. Clive stared frankly.

Hardass Martial Artist was mysteriously silent. There's a lot to be said for mysteriously silent. Makes it easier to hide how drunk you are, for a start.

Shaun came back, sat down. Everybody looked at him nervously and he grinned straight at me, looking devastatingly sexy even with the claw marks on his cheek. Especially.

"Hey Anna, you want to dance?"

Clive had a breakfast meeting, he made his excuses and left.

So we went out on the town and it was great.

The Spanish have a saying: take what you want and pay for it, says God. Replace God with the universe and that sums up what seems to happen. Not that there's justice, of course, justice is a human invention. But you never ever get something for nothing. Quite a lot of the time you get nothing for something. But never something for nothing.

Do you think I regret going dancing with Shaun and James and Denise? No. Not a single second of it. I had a whale of a time, despite the music only being familiar to me because of my sons. I wasn't properly dressed in my ultra conservative suit, until I took off the jacket and revealed the clever glittery little top - and somehow that was perfect. Denise turned out to have a strappy camisole under her conservatism. She had a stick with ultraviolet glitter in her bag which we put on in the Ladies like teenagers supposedly going to a church youth club. Since I didn't care who laughed at me, I could bop without restraint. And Shaun... Tattoo... he's such a great dancer... Our bodies knew each other so well, not just from the sex but from the training as well: we had that wonderful thing where you move perfectly together without having to think about it.

At some time in the evening, I nipped out the back of wherever we were for a fag and a cool-down and found Tattoo already there, carcinogens glowing away. Yes, there was a VIP lounge, but he hadn't been in it and I'd felt intimidated by the people already there.

I leaned against the wall that vibrated gently, ears ringing, smoked and looked at him, thinking, why is he so sexy? Since he could, as they put it, "open" a movie all by himself, I obviously wasn't the only one who thought so and perfectly straight men liked him too. So what was it? Not pheromones, because although the air in the alley was laden with them, they hardly help you on the cinema screen. Nor blue eyes. Plenty of men have blue eyes. Analyse it, take him apart, nothing there: big - so's Mike Tyson; fit – not much gut left; self-confident - considering how ruled he was by women, bit of a question mark there. Charming? Oh yes. That smile? Maybe.

"Anna," he said. The voice. Must be the voice.

"Mm."

"Thanks for coming."

I didn't know what to say. This is what makes cigarettes so good. You can be completely tongue-tied, but if you smoke instead of speaking, you look mysterious instead of klutz-like.

It was extremely dark, real mugger's paradise, somebody must have broken the streetlight just a little way down. Tattoo was a big shadow against only slightly lighter shadow.

"Do you know something?" he said conversationally.

"What?"

"I think I'm in love with you."

Was it the voice? He said it in such a surprised, considering way, as if he'd been standing there wondering what was wrong with him and this had been the only hypothesis that fit all the facts.

"Jesus," I said. Possibly I would have greeted the announcement he actually had a life-threatening illness more gracefully. No, definitely. That I could cope with. This...

"Jesus?" There was a smile in his voice.

"I...I... but..."

"It's not just that I want to fuck you every time I see you. That's not unusual."

I grinned to myself, drunk enough to find the alcohol-fuelled truth funny.

"Plenty of women do that to you, right?"

"Yeah, they do." He was quite serious, carefully doing what everyone finds so difficult, especially men, pulling up his feelings and looking at them and trying to name them precisely. Desperately difficult. I'm not very good at it myself. "I really love women."

"Uhuh." Nothing else you could say really. The darkness helped because we didn't have to look at each other. More like a phone conversation.

"But... you... And it's not just your tits and… stuff… you know? It's… I feel weird and out of sorts when I'm not near you. Everything's even more boring than usual. Nothing seems real or important. Then the world lights up again when you arrive."

He stubbed out his fag, found his pack, started to light another one. Whatever will we do to fill awkward pauses in conversations like this when smoking becomes illegal?

"It's bad," he said, carcinogens on track down his throat again "It's really bad. I can't concentrate, can't think."

Go on, admit it. You'd love to have somebody like Shaun Graham say something like that to you, wouldn't you? (Or Julia Roberts? I've seen *Notting Hill* too, you know. I liked the first half hour very much. Don't remember the rest.) But then when the actual etc actually does say it...

Thing is, not to forget to breathe. Very important. Fire needs fuel and air. So does respiration. Fact.

I concentrated on breathing that nice addictive cocktail of carbon monoxide, smoke particles, nicotine, tar and a few other jollies. What the hell could I say? He was waiting for me to say it, too, quite patiently.

"The thing is," I said slowly, not helped by the alcohol on account of I needed the judgement I hadn't got, "if you were just Tattoo the biker, I could... I could get my head round it. But you're not. And... seeing Nadia Shan Sen I wonder how much... how much it's due to me being just normal. Ordinary. Like I said. No..." What was the word? Brain tissues too fuddled to pull it out of the memory banks.

"Ambition," he put in for me and laughed. "Ambition should be made of sterner stuff." It was a quote, couldn't think where from.

"I dunno," I said, stomping the fag. "I dunno. I can't even think what to call you... Tattoo? Shaun? I dunno. Can't work it out."

He put his fag down carefully on the top of a wheelie bin, reached out for me, pulled me close, put his arms round me in the sort of hug that makes even cynical old bags like me feel briefly safe, protected, and kissed my nose and then my mouth, very lightly.

"'S mad isn't it?" he said, smelling of booze and reasonably clean sweat, which I think is a real turn on. "You work your butt off to make it, at least partly so you can fuck the most beautiful women in the world and then when you do, they bore you, and it turns out that the one everybody says is the most beautiful of them all is a psychopathic bitch. And the one I really want, the one who gives me a hard-on every time I even think of you… she's put off by what I've become. Hilarious."

"Oh Tattoo," I said, sadly. "If it was just fucking, that would be simple."

He made an amused "Huh." deep in his throat and I decided it wouldn't be at all naff to do it standing up in an alley, if only we could both keep our balance, which was unlikely, so on second thoughts, I just kissed him. It was a brilliant kiss. Brilliant. Absolutely mega, as Matt or Si might say.

At least there wasn't a microphone in the alley. Pity about the infra-red night-vision camera pointing at us though.

# Chapter 31

We walked back to the hotel, taking back routes to avoid the crowds. Jimmy had pulled a serpentine young man and Denise had had a call and disappeared somewhere. When we couldn't find her, we left a note for her at the desk saying she should take the car.

What did we talk about? Mostly, it's none of your business. I did ask him what had made him so unkind to Nadia.

"I dunno," he said. "It's stuff I've been thinking about ever since Lily died. In fact, since before. It just hit me suddenly that... everything's got to end. And... me too."

We both knew exactly when that had happened.

"I read a quote once by somebody, who said he'd always known everyone has to die, but he'd always assumed an exception would be made in his case."

"Yeah, exactly. That's it exactly."

"Comes as a shock to most people."

"I'll bet."

"Is Nadia like Lily?" I asked, the words popping out because I was so curious.

"Yes. Very like. Only Lily is much taller. Was."

"And Nadia has bulimia not anorexia."

"She *what?*"

"You know. Where you puke up after every meal and..."

"I've heard of it. Are you sure?"

"That's what she was doing in the bog after dinner, why she had to brush her teeth."

"Jesus."

"I felt so sorry for her. I did, really. It seems like such a brilliant solution and it turns into such a trap."

"Is that why she keeps fainting?"

"Probably. She'll damage her heart if she's not careful, not to mention her stomach and teeth."

He didn't say anything for a while.

"You haven't asked me what I'd do if you had a terminal illness," I said to him, worried he might think I was some kind of saint.

"Do I need to?"

"Just don't get one, OK? I may be a nurse and all that, but it's notorious how bad we are with our families when they're sick. Matt and Si used to get much more sympathy from their friends' mums if they had a cold than they ever got from me."

"Would you *consider your position?*"

I shuddered at the euphemism.

"No."

"That's all I need to know."

"Anyway, I told you, I'm not going to marry you or anything."

"Why not? Go on, I can take it. I'm not a kid."

Oh god. I swallowed hard. Heart did a drum solo. "The thing is, Shaun.... Tattoo... the thing is, I don't know if I love you or not or if I'm just overwhelmed or what. And even if I did love you, or I do, or whatever, I don't want to do something like marry you because the last man I fell in love with, I married, and it all went horribly wrong somehow, and he turned into Jim."

"Maybe he was just the wrong one."

"I don't believe that. I don't hold with that romantic twaddle about there only being one soul-mate for each person and you have to look until you find them."

"You don't?" Since I'd just blasphemed against probably the only religious dogma Hollywood knows, it wasn't surprising he was shocked.

We were walking along the Thames. Shaun stopped, lit the last two fags in his pack, gave me one and we leaned on the parapet to see the water, slippery and inky like obsidian below us.

"No and not just because Jim believes it, either. He's always said he thinks we're soulmates, married in the 17$^{th}$ century, born to be together in this one and so on and so forth. I don't hold with it because I think falling in love may be a matching up of immune systems or something to do with pheromones or bloody starsigns matching for all I know, but it's mostly made of insanity and illusion. The shadow of real love. Loving isn't something you feel, it's something you do... The soulmate stuff makes people lazy because if you're born to be together, why bother to be loving? And anyway, people lose soulmates all the time and I can't tell you how much misery it causes, this notion that there's only one..."

"Would you stop talking in generalities?" he interrupted. "I'm not interested in people or philosophy. Talk about you."

He turned to me and stroked his fingers along the side of my face and electricity went from his fingers into my cheekbone, zapped all the way down my spine. Words fled from my brain like startled pigeons.

"Immune system. Pheromones. Starsigns." He was teasing me. "Insanity and illusion."

Still no words came. The fingers curved round my jaw and my arms went round that big solid body under his jacket and I wished and wished I could just let go and tell him what he wanted to hear. But I couldn't. In case I was wrong. In case he turned into Jim.

"Excuse me," said a sharp mid-Western American voice. "But are you Mr Shaun Graham the movie star?"

I didn't turn to look at her. It was extraordinary, I thought, it was as though they believed he wasn't really real, as though he was a sort of android who stepped off the screen occasionally so they could see him in 3D.

"Hell no, ma'am," said Shaun, perfect Texas accent. "You got the wrong guy."

"Oh." She was hesitating. Go away you nosy old trout.

"Anything I can do for you, ma'am?"

"No. Thank you." She sounded embarassed. Androids don't have feelings, but if he wasn't Shaun Graham then he was a human being and she'd just gone straight up to him while he was in a clinch with a girl... People are very strange.

"He says he's not," she yodelled to her friend across the road as she waddled to join her.

"Sure he is," yelled the friend. "I recognise him."

Shaun suddenly grabbed my hand and pulled me along.

"I don't blame you," he said bitterly, as he hailed a taxi. "I wouldn't touch me with a barge pole either." He was tense and miserable.

"It's not that."

"Gives you to think, doesn't it."

"It does, but it's not that."

We sat in the taxi and Shaun kissed me but I kept wondering what the taxi driver would think and it distracted me. We couldn't talk either, or I couldn't, and Shaun had run out of fags and so had I.

We bought more at the hotel, Shaun saw me to my room very politely, kissed me good night, set off down the passage, weaving only slightly. I watched those broad shoulders and the way he walked and I suddenly thought to myself, what the fuck am I *doing...?*

I blocked the door open with my handbag and ran down the corridor after him, very undignified, Pam would have been shocked, grabbed him, turned him round, pulled his head down and kissed him on the mouth while I unbuttoned his shirt. Very expensive shirt. Very expensive trousers too. Shaun was the one who got enough of his brain operating again to manoevre me backwards into the hotel room and shut the door, but that bed was just too far away. Luckily the carpet was nice and deep and soft.

Oh use your imagination - this was your basic primitive satisfying simple poke. They don't look pretty, but they feel brilliant. God, I love that feeling when the man completely loses control and you do too and you can't see or hear or feel anything except stars exploding between your legs. Magic!

The floor was bloody hard though. After a bit, my back started complaining enough to make me eel out from under him. Once he no longer had a nice soft female body between him and the floor he made offended mutterings, felt around for me and woke up when he didn't find me.

"We could move to the bed," I suggested, all warm and cosy inside - nothing beats that just-been-thoroughly-humped sensation, does it? - and he sat cross-legged and examined his knees for damage. "Big baby," I jeered. "I've got carpet burns."

He kissed them better very nicely, but then instead of coming to bed, he pulled up his trousers again, buttoned his shirt.

"Why?"

"I've got to make sure Nadia's OK," he said simply and I sighed. "Don't I?"

"Yes, you do," I said, hating her, but liking him for feeling that way. Liking. Honestly, sometimes I wonder about myself, really I do.

So he kissed me night-night and I saw him to the door and off he went.

Fifteen minutes later just as I'd stopped wandering around telling myself I must get to bed it was terribly late and started brushing my teeth and so on, the phone rang.

"Anna." Shaun's voice sounded very strange. "Would you come up and... um... I want you to see something."

My gut swooped. Heartattack? Suicide?

"Are you all right?"

"I'm OK. Just come and look."

I left the wonderful Clothes where they lay and threw on a t-shirt and jeans, didn't bother with shoes, ran up the corridor to the lift.

Paranoia had reached its zenith when I knocked on the door. Maybe she was waving a knife? My heart was thumping. You think I'm overdramatic? A good friend of mine nearly got killed when a little old lady with Alzheimers decided she was being kidnapped by Nazis and defended herself with a vegetable knife.

Shaun opened it and one look at his face told me there wasn't going to be blood or corpses because it was more puzzled than shocked.

He showed me into a suite of Japanese-style rooms that seemed enormous. In the huge bedroom there was an indescribable mess. There was no sign of Nadia, all the wardrobes were open and the clothes gone, the walk-in closet empty, most suitcases gone, most traces of female occupancy disappeared, though nail varnishes, moisturisers and lipsticks lying on the floor in the bathroom said she'd just swept them into a bag with her arm.

That wasn't what was shocking. What was shocking was what she'd done to Shaun's clothes, of which he had a fair few himself. She'd had fun with the scissors, is what she'd done. All his jackets had the right arm cut off, every single one. All his trousers were suggestively ripped and shredded at the crotch. She'd emptied out the drawers with his shirts and underpants and she'd...

I couldn't believe it. I went over and examined the soggy smelly pile carefully. Yes, she had. She'd gone to the toilet on his shirts.

"Jesus," I said and sat down on the side of the bed.

Something stabbed me in the bottom and I leaped up shrieking.

"What?" Shaun picked his way over and pulled the covers off the neatly made bed. Between the sheets, glittering like the pretty crystalline tears she nearly shed for him when she thought he might be sick, was every tumbler and wineglass in the place smashed to jagged  smithereens and carefully sprinkled over the mattress. "*Fuck me!*"

I stared at the cunning booby trap with my mouth open. A mind that could come up with that...

"Boy, am I glad you didn't come back while she was here."

Shaun looked around himself at many many thousands of pounds worth of deliberate criminal damage and shook his head. I was examining my bum but luckily the duvet and my jeans had protected me from the sharp edge.

"I don't know whether to laugh or shit myself," he said to me.

"Don't do that. Nadia's ahead of you there. In fact, I think that's what you call... this. A shitfit."

He didn't smile, took a deep breath, blew it out again. "Why am I not angry?" he asked, blinking at his hands which were curled into fists. It was the same bewilderment I'd seen in him when Onion rejected him.

"Come on, love," I said. "Come and sleep in my bed."

I held his hand, led him out of the suite, he shut the door on it and we went down to my hotel room where he sat on my unboobytrapped bed and rang down to reception. He talked to the duty manager saying that Ms Shan Sen appeared to have had a nervous breakdown since she'd comprehensively wrecked the suite. Please don't let the chambermaids in until his people could take photographs and an inventory for the lawyers. Especially they were not to touch the bed. No, he didn't need another suite tonight, he'd be in room 434. He stopped and listened. Then he put the phone down.

"She left a message for me on voicemail," he said. "No hard feelings, but she's gone to see Lou. Sweet dreams."

I laughed. He laughed uncertainly. I kissed him on the cheek.

"See what I mean?"

He looked at me and nodded. "Yes, I do."

We got undressed in a very staid fashion, hanging things up conscientiously, got into bed and cuddled up. Nothing more. Shaun's skin felt cold when I hugged him tight. Metaphorical violence can be almost as shocking as the real thing and what she'd done... She didn't have to. She could have just dumped him. But she had to make sure she hurt him, and she had. Sure, no blood, but the shredded trousers and that bed sprinkled with glass would stay in my mind for a very long time.

At least, that's what I thought as I went to sleep. I didn't know, did I?

# Chapter 32

*To do: Sun.  Go see mum?  See movie?*

## "WHO'S THE FATSO, SHAUN?"

Do headline writers ever consider how people feel when they're sneered at in large bold type? At school they must be the ones who think of horrible nicknames to call people. Do photographers ever think how their own lardasses would look taken from an unflattering angle in a clinch? Using a night-vision lens? Or the hacks who write the sneering copy about the "plump" "well-covered" "cuddly" nurse (46" 40" 40", aged 49), still-married mother of three, that Shaun Graham had been comforting himself with during his nervous breakdown in darkest South Cornwall? No prizes for guessing who'd been busy on the phone that evening.

Second page (with frontpage teaser Shaun's Mystery Gal) national press. They delivered it with the croissants. I was still very tired and Tattoo had gone to sleep on my shoulder which meant my right arm had gone numb and was killing me with pins and needles.

I thought of all the people who would read it and believe it and laugh at me and my insides shrivelled. For a moment, I hallucinated my internal organs going all small and wrinkled, hanging there inside a chest gaseous with horror. Who was going to be first on the line? My mother? No, I thought she'd struggle internally between shock that I was such a fallen woman as to leave Jim, satisfaction that I was finally dropping the layabout (she'd been flutteringly pleased to meet a real author once) and delight at the spectacularly large fish I'd somehow managed to land after all hope was gone, though was he really a suitable choice? Plus the humiliating headline would be my fault because I hadn't followed her advice about diets. She wouldn't ring for a while, she'd have to sweat it out first.

Jim. He might ring. Depended how drunk he was and how much he wanted to crow. Pam. My boss. Jog. A patient. Lots of people knew my mobile number.

I put my head in my hand, grabbed hunks of hair and tried not to groan too loud. Nadia's shitfit, now this. I didn't cry. I was desperate not to start until I was in South Cornwall again because once I started I knew I'd cry for a long time. And I never ever cry.

Shaun was still fast asleep. Snoring slightly.

The phone went. I grabbed it, dropped it because my hands were shaking, stabbed the button.

"Hello?" I said cautiously.

"Mum! Mum!" It was Simon's voice, trembling on the edge of panic. "Mum, is it you?"

"Yes. What's up?"

"Oh mum. You've got to come home. Please."

"What's wrong?" He sounded as if he was in tears. Sick feeling. Going down Hampstead tube station lift.

"Dad's tried... he's tried to kill himself."

"What? When?"

"Now! Just now. He got the paper and he was shouting about the Whore of Babylon and he tore it up and then he said you'd never come back and then he went upstairs and took all the pills and then he went and slashed his wrists..."

"Christ. Jesus. Christ." Why do we swear by gods we no longer worship? "OK. Where's Matt?"

"Dunno. Sally's, I think."

Who the hell is Sally? "You alone?"

"Mum, what do I do?"

"OK. Stay calm." I took a deep breath. The selfish bastard to do this to Si. God, I hated suicide attempts. Every nurse does. How dare he? He had to live so I could kill him. "Where is he?"

"In bed. Upstairs."

"Is he breathing?"

"Yeah."

"How much blood is there?"

"Whh... what?"

"A bucketful? A bottleful? Is it spurting."

"Not spurting. A bottleful. Lots."

"In total? Say a milk bottle?"

"Yeah."

"No spurting."

"No."

"OK. Now ring the ambulance, say exactly what you said to me just leave out the stuff about the newspaper. Then ring me back. If you don't, I'll ring you."

I wandered around the familiar room grabbing my things, pushing them into my bag. The bag filled too full so I used the loudly-understated carrier bag as well. I was finished in five minutes, left most of my paperbacks behind.

I left the beautiful Clothes in the wardrobe. Somebody might get some use out of them, they needed dry-cleaning badly.

The phone went again. Si was sounding a little calmer.

"They say they're on their way."

"Where from?"

"Treliske."

"OK. It's going to be at least 40 minutes. Get two towels, go upstairs and try and stop any bleeding you can see. Make the towels into pads, press them on any cuts."

He gulped. "Y... yes."

"Has he been sick?"

"I think so."

People who take pills think they'll just die in their sleep. Not so. The body always fights and it reacts to the poison with a vengeance.

"OK, try and move him away from the worst of it and lie him on his side with his head turned downwards."

"Oh. Recovery position."

"That's right. Good boy. Then gather up all the empty pill bottles you can see and put them in a carrier bag on the bed, especially if there's paracetamol or prescriptions in them. Was he drunk?"

"Yes."

"Tell the paramedics that. If one of them's called George, tell him I'll be there this evening."

"You're coming back?"

I had to. What else could I do? It wasn't just Jim pulling a stupidly dramatic piece of emotional blackmail. In fact if it had been just Jim, I wouldn't have moved. It was the boys. And yes, it was the thought of what all the other tabloids would be saying... Of the wreckage in Shaun's suite. Of all the complications and questions and very public sneers by highly paid expert sneerologists.

But mostly it was the boys. I didn't want to go, but they were my babies, six foot tall, dermatological and hormonal disaster areas, but they were my babies.

"Yes," I said. "Go stop any bleeding."

"Yeah, OK. Hey mum. Did you really make out with that filmstar guy?"

"The one Matt almost puked on. Yes. Didn't Matt tell you?"

Silence of a 14 year old coping with the concept of his mother as a sexual being.

"Way cool, mum. What's he like?"

"Go stop your father from bleeding," I said gently.

I sat and thought for a long time. Mostly ways and means. No car. Train or coach. Train. Change at Penzance. I rang rail enquiries - yes a train, no seats.

Rang reception, get me a cab, please. Yes Ms Clements.

He was still asleep on the bed, sprawled, his head velvet with regrowth, chin stubbly, arms flung out, chest hairs gleaming as he breathed, the duvet not hiding the fact that he was rampant and ready for the morning. It was a very tempting sight. I wanted to molest him, despite everything, I wanted desperately to climb on top. Was that in love or in lust? Dunno.

I had to get home. I'd done wrong just walking out like that, very wrong. You can't do that when you're the tent pole. It's no good pretending they'll get along without you when they refuse to do it and they don't know how anyway.

Shaun was sleeping deeply and I didn't want to wake him because I didn't want arguments and uncertainty. I sat down and wrote him a letter. I explained that I had to get home, what had happened, everything. I signed it, "love?" That seemed terribly bold of me. I put that and the newspaper on the bed next to him, kissed him goodbye. He muttered and tried to grab me, then turned on his side, went back to sleep.

Reception said my taxi was there and so I picked up my bag, checked for anything forgotten, remembered to grab the phone and the recharger, handbag. Kissed him again. Looked at him. Tried to fix the picture in my mind. Everybody is beautiful when they sleep, adults even more heartbreakingly so than children because the contrast is greater. Major-league filmstars generally seen harding about with guns more than other adults, especially if his mouth is a bit open and he's smiling, because...

Oh god. I kissed him again and then ran out and slammed the door, ran to the lift. I managed to walk out of the VIP lobby and to the taxi.

I got the train with five minutes to spare. And yes, I'd bought a return, because, well, it's only a couple of quid more and you never know when you might need it and so on and so forth. I even found a seat that was only booked from Bristol to Exeter.

I left my bag in it to book it, went into the toilet and had a sniffle. Just a little one. I promised myself a proper one if Pam would let me borrow her shoulder.

Got back to find a teenage twat had moved my bag and sat down in my seat so I gave him my hardest hard look and after a moment, he moved. Then I settled down, used my bag as a pillow and went to sleep.

The phone woke me just as I was about to thrust the sword into Nadia's green snaky throat... Generally I find Xena the Warrior Princess hilarious, but my unconscious had evidently liked it.

It was Simon again. "Mum, they've pumped his stomach and given him the antidote and sewn up his wrists and they say he should be OK. They said I did just the right things."

"Well you did, first and foremost being not panicking."

"Uhh." Most teenagers can't really take praise. "Um... can you talk to the doctor?"

"Certainly."

It was a young thing of thirty, just qualified, knew everything. He tried to impress me with long words.

"Yes, we have been having marital difficulties, not least being his depression and alcoholism. He was taking an SSRI for the depression, I'm not sure of the exact formulation. Better contact his GP. He doesn't need to ring work because he's a writer. Sometimes."

I got back to Simon, said I was on the train and told him to get himself fish and chips if he had any money. I rang Pam, got an answerphone, rang work, got immense stuffiness and evasion from Mrs Curzon and eventually gathered that they'd wanted to sack me, but couldn't find a mug anywhere near as well-qualified and experienced as me to do the job for the ludicrous pennies they were prepared to pay.

I resisted the impulse to tell them immediately to stuff their job and said I should be back in a few days once I'd sorted out my personal life.

"Well, I do hope it won't take much longer," sniffed Mrs Pompous who rarely took less than two months a year off for her back. "We've been getting complaints."

It's emotional blackmail, basically. It's who cares least about the patients. Taking a break from it, no matter how unwisely, how irresponsibly, had given me an unexpected perspective: why was it my job to look after everybody? Why couldn't anyone else do it? Or a bit of it? Why did it all have to be me?

The answer was that it didn't. But...

I stared into space for practically the whole journey. Once I had to dash for the loo because tears suddenly started coming out of my eyes and I didn't know why.

My mother rang, just as we were getting into Truro. Luckily the signal was crackling, so I could ignore her delicate hints about things I could wear if I was going to be photographed with Shaun Graham, such as nice vertical stripes and an A-line skirt.

"Sorry mum, can't hear you."

The blessings of poor signal. The connecting train to Lyonesse from Penzance rattled out over some of the wildest and most beautifully lush scenery in Europe and I felt sick and grey and old, like a lifer who's been let out for a holiday and is now going back to jail. I felt exactly like that.

Of course, I'd hoped that Shaun would call, but he didn't. Couldn't blame him, really. I had run out on him when he needed me most. Just the sort of behaviour I'd got furious with him about when he'd done it to me. Still, I thought he'd survive, what with all Hollywood to shag. Training-wise, his spin kicks were already pretty good. In fact I was getting to the stage where I felt I needed to pass him on to someone who was better than me at the fancy techniques if Harris and the director decided they were necessary. I used the half hour it took to reach Lyonesse to call a Taekwondo mate of mine in London and track down the British champion, who was an enormous, charming and brilliant black Londoner who ran the most exhausting seminars I'd ever been to. That'd teach Shaun Graham to take up dangerous sports. I left his name, address and contact number on Denise's voice mail and gathered up my bags ready to get out.

Nobody was there to meet me, but then they never were. I got a taxi from the station.

The lawn hadn't been mown. The hedge hadn't been clipped. There were two black plastic bags sitting out the front waiting for the binmen who wouldn't come for three days. I stopped, looked at them, braced myself.

The front door was open, probably to let the smell out. The mess was... It was almost miraculous. I left my bags outside the door and walked slowly in, tripping over unopened mail, stepping across newspapers and pizza containers and beer cans and...

Gentle reader, when you see a place in a movie or advert which has obviously been designed by a very tidy designer in accordance with the stage direction "total mess" there's an almost comical lack of understanding of what that means. They scatter some clothes and a few papers and a can or two and think that's messy. Oh no. Shaun's suite had been a scene of wreckage all the more shocking because the underlying theme was tidy and minimalist.

Real mess is deep. It's archaeological in scope. It's just like those viking middens bearded boffins get excited about. I've only become tidy because you have to when you're a nurse, they make you, it's like the army. When Jim and I first lived together, we used to joke that we knew it was time to clear up because we'd forgotten what colour the carpet was. Often, the carpet had forgotten what colour it was.

Couldn't actually recall what colour our carpet was, now I came to think about it. I toed some Burger King wrappers and the TV control aside and found that it was newspaper coloured. Oh no, that was the supplement. Under that was... a patch of blue. With a coffee stain.

The smell was horrific. I went into the kitchen. Every single plate, cup, knife, fork we owned was there, sitting on the counters waiting for the washing-up fairy. Except for the ones in the dishwasher which I had loaded and nobody had bothered to switch it on to wash. They were mouldy. Flamboyantly so. Hence the smell. The sink was piled high with pans. More beercans. All the plants had died. The floor was sticky. More smell came from the corner where all Jim, Si and Matt's clothes were heaped in front of the washing machine as if the machine itself was going to grow arms and start stuffing them in, add powder and then switch itself on. But it couldn't because the vomity stuff I'd put in to wash a couple of weeks ago was still there, rancid with mildew.

Out in the garden I could hear digging, so I went out.

Matt and Simon were there, digging up my favourite flower bed. There was a nasty sweet gassy smell in the air that I recognised.

"What are you doing, boys?" I asked gently.

They turned round and I could see both of them were crying. "Oh mum!"

Two great rough oiks dropped the spade and fork they were ineffectually using, rushed over and flung their arms round me, both howling. They were frankly rather smelly themselves. I wasn't sure, but I thought Matt was still wearing the t-shirt I'd punched him in the middle of.

"How's dad?" I asked guardedly.

"Snff. He's better. He's awake. Snff. Snortle," said Simon.

"Why are you crying?"

"I'm not," said Simon, blowing his nose on his sleeve.

"It's Bilbo," said Matt, looking at me tragically. "He died."

Bilbo was the senile rabbit. "Oh?" I said. "What of?"

Matt started crying again, not so loudly this time. "We forgot him. I forgot him. His water bottle was all gnawed and his paws were bloody. He died of thirst. Oh mum."

I just looked at him steadily as he wept into his dirty hands. "We didn't even know," he added. "Until we smelled it. I forgot all about him. Oh mum."

Frankly, I'd forgotten too. Poor old rabbit. What a way to go.

"D...do you think he suffered?" Simon asked anxiously.

This was no time to offer the movie version. "Yes," I said. "He did. But probably only for a day or two."

I couldn't bear to watch them weep, it made my own eyes prickle and I knew if I started sobbing I'd never stop and besides, I'd end up digging the grave, burying whatever was left of the bloody rabbit and probably saying a pointless prayer as well. I'd done it before for hamsters and mice and guinea pigs, though those had mostly died respectably of old age or rodent illnesses, generally after many hideously expensive visits to the vet.

Sure enough, here it came.

"Could you help, mum?" sniffled Simon after some more ineffectual prods with the garden fork.

"No," I said, sitting on the patio wall with my arms crossed.

As one, they turned and stared at me.

"I walked through a house that has become a rubbish tip to find you burying a rabbit that you killed through neglect, all because your mummy-wummy wasn't here to tidy up for you and remember the fucking rabbit."

They blinked at me swearing. Let them blink.

"I was impressed with the way you handled yourself in London, Matt," I said to him. "Why did you revert to babyhood as soon as you got home?"

They looked at each other, sulkiness starting to creep back over their faces.

"I don't blame you entirely. I blame Jim who obviously saw no need to change the way he behaved just because his convenient skivvy wasn't there and I blame myself because I've let you get this helpless. Do you think it's somehow manly and attractive to be lazy, incompetent and useless? Well, believe me, it isn't."

I could see the shutters coming down, the instant switch-off at the sound of mum's voice. Obviously, I hadn't been away long enough.

"Don't stop digging." I said, "You can dig and listen and from the smell you need to get poor old Bilbo buried as fast as possible."

They started prodding at the ground again. Oh god, for the days of National Service when there were merciless army sergeants to teach them how to look after themselves and force them to do it too.

"If you think I'm going to spend the requisite three days mucking out that shit heap you've left in the house, you're obviously even dumber than you act," I said as viciously as I could. "And if you think I'm going to live like a pig just because I've got pigs for sons and a husband, then you've got your heads up your arses."

Their jaws dropped but they were afraid to stop digging now. I stood up.

"You smell. The house smells. I leave for a couple of weeks and everything goes to hell. Why is it my job to do every unpleasant boring piece of shitwork there is, eh? Why?"

As it had never occurred to them it was anybody else's job, they couldn't answer this question. It clearly attacked the very foundations of their world.

"I'm not back. I'm back in Cornwall. But I'm not coming back to this house until it's a civilized place to live. That means until it looks something like what it did when I left. Only better. Maybe not even then."

"But mu-um..."

"You, Matthew are nearly 16. You're fourteen and a half, Simon. Your grandfather was working at fourteen. I'll give you money so you can eat... In fact, I tell you what, I'll hide it somewhere for you so you can have fun clearing the place to find it. But I'm not living here until it's a place fit for humans again. Now get that fucking rabbit in the ground, Matthew."

I turned on my heel and left them trembling. I put a twenty pound note in the cupboard under the sink, under the bleach bottle. Then I went out to the front garden, gathered up my bags and went to the gate where the signal was slightly better, rang for yet another taxi, rang Pam. Thank god, she was there. I told her what I'd done and she gurgled with delight and approval.

The taxi roared round the corner and I climbed in and told him where to go. This whole personal life stuff was costing a fortune, but I'd just earned one, distant past, teaching Shaun Graham to kick. What the hell? And was I going to visit my poor suicidal spouse in his sickbed of pain?

Why the fuck should I?

# Chapter 33

What I did was ring Bertie Prince to tell him I was back and what had happened. He sounded amused rather than shocked by the tabloids which were full of the most incredibly unpleasant speculation about Shaun and quite extraordinary invention about me. None of it was actually news. Evidently Nadia had caught them before they started printing the papers. Unfortunately, although quite a bit of it was theoretically actionable according to Bertie, especially the ridicule bit of "hatred, ridicule and contempt", as I wasn't Robert Maxwell or Elton John and there's no legal aid for libel, I probably wasn't rich enough to get anywhere. This put paid to one of Pam's bright ideas. Another of her bright ideas bit the dust because after Shaun's crack about getting £20,000 for my story, I couldn't even think of it without feeling furious. Which was a bit of a pity because half a dozen people calling themselves reporters rang me up, offering improbable amounts of cash for my story. A sample will do.

"Anna Clements?"

"She's out."

"Anna, we really want to run your side of what happened between you and Shaun..."

"She's not interested."

"We could offer....£????" Fill in your own ridiculous amount in the space provided.

"No comment."

"Anna, is it true you were teaching Shaun tai chi for his..."

"No comment."

"If you don't talk to us, we'll have to run something and it may not be so accurate."

"What, you mean you'll make it up? You will anyway. Piss off."

Click. Beeble beeble beeble. "I'll ring back in an hour…"

"Piss off." Click.

Pam took me out to a seafood restaurant in Lyonesse and refused to let me pay. She said I was worth every penny and she hadn't been so entertained in years. She had me rocking with laughter at some of the school mums' comments, particularly the prettier ones whose lives were shattered. All their careful weight-watching and aerobics classes were as nought if somebody who looked the way I did could actually pull Shaun Graham while he was in South Cornwall. It was causing serious existential angst amongst women whose worst previous agonies had been over khaki or blue curtains for the kitchen (sorry, taupe and aqua). I was delighted to hear it. I'd always envied their fashionable figures, why shouldn't they envy me for a change.

But I couldn't stop answering the phone because Tattoo might ring. So our conversation was interrupted by two more "piss off" dialogues as above until I gave up and switched it off.

"What are you going to do about Jim?" Pam asked. "I think it's really out of order, him trying to top himself." Pam had been deeply affected by too much *Eastenders*, as well as *The Sopranos*. She was actually pure Cornish.

I thought about this. "You know," I said. "I really don't care. I know I used to care, but I just don't any more. It was so calculating. All the drama while Simon was there on his own, the booze, the pills, the wrists. Like a teenager, really."

"I've always said you've got three sons, but one's going bald."

"I know. I never ever wanted to be his mum, it just somehow happened. He is thinning, isn't he? I hadn't noticed before."

"Distinct corn circle happening at the top."

"I know there are men out there who get on with things, and contribute and all that, but…"

"Never met one?"

"Yes, I have. My dad was like that for a start. My mum was the helpless one."

"And you resolved never to be like your mum."

"Don't we all?"

"You know, I think that was a big mistake. After generations of women had spent hundreds of years convincing men that we were far too delicate and sweet to do anything hard, we go and get liberated and let on how tough and efficient we are. And then we're surprised that men plump for the sweet and delicate option in droves?"

I grunted and concentrated on scraping out a crab claw. "It's terribly bad for you, you know," I said. "Investing in being helpless, it's scary, it's depressing, it's what makes my mum such a trial."

"It only happens if people let it," said Pam thoughtfully, gnawing a crayfish.

"What?"

"It takes two  to make somebody helpless."

"Which two, oh wise woman who runs with the wolves?"

She waved the fat end of the crayfish claw at me. "You know perfectly well what I'm talking about. In the case of Jim, you and Jim. In the case of Matt, you and Matt. In the case of..."

"Why is it my fault?"

"Not exactly your fault. Just you slipping into the most convenient place for both of you."

"How the hell is it convenient for me to do all the shitwork?"

She looked at me consideringly. "Will you ever speak to me again if I say what I think?"

"Of course I will," I growled.

"All right, great wise woman who runs with wolves, she say this: if woman lie down like doormat, not complain if people wipe feet on her. If you're endlessly kind and supportive and patient and all those revolting saintlike qualities, naturally your loved ones will behave badly. It's that or puke."

"Are you saying I'm a martyr?"

"Yes."

"What?"

"Of course you are. I know, it's hard to spot because you're a very bossy and self-confident martyr. You do a difficult and very stressful and highly skilled job for peanuts. That's martyrdom. You tolerate a drunken barmaid-shagging layabout of a husband for far too long, that's martyrdom. You understand your school-shy slobs of sons far too well, that's martyrdom."

"I'm *not* a martyr..."

"Were you about to say, How could you say that to me?"

It's one of my mother's favourite lines, the quintessence of emotional blackmail and dishonesty. And I was about to say it.

I sat back, suddenly full although the magnificent sea food platter was only half-ravaged.

"Now what you say about Tattoo worries me." We'd used the codeword in case any tabloid reptiles were listening. Paranoia is easy if your bum has been plastered across the nation's newsagents with FATSO next to it. "I know he's rich and brilliantly talented and all that, but he drinks too much, he hangs out with women who sound crazy, he..."

"He's nothing like Jim. He works."

"Hm. For how long, once he discovers your supportiveness?"

There is something about ugly truth which digs you in the solar plexus. I looked down.

"You're saying, I'm the reason why Jim has never hit the big time."

"Not exactly," said Pam consideringly. "I'm saying, you have provided him with all the excuse he wanted for not trying very hard."

"Oh."

"You didn't ask enough of him. That's all."

"Do you think it's too late?"

"For Jim? Probably. He'd be outraged if you expected him to behave like an adult now. Not too late for the boys, though. It wasn't for Kenny and Tim, anyway."

"And Tattoo?"

"Has he rung?"

I shook my head. Well, he might have. I checked the phone for messages.

One from the boys. "Mum, we can't find the money for food."

I rang my number. "Matt," I said gently. "Have you cleaned the toilet?"

"Er... no." Probably hadn't cleaned anything, I thought darkly, probably hadn't even finished with the rabbit. I hadn't been able to contemplate looking in the bathroom.

"Clean the bathroom and toilet. Ring me when you've finished."

"Mu-um..."

Click.

Two journalists. Wipe. And...

"Anna. Call me."

Unmistakeable beautiful voice. Poured dark velvet. It was a real mystery how I hadn't recognised it immediately Tattoo opened his mouth. But in a way I had.

I took a deep breath and let it out again. Then I replayed it and held the phone out to Pam so she could hear him.

"God, you're lucky," she said, giving it back to me. "I'd give... obscene amounts to have him say "Pam" like that?"

I replayed it again for myself. Nor did I wipe it. I could get photos of him any time I wanted, none of them really looking exactly like him. But him saying "Anna." ...

"Anna, honey, wake up."

"Sorry."

"So call him."

"I don't know his number."

Pam nearly dropped a piece of squid in her lap.

"You're a very naughty girl," she said. "My nanna always said to get the young man's name and address first."

Pam's nanna was legendary in Newquay.

In despair I went through my phone address list - nothing under Shaun, nothing under Graham, nothing under filmstar.

"You idiot." said Pam, tucking into creme brulee. "Try Tattoo."

He'd put it in himself, of course. I fumbled the simple operation of getting the phone to call the number and had to start again.

"My, you're in a state aren't you?" Pam commented drily, clearly put out because I didn't want pudding. She screeched the waiter to a halt with her eyes, asked for the bill.

I called him. Denise's voice answered. "Oh thank god," she said when she heard my voice. "Listen, he's in make-up at the moment, he's going on in about ten minutes so he can't talk."

"On where?"

"On *McQuigley Live!*"

"What?"

"He told me to tell you, he's fighting fire with fire like you advised him. He also told me to tell you, Nadia's going to regret the stuff she said to the papers about you. He's very... What? Oh OK, I'll be right with you. See you, Anna, gotta dash."

"Yes but... wait..."

Click.

Pam was looking at me, her face almost comical with curiosity.

"What's *McQuigley Live!*?" I asked.

"Oh my god, is he doing that?" She checked her watch. "Bloody hell, we've only got about twelve minutes before it starts. Come on."

"What about paying..."

"Done that. Come on."

Pam on a mission was a frightening sight, truly terrifying. She waded through the tourists in Lyonesse, she swung out of her parking space like Action Man, she threaded the little streets and the skinny brambly lanes like a rally driver. How we didn't get stopped for speeding...

Her house was a mess she said, which for her meant that the papers were still on the coffee table and there was a dirty mug on the spotless counter in the kitchen. Ken and Tim were vegging out in front of the TV watching something about girls in bikinis and Pam marched over and changed channels.

"Mu-um." came the doleful cry.

"It's bad for you, makes you blind," she said. "Go get Anna a cup of tea and then come and watch Shaun Graham on *McQuigley Live!*"

They stared at me, fascinated, then uncertainly at her.

"Well, I couldn't not tell *them*," she said a bit defensively.

"It doesn't matter."

I'd actually never watched McQuigley Live! because of the bikini show and also because I was hardly ever home in time to see it. Apparently it was very hot, very successful. Boyd McQuigley only ever went live and as a rebellion against Chris Evans and Graham Norton and their ilk, he wore a very plain suit and tie. Gimmick, or what?

"Video!" yelled Pam, running around like a mad thing before she found a blank one, slotted it in, started it rolling.

"I'm not sure I'm going to want to watch this again," I said, full of foreboding. Tim came out carrying a tray with cups of tea on it, complete with saucers, sugar bowl, milk jug, spoons, biscuits. Maybe I could send the louts to Pam for training? I wondered briefly.

The phone went off. I fumbled to answer it, heard Matt's voice.

"Mum. We got the money."

"You found the bleach bottle then."

"Yeah. Why'd you hide it there? Listen mum, is it OK to order a curry delivered?"

"Blimey, do they do that now?"

"Yes. Just birianis and stuff. Can we?"

"Sure." I said, watching the screen. Boyd McQuigley was there in a natty blue suit and a regrettable tie involving Simpsons strangling Mickey Mouse, still bald from his stunt the week before, saying something about a media feeding frenzy.

"Look I'm busy watching McQuigley Live at the moment. I'll call you back."

"What?"

Click. I switched the phone off.

I knew it wasn't quite live, they had a loop to add beeps if people swore or punched each other. I'd read something about McQuigley being the new Parkinson, the British Letterman, giving people a chance to talk. They played a movie after his show so it could go over time if things were going well.

"And here he is, the biggest thing from Australia since Russell Crowe, *Shaun Graham.*"

It was like being thumped in the pit of the stomach to see him stroll out from between the screens, last remaining black suit, red t-shirt, silver belt buckle dealing with somewhat shrunken but still existing gut. He was a suede-head - very fashionable. They were playing the music from *King Alfred.*

One of the odd things about filmstars. They genuinely do look better on camera than in real life. Bigger, somehow. Presumably that's why they're filmstars. If they can act, it's a bonus.

He shook hands with Boyd McQuigley, waved at the audience who were wolf-whistling and cheering him, sat down on the sofa and crossed his legs at the ankles. Then he gave McQuigley one of his special hard look jirugis and I suddenly knew he was nervous. So was I. What the hell was he planning?

McQuigley: How's it going, Shaun?
Graham: Well, I've known it better, Boyd.

Strong Aussie accent. Not because he was under stress, though that did bring it out, but because he did it deliberately. He wasn't going to be mistaken for just another Yank.

McQuigley: Your private life's causing a bit of comment, isn't it.

Graham: You could say that.

McQuigley (leaning forward, patting a pile of tabloids): What's going on?

Graham (Slow smile, blue look direct to camera): Well, you know all the press comment and speculation, specially in the British tabloids. Not to mention some of the stuff that's been going out on the Internet.

McQuigley (knowing look): Oh yes. Dynamite.

Graham: I always reckon that's fair dos for me. It seems it's part of my job, isn't it? You might say, who the hell cares who some overpaid actor's in bed with when there's famine here and a civil war there, but it sells newspapers.

McQuigley: And cinema tickets. Don't forget that, now.

Graham: Sure. So I say, you can write what you like about me, call me what you like so long as you don't tell lies. I'll just sit back and count the noughts on my next contract, doesn't worry me.

My goodness, he was a good liar. He really had cracked faking sincerity.

McQuigley: Is it a 'but' I hear in there?

Graham: Oh yes. (leans forward)  Boyd, tell me, how would you like it if somebody called a friend of yours, fatso? Or some of the other things they've said in the tabloids? Somebody who doesn't have any interest in publicity, who doesn't want to sell her story? She isn't in the film game at all.

McQuigley: I wouldn't like it one bit...

Graham: Now I've spent the afternoon talking to lawyers. One of the things they pointed out is that the picture that the scumbag paparazzo got with his fancy lens...

(Show picture full screen)
Oh god, please don't.

McQuigley: This one. With the famous headline.

Graham: Yeah. This picture's been altered. My people got hold of an original from the photographer and we've compared them.

Both photos side-by-side. In the original one I looked OK, though it wasn't exactly a flattering shot, but in the other one I was ten-ton-Tessie.

Graham: There. See? They morphed it to make her look fatter so it was a better story.

McQuigley: You're right now, they did.

I was amazed. They'd had to fake it?

Graham: That's not what she looks like. She's not anorexic, she's not a skeleton like some people, she's a real woman with real curves. But that picture's been altered to make her look obese and that's a lie.

McQuigley: Bad news for the paper.

Graham (hard look): Very bad.

Mcquigley: I'd feel sorry for them if they hadn't had a go at me a while back there.

Graham (nasty grin): Don't waste your sympathy, mate.

Mcquigley: Speaking of which, where is the... lady?

Graham: I'm not sure. She's done a bunk. Can't blame her really.

"Blimey," breathed Pam. "Boyd McQuigley must think he's died and gone to heaven."

"Shh," I hissed.

McQuigley: Now, the lady in the picture. How did you meet?

Graham: It's quite a long story. I wonder if any of you remember Lily Bates? She was a model, years ago.

McQuigley: Oh yes.

(sequence of pictures of Lily Bates, modelling, catwalk pics, her one disastrously wooden film role)

Graham: I went out with her for a while. 'Course, being a young idiot at the time, I didn't appreciate her. She helped me, introduced me around and then...

McQuigley: You met Carol Tulling.

Graham: And she met somebody else. That's how it goes. I always remembered her and when she dropped out of sight, I heard a rumour that worried me. So I tracked her down.

McQuigley: And? Whatever happened to Lily Bates? Don't tell me she's a mum somewhere.

Graham: No, I'm afraid she's dead. Died last month.

(audience gasps).

McQuigley (he's shocked too): How? What of?

Graham: Cancer. Fourth stage, multiple metastases. Very ugly, though funnily enough Lily was beautiful almost to the end.

McQuigley: Oh.

Graham: When someone gets that sick, she needs a lot of looking after. Lily had a whole bunch of friends looking after her, like family. And the lady the British tabloids have been having their fun with today, is a nurse who takes care of people like that, terminal care in the community.

McQuigley: Phew.

I really didn't like the syrupy sound of that.

Graham: Now when I went to see Lily, I didn't want to bring a pack of journos with me on a feeding frenzy, I didn't think she'd appreciate it. So I took steps to try and hide who I am.

(full screen picture of Tattoo in all his glory, for the party)

McQuigley: Did it work?
Graham: Yeah, it did. That was taken at the party I gave in memory of Lily. A few days earlier some locals wanted to beat me up in a pub while I was there because they didn't like my face. Luckily, Lily's friends told them I wasn't really a brutal cockney punk.
McQuigley: You do look a bit rough there.
Graham: Thanks. Anyway, that's how I met Anna, when she was taking care of Lily, and you may not believe this, but she didn't spot me at all. She's very highly qualified, very dedicated, she's the most gorgeous fantastic woman and she thought I was just some ugly bruiser from Lily's past.
McQuigley: Pretty romantic.
Graham: Bloody great, mate, I'm telling you. Got me past all the bullshit. Course, it was a while before I could get her to talk to me because she thought I was this lowlife biker.

(audience laughs)

Graham: But she came round in the end, I'm happy to say.

I could feel myself blushing. I put my head in my hands. Shut up, shut up.

McQuigley: Sounds like you've got it bad.
Graham: Acute, chronic, you name it. She's the most beautiful woman I've ever met, bar none, she's the most intelligent, the funniest. Maybe I'd better stop before everybody chunders.
McQuigley: I hope she's watching.

Graham: If she is...

"Look up!" shouted Pam.
Well I had to, didn't I? Blue eyes looking out of the TV, melting me like chocolate.

Graham: If she is... Anna, I love you. Come back.

The audience whooped.

McQuigley: Shaun Graham, thank you very much.
Graham: Thank you for letting me set the record straight. G'night.

Pam had her arms around me. I wasn't sure whether I was furious or helplessly overwhelmed or what? What a performance! What an outrageous fucking performance! What do you do about something like that? When you can't actually kiss or hit the bastard yourself?

Obviously, you cry. Even if you never cry.

I was dimly aware of my phone going and Pam answering it. I couldn't believe what she said or the icicles dripping from her voice.

"Yes, Mr Graham, we were watching. She's a bit upset at the moment."

Silence while she listened.

"Yes, we thought it was an amazing performance. I said performance. Don't shout at me."

More silence.

"No, Mr Graham. If you meant what you said, you come and get her."

And she put down the phone. I gobbled at her.

"Trust me," she said. "Wise woman who run with the wolves, she say: make the bugger work."

"But... but..."

"And I don't care how mad he gets, it was a performance and quite a self-serving one. I'm not sure if I like him now. All that stuff you told me about him not wanting to talk to the press and then he pulls a thing like that."

There was truth in what she said. I nodded, blew my nose again.

"He sounded like he meant it."

"Hm. Also, you need time to decide if you love him back. I won't have you railroaded."

"I don't know," I wailed.

Tim handed over another box of kleenex and I blew my nose. Red eyes, blotches, industrial amounts of snot. Most romantic moment of my life and I turn into a mucus fountain. Actually, if there was a God, I'd want to have a serious word with him on the subject of mucus and its position in human relationships. We are not sea slugs, I would tell him, we need less of it or to start admiring the stuff.

"Of course you don't. But you soon will. Now what I get from that is Mr Shaun Graham is very angry indeed, and is about to send a posse of lawyers to do battle for you in court. In the meantime, at least he's seen off anyone else who wants to widen your bum in the national press."

"Do you think they really did that?"

"Sure they did. You're not that wide. Did you think you were?"

I nodded. Pam shook her head. "You know what," she said. "you've got that thing anorexics have where they think they're still fat, you can't actually see what you look like."

"Me? But I'm not ano…"

"Do you think Graham would have gone after you like that if you were as ugly as you think you are?"

"I thought he just liked my personality."

Pam hooted in a very coarse fashion. "Anna, sweetheart, he's a *bloke*." I had to laugh with her. "All right. You stay here tonight, but you'll have to ring the boys and warn them."

Pam's landphone went. It was Matt.

"Mum, mum! Did you see it?"

"Er... yes."

"He was great. He's cool, I like him."

Poor Jim, I thought, even your sons are star-struck. "Well, good. Look, Matt, there are going to be journalists at the house in a few hours, trying to get interviews. Tell them no. Make sure the place is locked up tonight."

"Well, Sally's mum just rang and asked if me and Simon would like to stay over."

"Brilliant idea, you do that. What's her number."

Sally's mum wasn't as good a friend as Pam but I remembered now that I knew her from the days when Sally was an adorable little ginger-haired minx who had Matt twiddled round her tiny finger. It seemed she still did. Sally's mum was full of envy and admiration and excitement and only too delighted to have the boys over.

"Don't take any nonsense from them," I said. "Make them do the washing up and carry the bins and anything that needs muscle and no brain. Don't mollycoddle them."

"Will do. God, this is so exciting."

"Mmm."

Ken and Tim were so heroically tactful that I ended up telling them about teaching Shaun Graham to do taekwondo. Pam roared with laughter when I mentioned ticking him off for kicking the board without permission.

"Probably the first time a woman's done that since he was ten."

"No, I think he goes for strong women. Nadia Shan Sen certainly slapped him around."

"Can I have him if you don't want him," Pam said. "Or when you've finished with him? Please?"

"I thought you said you didn't like him any more."

"What's like got to do with it?"

"Mu-um," protested her boys in chorus, running away as she paraded up and down, hand on hip, intoning, "Have him stripped, washed and brought to my tent."

I laughed so much I sneezed revoltingly.

"I suppose you might wear him out," said Pam.

"No sign of that," I said reminiscently. "Far from it."

"God," said Pam enviously. "Do you know how long it's been for me?"

"Since Lloyd?"

"Yes."

"Dear oh dear."

"Dearohdear is right. In fact, I want to change the subject now. You've got to go to bed so you're rested in the morning."

"Well, but..."

"But nothing. Come on, off we go."

She practically frog-marched me to her annexe where everything was clean and tidy and there were fresh sheets on the futon. She hung up my clothes, she got me a drink of water, she fussed over me like a mother which was so nice and such a change, it almost made me cry again.

Took me ages to get to sleep though.

# Chapter 34



Next morning, seven oclock, Pam was at the door, in her dressing gown, holding croissants and coffee and some tabloids, and my phone.

The first tabloid said "SHAUN'S ANGEL". There was a picture of me and him dancing at a club, another one taken with a long lens of me going into the restaurant with Denise and in fact with the Clothes, I didn't look too bad at all. Another one had a delightfully poisonous interview with Nadia, Happy At Last With Bud, in which she went on at length about Shaun Graham's sex addiction, alcoholism, bad temper, habit of disappearing and running around in disguise having nervous breakdowns, and general impossibility. She said she thought it was a good thing he'd taken up with a fat nurse, because he'd need a lot of looking after. All of them reported the McQuigley interview as if it were news. *The Guardian* ran a short piece which looked as if it had been cut by a libel lawyer in which it was snidely alleged that a certain filmstar had been seen surfing and smoking dope in South Cornwall and that he'd double-parked a Harley, causing a retired teacher to get a parking ticket.

"There's a Mrs Curzon on the line," said Pam, handing the phone over.

"Well," she said. "Are you ready to come back to work, Anna?"

"Eh?"

"You see Gina's just rung in sick and everybody's on a conference. Can you do Gina's patients as well as your own?"

"I don't know if I..."

"We're really desperate. We didn't realise...."

How much I do, eh?

"...what a problem your being away would be."

"Are you sure?"

"Oh yes." It sounded as if she hadn't read the papers yet. No doubt she would eventually, and be shocked and horrified and envious. Bad backs didn't get you into the newspapers. "I'll have the list of appointments ready by 8.30 if you come and pick them up."

"Well, I..."

Actually, I thought it would be nice to meet reality again. You do get sort of insulated from it in a filmstar's world. And it would keep my mind off things.

"All right. As a favour to you. I'm still supposedly on holiday, aren't I?"

"I suppose you are."

"Last year's holiday, in fact."

"Um. Yes."

"See you at the office."

"I won't be there, I'm afraid. My back's giving trouble again. It's in the fax."

So I showered, put on my uniform – encouragingly loose on me - drove to the office, picked up two pages of fax with a completely insane itinerary on it - Judy Curzon did not really understand the concept of scale on maps - rang a couple of people to make it more feasible and was just hitting the A30 when the phone went again. I pulled into a layby to answer it.

"Good morning to you," said Bertie Prince. "Now. A company called Graham Productions have just paid £50,000 into my client account to be used by you if you decide to pursue a libel case against the various newspapers who were so unpleasant yesterday. This is on account for my fees and expenses. They have faxed me with a full dossier of offenses and possible London counsel to brief, as well as faxed an opinion by Mark Graves QC on the subject. Your young man has added a note to say that he wants me to gut them on your behalf, but it has to be your decision."

"Blimey," I said. All right, I've watched Eastenders too. "What do you think, Bertie?" Bless him, who else would call Shaun Graham my young man?

"All court cases are gambles, there are never any guarantees, particularly not in libel cases. However, in this case, the QC thinks, and I humbly concur, that you stand a reasonable chance of making them cry. And frankly, anybody who can get a QC to function in under a week, let alone 8 hours on a Sunday has my sincerest admiration."

I sat there while lorries thundered past, my heart thundering back.

"What about the divorce?"

"Well, as far as I'm concerned, I've had no further progress."

"No, I mean, won't that make it more difficult?"

"Thinks have changed, Anna. It's not relevant that you're a scarlet woman, though no doubt they'll run something nasty about you and Jim just as soon as Jim gets through to his agent."

There was that. I took a deep breath.

"OK, Bertie. Go get 'em."

"Lovely. I haven't had fun like this in years. I'll be in touch."

The phone rang again as soon as I put it down.

"Hello?" I said, expecting my mother, Jim, maybe Matt or even Shaun.

"Um..." said a nervous young voice, slightly familiar. "Um... is that Anna Clements the nurse?"

"Possibly," I said warily.

"Um... the one in the alley...?"

Understanding dawned. I'd left my mobile number with the social worker. "Is that Yarrow?"

"Um... yes."

"How's the baby?"

"Oh she's lovely, she really is... Listen."

She moved the phone and I heard the unmistakeable "glug glug ahhh, glug glug ahh" of a baby latched on and drinking milk with every fibre of her being. Made my own breasts prickle reminscently.

"There. She's really greedy."

"Good," I said. "How are you? They treating you right?"

"Um... yes, sort of."

Meetings going on right now, no doubt, trying to sort her out with accommodation.

"Um... listen.... I wanted to say thanks."

I was ridiculously pleased and surprised. I'd expected nothing of Yarrow, certainly not good manners.

"You're welcome. I was glad to be there."

"No, but... um... I mean... I wanted to thank you anyway, but I... I just wanted to know if... um..."

"Yes, it is me."

"In the papers?"

"Yes."

"Who Shaun Graham was talking about on the TV?"

"Yes."

"Oh fucking wow man. I mean... wow! You're really Shaun Graham's girlfriend?"

"Sort of."

"Um... Wow. Why didn't you say?"

"Didn't have time."

"Um... can I call her Anna?"

I felt a silly pleased prickle at the back of my nose. "Of course you can." A lovely idea occurred to me.

"Listen, Yarrow. You've got the chance to make some serious cash here."

"Yeah, one of the nurses said her boyfriend's on the *Sun* and they'd give me five hundred quid for the story. Do you think that's right?"

"No."

"Oh." She sounded very sad.

"I think they should give you at least several grand for it and maybe more. Now listen, I'm going to get a woman called Denise, who's Shaun Graham's publicist, to ring you in about ten minutes. Stay by the phone. Don't talk to anybody else. Can you do that? She'll make sure you don't get cheated and she'll organise it all if you'll let her."

"Sev… several grand?"

"I think so. Don't take any less. But only if you act now. They'll have forgotten all about it in two days. Are you willing to be photographed with the baby?"

"Oh yes."

"Right."

I got her number, rang Denise, spoke for five minutes and then listened to a minute of silence.

"So that's where you were."

"Yup."

"The press will want to know why you got out of the car."

"I got tired of trying to stop Bud Anderson from grabbing my tits. It was too boring for words. That's why he stranded me."

"Oh I see." She didn't sound in the least surprised. "He's horrible, isn't he? Can I quote you on that?"

By the way, children, this was all long before MeToo and nobody gave a toss about famous and powerful men trying to grope people.

"Certainly. I was carsick as well but you can leave that out."

"Right. I'll get onto it."

"Make sure they don't screw her, she's been screwed enough."

"Don't worry, Anna. This is great, you know."

I clicked off the phone and sat back, fag, stared through the window at the lorries booming past, very satisfied with myself. In the last few weeks, I'd learnt an awful lot about the tabloid press. Mentally, I thought of them as a sort of Greek chorus of pantomime dames and female impersonators, all going "Oo Missus!" with hypocritical horror every time a celebrity got caught with his pants down. And you couldn't win. Whatever you did was wrong. Yes, it sold cinema tickets, as Shaun had said, but there was a nasty lickerish edge to it. The tabloids are the spiritual heirs of the frustrated old biddies who used to twitch their net curtains and ruin reputations. They still do in Cornwall, retirement Mecca for those who want to prune roses in their old age. Whatever I did, Yarrow was going to tell her story - at least this way she would get something for it. And nobody needed money more than Yarrow, though I really hoped she wouldn't just put it up her and Jesus's arms. I wished I could watch when Bud Anderson read about how boring he was. As for Nadia... Don't take me on in the holier-than-thou stakes, honey. After a few minutes wondering how Shaun would react to it, I drove off.

I was very nervous going to see the patients I'd so selfishly left in the lurch a few weeks before. I thought they could legitimately ask what I'd been playing at and how dare I just take off like that when they were dying and I wasn't.

Gerry was dealing with his two children for the weekend and seemed quite happy and calm, new medication working well and several sorts of alternative therapy booked. He was even doing preliminary plans for somebody's new extension. He said, not to worry, he'd liked Gina almost as much as me. He should. I'd trained her.

All the others were just lovely. Even the selfish old ladies were basking in the reflected glory of my romance with the great Shaun Graham. I had requests for autographs. I had questions about what they saw as the high life in London.

Mrs Tredurgan wrote a note for me with a mischievous grin.

"Any journalists who want to interview one of your patients, send them to me."

I smiled.

"I mean it," she scribbled. "I'll give 'em what for."

In fact I did pass her name on and she eventually did a wonderful interview for a woman's magazine. I zipped round Cornwall at a terrible rate, calling in on people, drinking tea, answering exactly the same questions each time (Was he really as big as he looked, did he sound like he did on TV, what did he have for breakfast?) Only one (Mrs Bosteagle) asked if he was good in bed and I told her he was. She heaved with hilarity and then started to cough so I got busy with her breathing mask and we couldn't talk any more.

I told every one of them I was thinking of giving up nursing and every one of them said they weren't in the least surprised and I'd be mad not to. Except for Robbie who clung to me and cried.

Oh and my mother rang four times, the last time agitating to know what she should wear to the wedding. My brother thought the whole thing was very shocking, but quite funny. Mrs Curzon caught up with events very late in the day and wanted to know if this was going to interfere with my work again. I said with unaccustomed daring that for the moment, I thought she should treat it as if I had a bad back and she went quite quiet.

I dropped in on Sally's mum because I was visiting somebody else in the same village, she gave me tea, I found that the boys were at the beach with her husband and she asked me if Shaun Graham was as big as he looks. She didn't ask me what I was doing working like a dog in Cornwall when Mr Filmstar was declaring his love for me to millions of viewers, but I could hear her thinking it.

I didn't know either.

All I knew was that I had this peculiar empty feeling all day. You know when you go on a diet and after about a week or so, you get this odd sensation (yes, of course, I've been on diets, dozens of them in my teens) of not being exactly hungry, just perpetually obsessed with food. Everywhere you go food lies in wait for you, sneering at you. It was like that with Shaun: everywhere my eyes moved, it seemed, there was a poster of him or a video or a piece in the paper. I nearly had an accident out by Trenever because there was an old poster of him on the railway bridge, being nobly wistful in *King Alfred*, and the blue eyes mesmerised me. I used my compartmentalising skills: I put him in one compartment and tried to concentrate on all the patients in the other compartments but every time I opened a new one, there he was, metaphorically, sitting invisibly next to my patient.

I wished he was in the car with me to sing stupid corny songs with or argue back with the idiot DJs or have a fight with about which road to take. I wanted to put my arms around him, feel that lovely warm bulk that a big man has. I suppose it was a lot like the odd yearnings you get when you're pregnant when you simply must have sardines and marmalade or you'll die.

The itinerary finished at Treliske at 6pm and although I got there well after 7, I thought, as I'm here, I'll go and see Jim.

It was on the principle of crossing him off my list, really. It wasn't just the thing with Tattoo. I realised that something like Tattoo had been waiting to happen because Jim had simply worn me out. What Pam had said was true: I had been a martyr, I had let him get away with it, but he'd wanted to get away with it. It may have been a conspiracy of two, but somebody had to do something to break the deadlock and Jim was too comfortable. He claimed to be in agony, but really he was living in a free hotel that paid him, where he could live inside his own head as much as he liked. The trouble with living inside your own head is it's very lonely there. You need reality. I'd protected him from the stuff for too long and now I had to throw him out into it.

I found him in the patient's waiting room, fully dressed. He looked bad. He was at least shaved and clean, but his eyes were sunken in his head, he looked as if he'd lost weight, he was pale grey. I wouldn't have sent him home myself, but no doubt they needed the bed.

I stopped by the door.

"Jim," I said nervously. Last time I'd seen him, I'd written YOU ARSEHOLE on his bum, remember. The last words I'd heard from him had been "you fucking bitch."

He turned his head, looked at me and a flicker of something went across his face.

"Oh," he said. "I was waiting for Suzie."

"Who's... Oh."

"She's late."

I could hardly get hoity toity about Suzie considering my own activities. I found and started to light a fag, then spotted one of those smug little notices declaring Treliske a cigarette-free zone. Well, they're right, of course. I put it away.

One of the nurses came in. "You still here, Mr Stukely?" she said brightly. "Shall I call you a taxi?"

"No. A friend is taking me home."

The nurse gave me a meaningful look and I followed her into the passageway.

"He says his girlfriend's coming, but she's not. Do you know him?"

"Husband. Ex-husband. To be."

"Oh dear. She rang earlier and said, and I quote, she wasn't bloody going to run around after him any more or come and get him and would I tell him so."

I laughed. Suzie evidently had more sense than I'd had at her age.

"Did you?"

"Three times."

"Are you sure he's OK to be discharged?"

She shrugged helplessly. "There are three old men in A&E on trolleys who need admitting tonight and I've got to have the bed."

"Suicide risk?"

She shrugged again. "Psychologist saw him this morning, thought he seemed rational, prescribed for him. That's about all we can do."

I went back to the day room.

"Jim," I said. "The nurse says Suzie's not coming and that she's told you."

"Oh," he said. Doleful note. There's something about the voice of depressives, you can always spot it. It's not just a monotone, it's a special kind of monotone. You can actually hear the black clouds. This had a higher pitch in it, put my teeth on edge.

His wrists were bandaged, not very heavily. Obviously, he hadn't been able to cut deeply. Thank goodness. I wasn't sorry he'd survived, though he was still a problem. What do you do with someone who resolutely won't help himself? Not can't. Won't.

I couldn't help myself either.

"Shall I take you where you want to go?" I asked. "I've got the car."

He looked at me distantly. "That's kind of you. Where shall I go, though?"

"Home?"

"Oh yes. Home."

"Might be journalists there, though."

"Huh?"

"You know."

He shut his eyes. I felt sorry for him. He was so limp, so exhausted, so different from the Jim I'd married. And his life had turned putrid, after all. Even if so much of it was his fault, you still had to feel sorry for him. He stood up, I noticed his hands shaking as he put the newspapers on the couch, spread out of course, not folded. Jim had never folded a newspaper in his life. He'd been reading the interview with Nadia, I noticed.

We went out, walked across to the staff carpark where I'd parked. He got in, I got in. I drove off. Headed southwest on A30 towards Penzance, dual carriageway all the way. Jim sat there in silence, radiating gloom.

They do, you know. Depressed people radiate gloom. It's like a black hole. Not only are they stuck in it, they suck you in so you can feel miserable too. And it's no good trying to cheer them up, only makes them worse. Nor is it any good being sympathetic; any amount of sympathy you can generate, they can suck in. Your sympathy glands will be exhausted, wrung dry, wrinkled like raisins, (mine were) and you won't have got anywhere near the amount of sympathy they want. Brisk produces more dolefulness. Neutral more gloom. There is nothing whatever you can do to help, except sometimes, very occasionally, at the randomly selected right moment, shout at them. But usually not.

Nothing is more frustrating than being married to a depressive. In the great Sylvia Plath v Ted Hughes controversy, I am firmly on Ted Hughes' side. He had to do a runner, it was the only way he could survive.

I should have done my runner years ago. Years and years ago. Paradoxically, the shock of it does sometimes do the trick. Not always, of course, because sometimes they top themselves like poor dear Sylvia.

It was true what Pam had said. I had given him the excuse he needed, and the leeway, to let himself down into the pit. Pit and Pity - interesting. Pity I'm not a poet, I might make something of that.

Defiantly, despite his radiating gloom, I started singing a Steeleye Span song. God forgive me, I loved Steeleye Span once. Don't ask, if you're under 35.

"I hate that song," Jim said.

"Sorry," I said.

Well, that scotched that attempt at cheering myself up. I put the radio on. Jim switched it off.

"Inane rubbish," he said.

I sighed. We drove in silence, black hole and me, through beautiful countryside, late wild-flowers making purple and pink explosions in the green-furred walls, sheep and cows munching peacefully... The sunset was just draining down, a huge child's exuberant paintpot of purple and gold and pink and blue. Shaun had been right.

"Isn't it beautiful?" I said stupidly.

"Is it?"

It's a waste of time trying to be cheerful. They don't like it. If they're miserable, why aren't you? I could feel all my energy and optimism draining out through the black hole next to me. Half an hour with him and I felt old and grey again.

I drove round the village carefully once, looking for journalists. None visible. It rather looked from the footprints all round the house that they'd tried to get in and found it was indeed empty and pretty smelly too. I unlocked the front door, found a full binliner there, stepped over it.

Well, the boys had tried. They'd put the dishwasher on and washed the mouldy plates. They'd run the washing machine and rewashed the mouldy clothes, and (god almighty) hung them on the line. They'd emptied and refilled the dishwasher but forgotten to run it. They had sort of cleaned the toilet. Curry cartons littered the living room on the top layer of detritus, but they had attempted to clear the kitchen. It was far more than I had expected.

Jim looked round at it.

"I'll help you clean up," he said dolefully, picking up a plate from the sitting room and one curry carton and carrying them into the kitchen where he left both on the counter.

I folded my arms.

"You'll help *me*?"

"I'm sorry it got this bad."

"Oh. Are you?"

He sat down in the sitting room, where the sofa and armchairs had indeed been swapped round, sighed and switched the TV on. Yes, folks, he honestly did.

"Where are the boys?"

"Staying at Sally's house."

"Oh right. Now you're back, I suppose I'd better do some writing soon."

"Jim," I said to him. "Jim, you're missing a screw. I'm not coming back. I'm not staying here."

"Why not?"

There was a note of panic in his voice.

"Why should I? To be your slave? To clear up three weeks of shit? To work my arse off all day and come home to work my arse off some more. For no thanks and plenty of complaints. For no affection, not even friendship? Why on earth would anybody want to?"

"But I thought you'd come back to me."

"I'm in South Cornwall, sure. I came back because I had my little boy Simon on the phone yesterday morning terrified because his dad had tried to commit suicide. I came back for them. Not you. Why should I come back for you?"

"I'm sorry about Suzie. She's gone anyway. Very selfish girl."

"Oh you silly prick. I don't care about Suzie. If she wants you, she's welcome to you. Suzie just clarified things a bit. Such as your selfishness and dishonesty."

"I'll try harder."

"Please spare me the trembling voice and the doggy eyes."

"I can't compare with that... with that filmstar. I'm not rich or successful. I know my books have never done very well, I've never had that much luck but I..."

"I don't care about your books either. If you'd occasionally cooked me a meal when I came home knackered, or listened to me talking about my work problems instead of constantly boring me with Job Gurney, maybe I'd consider it."

"But I need you."

"That's a pity. I don't need you. Like Pam said, what are you for?"

"But we're married."

"I know. Bertie Prince is working on it. And remember, you started proceedings."

He started to cry. "But I can't live without you. I can't write, I can't think. I love you. You're my other half."

That bloody stupid soulmate notion again.

Oh yes, once my heart would have melted and I'd have cuddled him. Now all I could think was how fake it seemed, or if true, entirely self-serving. I sat down to face him.

"Jim. How do you love me?"

"What?"

"You say you love me. How do I know? How do you show me that you love me?"

He looked stunned. He thought love was a feeling, not what you do.

"Do you make love to me? Do you smile at me, talk to me, share things with me, help me? Do you do more than the minimum possible you can get away with?"

"But that's not what I mean."

"Isn't it? Then what do you love in me? Do you love the way I clear up after you, cook for you, earn money for you, deal with your sons for you? Wash your clothes, change your sheets, listen to your complaints? Is that what you love?"

"You try very hard. I'm sorry I'm not cheerful enough. I'll try and be cheerful."

He fixed a rictus of mirth on his face.

"You see, I don't think you do love me. You love my convenience. That's all. You don't even particularly love my body any more. You just like the service. You're dependent on me. Why on earth should I want to stay for that? It's not the 19th century."

"I'll help more round the house, I will, I promise." He sounded panicky, bewildered. He just couldn't work out what the problem was.

We'd had this conversation before, in different forms, many times. I wondered if he remembered any of them.

"No, Jim, you won't help. You'll be doing it. Not me. You. Because I won't be here."

"But... but what about my writing. I can't do housework when I'm writing."

"What writing? You haven't done a word for months, you've been too busy fucking Suzie."

"But she's gone now... What am I going to do?"

I lost it. Completely. "And she's right, you miserable idle selfish limp-dicked piece of shit!" I bellowed. "I'm not sticking around as your skivvy while you fuck every bimbo in Cornwall…"

His face crumpled like a child's and he whispered, "Oh Mrs Gurney, what will I do without thee…"

I stuck my face in his and whispered back, "Do you know when I got tired of your fucking stupid theeing and thouing? Around the time you got your second Job Gurney book published. Do you know something? You're not living in the 17<sup>th</sup> century. I'm not Mrs Gurney, you're not Job fucking…"

He slapped me. Big open-handed roundhouse swing to the face, rocked my head on my shoulders, made me gasp. Funnily enough, it didn't hurt that much. It was the impact more than the pain that took my breath away. I gawped.

"Say sorry." This was so outrageously dumb I carried on gawping. Jim was breathing hard through his teeth. "How darest thou berate me so?!"

"Fuck off." I turned to go, he caught my shoulder and slapped me again. But this time I blocked his arm, stepped in and palm-heeled him hard on the chin. Brilliant strike. Best of my life. I got him right on the pressure point in the chin, his eyes turned up and he fell backwards, crashing into a coffee table and landing in a litter of magazines and newspapers.

Now my face was starting to burn and ache. I looked down at him, thinking what a baby he was and how easy it had been. "That's it," I said. "Finished."

He just lay there with his mouth open, stunned, tears on his cheeks and some stupid show with a dayglo orange and green set cavorting on the TV next to him.

I went upstairs, found the suitcase on top of the wardrobe, the traditional huge one you buy for your one and only family holiday in Spain. Then I started packing properly, emptying the drawers, only taking the newest stuff, leaving behind all the drab boring outsize clothes. I heard him coming up the stairs and ignored him.

Like I tell my self-defence classes. Never turn your back on a man you're not happy about. Especially not your husband.

# Chapter 35

I think he hit me with Simon's baseball bat. He hit me twice because he was scared of me, right on the back of the head, and I went down.

Now we live lives so cossetted and protected some of us go entire lives without ever seeing any violence at all, except on the TV. We hear about fights and people getting beaten up and so on, but we never see it, never experience it, except the TV and film kind. We're afraid of it, much more than we should be, because it's so strange to us.

That's why I froze when Mr Wife-beating accountant attacked me. The thing was just so strange, I couldn't believe until it was way too late that anyone actually would lash out at a woman, at *me*, grab *me*, ram *my* head against a wall, punch *me*, kick *me*. I didn't even put my hands up, I simply froze. It's easier for men. Jim had gone through his lad stage at university, as many men do, he'd paid his share of fines and emptied his share of fire extinguishers, had a few fights in bars when so drunk he could hardly see to punch crooked, let alone straight. These fights always improved immmensely in the telling, of course.

But me, the last fight I had before the patient's husband did me over was with Katy-Ann Simpson in Year 1 about who got to be the Angel Gabriel in the Nativity Play. Sure it was vicious, sure fists flew, but at six years old, you don't do that much harm. Mrs Scarfe's legs took the most damage when she separated us.

Mr Wife-beater cracked my cheekbone and a couple of ribs and I was a jelly for a week. I remembered lying in bed crying, yet again, trying not to make too much noise, and deciding that under no circumstances was I going to let it happen again. Either quit nursing which was getting more dangerous, or learn to fight. Hence self-defence, hence taekwondo, as I'd explained to Shaun. Jim hadn't liked me going out so often to train and he did his level best to make me feel guilty about it, but he hadn't stopped me.

But it never occurred to me he would ever... well, hurt me. We'd had fights, early on, where he broke furniture. Once he threw a saucepan at a wall and made a dent. Once he slapped me because he thought a consultant was trying to get me into bed (he was right, though it wasn't my fault). I told him if he did it again I would leave. Since then, a whole lot of psychological bullying which I had only just recognised as such, but no violence. None.

What I'm trying to explain is why it happened to me, taekwondo black belt, martial artist extraordinary. I was a lot tougher than I had been, I'd sparred, I'd got hit and discovered it actually wasn't the end of the world. No way would I freeze again, ever. In a film it would never have been so easy for him.

And of course, the fact is, it can happen to anyone at all if you don't expect it, if someone comes up behind you with a big stick and hits you as hard as he can with it, flesh and blood lands on the deck.

We don't understand concussion any more either. We see James Bond or Mel Gibson or, god help me, Buffy, get hit on the head, and they're unconscious. A few minutes later, they blink, wake up, go "Ooh my head." then up they get and off they go, ready for anything again.

No. Concussion is what happens when the meaty jelly that is your brain bangs the inside of your skull hard enough to completely disrupt what's going on in it. You can die of concussion. People are often brain damaged by it. There's an appreciable chance of epilepsy as a result. You will inevitably lose a fair number of neurones.

For instance I don't remember if Jim talked to me or if he just hit me. Don't remember anything for about half an hour, as far as I can guess. It's gone, blank. There was a peculiar tearing sound. There was the feeling of my head being a rushing whirlpool, of light and shade spinning past, of a horrible sick headache that somehow seemed bigger than my head.

Somebody was doing something weird to me. I was sitting propped up against a wall. I knew that my head was hanging because it was so heavy. The sick whirling got worse and worse and I retched.

Somebody was breathing hard nearby. I couldn't move my hands which were somehow strained behind me in a way which hurt. Feebly I tried to get them to my head and couldn't. Why not? Tried again, feeling of stickyness round them. Spider's web? No. The tearing sound again.

The person who was panting for breath was wrapping gaffer tape around me. He'd used the stuff to hold my hands behind me, now he was wrapping it round my arms and body, like a cocoon.

*Wake up*, roared something inside me, *wake up, this is serious!* More sick whirling, more retching, nothing left. The taste of bile was awful.

Get an eye open. One. Now the other. Couldn't see. Everything blurred, like a windscreen at a carwash. Blink. Focus. Sick whirling. Retch. Focus again. Not at all like being drunk, like nothing at all. I'd never seen double before.

Jim's face doubled up, close to mine.

"Jim," I said wonderingly. "Jim, zhat you?"

"He left a message on your phone," Jim said, quite a normal sort of voice, really. In fact he sounded happier than he'd been in months, years perhaps. "He said, he'd meet you out by Onion's place. That's at MiniWonders isn't it?"

"Wha'?"

"Your lover, the film star."

My head was rocking because I was trying to focus. I didn't understand.

Jim's face came close to mine. "Thou art an adulteress. Thou art filthy with sin, thou hast played the whore again and again. Thou hast done iniquity in the sight of God and in my sight. Everybody's sight. You're all over the papers, you tart. You made it as public as you could, so you could rub my nose in it."

I blinked. "Sinned? Wha' the fuck you talking about?"

He slapped me, quite hard. "Watch your language. When thou commitedst the sin of fornication with thy film star, thou didst sin. The sin of adultery."

"Oh and you didn't when you were up to your bollocks in little Susie?" I snarled. How dare he slap me?

"That's got nothing to do with it," he said. "I've atoned for that sin, many times. I was weak, I should not have taken her to my bed, but the woman tempted me and I fell."

"What?"

"But you... you fornicated with your film star, you went off to London with him, leaving me alone, thou didst dwell with him in sin, and thou didst sin with him."

Awful, awful fear, not the little tinctures you get on rollercoasters, not the thumping silly fright of horror movies, but the kind that spreads like an octopus across your bowels and squeezes tight, the kind you get when your little boy flings himself off the top of a climbing frame and you don't quite catch him and he lies still... That kind.

"Jim?"

"And for thy sin, thou must repent," he said.

"Jim, what are you talking about?"

"And thou shallt atone."

Has he flipped, does he really think he's turned into bloody Job Gurney, the 17th century Puritan, or is this some kind of scam? Surely he's faking it? Was he drunk, like that time when he was going to smash the vicar's car? He didn't smell particularly drunk.

"OK, I repent, I'll atone. Let me go."

"No. I think we'll go and meet him."

"Why?"

"I want to talk to him. I want to ask him why, when he had so much, he had to steal my wife."

"He didn't steal me," I said between my teeth. "I'm not a fucking car. I went with him. He treated me like a human being, not a slave, so I sort of liked him for it. What the fuck do you think you're talking about, sin, atone, I never heard such fucking crap in my life, do you think you're Job Fucking Gurney or something...?"

He shook his head sadly, then what he did was this. First he hit me again. Then he held my nose really hard with his fingers and when I opened my mouth, he pushed a sock into it, I don't know whose but the gorgonzola made me want to puke again, and then he stuck more gaffer tape across my mouth.

For a moment I couldn't breathe at all, not even a bit and my eyes went black but then I got a bit of air through my nose and a bit more.

Somebody was holding my hair and there was something metal digging in my cheek.

"Stop making such a fuss," said Jim.

Fuss? I can't breathe. But I could, just. I flared my nostrils, blew snot, breathed again. There are only two options for getting oxygen and one was closed.

Froze again. The metal thing was a screwdriver right next to my eye.

"If thine eye offend thee, cast it out. And if you don't do as you're told, as a proper wife should, I'll put out your eye," said Jim conversationally. "With this. And if you try to kick me, I'll hit you on the nose and you'll suffocate. Get up."

My head was whirling and sick still, I could hardly feel where my feet were. He pulled up on my hair and I lurched up, sideways, banged the wall, up more. Panting for breath because I was so scared I was nearly wetting myself, honest to God, I had to concentrate just to keep my sphincter shut, and my head was whirling. I retched again. terrified I'd inhale that disgusting sock.

"Stop it," he said. "Now we're going downstairs and out to the car."

Please let there be a journalist out there, please let there be a hack watching the place for the ones in the pub, please let him not be asleep, let Mrs Nosey Parker next door be at home looking out of her windows and call the police, please, god, please...

It was surprisingly late. I must have been unconscious for longer than I thought, which tallied with Jim getting messages off the phone, come to think of it and...

Why were we going to meet Shaun? Why? What the hell did he have in mind? This was mad, ludicrous.

When did he flip? I asked myself frantically, when he tried offing himself or when I said I wasn't coming back? Or earlier? Or when.

We were at the top of the stairs. Right, I thought, when he's concentrating on the stairs, I'll do him with a side kick and run out, run like fuck...

Could he read my mind? He stopped there.

"Hmm," he said. "Sit down on the top step."

Wobbling, I sat. Then he shoved me in the back with his foot and I went down the stairs sideways, banged my elbow, banged my shoulder. Landed at the bottom, tried to get up and run and he caught up with me and punched me under the ribs.

I wanted to whoop, but couldn't, nearly pitched over again. He got hold of my hair again, big knot of it in his fingers. There's a way you can deal with that, but you need a hand free. My legs were shaking, fright, lack of air, the punch. I kicked sideways anyway, maybe I hit a kneecap, kicked again. He shoved me over easily and kicked my back, my bum, only funnily enough that didn't hurt so much because the world faded a bit.

He's going to kill me, I thought, trying not to be sick, locked inside the world with the sock taste and the blurry vision. He'd never do this if he thought I was ever going to be able to come back at him, he's decided he's going to kill me. (No, can't believe it. *Jim?!*)

He hauled me up by the hair again, and we went out to the car, me bent over, my feet turning over and tripping and my knees soft. He shoved me in the front passenger seat, looked at the gaffer tape roll which was getting a bit skinny, and then he put a few turns around my neck and the headrest, put the seatbelt on.

I felt I was strangling, heaved and fought. The headrest ground into the back of my head where it was raw and swollen. He stripped off the gaffer tape round my mouth, and I managed to spit the sock out, retched again, coughing. The tape against my throat felt too tight for me to breathe, but I could. Just. For a while I did that, breathing, gasping in fact. Heavy oxygen debt. Often burglars do this sock and gaffer tape thing to old ladies and they croak immediately, because their hearts won't take the oxygen debt. Fear makes you breathe faster, use oxygen faster. Stop the intake of oxygen and ... Anyway, there are burglars doing time for murder who only wanted to shut the old dear up. If you're a burglar, bear this in mind.

Jim was getting in the driver's side, starting the car up. There weren't any journos there, of course, they were all in the pub or bothering Pam or Sally's mum or something. Never a hack there when you need one.

"Jim, what do you think you're doing?" I asked as he drove. My lips were terribly sore, they felt like they'd been sunburned. Did he drive like a maniac? No, he didn't, he drove sedately out of the village, pausing to post a letter at the postbox, then quite slowly and sensibly along the dark lanes. He was a good driver, I remembered. "Why are you doing this?"

No answer.

"You won't like it in jail," I said. "You really won't..."

He laughed softly. "I'm not going to jail. I know my life's over, it's just a question of getting it right. As for you... As for him...."

Deep breath through his nose. "What was it about him? Money? Fame? Big dick?"

I nearly said, big dick, but thought better of it. Men are so obsessed with willies and their comparative sizes, he might have believed it. Anyway, there was nothing wrong with the size of Jim's dick, when it was operational. And the fact that for most of the time it wasn't, hadn't mattered so very much because I was always so tired.

What had it been about Shaun?

"Do you want an honest answer to that?" I asked. "Or just something that confirms your prejudices?"

He looked sideways at me. "You could try honest," he said.

"OK. When I saw him first, I didn't know who he was because of the shaved head and the tattoo, like it says in the newspapers, right? I didn't recognise him. I thought he might be a drug dealer in fact."

Jim laughed. First sign I'd had of anything sensible going on inside him. All right, talk to him, try and get through to the sane bit. My throat was sore with all the retching and... I can't tell you how much everything else hurt, because as you find in competitions, your mind sort of edits things when it has to, and you don't feel stuff that's not important.

"So it was true what he said on the TV?"

"Yes. I thought he looked horrible."

"What converted you?"

"He's a gentleman," I said. "He looked after Onion - that's Lily Bates - he cooked for her and the boys, no big song and dance, just some tapas occasionally - he helped with all the tedious unpleasant stuff you have to do when someone's really ill, he took his turn. No big star bullshit at all."

"Probably it was a bit of a thrill for him, doing ordinary things."

I considered this, as well as I could. "Yes, perhaps it was. Maybe you should try it."

Stupid thing to say. Stupid stupid. I waited for him to do something awful, but he didn't. He drove on in silence, radiating... not black hole. Something else. A nasty kind of self-satisfaction?

My hands had gone to sleep and I tried to work them, get the blood into them. Pins and needles. My shoulders were hurting. Every time Jim slowed down, the gaffer tape pressed against my voicebox and made me feel sick. When he accelerated the headrest hurt the tender back of my head.

And I couldn't believe what was happening, couldn't. It wasn't even a nightmare. I'd never had a nightmare this bad, I'd never had one where somebody familiar and trusted, whom I'd loved, still sometimes loved no matter how impatient he made me, the father of my children, had suddenly turned into a monster. As if an alien was inhabiting him in some paranoid fifties film. A terminator was impersonating him. For fuck's sake, this was the man who'd held me while I sweated and gasped through two labours, who'd told me to blow so I wouldn't push, who'd been the first to see both our babies, who'd wept over both of them because they were perfect. What could be more intimate, more trusting than that? I couldn't believe it. When did it happen? When was the monster born?

Oh god, what would this do to Matt and Si?

To my fury, tears started welling up in my eyes and dripping down my face. God damn it, why the hell now? I don't normally cry. Jesus, I laughed at Watership Down, even.

"Oh stop it," sneered Jim. "I know it's fake."

I tried desperately to swallow down huge lumps of sadness in my throat. "I was just thinking about Matt and Si."

He contemplated this. "They'll recover," he said coldly. "They'll be better off without us."

The terror octopus squatting in my guts tightened its grip and went a few degrees colder. I was right, he was going to kill me as well as himself.

Why hadn't he done it when I was out cold? He could have kept on bashing my head with the baseball bat and I'd never have woken up? Why all this complication?

Suddenly I knew. Shaun had phoned, and that had broken the spell. He'd got the message and he'd decided he wanted the famous lover too. Make a clean sweep and incidentally, perhaps, acquire a bit of notoriety, even if he was planning to be dead and wouldn't be there to enjoy it. Everyone's heard of John Hinckley, haven't they?

Oh Jesus. Shaun would be waiting for me at MiniWonders. Ohgodohgod.

The octopus had a friend in there now. I'd been terrified for myself, now I was terrified for Shaun as well. And he wasn't a tough soldier or a cop, he was an actor, and he wouldn't be expecting anything bad, he'd be expecting to meet me where he could reasonably hope there were no journalists...

"Jim," I said, trying to speak gently. "Jim, couldn't we just work this out between us?"

"It's gone too far," he said, quite objectively. "I can't allow it."

"Well, maybe. But... but why do we have to involve anyone else? This is our problem..."

"Because he has made love to you, because he is filthy with thy sin."

The doleful self-righteous voice, the antediluvian attitudes, they infuriated me. Had Jim always been this jealous? I'd never had a lover before so I didn't know.

"And because he said he loves thee."

"He probably only said it for effect."

"I don't think so. You see, me and Suzie, that was physical. You and... and the filmstar. That's more. You love him back."

"No it's not. I don't love him. It was just physical." God forgive me, I did say that. You would too.

Jim looked at me slowly, then turned his attention back to the road. "I know you, Anna," he said quite gently. "I know when you're happy."

"He's fun... He's interesting.  It's not the same as..."

"You love him. I can't allow that."

"But why not, for Christ's sake?"

"Don't take the Lord's name in vain."

"Jim, you're not the guy in your books. You're not Job Gurney. You were born in the 20th century, not the 16th."

"17th century, Job Gurney was born in 1603, on the day Queen Elizabeth died. Don't you even remember that?"

"I was confused by the 16. But you..."

"I think they had it right in the 17th century. I think things were better. Everybody knew where they were."

"Women knew their place, eh? Under their husbands?"

"You can't understand, can you? It's just a matter for joking to you. I know a cuckold is always funny. Sorry, I don't see the joke."

He stopped the car in a layby. He got out, opened the passenger door, picked up the sock and stuffed it back in my mouth, put the gaffer tape on. It didn't taste any better. I breathed carefully through my nose, trying desperately not to cry again because that would stuff my nose up and I'd suffocate. I was trembling all over.

"It's all right," he said, getting back in the driver's seat. "It'll soon be over."

Then he drove in through the broken gate of MiniWonders. Somehow, I expected it to be exactly as it was when I left the party with Matt and Si, as if no time at all had passed in the interim. But of course, everything was cleared away, apart from the trampling effect of all those feet, even the fairy lights.

Maybe Jog and the boys will... No. They weren't there. They were up-country for a festival, I remembered, I'd been hearing about it from my patients. All the long-haired layabouts  who cluttered up South Cornwall would be cluttering Newquay for the big surfing carnival. No way would Jog and the boys miss the highlight of their year.

We passed the ghostly Eiffel Tower, the White House, the Taj Mahal... A sleek shiny new car was parked in the car park where Onion's old caravan still stood. Tattoo's camper van and his Honda had been picked up and dealt with by some people. There was nothing except the caravan, some patches on the grass where tents and benders had been and the automated lighthouse with its evil sigils. A new one caught the headlights, very beautifully painted: ONION RIP. People would puzzle for years over what that one meant, I thought, getting lightheaded again.

Where was he? I tried telepathy, desperately. *RUN AWAY*, I thought at him silently, *FUCK OFF, RUN!*

He was near the cliff edge, looking out at the sea which was quite quiet. Well, it was a beautiful sight, stars thick as daisies, water inky and mysterious with some silver fretting. A bit of surf. He heard the car, turned towards us smiling, confident and relaxed in his leather jacket and jeans, smoking a fag. Had he brought any people? A driver, Steve or Yori. Harris would be nice, for instance. No, why should he? And of course, he knew my car, why should he think there was a problem?

I kicked desperately with my legs, trying to get them up to the windscreen, screamed as loud as I could only making a sort of "wuffle" noise, tried to lie on the gearstick. Jim punched sideways at my head. I saw Shaun Graham in the headlights as Jim spun the wheel, drove at him, saw him turn to run, then see me, hesitate fatally. His mouth opened, he took a step towards the car...

Sam Peckinpah is right, things do go to slow motion. Jim accelerated, the wheels spun in the grass, the car speeded up. In the last possible second, Shaun did what he'd learned to do for stunts, he threw himself up and sideways, fag end flying. He rolled across the bonnet and hit the windscreen sideways on, cracking it into snowflakes. Jim handbraked the car, got out with the baseball bat, I screamed and screamed into the sock, heard Shaun's dazed voice, "What the fuck..."

Then a thud, a cry of pain. Silence.

Don't cry, I ordered myself, don't cry. You'll suffocate.

Jim opened the boot, got something out of the back.

I couldn't see because I'd slipped down and the gaffer tape holding my neck to the headrest was strangling me. I shoved myself up desperately and saw in the headlights, Jim bending over Shaun. Don't kill him, I shrieked, but the sock got most of it.

Now he was pushing Shaun along, left arm twisted up behind his back. Jim's reasonably big and strong even though he's not fit. Shaun is big, and fit, but he'd been hit by a car and a baseball bat. I saw him try and escape from the lock, but Jim kneed him in the crotch and he fell to his knees.

I knew this was my chance. One of him, two of us. I tried wriggling my hands which no longer seemed to belong to me, wrenching my shoulders back and forth, sweat pouring off me. It didn't help, gaffer tape's very tough. And Jim had watched plenty of movies, after all, he'd seen *Reservoir Dogs*, he knew what to do.

The seatbelt was still on, my neck was still being strangled. I lifted my foot sideways, careful, careful. Cramp. Why now for fuck's sake? Augh, cramp.

In the wing mirror I saw Jim open the caravan door, he had Shaun in a neck lock now, screwdriver next to his face I think. Shaun had his feet under him, but he looked badly banged up, blood all over his face, and his right arm... Oh god, it was hanging limp. It was broken.

They disappeared inside. I brought my foot down on the horn and rested it there.

"BEEEEEEEEEEEEEEEEEEEEEEEEEEEEEP." Up again. "BEEEEEEEEEEP!"

I heard a scuffle, a moan. Somebody was there.

"Uhh," said someone, coming out of the bushes around the Taj Mahal, in the headlights it looked like a tramp with flopping brown hair. It came up to the passenger window, peered in, bloodshot pin-hole eyes blinking slowly. "Anna."

Good god, it was Benjy. They must have kicked him out... Sorry, he must have been referred for care inna comm*uni*dy. From the look of him he was back on whatever had wasted his brain in the first place. Probably a nice cocktail of uppers and jellies.

I mooed at him desperately, call the police, Benjy, run down the road now and call them, or better still let me out of here...

He couldn't work it out. He looked at me, trussed like a chicken, mouth covered with gaffer tape, head bloody, face swollen, utterly desperate, and he couldn't get his head round it or work out what to do.

"You come to see Onion?" he asked with a goofy smile, such a child's expression in a desperate young man's bearded face. "She's in the caravan."

"Mmmmaaaa... uhh," I mooed. "Mmwwwwwugggh!" He didn't understand, couldn't.

More footsteps, the baseball bat swung and Benjy went down. Jim hauled him out of the way, thought about it, then hauled him a bit further and rolled him over the cliff edge.

He came back to the car and leaned on it, getting his breath back. Then he opened the passenger door, punched me in the nose.

I started to die. I did. There was that awful starry sharp, almost sweet pain of my nose going, the blood coming, but when I tried to breathe through my mouth, the sock was in the way and it didn't matter how much I heaved and fought, I couldn't get... any air...

Sparks. Eyes going black. You have two minutes and counting, boomed a voice in my head. Ripping sounds, something dug into my neck. I think he used the screwdriver to release the gaffer tape round the headrest, undid the seatbelt, pulled me out and onto the ground by my hair. He was gasping for breath too, this was all very much harder work than poking at a computer console. Or a barmaid. But I was dying. He started pulling me towards the caravan by my hair and collar and the lights flashed, I went limp with the surf roaring in my ears.

Air like wine. The sock was out. I heaved in breath, coughed, breathed some more. Felt wonderful. Comparatively.

"All right. Walk," gasped Jim's voice and I felt the metal next to my eye, the hand gripping my hair. Sometimes it's good to be heavy. I managed to stagger along, head throbbing, nose throbbing, still not able to believe this. I know, it sounds drippy, but I still couldn't believe it. So baroque. So mad.

Be grateful he didn't just drive straight off the cliff, said the voice inside which I told to shut up. Somebody had to stay sane here.

Up the metal steps, into the caravan. Somebody had come and taken Onion's hangings, stripped out what was useful. It was now just a bare compact little caravan, with a bed and a sink and a cooker and a tiny table and the chair. Shaun was hunched over the sink, his knees braced against it, his left hand tightly gaffertaped to the taps, his right hand hanging, going purple. His face was just awful, Jim must have hit him in it with the baseball bat, his mouth was bleeding, the side of his face was puffing up. He could hardly stand.

In a movie, Mel Gibson or Russell Crowe or Shaun Graham himself would certainly have had something witty to say, some wise to crack, but you don't, you know. You really don't.

Jim hauled me into the director's chair which was still there on account of being broken. He used the last of the gaffer tape to wrap around me, make sure I stayed in it. He shut and locked the door. Then he sat on the bed next to a cardboard box somebody'd left there, baseball bat in one hand, screwdriver in the other. A sleeping bag rolled in the corner. Benjy must have been sleeping there... yuk... That was the cardboard box which had held Onion's ashes before Jog and Tattoo emptied it into the sea from the rocks near the surf beach on the morning of the party. Shaun had told me about it, how neither of them could think of anything to say and how the seabirds had shouted and gone diving after the fragments in the hope of fish.

Weird how your mind works when you've been hit on the head. I couldn't concentrate. Couldn't think. Benjy dropped off the cliff... No reaction.  Couldn't think of anything except seagulls.

We just stayed where we were, all three of us, panting and gasping for breath, Shaun occasionally spitting blood, me just bleeding steadily from my nose.

I caught myself thinking, it's all right, Shaun will think of something. But why should he? He's an actor, a professional fake. When he thinks of something, it's in a script, when he does something heroic, there's usually a stuntman or a computer involved.

He looked so bad, breathing harshly, I could see his legs shaking. Under the blood, he was white, and not just because there was no light in the caravan except from the car's headlamps and my night vision was coming in. Was it shock? I wondered if he'd busted something inside when the car hit him, as well as his arm. Spleen, possibly. Medical emergency. Can kill you. Oh god.

But Jim's going to kill us first, said the voice, all of us.

Shaun looked at me, then at Jim. He gripped the taps and braced his legs again. One reason for the notable absence of wisecrackery was because talking out of that mouth would hurt. He looked at me.

Don't ask me, I don't know what to do, his scared eyes were saying, one of them going purple and shutting, I've got no experience of dealing with a mad husband.

Well, I have, and he pasted me. No experience of this particular mad husband either. I dunno either.

Why do husbands go mad? Is it that thing of being a pea up your nose? Or what?

"Now we can talk," said Jim in a self-satisfied way.

We exchanged glances, me and Shaun. Let him talk, we both thought, the longer the better, give him time to think, time to sober up or sane up or whatever. With the dawn, somebody might see the car, wonder why it was there. Maybe Benjy's body would be found. You never knew. There was a funny taste in the quiet sea breeze, worried me, couldn't quite work it out, sort of acrid, reminded me of smoked mackerel.

"What I want to know is, why?" said Jim to Shaun. "When you've got every tart in the world after you, every film actress in Hollywood spreading her legs for you, Nadia fucking Shan Sen, even, why do you want mine? I've only got one, you've got thousands. So why steal mine?"

I really didn't like being talked about as if I was a resource, an oil well or something. A mucus well perhaps?

"He didn't steal me..." I started furiously.

Jim reached over and poked Shaun viciously in the right arm with the baseball bat, where it was broken. Shaun yelped, flinched back. His eyes were wide, you could see the whites. He was as far away from Jim as he could get. Were there tears of pain in his eyes? I didn't blame him, you can't stop them sometimes. What you realise when you're a nurse is that nobody acts like they do in films in a real crisis, it's totally unpredictable. I once talked to someone who'd been in a plane that was going to crash and he said, he would have been happier if there'd been screaming like there is in movies, but there wasn't. Everyone was totally silent because they were too frightened to scream.

Real pain is very different from special effects gore; the fact that Shaun had acted tough for millions of people, didn't mean he was tough. And I didn't care anyway, I just didn't want him hurt any more because it twisted inside me so much.

"You," said Jim to Shaun. "You talk to me, shit-head, or I'll hit her in the face with this."

"Wh... What do you want me to say?" Shaun asked. He didn't sound as beautiful as usual, his voice was hoarse and his words were mushy because one side of his mouth was swollen and bleeding. Very Aussie accent.

"I want you to tell me why you stole my one little ewe-lamb."

What was he jabbering on about? There was something vaguely familiar about that. What?

"I told you," I hissed. "He didn't steal me. I went because I love him."

"Shut up," Jim said to me. "Or I'll break his other arm."

I shut up because I didn't want him to hurt Shaun any more, though Shaun hadn't seemed to hear what Jim was threatening, he was just standing there staring at me.

"Well?" said Jim. "You got any notion what I'm talking about?"

I saw the puzzlement in Shaun. Then he blinked, he'd worked it out, somehow. He braced his knees again, swallowed, spat a bit of tooth, turned to Jim. Something had changed. What?

"You're not Uriah the Hittite," said Shaun. "And I'm not King David."

What? What the hell was this, Sunday School?

No, by god, it was a Bible quote that formed the theme of one of the first Job Gurney books - a long time since I'd read it. Something to do with King David lusting after Bathsheba. Uriah the Hittite was Bathsheba's husband, sent off to get killed by King David. How had Shaun managed to spot that?

His voice was quite soft, almost gentle. And it was steadier. Suddenly, I knew what he was doing. He was doing what he knew how to do. He was acting brave. Well that was enough. That's all brave is, after all, pretending to be steady when you're shitting yourself.

"You know, I was thinking King Alfred," said Jim with a nasty edge.

"What?"

"That affair his Queen had with the Viking? You know?"

"That was a film. A story," said Shaun carefully after a pause.

"It happens all the time. So why did you do it? Why did you fool her into loving you?"

"Because I love her," growled Shaun. "Because she's beautiful."

Oh god, don't say that. Lie, you idiot, fake it. Say it was just physical, say it was just an affair, say it's over.

"Because she's beautiful?" said Jim, wonderingly, looking at me. "She was when I first knew her. But now? I'd say she's a bit old and fat for you, don't you think?"

Silence. Shaun spoke very quietly. I recognised in his voice that he was holding onto his temper. Good. Doesn't matter what Jim says, just humour him, stay calm, keep him talking.

"No, she's beautiful. But if you can't see it, if you don't want her, why can't I have her?"

"Because she's mine. And I do want her." There was a snuffle, not from Shaun, not from me. Good god, it was Jim, he was crying. "I love her."

"Really?" said Shaun, tilting his head at me, not taking his eyes off Jim. "How'd all that damage come about then?"

I supposed I looked pretty ugly, I felt terrible. I wanted to shout that they shouldn't talk about me as if I wasn't there, but I didn't dare. There was something dimming the headlights as well, and an acridness in the air again. What was it? I couldn't smell anything because my nose hurt and I couldn't breathe through it, but I could taste it. Like a barbecue. My concussed brain couldn't hold onto what it might mean, the idea kept slipping away and Jim and Shaun were too intent on each other to notice.

"She was leaving," sniffled Jim. "She was packing to go. I thought she'd come back to me, I thought she'd dumped you, but then I saw she'd just come back to get her things and... I couldn't allow that. She's mine. She's not allowed to love you. We've been married for 20 years. I can't let my Mrs Gurney go."

His face had a strangely tender, pleading look.

I could hear Shaun swallow again. He took a shaky breath. His legs were still trembling but his face was calm. How was he doing it?

"But she…"

Jim's expression flickered. "Big star like you," he sneered. "You probably don't know what it's like when you love someone and they don't love you back any more. They just don't. They talk to you kindly and they let you have sex with them and they look after you, but they don't love you any more. They love the kids, or someone else, not you. You've got no idea how I've suffered."

Shaun stared and then he said, "You're a moron. You really can't see past all the film star shit, can you? You think it's real. Well, I've been dumped. Everybody has. If they've had a life." His voice strengthened, he sucked and spat. "You hear about Lily?"

"Oh the woman who died."

"Yes, the woman who died. I loved her, you know, bloody worshipped her, if you're interested. Didn't care what she did, how badly she behaved, I just wanted to be with her. Then she decided she was bored with me, said, "Goodbye Shaun, you can piss off now.""

Now that was a different story to the one he usually told. Sounded more realistic, I had to admit, but he might have been making it up for the occasion. No, I didn't think so, somehow.

"So what did you do?" said Jim in a bored voice.

"Well I didn't beat her up," said Shaun softly. "I could have, I was angry enough, but I didn't. I like women, you see."

Oh god, don't go too far. Don't make him madder.

"Really?"

"Yeah. I went and got drunk for about a week and lost a job because of it, which was pretty stupid of me. But I didn't do that to her."

"Are you saying, I don't like women?"

"Funny way to show someone you like her."

"She's my wife."

"We're not in the 17th century. You can't beat her because she's lippy or not willing enough. Those days are gone, mate. Your Job Gurney would be in jail today."

Now that was clever, I thought, wondering distractedly in my concussed state what was crackling outside. It was a good tactic, talking about the books. And he was right. Job Gurney does, occasionally, 'chastise' his wife, as was the custom then. Christ, we'd even re-enacted the scene with a hairbrush and a basque during one of my magazine-inspired efforts to revitalise my marriage. And Jim's as vain as all writers, as obsessed with the world he creates as any of them.

Shaun understood ego, after all, he had one himself.

"You've heard about them?"

"I've read them. All of them, soon as Anna told me about them."

"I thought Hollywood actors don't know how to read."

Shaun paused, you could see him very carefully not rising to the bait. "Well, I read. And I liked them. Bit complicated, a bit dour and Gurney wouldn't be an easy part to play, he's not naturally very sympathetic, but they were good."

Yes, he'd noticed. While he was talking, I saw his eyes move, held-down panic in them, he'd seen something bad out of the window. And the light had changed inside the caravan, gold and red not just white.

"Oh." Just for a moment I could hear the pleased smugness in Jim's voice, the praised writer voice, the really-I'm-modest-about-it-but-please-tell-me-more-about-how-you-liked-it.  Then it soured. "I suppose you think if you flatter me, I'll let you go."

"No," snapped Shaun, fear and anger poking through. "I'm not flattering you, because I think you're a worthless piece of shit. I was saying I liked your books. The books are a lot better than you are, even your fucking character's better than you. She's kind to you, she lets you have sex with her, she looks after you." That beautiful voice mimicked Jim's voice mercilessly, the drone, the self-pity, the sloppy Oxford graduate sound. "What the fuck do you want, you arsehole? She stuck by you. She wasn't even going to go to bed with me until she saw you fast asleep on top of your girlfriend."

Oh shit! I thought, oh no. Don't deliberately make him angry, don't tell him, he doesn't know...

"You *saw* that?"

Jim was up off the bed, baseball bat in hand, coughing because there was smoke coming into the caravan, curling up through the floor, whisping through the window-seal and round the door. Shaun was coughing too. Christ Jesus, I thought, as I suddenly understood, some way behind Shaun. The gorse is on fire. The headland is burning. Why? His fag-end? Benjy? (Doesn't matter why, we've got to get out!)

Jim advanced on Shaun, prodding at him with the end of the baseball bat. Shaun saw it coming, hunched over. Jim slammed the end of the baseball bat into Shaun's stomach. To do it, he had to come between me and Shaun.

I suddenly understood what Shaun was playing at. He was drawing Jim towards him the only way he could. He knew the director's chair was broken, he was gambling on me.

"That must have been a good laugh for you," hissed Jim, prodding at the broken arm.

"Yeah," Shaun's voice creaked breathlessly. "It fucking was. I nearly pissed myself laughing. Specially when she wrote, 'you arsehole' on your bum and you didn't wake up because you were drunk, I thought that was fucking magic...."

Jim was up close to Shaun, raising the baseball bat to hit him again, his back turned to me.

I stood up, director's chair and all, turned slightly and side-kicked him on the side of the knee, stepping through, breaking power.

His knee buckled. Same instant, Shaun head-butted him, full on, right on the nose.

Jim flailed with the bat, I kicked him again, same place, breaking the hinge, he screamed, Shaun kneed him in the crotch, I axe-kicked the baseball bat out of his hand, Jim slid down to the hot floor, Shaun's boot came down as hard as he could on Jim's fingers, I could hear the crunch even through the greedy crackling all around us.

The caravan was well and truly on fire.

"Get out," yelled Shaun. "Get the fuck out of it."

He was twisting and pulling desperately at the tape holding his left hand to the tap, pulling and yanking. He tried to move his right arm up to it, his eyes rolled and he nearly buckled because he couldn't use it, the pain was too bad. The caravan was full of smoke, there were flames licking round the joint with the roof.

"Anna, please, will you fucking get out." He was panting, desperate, his voice broke across the middle. "Get out NOW!"

No, I thought, quite clearly, no, I don't think so. Jim moaned, tried to move, I kicked him, tried desperately to think. My hands were tied and I couldn't feel them anyway. All you needed was something to cut the gaffer tape with. Screwdriver. Jim had brought the screwdriver.

Where the fuck was it? Coughing and heaving, I looked. It was lying on the bed, next to the box which had had Lily Bates' ashes in it. Looked like she was almost going to get her wish: go up in flames with attendants to serve her in the afterlife. Pity she wasn't here to see it, really. OK, concentrate, stay calm, plenty of time.

Not actually. Not plenty of time. The roof was alight and bits of melted plastic were dripping and setting light to the floor and the smoke was black and poisonous. Shaun was coughing, while he wrenched at the tap, kicked the sink. He bent down to it, tried to get his teeth on the tape.

I held my breath, leaned carefully over the bed, picked up the screwdriver in my own teeth, lucky I still had them really, stepped over Jim, pushed past Shaun, started prodding with the end of the screwdriver at the gaffer tape, blood came, I wasn't prodding very accurately, but once you've made a hole or two and somebody strong is pulling very hard indeed, it starts to part, I prodded again, it came away.

The door was shut. Shaun tried to open it, snatched his hand back - too hot to touch. Molten plastic fell on my shoulder, on him, we both screamed.

Of course we kicked through the door, it was only plywood, god how we kicked. Fire outside, fire leaping up from the gorse and grass, heat on our faces, heat around us, director's chair still attached to me.

Could both me and the chair get through the narrow door? But Shaun had picked up the screwdriver left handed, he was chopping at the tape, the thing finally came off, fell on Jim who moaned.

The caravan was burning, and the gorse and everything around, a wall of flame. Some of it smelled quite sweet, must be a fortune in cannabis going up with that little lot. Somewhere beyond I glimpsed a scarecrow shadow leaping.

I was crying with fear. Shaun's good hand gripped my shoulder.

"Anna," he said. "It's like a pyro. You go through it fast enough, you don't even feel it. Just stay upright."

"Oh shit!" I squeaked.

"One two three, go!"

He shoved me through ahead of him, I heard him jump, we ran, ran blindly through smoke and fire, eight, nine steps and into the carpark.

Then I stopped, turned. "Jim!" I shrieked. "Jim, get out!"

Benji was standing there, throwing bits of glass with torn and bloody hands. Then he stretched his arms up, laughing and shouting and cheering at the flames climbing him. He walked to the door of the caravan, climbed in.

"Benjy!" I screamed.

I started back towards the caravan and Shaun cannoned into me low down, knocked me over, just as the butane gas bottle exploded.

Everything faded again as I hit the tarmac, so I came round to look at black, red, orange, a soft summer night, and smoke billowing everywhere. Felt like broken glass in my chest when I coughed.

Jim and Benji were burning to death. Dear god, who isn't there, let Benji be too drugged up to feel it, let Jim be unconscious, let him not know, let the smoke get him so he can't feel it. Poor Jim, poor Job Gurney. Unworthy little thoughtlet: Thankyou god that it's them and not me and Shaun.

Where was Shaun? I was lying on my side, I was sure I hadn't landed like that. I coughed, coughed some more, the black smoke had got into my lungs, they felt like they were burning up still. Somebody was coughing in the background.

I turned, squinted, didn't have the energy to struggle upright. Shaun was over by his car, leaning on it, he had his mobile on the roof, he prodded shakily with his left hand, croaked into it, coughing painfully, tears streaming from his eyes. That cough should convince them he wasn't joking if nothing else did.

Fire surrounded us, smoke billowed, and between its clouds you could see the dried up gardens and little cement covered garden sheds of MiniWonders catching light one after the other. The Taj Mahal burned round the inside, looking ethereally beautiful as the fire ran through its wooden structure and the white snowcem held longer than the wood, so it seemed as if a golden worm was eating it from inside. All Benji's beautiful work, the cave of jewels he had made for Onion, all smoke and ashes.

Shaun came back, I heard his feet stumble. He knelt down next to me to pull off the sticky gaffer tape holding my hands behind my back. I'd nearly forgotten about them because although my shoulders were killing me, my hands were completely numb.

He stripped off the tape left handed, helped me into a sitting position and I knew he was having trouble because he was panting, breathless again.

"It's all right," I said. "Rest."

"Gotta get it off you," he croaked. "Your hands are purple."

The last bit came away and my hands just sort of stayed where they were. They'd been there for a long time, they were stuck. He rubbed my shoulders gently with his left hand, gradually I got them round and he was right, they were very purple and swollen indeed. Couldn't move them at all. Couldn't help him or make a sling for him or anything. Then pins and needles started.

I was still crying. Bloody fountain. "Poor Benji," I said.

We both looked at the pillars of smoke and flame from Onion's court and the Taj Mahal and thought of her talking about worms and fire, climbing inside poor Benji's defenceless head. He'd loved her so much. Insanity and illusion.

"Well, that should please her," said Shaun and I shuddered and hid my face from the roasting smell where Benjy and my husband were turning into carbon and carbon dioxide and water and trace elements and a few bits of calcium carbonate. "Selfish bitch."

Just because I'm an atheist doesn't mean I'm not superstitious. "Don't say that," I whispered into his leather jacket which was covered with hard drops of molten plastic. Everything hurt so much, I was so exhausted and the coughing felt like my ribs would break. Shaun sat next to me, holding me tight with his good arm, also coughing. Blood was still oozing from the holes I'd made in his hand with the screwdriver. His face was just horrible, like a gargoyle's, plastic burns on top of the baseball bat damage. I kissed it, hurt my poor nose, cried some more, kissed again. Total basket case.

"It's OK," he whispered. "Don't cry."

"I'm crying because my hands are hurting," I told him which was true, they were. Also I couldn't breathe properly again, felt as if I was suffocating. It was hot, the fire all around was burning high up around us. Suddenly I knew what the matter was. It wasn't OK. Not at all.

"Shaun," I said. "The fire. It's taking all the oxygen." Terror got me on my feet again.

"Oh shit," he croaked. "Don't believe it."

He got to a crouch, paused there panting. I squatted down, in the light from the flames I could see how white he was, how sweaty.

"Is it your arm?"

"Gut."

Oh god, his spleen.

I'd thought we could just wait for the emergency services or for the fire to burn out, but we couldn't because in the still night, the fire around was too hot, it was burning up all the oxygen, we'd die like forest animals hiding in the river sometimes do. The tarmac round the edges was starting to buckle and it wasn't that big a carpark.

My car had a broken windscreen. His car was intact. I got my shoulder under his arm and we lurched up together, panting and dizzy, hacking and coughing from the smoke around us, felt our way to it. BMW, not a soft top, thank god.

"My hands won't work," I cried, trying to open the door.

He did it for me, got in the driving seat, which I wasn't happy about at first because I thought he looked ready to pass out. Then there was one of those stupid hitches that you never ever get in movies. The key was in his righthand pocket, but he couldn't move his right hand and he reached across with his left and couldn't get at it.

So I climbed out of the car, coughing, head whirling again, went round to get the keys out of his pocket. Only my hands wouldn't work properly. It would have been funny if it wasn't so fucking dangerous with the fire and the smoke and the suffocating breathless feeling. Useless bloody hands, I shook them. Tried again. Scrabbled. Sausages attached to the ends of my arms, no connection to my brain. The keys came out of his pocket, fell on the ground. My hands just wouldn't perform the perfectly simple operation of making a pincer and picking them up. I picked them up in my teeth, put them in his left hand, looked up at him and said, "Woof?"

For a second, the moveable half of his face grinned at me. He fumbled the key in the lock left-handed, the engine roared.

I waited while he picked up his broken right arm and put it in his lap. He shut his eyes to do it, panted like a dog. I prayed he wouldn't faint. Eyes open, he's OK. Then I slammed his door with my foot, ran round, climbed in, couldn't slam the door. He reached across me, gasping, pulled it shut. I shoved him upright again. Feminists may ask why I didn't drive? My hands, girls, remember? It isn't true that you can be tied up for hours and then function perfectly well afterwards. What's more, even if they had been working, and my head hadn't felt so woozy, I would have wanted Shaun to drive because... well, I'm sorry, some things men are better at.

Maniac driving, for instance. Me, I'd have gone cautiously, frightened of hitting something, making a mistake and maybe we'd have got through before the tyres melted or the petrol in the car's tank got hot enough to vapourise and explode, maybe not. It was a BMW, they're very well built.

Shaun put the car in gear, did what I believe is technically known as gunned the motor, took off the handbrake, held the wheel one-handed cross-wise, snarled and put his foot down. We screeched across the melting carpark, heading downhill, dove straight through the fire, flame, stink of burning rubber, screech, we were on the road, engine screaming in first because he couldn't change gear without letting go of the steering wheel, bucketing round the curves designed to show off the gardens and the MiniWonders and a great arching cathedral of burning trees on either side of us.

A burning tree had fallen across the road, blocking the way ahead; jerk off the road, missing trees by inches, undergrowth in flames, a blazing Cheops pyramid looming insanely through the mirk, crush a bench, skid round another tree, back on the path, through the gate and then out onto the dark road with bits of burning undergrowth still stuck to the car.

He stamped on the brakes just in time to stop us crashing into the side of a fire engine, swerved into some soft earth by the side of the road and came to a halt. Firehoses sprayed the car.

And we just sat, limp, waiting for them to come and get us out, breathing proper air not smoke, coughing painfully, gasping, very very happy to be breathing at all. My swollen right hand found his left. He leaned his head back, made a funny noise in his throat that I finally identified as a wheezing laugh.

"What?" I croaked.

"You... said it. I heard you."

"What?"

"Took a madman with a... fucking baseball bat to make you... say it... but you did."

"Said what?"

There were firemen outside, trying to open the door, but the metal had seized shut with the heat.

"You said... you love me."

I blinked, tried to think. Oh yes. When I was telling Jim why I went off voluntarily with Shaun. Bloody hell. How had that slipped out?

"Yes I did. Damn it."

Shaun shut his eyes. Waited.

I gripped his hand so tight I'm sure I hurt him, chest pounding, it felt like I was doing one of those James Bond stunts, you know, hanging out of a helicopter, over Niagara falls, held only by Shaun's hand...

The firemen were using jemmies.

Jim and his baseball bat had made it easy. I gulped, wished I could think straight. Did I love him? Or not?

Fuck it.

"Shaun," I whispered, and he looked straight at me, blue eyes punching a hole through my heart. "Shaun, I l...love you."

"Ripper," he croaked, lifted my swollen hand to his lips and kissed it, leaving a blood print. "I love you too."
The fireman opened the driver's door, looked in, blinked.
"Hey, you're Shaun Graham!"


THE END

Hi – my name is Patricia Finney and I want to bribe you to sign up for my email list.

Even if you've already signed up for my list through my website or a Carey novel, I want you to sign up again because this is a different list.

LUCKY WOMAN is a romantic comedy thriller, sort of thing – and more or less contemporary. No, I don't count the early 2000s as historical. Sorry.

The Carey, Enys and Elizabethan Noir books are historical novels.

So – two lists. One for historical novels, one for everything else. I hesitate to use the word "contemporary" because I might write SF or fantasy or something. I don't know what the Interstellar Idea Bats are planning, do I?

You know I won't anxiously spam you with loads of emails – if I send you one it'll be because I think you might be genuinely interested in it.

So if you want to sign up for my everything-else fiction list, go to this URL (you'll have to type it in!)

https://www.subscribepage.com/ambrosestory

You'll get exclusive access to a short story called AMBROSE THE GAY POSTMAN. I dare you!

Also, when you've finished the book of course, could you please write a review?

Thank you.

AFTERWORD, TWENTY YEARS LATER

Sometimes books attack you sneakily from behind. Sometimes they land on the roof and wait patiently for their turn to be written. Sometimes you get some images or a phrase grabs your attention and then you build the story from there.

I'm a natural Pantser rather than a Planner – oh sorry, writer-jargon. Most writers seem to plan their books before they write them, sometimes in extraordinary detail. I've tried writing books that way and I just can't hack it: I get bored and midway I have to change who the villain is and sometimes who the hero is, which is a lot of work, let me tell you. I have respect for writers who plan but it's simply not for me.

A Pantser is one who flies by the seat of their pants – doesn't know what the plot is, might not know what happens at the end, possibly doesn't even know what's happening next and has to write the scene to find out. A politer term is a Discovery writer.

I don't think you can tell which one the writer is by reading the book – although if it's a bit chaotic, probably a Pantser wrote it and if it has a plot which works like a machine shoving the characters around, likely a Planner wrote it.

So when I write a book it's as if I'm flinging myself off a cliff with a half-finished hang-glider in my hand which I have to finish before I hit the ground. Luckily I get lots of goes. If you're a Pantser you have to trust your unconscious, which is where your creativity lives anyway.

But sometimes… Sometimes it's different.

LUCKY WOMAN started with me suddenly falling in love with an Irish folksong called "The Gypsy Rover" and singing it loudly everywhere I went (I am unfortunately not able to sing quietly). There was a motorbike and a bloke and a nurse looking after a mysterious cancer-stricken woman in a caravan, that a friend had told me about…

The book dropped straight into my head (probably from a stray Interstellar Idea Bat) – KABOOM! – and there I was helpless in its grip, wandering around singing, laughing mysteriously, and that was just the thinking stage. I started writing it as fast as I could: partly because I had the whole book there in my head at once which is very uncomfortable and interferes with my sleep and partly because I had three children and a husband at the time and a hell of a lot of things to do because the youngest was only three.

This was when my daughter was asked by a well-meaning person if she liked having a writer for a mum. She answered "Yeah well, if you like having somebody with eyes like boiled eggs in tomato sauce banging baked beans on toast in front of you for the fifth time that week and then going and typing more."

Or words to that effect. I wasn't paying attention. I was writing.

The first draft took about six weeks of madness and needed a lot of work.

Various other things happened, including my husband getting lung cancer in 2000 and dying 18 months later.

Yeah, spooky. I prefer not to think about that.

I was totally confident that the book would sell in an auction to a trad publisher and make me loadsamoney.

It didn't. I still don't know why. The best anybody could suggest was that it was funny and romantic and a thriller combined and that seemed to upset publishers and make them nervous.

I don't know, guv, I just write 'em.

This is my orphan book. It slammed into my life, disrupted it, messed me about. As I was supposed to, I faithfully wrote it to the best of my ability and waited for my reward.

I'll let you know what happens next if you sign up to my contemporary fiction email list. Here's the link to type in: **https://www.subscribepage.com/ambrosestory**

There's a bribe for you in the form of a short story called "Ambrose the gay postman."

In the meantime, South Cornwall has become a place I know quite well - although it doesn't exist - and I'm getting tickles in my head (and nudges from Idea Bats) for more books set there. So this is the first Tale from South Cornwall.

I, JACK is also set there but that's a children's book, written from the point of view of a dog. In Doglish. I'm at the start of the process of reissuing it and eventually the Jack books might take their place as "Tails of South Cornwall."

Sorry.
Not sorry.

Cheers!

Patricia Finney